THE DED

BRITISH FANTASY:

the 19th century

Compiled with an
introduction and notes by
Brian Stableford

DEDALUS

Published in the UK by Dedalus Ltd. Langford Lodge, St Judith's Lane,
Sawtry, Cambs, PE17 5XE

UK ISBN 0 946626 78 2 (paper)
0 946626 84 7 (cloth)

Introduction, notes & compilation © copyright Brian Stableford 1991

Printed in England by Billings & Sons Ltd,
Hylton Road, Worcester, WR2 5JU

Typeset by 'Wideyed', 25 Kemerton Road, London, SE5 9AP

Cover picture is Richard Dadd's The Fairy Feller's Master-Stroke
reproduced by courtesy of the Tate Gallery-London

THE EDITOR

Brian Stableford was born in Shipley, Yorkshire in 1948 and studied Biology at the University of York, before doing a D.Phil in Sociology. He is one of the UK's leading writers of science fiction and fantastic fiction and his recent novels include *The Empire of Fear* and *The Werewolves of London*. His non - fiction books include *The Sociology of Science Fiction* and *Scientific Romance in Britain 1890 - 1950*.

He has edited several books for Dedalus including *The Dedalus Book of Decadence, Tales of the Wandering Jew* and the forthcoming *The Dedalus Book of Femmes Fatales*.

LITERARY FANTASY ANTHOLOGIES FROM DEDALUS

As part of Dedalus' Europe 1992 Programme we are anthologizing European Literary Fantasy.

Volumes currently in preparation are:

The Dedalus Book of French Fantasy
editor Christine Donougher

The Dedalus Book of Belgian Fantasy
editor Richard Huijing

The Dedalus Book of Dutch Fantasy
editor Richard Huijing

The Dedalus Book of German Fantasy (2 volumes)
Editor Mike Mitchell
Volume 1: **Austria: The Meyrink Years 1890 - 1930**
Volume 2: **The Romantics and Beyond**

LIST OF CONTENTS

INTRODUCTION

Modern publishers and booksellers recognise three genres of fantastic fiction, and label their produce accordingly as science fiction, horror or fantasy. Although the world's best-selling contemporary author, Stephen King, is marketed under the second label the genre which has the largest following is fantasy.

This is slightly surprising, given that fantasy was not demarcated as a publishing category until the late 1960's, in the wake of the astonishing success of the paperback editions of J.R.R. Tolkien's *The Lord of the Rings*. Before that date, paperback books which would now be labelled fantasy had sometimes been published on the ragged edge of publishers' science fiction lists, often under the heading "sword and sorcery" , but the sub-genre was not reckoned to have much profit making potential. Fantasy novels were regarded, by readers as well as by publishers, as perfectly appropriate reading for children but not for adults. The elevation to fashionability of Tolkien's trilogy changed that dramatically, restoring the respectability of the fantasy novel as something that adults might read without being deemed childish. Once granted this licence, millions of readers queued up for more.

The Lord of the Rings is the parent of the modern publishing category, but Tolkien's work has a long and complicated ancestry of its own. The wave of fashionability which snatched up *The Lord of the Rings* was largely an American phenomenon - it began on American campuses during the brief heyday of flower power and the counter culture - and it has been American writers who have supplied the publishing category it inspired with most of its best-sellers: Stephen R. Donaldson, David Eddings, Terry Brooks, Katherine Kurtz, Tad Williams, Melanie Rawn, and many others; but the tradition of fantastic fiction from which *The Lord of the Rings* descends, and which provided Tolkien with his inspiration, is a distinctly British one.

Other nations, including America, have their own

fantasy traditions, but these tend to be distinct and markedly different. It is inevitable that this should be the case; because they are rooted in particular folkloristic resources the fantasy traditions of different nations lend themselves rather more readily to treatment in isolation than traditions of science fiction and horror, whose inspirational roots are universal. It is true, of course, that fantasy writers frequently borrow from alien folkloristic traditions, and that some folkloristic materials have themselves been transmitted from one oral culture to another in days long gone by, but each nation does tend to have some essential kernel of uniqueness within its popular mythology, embodied not only by a particular fondness for certain tales but also by a more general attitude of mind.

This book traces the development of the British fantasy tradition through a period of great importance : the nineteenth century. This was a key phase in the evolution of fantasy in all nations. The century began with an upheaval of attitudes associated with a general revival of interest in the imaginary and the supernatural associated with the Romantic Movement. The Romantics renewed the respectability of the fantastic and stimulated a good deal of discussion about the possible artistic uses of fantastic material. In Britain, however, the cultural environment to which that renewed interest had to adapt came to be determined and defined by the unique and specific conditions of Victorian publishing and Victorian moralising.

British writers of fantasy did not find it comfortable to labour under the stresses and strains of Victorian attitudes. Fantasy is by its nature subversive of "common sense", and the more rigid the moral attitudes which pass for common sense become, the more anarchic and dangerous fantasy may seem. The new interest in the fantastic inspired by the Romantics faded somewhat as the moral climate shifted and esoteric poetry gradually ceded its cultural centrality to exoteric prose. Fantasy was largely banished to the margins of the literary landscape as the realistic novel moved into the foreground, but it did not disappear and it continues to play an important if subsidiary role.

Whatever is deemed unsuitable for discussion in "realistic" fiction tends to become the subject matter of supernatural fiction, albeit in disguised form. The fierce moralists of Victorian Britain were uniquely extravagant in deeming topics unsuitable, and it was inevitable that their repression would call forth some uniquely extravagant, and sometimes rather peculiar, responses. Some of these responses were apologetic; some writers of fantasies took care deferentially to excuse what they were doing and to demonstrate that fantasy could be placed in the service of Victorian morality. Others were, in various ways, subversive: some writers did what they did unrepentantly, cleverly challenging and undermining the moral order of Victorianism. As the end of the century approached, and a second upheaval of values swept away the Victorian verities, the advent of a new liberalism was reflected more clearly in fantasy than in any other kind of writing.

The philosophic and scientific revolution of the seventeenth and eighteenth centuries was a triumph of wisdom over superstition, and of tolerant scepticism over mean-spirited dogma. It brought about a new confidence in the power of the human mind, and fully deserved to be reckoned an Age of Enlightenment. The new power of the mind was reflected in a far better understanding and control of the environment than men had ever enjoyed before. A new science fed a nascent industrial and technological revolution, and the effects of this intellectual and material progress were nowhere more evident than in Britain. But any increase in power is always accompanied by a certain sense of frustration: progress in one arena always increases awareness of its absence in others.

The Enlightenment had the effect of lighting a lantern in the twilight; as well as adding to the sum of illumination it also separated out light and darkness, throwing that which was not bright-lit into a deeper and more threatening gloom. It created opposition where before there had been

9

permeation. This is clearly reflected in the literary produce of the aftermath of the Enlightenment, where we find the gradual emergence of a new Realism in dialectical opposition to a new Romanticism. It is evident, too, in the paradoxes of Victorianism, which was the culmination of a peculiar amalgam of moral confidence and moral anxiety.

The uneasy and fearful aspect of Romanticism was exhibited in the Gothic horror stories which were so popular in the late eighteenth and early nineteenth centuries, but horror is not the only expression which anxiety can find and Romanticism also had a celebratory element which took a certain comfort in the failure of Realism to secure its dominion absolutely. It is in fiction much more reminiscent of the modern fantasy genre than the modern horror story that we find this second aspect of Romantic dissent: the comic, the sentimental and the mystical.

Because these aspects are several, fantasy - considered as a genre - is less easy to define than the other two genres of imaginative fiction. Horror fiction can be characterised by its ambition to frighten and disturb the reader; science fiction by its attempt (or at lease its pretence) to remain within the bounds of hypothetical possibility. Fantasy seems to be more easily characterised, at least in the first instance, by means of a series of negatives: it is that fiction which is not mundane, yet does not belong to either of the other two genres of supramundane fiction.

It is incorrect, however, simply to consider fantasy as a kind of residual category. Hindsight does allow us to perceive a fantasy genre emerging in the nineteenth century, possessed of some degree of coherency in spite of its hybrid nature. The writers and critics of the day did not think in terms of literary genres - not, at any rate, in terms of the genre categories we recognise today - but that did not prevent writers of fantastic fiction being influenced by one another and recognising a degree of common cause in what they were doing. The later writers included in this anthology would all have been familiar with the work of the earlier ones, and would have recognised some degree of kinship between their own works and those previously issued. Although they did not call themselves "fantasy writers" - and only a handful of them specialised in fantasy - their fantasy works were part of a developing tradition of discourse. What we see when we look back at the fantasies of the period is not an amorphous mass but an assembly of texts grouped around certain key themes, which evolves certain characteristic methods in the course of its progress.

Most of the stories which are nowadays written for publication under the modern fantasy label belong to a subclass which J. R. R. Tolkien, in his classic essay "On Fairy-Stories" describes as "Secondary World" fantasies. These are stories set in imaginary worlds whose spatial and temporal connection with the real world are frankly mysterious, but whose nature and contents are intelligibly related to it. Lin Carter, who became the most ardent champion of adult fantasy in the world of American publishing after the success of *The Lord of the Rings*, argues in his book *Imaginary Worlds* that Secondary World stories constitute the hard core of the fantasy genre.

The "purest" fantasy, for both Tolkien and Carter, consists of stories set entirely within a Secondary World. In many stories of a closely related kind, however, the characters must move from our mundane world into the Secondary World, and may move back and forth across the boundary between the two. Any reasonable definition of Fantasy must obviously accommodate these works. A broader definition, though must also take in stories in which a part of the mundane world is briefly infected or transformed by a limited incursion from a Secondary World, even if the Secondary World is not formally allotted a space of its own. Such incursions are frequently likened to (or "explained" as) dreams and hallucinations; many actual examples are concerned with the displacement from a hypothetical Secondary Word of a single magical character or object. Horror stories typically deal with similar disruptions of the normal course of world affairs, but in horror stories

11

the intrusions are necessarily threatening; where the effect of the temporary incursion is at least partly enlivening or life-enhancing then the work is usually better classified as a fantasy.

Carter alleges in *Imaginary Worlds* that what differentiates Secondary Worlds from the mundane one can be adequately summed up in a single word: magic. This serves well enough, but there are certain other characteristics worth pointing out. Secondary Worlds usually resemble our own world in very basic ways (atmosphere, gravity etc.) but the details of their geography may be very different. Their flora and fauna are usually augmented by an assortment of creatures borrowed from ancient mythologies. They are usually technologically primitive, and their social organization is likely to be feudal, supported by some notion of the divine right of kings.

Secondary Worlds of this general kind are essentially composite versions of the world that our remote ancestors once believed in, but which has been displaced by modern knowledge. Other Secondary Worlds whose existence is either featured or implied by fantasy stories tend to be worlds which our ancestors believed to exist in parallel with our own: the Underworld, the land of Faerie, Heaven, the Land of Dreams. Fantasy is deliberately archaic and anachronistic: its central feature is that it deals with that in which we have ceased to believe. For this reason, fantasy often seems nostalgic, and is often redolent with sentimental regret for lost illusions.

It has always seemed pointless to some critics that anyone should be interested in reading stories about the power of magic in an era when mature and reasonable adults have ceased to believe in its workability. Some nineteenth century educationalists were, in fact, sternly opposed to fairy stories and other tales traditionally told to children on the grounds that such fictions could only mislead and confuse, and would handicap intellectual development. This puzzle sometimes invites a simplistically uncharitable solution; the argument that a taste for fantasy is symptomatic of a failure to cope with the rigours of real life was largely responsible for the pre-1970 notion that fantasy was only fit reading material for children.

The idea that fantasy is essentially "childish" tacitly assumes that our remote and ignorant ancestors believed in the efficacy of magic because they were simple-minded, and that only people who are similarly simple-minded can take stories about magic seriously. Its adherents reason from this supposition that we may grant a tacit licence to children, permitting them to believe in magic until they are old enough to "know better", but holds that modern adults ought to have "grown out of" such silly fancies.

The first tacit assumption on which this line of argument is based is dubious; the second is clearly ridiculous. It is a grotesque misunderstanding to assume that in order to read and enjoy fantastic fiction one must be prepared to believe in the actual workability of magic. Most commentators follow Coleridge in referring to what is actually required as a temporary and limited "willing suspension of disbelief", but Tolkien goes further than this, characterising the contact between writer and reader in more positive terms, as a demand for a distinct species of "Secondary Beliefs". Using this observation as a prelude to explanation, Tolkien opens the way to a more sensible discussion of the psychological utility of fantasy.

Tolkien's essay refers to three functions of fantasy, which he calls Recovery, Escape and Consolation. It is an essential part of his thesis that fantasy is the natural partner of reason, neither "insulting" nor undermining it, and that our sense of what *is* necessarily has as its logical counterpart a sense of that which *is not*. He argues that the ability to take up a fantastic viewpoint for the sake of comparison helps us to put real things in a better perspective; what we "recover" in fantasy is a clearer sight than we normally employ in viewing the world, because it is a less narrow sight - a sight which does not take for granted the limitations of mundanity.

To argue thus is to assert that we cannot see reality clearly enough if we are trapped within it, and that it is only when we can perform the imaginative trick of moving outside the actual that we can properly appreciate its bounds. This is the fundamental task of the literature of fantasy, and in the nineteenth century evolution of the genre we can see the principal contributors of the genre developing a series of literary devices adapted to this purpose.

Seen from this viewpoint, offering fantasies to children is not at all a matter of granting them temporary licence to believe absurdities. It is instead an entirely appropriate means of helping them to arrive at a sensible distinction of the real and the unreal. It is not surprising, therefore, that one of the motive forces which we see at work in the evolution of nineteenth century fantasy is a campaign to rehabilitate and revitalise those fictions useful (perhaps even essential) to the education of the developing mind.

The function of Escape is seen by Tolkien in much the same light as the function of Recovery. He asserts unhesitatingly that the escapism of fantasy is to be evaluated as if it were the escape of a prisoner rather than the desertion of a soldier; it is a liberation, not a moral failure. This statement is not without qualification, however, because Tolkien proposes that if it is to be genuinely rewarding, the escapism of Fantasy cannot be content simply with drawing the reader away from oppression; it must also lead to some kind of goal. This is where the third function of fantasy - that of consolation - emerges.

Tolkien calls the consolatory goal which he believes a fantasy story should have a "eucatastrophe". By this he means a climactic affirmation of both joy and right: pleasure alloyed with moral confidence. This does not mean that fantasy cannot or ought not to be tragic, but it does mean that in Tolkien's view fantasy should not be despairing (as speculative fiction and horror fiction sometimes are); according to this argument, the work of fantasy is essentially committed to the cause of moral rearmament.

There is nothing surprising in the intimate alliance between fantasy and moral fabulation; such an alliance is already implicit in the idea of magic, whose workability is the central premise of fantasy.

In preliterate societies, where belief in magic is still sustained there is always an intimate connection between magic and morality. Magical explanations and magical practices are invoked on precisely those occasions when the real world fails to measure up to the ideal. The hunter in search of meat makes magic against the possibility of failure, but he may fail if he has broken a taboo. The crop-grower makes magic to bring the rain which he needs, and magic to fertilise the soil, but if the tribal ancestors have been offended by the wickedness of their children the rain will not come and the soil will not bear fruit. The medicine-man makes magic to fight illness and oppose the evil of witches who would bring all manner of misfortune upon the tribe. Magic is an expression of desire; it is the attempt to create, at least in the imagination, a world where the human will is the master of fate. But desire without moral responsibility is itself an evil, and magic of that kind is black magic. Institutionalised magic is intimately bound up with the question of whether men truly deserve to succeed in their endeavours.

Magic does not, in fact, work - but that does not mean that it is not useful to those societies which practice and believe in it. The real utility of magic does not lie in the practical arena of human endeavour but in the theatre of the psyche, but it does have a real utility, and that is why it is wrong to regard belief in magic as though it were simply a silly mistake. Institutionalised magic builds confidence and morale; its operations are of purely symbolic value, but it nevertheless opposes defeatism and despair, and conserves hope. Magic - or some psychological substitute - is vital to all human endeavour at a causal level, because confidence may be a necessary condition of success, and despair is generally a guarantee of failure. In all societies where belief in magic is sustained (and ours has by no means been entirely purged of such ways of thinking) forms of magical practice and magical belief are largely defined by moral priorities, dependent upon notions of reward and punishment.

The characterisation of magic as an expression of desire is ironically inverted in Jean-Paul Sartre's theory of the emotions, which attempts to characterise emotion as a "magical" form of sensation. How we feel about an object, Sartre suggests, reflects the relationship we would have with that object if the world were indeed magical, and the emotions fill a spectrum which extends from a conviction of our own omnipotence to a sensation of utter helplessness - from megalomania to paranoia. The emotions, of course, have a moral gravity of their own whenever passion moves us, there is a moral danger.

If we look at supernatural fiction in general from this perspective, we will recognise that horror fiction exemplifies the negative end of the emotional spectrum, while fantasy exemplifies the positive. Horror stories characteristically deal with the frustration of desire, or with temptation leading to destruction; fantasy characteristically deals with the measured victory of desire, or with constructive temptation. Horror stories frequently built to a climax which involves the escape of the characters from whatever has threatened them, but such an ending is a matter of relief rather than achievement. By the same token, fantasy stories often contain a partial negation of their own logic, which shows not only in occasional tragic resolutions but also - more frequently - in a bittersweet undercurrent of irony. The lovely sadness of knowing that fantasy is, after all, fantasy, supplies a characteristic savour to the masterpieces of the *genre*.

In all supernatural fiction matters of morality are at stake. Good and evil are in the balance, and the question at issue is whether and how the characters will be delivered from evil. Horror fiction tends to emphasize the threat, and to build suspense upon the question of whether deliverance is possible; a happy ending, in a horror story, is a restoration

16

of normality. Fantasy, although it is often comical and calculatedly quaint, conceals beneath its relative lightness of tone a greater ambition; in fantasy, normality is never enough, and though the preferable ideal may in the end turn out to be unattainable - or attainable only at a terrible price - fantasy nevertheless moves in search of eucatastrophe, in the hope of improving the quality of life. Horror stories comprise the fiction of fear; fantasy stories comprise the fiction of hope.

Nineteenth century fantasy is so various that it is not a simple matter to isolate its key themes or point out the coherent undercurrents guiding its evolution. However, Tolkien's identification of the three key features of Secondary World fantasy does offer a set of analytic instruments which help to make these unifying themes and methods a little clearer.

Tolkien is clearly right to argue that recovery of a clear view of the world is something which requires imaginative effort. Such an effort is required to make us look beyond and through the triteness of the taken-for granted, and to discover new perspectives from which the familiar looks odd. Tolkien, borrowing from G. K. Chesterton, calls this kind of effect "Mooreeffoc", after an odd thrill reportedly felt by Charles Dickens upon observing from the wrong side the phrase "Coffee Room" inscribed on a glass door.

We have all experienced similar thrills and fascinations. It is not only words spelled backwards which sometimes acquire this mysterious aesthetic appeal; most other kinds of wordplay can do it, whether they consist of sophisticated exercises in rhyming and punning or the malapropisms and naive misunderstandings of children. Language, as a map of the world, is mutable in all sorts of ways which introduce happy absurdities and discontinuities into its work of reference. The same is true of fiction, which maps human experience in a fashion analogous to the way in which language maps reality, and which generates many of its happy absurdities and discontinuities in the form of fantasy.

A large number of nineteenth century fantasies work in this fashion, creating new viewpoints which administer a series of shocks to our conventional assumptions about the way our world works. The characters which Alice meets in her odysseys underground and through the looking glass use the instruments of wordplay to do this, but there are other ways in which the trick can be worked. There are, for instance, wonderful visits paid to our world by the ambassadors of others ways of thought: more-or-less amiable demons, or angels, or various creatures and characters borrowed from pagan belief. Then again, fantasy provides the opportunity for personalities to be displaced by trading places. All such stories serve the function of showing their characters and their readers the world's stage lit from an unconventional angle.

The daydream fantasies which we make up for ourselves in order to escape temporarily from everyday life are often described as "idle fancies", mainly because they come to us in moments of idleness and may be used to distract us from burdensome matters of duty. But our everyday fantasies are often idle in another way too: they fall readily into stereotyped patterns, and we rarely elaborate them beyond the point of enjoying their vicarious satisfactions. For the most part, we obtain gratification from our fantasies quite easily; we usually do not put a great deal of effort into their formation. We may, of course, enter into collaboration with writers in the construction of our fantasies, appropriating their efforts to make our daydreams more detailed and more lively, but the best writers inevitably do this kind of job more thoroughly and more artfully than the vast majority of their readers, and if we draw too heavily on their resources we may find our daydreams reduced in value because they are not specifically tailored to link up with our particular feelings and frustrations.

There are some kinds of fiction which apparently exist largely to fulfil this kind of daydream-fuelling purpose; pornography is the most obvious example. Those who despise fantasy as a genre often speak of it as if it had no other functions, but that is an obviously mistaken view, and fantasy stories which do deal with the theme of wish-fulfillment usually do so in order to issue cautionary warnings against the perils of idle daydreaming. This can most easily be seen in parables which inform us that wishes which are granted (such wishes traditionally come in sets of three) will always, perversely, lead us to disaster. Nineteenth century fantasy contains many examples of such stories, which show us ill-advised wishes going absurdly or tragically wrong; it is also rich in accounts of dream-worlds where characters are educated in the folly of their fancies.

Where writers are more generous in their treatment of daydreaming - as they often are in childrens' stories - they remain very conscious of the temporary nature of such fantasies, careful to emphasise that daydreamers must always return from their fantasies to deal with the world from which they fled. Usually, fantasy stories which are sympathetic to the stuff of daydreams make their apology on the grounds that a daydreamer may return to the vexing problems of real life refreshed, or having learned some lesson which will make those problems more tractable.

When nineteenth century fantasy writers lead us into Secondary Worlds they are facilitating an escape from our imprisonment by mundanity, and we may often feel ourselves to be tourists out for enjoyment rather than earnest seekers after knowledge avid for instruction. Nevertheless, the authors invariably have some didactic purpose in escorting us upon such odysseys. Even when they boldly declare that they are peddling pure nonsense they unobtrusively guide us towards an entirely proper irreverence for the sordid habit of taking things for granted.

The most significant of the nineteenth century journeys into the land of Faerie and its many analogues were authentic voyages of exploration and discovery, undertaken by writers who were concerned to learn as well as to teach. The authors too were trying to escape, and though they were

19

usually uncertain where their destination truly lay they were nevertheless eager to make progress in their journey towards it. The writing of many of the most effective fantasies must have been acts of catharsis on the part of their authors: attempts to purge confusion.

Inevitably, the purgation can only have been half-effective. Allegory, though it can be a valuable instrument of thought, can produce no real solutions to the the moral problems which it brings into sharper focus; but we must not underestimate the value of that half -effect simply because it is, in functional terms, entirely magical.

The magical worlds devised by fantasy writers, whether they lie in a hypothetical past or in some parallel dimension, often seem to lie closer to the world of Platonic Archetypes than to the real world of the nineteenth century. They are dramatically purified worlds, where good and evil are more clearly polarised and whose characters very often embody single virtues and vices. They are worlds where rewards and punishments are more extreme, where social roles are generally very distinct. For the heroes who move through them, though, they remain problematic, and no matter what success the heroes attain in material and spiritual terms those problematic features can never be entirely resolved. Often, the conclusion of the story is a dissolution of the dream which leaves the protagonist with mixed feelings - richer in experience and understanding, but no more certain than before what the answer is to the question of how men and women should live.

For this reason, even the most positive and constructive of nineteenth century fantasies do retain a darker and more anxious side. The quest for eucatastrophe is haunted by the awareness that success rests on compromise. Fantasy is by no means as simple-minded or ritualistic as its opponents sometimes claim, and serious fantasies inevitably bear adequate testimony to the moral doubts as well as the moral determination of their authors.

Given all this, there can be no doubt that the Tolkienian function of Consolation, as served by nineteenth century fantasy, is by no means to be dismissed as a mere literary equivalent of the compensatory consolations of private daydreams. The Escape which it offers is by no means a cushioned refuge which simply insulates its readers from the stresses of confrontation with the real and the weariness of social conformity. Both these functions remain associated with (and perhaps subservient to) the function of Recovery, in which we are allowed to regain a proper reverence for the strangeness of our own world by confrontation and intercourse with imaginary ones which, because they are magical, are less strange to the emotional aspects of perception.

Like any other genre, fantasy derived its instruments largely from pre-existing forms. Writers throughout Europe borrowed from the folkloristic material which had been adapted into fiction, and moulded to the cause of *bourgeois* moralising for the purpose of "civilising" young minds, by the likes of Perrault and the Grimms. Fantasy writers of all nations also borrowed from the chivalric romances of the late Middle Ages, which had in the latter part of their history begun to escape (albeit rather halfheartedly) from the straitjacket of moralistic and pietistic allegory into which they had earlier been crammed by the monks who controlled the distribution of literacy in Medieval Europe. Other rich sources of material were provided by the Oriental fantasies which (aided by a less rigorous style of moralising) had become popular in the wake of translations of the Thousand-and-One Nights, and by the ancient religious systems of Europe, especially the Greek and Roman mythology which was so richly interwoven into the texture of Classical literature, and thus into the ideological heritage of Western Europe.

When we look at British fantasy in isolation, we can easily identify several distinctive strands which are of cardinal importance. These are, of course, the contributions made to it by native British folklore and legendary. These are complicated, first because Scottish and Celtic folklore are

21

in many ways distinct from English folklore, and secondly because of the legacy of Norman invasion of 1066. The Normans imported a strong Gallic element into the reporting of English folkloristic materials, which were mostly committed to paper for the first time by Anglo-Norman chroniclers of the twelfth and thirteenth centuries, although Scottish and Celtic materials were less-heavily polluted.

Gallic intrusions are evident to a fairly limited extent in the mythology of Faerie which provides one of the principal fountainheads of British fantasy, but they are glaringly obvious in the pseudohistorical legends deployed in one of the first and most enduringly popular English printed books, Malory's *Le Morte d'Arthur* . Although Arthurian legend may reasonably be reckoned specifically British, in that it refers to a pre-Norman king already recognised in British legend, Malory's "Arthurian Bible" is cast in the form of French chivalric romance, and borrows several of the central themes of that genre, including the chivalric code and the quest for the Holy Grail.

It is important that while we recognise the importance in British fantasy of folkloristic materials which are specifically British, we also recognise that works by British writers which use Oriental or Classical sources are no less authentic or significant as participants in the evolution of British fantasy. The uniqueness of British fantasy is a matter of attitude rather than choice of materials, and part of the delight of fantasy is its readiness to deal with the strange and the alien. The native folkloristic tradition is a major contributor to the distinctive flavour of British fantasy, but it was never a straitjacket setting boundaries of parochiality.

In nineteenth century Britain, Victorian morality came to exercise a powerful dominion over the written work, and this dominion has very clear effects on the development of British fantasy. Early in the century one can find Shelley attempting to claim for the poets the privilege of being the world's true legislators, and Keats proclaiming the equivalence of truth and beauty. Both writers practised what they preached, and their work is replete with fantastic themes whose exoticism is openly celebrated, and which champion a liberal morality. But British fantasy - especially prose fantasy - was quickly and conspicuously chilled by the icy winds of moral oppression. By the time Victoria came to the throne in 1837 fantasy stories were already becoming prim and conservatively moralistic, and this primness became exaggerated almost to the point of grotesquerie in the work of the most ardent disciples of Victorianism.

Victorian painters were able to use fantasy motifs as a means of sidestepping moral restraint. There was a mid-century fashion for fairy painting, occasioned in part by the fact that one way to present images of female nudity while insulating the artist from accusations of indecency was to add a pair of gossamer wings to the figures in question (a similar exception was made for female figures in paintings illustrating scenes from Classical myth). Writers found no such parallel move available; verbal indecencies and indelicacies could not be excused by context. Thus, the most obvious response to Victorianism in supramundane fiction was the development of a highly stylized and carefully chastened school of fantasy best exemplified by the works of Mrs Craik, George MacDonald and William Morris. This was not, however, the only response.

The anarchic spirit which remains submerged in Victorian fantasy tended to sidestep confrontation with official morality by displacing its energies into a more radical confrontation with logic and reason, best exemplified by the nonsense poetry of Edward Lear and the works of Lewis Carroll. It was not until the 1880's that this kind of deliberate trafficking with absurdity began to confront issues of behavioural morality in a less elliptical fashion - very cautiously in the works of Walter Besant and F. Anstey, more calculatedly in the deceptively light fantasies of Richard Garnett and Oscar Wilde. Even then the forces of repression remained sufficiently powerful to destroy Wilde for his

23

temerity. Beneath the surface of all the classic Victorian fantasies, though - usually hidden by a veil of grotesquerie or humour - bitter responses to the pressure of Victorian moral extremism can be discovered; a sensitive decoding of the allegories of Charles Dickens and John Sterling, and even those of George MacDonald, reveals a full measure of confusion and pain.

As might be expected, this history contrasts strongly with the development of fantasy in other nations. The contrast is most obvious in the case of France, which had been the first European nation to develop an elaborate supernatural literature which had relatively little horror in it. Long before the revolutionary period, France had been the home of the chivalric romance, and in the eighteenth century French writers - aided in their inspiration by the examples of Perrault and the Galland translation of the Arabian Nights - produced dozens of exotic romances which combined the whimsicality of fairy tales or the lushness of Arabian mythology with the *politesse* of French courtly manners.

The nineteenth century French Romantics continued to carry these themes forward, and never doubted the respectability of producing fantastic fictions. Charles Nodier, Théophile Gautier and Anatole France became the leading producers of prose fantasy, but French poets were also extraordinarily fond of the exotic, and they continue to celebrate and explore it throughout the century. French writers were fascinated by "the Orient", and with the interface between Classical antiquity and mythology. It was France which produced, in the work of the forefathers of the Decadent Movement - Baudelaire, Lautréamont and Rimbaud - the most explicit challenges to the oppressive "official" morality of Christianity. This challenge overflowed into prose fantasies to such an extent that many of the leading examples of French fantasy were considered far too indecent for early translation into English. Fantasy in France became an extravagantly eloquent champion of a warm and humane liberalism, frequently celebrating the power of erotic attraction.

American supramundane fiction was rather more heterogeneous than that of France or Britain, and that heterogeneity could be found within the work of all its major writers, In the works of Washington Irving, Edgar Allan Poe, Nathaniel Hawthorne and Fitz-James O'Brien we find the comic rubbing shoulders with the horrific and the sentimental, and though the authors pull in different directions - Irving towards the grotesque, Poe the paranoid, Hawthorne the moralistic - their canons each present the appearance of a mélange with less internal consistency than is exhibited by any European author.

To some extent this variety reflects the fact that America had only the most meagre resources to draw upon in terms of a native folklore, and its writers tended to take their pick from a wide spectrum of European sources. One could argue with reasonable conviction that American fantasy stood in a similar imaginative relationship to Europe as the relationship which existed between French fantasy and "the Orient". Europe was, from the American viewpoint, a kind of Antiquity, and when American fantasists came to mine its resources they tended to adopt the same Open Door philosophy which was subsequently to be formally articulated as an item of immigration policy. The distanced haphazardness of American borrowings from folkloristic sources, coupled with a marked irreverence in the invention of "new" folklore by writers like Irving (which seemed entirely appropriate to authors working in the thoroughly disenchanted milieu of the newborn nation), gave early American fantasy a heavily ironic flavour. Writers of madcap comic fantasy, including Mark Twain, Frank R. Stockton and John Kendrick Bangs, had gained ascendancy within the American genre by the end of the century.

German fantasy began to crystallize out in the theoretically-supported *kunstmärchen* ("art fairy-tales") of Goethe, Novalis and Fouqué, but German Romanticism always leaned so far toward the anxious pole of the magical spectrum that the greater part of its prose fiction belongs to the horror *genre*. If one can judge the matter accurately from the relatively sparse translations which exist, it seems to be the case that writers in Germany did not make much of the opportunity to construct moralistic fantasies either uneasily to support (as in Britain) or flamboyantly to oppose (as in France) the dominant morality of the day. Nor were German writers drawn to the kind of humorously sceptical fantasy which came to be produced in some quantity in America.

All of these rival traditions - even the weak German tradition - had some slight influence on the evolution of British fantasy in the latter part of the century; but in the main it is the differences of attitude which stand out. Even when it draws on the folklore of other nations British fantasy usually stands in stark contrast to the nineteenth century fantasy of those nations. Tales of terror from France, Germany and America exerted a far greater influence on British horror stories, and have far more in common with them, than foreign fantasies have on and with British fantasies.

The intellectual environment in which nineteenth century fantasy developed was by no means constant in its scepticism. The Romantic rebellion against the empire of Reason gave birth to some strange progeny, and certain kinds of magical beliefs - refined and refashioned by the processes of ideative natural selection - made a considerable comeback in the latter part of the century, when there was a remarkable resurgence of credulity with respect to the occult.

The manifestations of this resurgence were many and varied, but they included Baron von Reichenbach's championship of the healing powers of magnetism and the subsequent clinical uses of hypnotism; the cult of Spiritualism associated with those dishonest conjurors who set up in business as mediators between the human and spirit worlds; the Theosophy of Madame Blavatsky and

26

Annie Besant; and the neo-Rosicrucianism of such would-be ceremonial magicians as "Eliphas Levi" and the founders of the Order of Golden Dawn.

The scholarly fantasies inspired by these overlappping cults attracted the interest and involvement of a good many notable persons, including both scientists and literary men. Many writers began to import the ideative flotsam and jetsam of these cults into superstitious didactic fantasies which took their place within the nascent tradition of moralistic fantasy. Their influence can clearly be seen in dozens of mawkishly optimistic literary accounts of the afterlife, which were mostly devoid of any merit whatsoever, but did help to open up imaginative space in Britain for the later development of a more philosophically-inclined subgenre of posthumous fantasy.

Almost all occult fiction is awful; the missionary zeal of its authors frequently leads them to set matters of literary competence firmly aside. There were, however, some good writers among the credulous, and there were other writers who were prepared to borrow the vocabulary of ideas popularised by the credulous, without necessarily committing their own faith. There is little point in quibbling over such questions of definition as whether a credulous occult romance really qualifies as fantasy if its author believes religiously in the possibility of all that he (or, more often, she) has set forth. It is certainly true, though, that the literary interest of such works tends to stand in inverse proportion to the degree of conviction which the author has.

This is not to say that credulous occult romance was not popular - the author who out-sold all others in Britain during the last few years of the century was Marie Corelli, who was by far and away the most fervent and most earnest of such writers - but its writers occupy a curious position in literary history. We can only try to account for their popularity in psychological terms; any estimation of their literary merits is bound to be confused and compromised by the knowledge that the items of faith which they sincerely and strenuously assert are irredeemably stupid.

Credulity is not incompatible with the ability to tell a convincing horror story, but it does not lend itself effectively to the construction of a story whose ultimate intention is to be consolatory or uplifting. We know only too well that we are being paid in false coin when an author asks us not only to recognise the moral propriety of what he or she is saying, but also to believe that the world really is like that. Life in Heaven is a eucatastrophe in which many people try to preserve real belief, but such real belief is likely to be threatened and undermined by attempts at literary description, which inevitably raise more questions than they answer.

The most effective moral allegories are produced by sceptics who need not be confused or weighed down by matters of dogma. Nowhere is the difficulty of writing fantasies based in sincerely held faith more obvious than in the "new legends" produced by devout Christians attempting to elaborate a mythos which is still, for them, sacred. Works in this vein offer clear evidence that serious and efficient literary investigation of the moral tenets of a sincerely held faith cannot leave that faith unaltered, and when the believer resists the loss of his belief he is inevitably led towards an uncomfortable heterodoxy. The mid-nineteenth century fantasies of George MacDonald offer clear evidence of this kind, as do later works by Laurence Housman.

Having said all this, though, it must also be said that any straightforward attempt to separate out the attitudes displayed to the motifs deployed in nineteenth century fantasy into the credulous and the incredulous is bound to fail. The "secondary belief" required of readers is required of writers too, and may become for more serious fantasy writers a matter of considerable importance. They may acquire a strong proprietary interest in their own inventions, or in the borrowings which they deploy. The relationship between fantasy writers and their folkloristic sources is far too complex to be reduced to a mere matter of belief or unbelief.

A "conservationist" regard for the value of folklore is

frequently to be found in cultures which have come to fear their own erosion, as can be seen in those parts of the British Isles whose language and folkways were reduced to marginality by virtue of the economic and political dominion of the English. Several Scottish writers of the nineteenth century used fantastic fiction in a way calculated to capture and preserve something of the spirit of their eroded mythos. Yeats and others did the same for Ireland, and the Welsh mythology of the Mabinogion has similarly been redeployed in more recent times.

Nostalgia generated by the erosion of mythos and mystery is correlated in much nineteenth century fantasy with the notion of the banishment of superstition by the march of reason and the corollary feeling that there is something to be regretted in this banishment. There is a depth of tragic consciousness in parables which describe the exile of the fairy folk from England, or the sad fate of other outdated objects of worship. Nostalgia is also a key component of one of the more popular sub-genres which lie on the margins of nineteenth century fantasy: the lost race story. Lost race stories rarely give a prominent role to the supernatural, but their internal dynamic takes them beyond the map into those exotic regions of the Earth where men may seek a romantic destiny outside the possibilities of actual society. Like the more admirable Secondary World fantasies, the best lost race fantasies offer no easy solutions by this route, and the eccentric masterpiece of the sub-genre - Rider Haggard's *She* - is paradoxically determined in its uneasy ambivalence.

The uneasy play of nineteenth century secondary belief is also complicated by a burgeoning of interest in the altered states of consciousness associated with hallucination and delusion. This has its straightforwardly clinical side, but its more interesting exhibitions are to be found in hallucinatory grotesques moving in the direction of surrealism and absurdism. Such themes are historically linked to ideas associated with mesmerism, animal magnetism and hypnotism, which are staples of credulous

29

occult romance, but they are by no means imprisoned by the constraints of pseudoscholarly fantasy.

Consideration of the relationships which exist between fantasy and the fashionable ideas of the nineteenth century should not be concluded without amplifying the observation that, with very few exceptions, nineteenth century fantasy existed on the periphery of the Victorian literary world. It never became fashionable in its own right.

If we leave aside children's books, which compete in a specialised marketplace, the best-selling novels of nineteenth century fantasy are very few in number, and they all appeared at the end of the century when the long reign of the three- decker novel came to its end; they are *She*, the romances of Marie Corelli, and Anstey's *Vice Versa*. On the other hand, there were a few nineteenth century fantasies of a briefer kind which were spectacularly successful because they created - or at least colonised - their own market niches. Dickens' *Christmas Books* helped to create a norm by which the Christmas annuals issued by British publishers in association with their periodicals were licensed to indulge in supernatural whimsy and other fanciful tales. This licence was shared by many of the annual volumes which were issued to take advantage of the Christmas present buying season: *The Keepsake; The Continental Annual and Romantic Cabinet; Friendship's Offering* and many others.

Periodicals were vital to the promulgation of all kinds of imaginative fiction in the nineteenth century, because so much imaginative fiction works best in short fiction forms. Despite the fact that literacy spread more slowly in Britain than in France or America, the relatively large population of Britain - and especially of London - meant that British writers were at least as well supplied with outlets as their French and American counterparts. Blackwood's *Edinburgh Magazine*, which was consistently hospitable to all kinds of imaginative fiction was a vital outlet for many English writers as well as Scottish ones.

The more downmarket a mid-nineteenth century journal was, the more space it was likely to give to supernatural fiction. Popular British magazines like *The Olio, or Museum of Entertainment* (founded in 1828) and Vickers' *London Journal* (founded in 1845) are replete with stories of the supernatural, though almost all of them were either reprinted from familiar sources or of negligible quality. Penny fiction periodicals often featured fantastic tales and "legends" based in or masquerading as items of authentic folklore. Writers with higher literary ambitions usually had a hard time finding markets for their more enterprising and unusual work, and many of them obtained a significant start by publishing their works in their own periodicals. Edward Bulwer-Lytton, John Sterling and William Morris all contrived to publish their early fantasy work by such means, as did the notable Irish writer of horror stories J. Sheridan LeFanu. Had there been a recognised publishing category of the kind which now exists, the tradition of nineteenth century fantasy would undoubtedly be far richer and far more coherent.

The end of the nineteenth century was an important watershed in the history of fantasy, whose importance can hardly be overstressed. In 1900 Sigmund Freud published *The Interpretation of Dreams*, a book which was to bring about a dramatic change in attitudes to the activity (whether private or literary) of fantasizing. Whether Freud's account of the logic of dreams was actually true, or how widely it was believed, were matters of little significance in bringing about this change. The point was that a set of ideas had been produced which could not be entirely ignored, and whose attempt to penetrate the symbolism of fantasy - even if it was to be deemed entirely fatuous - could not help but make writers and readers more self-conscious in their fantasizing.

The Interpretation of Dreams was the first of a series of highly significant works in which Freud worked out his theory of the unconscious and his ideas regarding the process of repression. It argued strongly that dreaming

31

operates as a means of vicarious wish-fulfillment, in which the wishes and the means of their fulfillment are often disguised even from the fantasist by their encryption in a pattern of symbols. It went on to link the fountainhead of fantasy, and its internal symbolism, to the libido. In Freud's view, literary fantasy could be treated in much the same way as dream-fantasy. Once literary fantasists had heard of this theory, therefore - even if they heard of it only in its popular extensions as rumour and jest - it was unforgettable. Its central theses might be rejected, but they could not be disregarded.

It was, of course, well known to many literary fantasists of the nineteenth century that their creative work might involve symbolism and that symbols could be used to convey sexual meanings whose direct expression was taboo. When Christina Rossetti wrote in "Goblin Market" about "forbidden fruit" she used the euphemism quite deliberately, and it may have been in her mind when she wrote of the goblins trying to force their fruit past Lizzie's resistant lips that the word "lips" is susceptible of more than one meaning. But in making such symbolic wordplay, the poet was not referring her practice to any theoretical context which spoke of the intrinsic nature of fantasy; she was simply making a fantasy of one particular kind. The way that twentieth century writers came to handle sexual symbolism in their fiction could not help but be different.

Freud's theory changed the way in which nineteenth century works were henceforth read, as well as the way in which subsequent works were composed. Many nineteenth century fantasies have erotic themes, subtly veiled by humour and sentimentality, but those themes tend to be treated innocently and reverently; it is nowadays difficult to read them with a similarly reverent eye. Thanks to Freud all twentieth century innocence has come to seem like shallowness where it is not mere pretence, and reverence a stylistic affectation. Just as dirty jokes came to be accompanied by a ritual nudge and wink, and sentimental displays with a mime of mournful violins, fantasies began to be packaged with token acknowledgements of their own particular artificiality; naive literary dreaming was very largely replaced by a form of "lucid dreaming" whose lucidity was supplied by theories of natural symbolism.

We now know, of course, that Freud's *Interpretation of Dreams* is not true in any strong sense; as a whole and coherent scientific theory it is quite exploded, although its remaining adherents still nurture the hope that its bare bones might yet be fleshed out into a theory which, though falling short of a general explanation of the phenomenon of dreaming, might still have some relevance to the business of thinking seriously about the psychological utility of fantasy. Freudian theory is itself, therefore, no more than a fantasy about fantasies, exactly on a par with many of the literary works whose composition and substance it overshadows. Freudian theory cannot *explain* fantasies any more than it can really explain dreams, even though it has altered forever the terms in which we think about fantasy, and the way in which writers go about the business of creating a fantasy.

It is worth noting that Freud's theory is itself merely the latest in a long series of images which represent the human psyche in terms of a crucial division and opposition. In Freud's terminology, the *ego* must somehow negotiate between, and if possible reconcile, two sets of contradictory pressures: the anarchic and amoral bundle of appetites which is the *id*; and the censorious and orderly *superego*. In the conflict between these forces we can see one more version of the battle between passion and reason which has been recognised since the birth of philosophy.

Plato, one of the first great champions of reason, imagined the human soul to be purely rational, but when embedded in its material shell it had perforce to be associated with irrational impulses. Even in Plato's view this was not entirely unfortunate, for there were some impulses which were noble ones - ambition; the desire for power; righteous wrath - but the rest of these passionate forces were "lower" in kind, to be feared, despised and

33

disciplined. Their temptations ought, in Plato's view, to be subject to a ruthless tyranny of the intellect. From the ideal society outlined (without irony) in the *Republic*, poets were to be cast out, because their work "nourished the well of the emotions" while the true aim of a civilised society should be to dry it up.

Few of Plato's successors were as ruthless as this in their opposition to the emotions, but their more moderate views were usually aligned on the same side. Aristotle felt that emotions and the vulgar passions connected with basic bodily processes, which constituted the "animal part" of man. Among later Greek philosophers the Stoics shared Plato's suspicions to the full, regarding the passions as perturbations of the mind, almost as a kind of mental disease. Their rivals the Epicureans took a different view, insisting on the naturalness of pleasure and preaching a kind of hedonism but their search was for a purified, rather cerebral species of joy, fit for connoisseurs, and one of their mottoes was "Nothing to Excess".

For Christian philosophers of a later period the passions were temptations of the devil, and giving way to them was the very essence of sin. True godliness was based in asceticism, and those emotions suited to life in Heaven would be very stringently purified, consisting mainly of love of God and a joyful knowledge of that Divine Love which would be returned. When rationalist philosophers set to work again within the Christian tradition they tended to do little more than secularise this view. Descartes considered the passions as excitations of the soul caused by the movement of "animal spirits"; Spinoza, in laying down the foundation stones of his system of Ethics, accepted it as axiomatic that human freedom was based in the rational power of the intellect, while the opposing power of the emotions must be reckoned a burdensome kind of servitude.

Many writers of the nineteenth century proposed new terminologies which pretended to be more scientific, but the dualistic story which most of them told was much the same. Darwin, meditating upon *The Expression of the Emotions in*

Man and Animals (1872) , considered our appetites and passions to be part of our evolutionary heritage, operating independently of the will, as an "undirected flow of nerve-force". The psychologist Havelock Ellis, in *Studies in the Psychology of Sex* (1897), identified two "great fundamental impulses" supplying the "dynamic energy" of all behaviour: hunger and sexual desire; like Freud he was to become preoccupied with the idea that the latter might easily be transformed by "sublimation" into other kinds of creative endeavour, including literary work.

Some other nineteenth century writers tried to make fundamental connections between the divided nature of man and the exercise of artistic creativity. Notable among them was Nietzsche, whose account of *The Birth of Tragedy* (1872) contrasted the "Apollonian" and "Dionysian" elements which, in fusion, formulated the world-view of tragedy (whose subsequent death was procured by the victory of rationalism). Later writers were to borrow this dialectical pair to describe phases throughout which whole cultures might pass, in the one striving for the rule of calm reason, in the other for the wild abandonment of ecstasy.

Throughout the history of these dualistic accounts of human being there emerged only a handful of true champions of the passions. The most prestigious was probably the eighteenth century French philosopher Rousseau, who firmly believed in the nobility of savagery, and became the father figure of the cult of *sensibilité* . In his later writings, though, Nietzsche remade his image of Dionysus, making him a symbol of a healthy reconciliation of the Apollonian and the Dionysian: passion sublimated into creative endeavour. In this view reason is a counterpart to rather than an enemy of the passions, and the real contrast is between the harshly repressive dominion of ascetiscism and a benevolent quasi-Epicurean acceptance of passionate purpose and rational method.

The principal process of ideological evolution which is visible in the fantasy genre as it moves from the nineteenth into the twentieth century is perhaps best summed up (though any summing up is bound to be an oversimplification) as the discovery and championship of an essentially Nietzschean position. We can find the earliest evidence of this evolution in the lushness of nineteenth century French fantasy, but we can see its emergency in some of the British *fin de siecle* writers - most notably Richard Garnett, Oscar Wilde and Vernon Lee.

In the Sartrean theory of emotion - which is itself an unmistakable product of twentieth century thought, and might well be reckoned another of its scholarly fantasies - passion ceases to be defined in quasi-mechanical terms. The ideas of "animal spirits" and "nerve-force" are consigned to the same dustbin. Sartre urges us instead to view emotional experience as a kind of perception, characterised by a "magical" world view which contrasts with, but also complements, the "instrumental" world-view which underlies our scientific understanding.

In this view we see the world in two ways, which overlap but never quite come into perfect focus: we see a world of objects to be manipulated, and a world of objects of desire. These two worlds are differently conceptualised and differently evaluated, but we live simultaneously in both. We can no more force our experience into a repressive existential straitjacket which recognises only one form of perception than we can separate ourselves into two distinct individuals. Our task instead - and this is what mature fantasy fiction also asserts, both in its most interesting fictions and in its theory as articulated by Tolkien - is to reach the most life-enhancing compromise we can. The Nietzschean image of the reformulated Dionysus is as apt a symbol as any for that goal.

This is the *zeitgeist* of modern fantasy literature, within which many and various writers are trying to find their moral bearings. The writers of the twentieth century inherited this task along with the tradition from their nineteenth century forebears, and there is little among their materials that is authentically new. Twentieth century usage of these materials is different because it is far more

36

self-conscious, but the essential mission of twentieth century writers remains the same as the mission of their nineteenth century forebears, which was - whether they knew it or not - to reconcile more intimately and more cleverly the two modes of our experience: the emotional and the rational; the magical and the instrumental; the fantastic and the mundane.

THE DEDALUS BOOK

of

BRITISH FANTASY

NATHAN DRAKE (1766-1836) was a country doctor
and literary scholar whose works include two notable studies
of Shakespeare and a curious patchwork of essays, poems,
tales and meditations called *Literary Hours* (1798). The last
named includes an essay in which Drake appointed himself
an early apologist for the Gothic imagination. This item is
almost exactly contemporary with Coleridge's "Rime of the
Ancient Mariner" and their publication was quickly followed
by Matthew Gregory Lewis's two collections of ballads
mingling elements of chivalric romance and Gothic horror -
Tales of Terror (1799) and *Tales of Wonder* (1800) - the
latter of which featured the earliest published poems by
Walter Scott.

In his apologetic essay Drake observes that Gothic
literature has two distinct strands, which move in different
directions; he calls them the "terrible" and the "sportive".
The former, he argues, is organised around the central motif
of the spectre, the latter around the fairy. He also notes that

the recent resurgency of the Gothic in literature had been supplemented by a similar resurgence of the Celtic imagination, by virtue of the publication of James MacPherson's *Ossian* (whose authenticity Drake had no reason to doubt).

Having called attention to certain faults which he deemed to be present in recently published works, Drake boldly set out to demonstrate how the job ought to be done, conscientiously attempting to practise what he had preached. His essay on the Gothic is followed immediately by an "Ode to Superstition", and then by "Henry Fitzowen", in which he set out to find a proper balance between the terrible and the sportive. He was to write other tales and verses of the same type, but this first attempt remained his most interesting exercise in leavening the tale of terror with the charm of fantasy.

HENRY FITZOWEN

by
Nathan Drake

I

But when he reach'd his castle-gate,
His gate was hung with black
Percy's *Reliques* , Vol iii

In the north of England, toward the commencement of
the reign of Edward the Fourth, lived Henry Fitzowen. He
had lost his parents early in life, and had been educated with
an only sister under the care of his guardian. Henry was the
heir of considerable property which had been under his sole
management for near four years, having arrived at that
period of life when the character of the man fully unfolds
itself, when at five-and-twenty he had gratified the wishes
and fulfilled the predictions of his friends. Possessed of an
active and liberal mind, of a tender and grateful heart, he
was equally an object of love and esteem to his companions
and his tenants; and combined, likewise, the energies of
youth, its vigour and vivacity, with, what were rare
attainments in that age of anarchy and ignorance, the
elegant accomplishments of the scholar and the poet. In his
person he was rather athletic, yet was it gracefully formed,
and had much of that chivalric air so highly prized at that
time when warfare and civil discord still raged throughout
the island. When rushing into the field, no hero in the army
of the youthful Edward burnt with superior ardour, or
managed his horse and arms with equal ease and spirit;
when seated mid the circle of his peaceful friends, none could
rival his power of intellect and sweetness of manner, the
courtesy of his demeanour to the men, the gallantry of his
attentions to the fair.

With his sister, who superintended the economy of his
household, and a few friends, he spent the major part of the

41

year at his paternal castle in Yorkshire, a piece of fine old Gothic architecture, and seated in the bosom of a romantic glen. Here, in his great hall, hung round with the arms and trophies of his ancestors, and presiding at his ancient, oaken, and hospitable table, he delighted to accumulate his neighbours, and view the smile of satisfaction and pleasure play mid the charms of innocence and beauty, or gladden the features of industrious dependence. Here, also, on a visit to his sister, and usually accompanied by her mother, would frequently appear Adeline De Montfort. Adeline was the only daughter of an officer of great worth and bravery, and who fell contending for the Yorkists at the dreadful battle of Towton. Dying, however, in embarrassed circumstances, his widow was unable to support the establishment they had hitherto maintained, and therefore took a small but elegant house on the skirts of the forest adjoining to the Fitzowen estate. A short time sufficed to produce an intimacy between the two families, and from similarity of disposition and pursuits. Adeline and Clara Fitzowen soon became almost inseparable companions. The daughter of Montfort was in her twentieth year, and had been gifted by nature with more than common charms, her person was elegantly formed, her eyes blue as the sky of summer, her hair of a nut brown, and her cheeks

> The roses white and red resembled well
> Whereon the hoary May-dew sprinkled lies,
> When the fair Morn first blusheth from her cell,
> And breatheth balm from opened Paradise.

The most unaffected modesty, too, and a disposition peculiarly sweet, united to the graces of a mind polished by unusual taste, rendered her personal beauties doubly interesting; and there were few of the opposite sex who, having once witnessed her attractions, did not sigh to appropriate them. That Henry, therefore, who had such frequent opportunities of conversing with this amiable girl, should admire and love her, was an event to be expected;

42

indeed, such was his affection for her, that, deprived of his beloved Adeline, existence would have lost all its allurement.

To love thus ardent and sincere, and professed by a youth of the most winning manners, and superior accomplishments, no woman could long be insensible, and in the bosom of Adeline glowed the sweet emotions of reciprocal passion. Amid the wild and picturesque beauties of Ruydvellin, where the vast solitude and repose of nature, or the luxuriant and softened features of the secluded landscape, awoke the mind to awful or to tender feelings, the sensations of mutual attachment were for some time cherished undisturbed, and an union that would, probably, fix for life the felicity of the lovers, had been projected and determined upon; when an incident, accompanied with circumstances of the most singular kind, threw a bar in the way of its completion.

At the distance of about twelve miles from the castle of Ruydvellin, resided Walleran Earl of Meulant, a nobleman of Norman descent, and of great hauteur and family pride. He had reached the age of forty, was unmarried, and though, from motives of ostentation, supporting a considerable and even splendid establishment, his disposition was gloomy and unsocial. In his person he was gigantic and disproportioned, and his features betrayed a stern and unrelenting severity, whilst from his eyes usually darted so wild and malignant an expression, that the object on which they fell, involuntarily shrank from their notice. His habits of life too were such as to excite much wonder and very horrid reports; he constantly inhabited one turret of his extensive castle, where, all night long, for many years, the glare of torches had been visible, yet his servants declared that, notwithstanding this perpetual illumination, his agitation and terror were, frequently, as the twilight closed, so dreadful, that they fled his presence, and often at midnight from his chamber, in which he always locked himself up and forbade interruption, half-stifled groans and wailing sounds were heard, as from a person under torture. At stated periods he visited a forest of very antique oak, which stood about a mile from the castle;

43

such was the massy size of these trees that they were generally esteemed coeval with the druidic times, and the gloom of their foliage was so dense and impenetrable, that the country people feared to approach the wood, and believed it to be haunted by preternatural beings; for often at the dead noon of night, shrill and demoniacal shrieks, and appearances of the most ghastly and tremendous kind, had terrified the belated traveller, and once, it is said, when one of the servants of Walleran, from motives of curiosity, had traced the footsteps of his master to this enchanted forest, he dared to enter its infernal shade, and since that hour no eye has witnessed his return.

Though Walleran was thus an object of dread and awful surmise to all around him, yet, from being possessed of very large property, and having numerous relations whose interest it was to pay him every respect, his castle was occasionally filled with the first ranks of society, who were banqueted in a sumptuous manner, and amused with the most splendid diversions of the age, such as tournaments, mysteries, the chase, etc. On these occasions the neighbouring families were invited to the castle, and Henry Fitzowen, with his sister and Adeline, usually graced the festival. Henry was one of the most expert and elegant tilters in the school of chivalry; and when Adeline's Champion, and, according to etiquette, by her conducted into the lists, he performed prodigies of valour, and unhorsed almost every opponent. Adeline had then to bestow the envied prize on the object of her affections, and in these moments her features were lighted up with peculiar animation, and her form displayed the most fascinating allurements. None beheld her without emotion; but in the breast of Walleran burnt the most intense desire, and, accustomed to overcome every opposition in his amours by open force, or insidious stratagem, he had long determined, and without the smallest scruple or compunction, to get possession of the person of Adeline, for in her heart, such was the brutality of his appetite, he had neither wish nor hope to find a place. Indeed, he was well acquainted with

44

the connection, and had heard of the approaching union between her and Henry, and the latter, on this account, became an object of the most malignant hatred. Frequently had he meditated on the means of conveying her from her own villa, or the castle of Ruydvellin, and one attempt through the medium of his servants the vigilance of Henry had already rendered abortive, who suspected, though he could not prove, for the villains were disguised, the machinations of his infamous and too potent neighbour.

Apprehensive, at length, he should for ever lose her, if the nuptials, the day for which was fixed, should take place, the Earl became resolved, whilst Adeline was now at Ruydvellin, to seize the earliest opportunity, and to employ all the resources of his art in effecting his diabolical purposes. It was not long ere the opportunity he had so anxiously awaited was given; for, in about a week after, Henry, with a large party of his friends, the nobility and gentry of the neighbourhood, met together for the stag-hunt, and were, as usual, joined by Walleran. The morning chase afforded the finest diversion, but was very long, and carried them to such a distance from home, that they agreed to dine in the forest upon the provisions which they had providently brought with them, and endeavour to start fresh game after their meal. Walleran, it was observed, had retired before dinner; but as this was no extraordinary occurrence, little attention was paid to it, and, a stag being shortly after roused, the chase was resumed with fresh vigour and alacrity. Nothing could exceed the spirit and swiftness of the animal, and Henry, who was generally foremost on these occasions, so far outstript his companions, that, having pushed into an intricate part of the forest with a view to reach the stag in a more direct line, and being led farther into its recesses than he was aware, at length neither the sound of hounds, horses, nor men, any longer reached his ear, and perceiving his path more difficult as he proceeded, he paused, and listened with deep attention, but nothing, save the sighing of the evening breeze, as it rustled through the branches of the oak was heard. The sun was now

45

approaching the horizon, and had shot his fiery beams into the forest, when Henry, reflecting on the distance he was, probably, from home, and on the impending gloom of night, immediately determined to retrace his steps, and regain, if possible, the open country. With this intention, therefore, he turned his steed, and carefully pursuing the path he came, at length reached the plain, when, to his great surprise, he once more beheld, and in a direction directly contrary to what he could have expected, or thought possible, the very stag he had been chasing so long in vain. He appeared lightly bounding at a distance, and as the sun shone upon his dappled sides made a pleasing and conspicuous figure. Neither dogs, nor horses, nor a single human being, were in view, and Fitzowen, more from curiosity than any other motive, put spurs to his horse, and pursued him. The animal seemed perfectly at his ease, and went on gently, as if holding his chaser in contempt, when, crossing the dale, he turned into a narrow road, with Henry almost at his heels, who followed him in this manner, between three and four miles through a series of winding and intricate lanes, and had just reached him, as he conceived, when he suddenly struck to the left, and, the lane closing, a vast and apparently interminable heath rushed upon his view, but to his utter astonishment, for no shelter, or cover of any kind was present for concealment, not the least vestige of the animal he had so closely pursued could now be seen. All was nearly silent and sunk in repose; twilight had spread her grey tint over the plain, and scarce a breath of air moved the thistle down. Some clouds, however, gathered dark in the west, and were tinged with a dusky red, whilst a few large drops of rain were, now and then, heard, as they fell sullen and heavy on the heath, or shook the withered broom.

Unable to ascertain the distance from Ruydvellin, and unacquainted with the features of the country, Henry now rode impatiently forward, in hopes of discovering some road or track which might lead him to a cottage, and give him a chance for enquiry. The strangeness of the preceding incident too had occasioned some uneasiness in his bosom, and he more than once adverted to the arts and designs of Walleran; the night also was approaching, and threatened to be stormy, and he dwelt upon the anxiety of his female friends. Whilst thus meditating, he had reached a spot where several rugged paths seemed to stretch across the heath, and one appearing more beaten than the rest, he was about to enter upon it, when he thought he beheld, at a distance, a human figure, as of a man wrapped in dark garments, and walking swiftly on. Highly pleased with the circumstance, and anticipating ample information, he immediately quitted the track, and pushed after him. As he drew near, the figure, which appeared to dilate into more than common proportion, had the garb and aspect of a monk, and glided on with such rapidity, that Henry found it necessary to quicken his pace, when the plain gradually contracting, and some trees shooting up in the horizon, afforded him hopes of its termination. He now called loudly to the monk, requesting him to stop, but no answer was returned, and his form, dimly seen through the increasing gloom, still glided noiseless along the heath, till having reached its verge, where rose the skirts of a pine forest, he, for several minutes, hurried along its border, and then suddenly disappeared. Henry was, by this time, convinced that the being he had so long endeavoured to overtake, was nothing human, and resolving, if possible, to return to the track he had so rashly quitted, was wheeling round, when a light not far distant glimmered among some trees, and though nearly in the same direction the delusive monk had taken, yet once more animated with the hopes of obtaining a guide, he again ventured to trust his senses, and made immediately for the spot whence the rays appeared to stream.

The light, as he advanced, glowed steady and brilliant, but required more time and effort to attain than he expected, for having left the common, he was now amid cultivated land, which consequently opposed many an obstacle to his progress. At length, however, he approached within a few hundred yards of it, still flattering himself it issued from

47

some neighbouring hamlet, when, rising slowly from the ground, it began to expand and yield a very vivid light, then diffusing itself, and melting into air, it gradually assumed a paler tint, and disappeared.

The night now became extremely dark, the thunder growled at a distance, and the rain fell heavy, whilst Henry, shocked at the delusions he had been subjected to, and tormented with apprehension for the safety of his beloved Adeline, wandered from field to field, his imagination busy in suggesting the most dreadful events, and filled with horror and resentment as he called to mind the wild and lawless character of Walleran, to whose infernal machinations he could not avoid attributing the singular incidents which had lately befallen him.

Whilst thus situated, and in little hope of receiving either information or shelter until break of day, his attention was aroused by the barking of dogs, and making up to the sound with as much precision as the storm would permit, to his great joy he discovered a farm-house, whose inhabitants welcomed him with the utmost promptitude and kindness. Here he learnt that he was better than twenty miles from Ruydvellin, and that it wanted scarce an hour of midnight, but that the principal road, and which would soon lead him into that which went direct for his castle, ran within two miles of their cottage. Highly delighted with this last piece of intelligence, and extremely anxious to hasten forward, he engaged one of the farmer's sons to conduct him to the road, and then partaking of some refreshment, and heartily regaling his steed, he made many acknowledgments to his host for his well-timed hospitality, and departed.

The rain beat furiously on our travellers, and the lightning played strongly in the horizon, whilst the thunder continually muttering, and pealing louder as they advanced, gave token of a dreadful tempest. The road, however, was now before them, and the young farmer parting on his return, Henry rapidly pursued his journey, and within two hours, notwithstanding the darkness of the night, reached the border of his own domain. With a boding mind and palpitating heart he passed the well-known grounds, every now and then vividly illuminated by the glare of intense lightning, whilst the thunder rolled awfully along the vault of heaven, or burst over head in loud and repeated claps. He had now approached within view of his castle, whose numerous towers and turrets, as the lightning flashed, were distinctly seen, and made a beautiful appearance; but in the pitchy darkness which immediately succeeded, no lights could be distinguished in any part of its vast extent, a circumstance which occasioned him much surprise, and added not a little to his apprehensions. These, however, were increased to a painful degree, when, on his arrival at the fosse, no wardens were perceived on the walls, nor was any porter at the barbican, which being open, he hurried over the draw-bridge, and was about to strike upon the great gate, when, starting back with horror, he observed, as the lighting glared, that it was hung with black. This, in periods of chivalry, being a signal of misfortune, was sufficient to strike terror into the stoutest chief, when returning to his castle, he beheld the portentous monument of disaster; and Henry, whose fears had been long alive, now felt that all his hopes were blasted; for that some dreadful event had taken place he well knew, and the uncertainty of the moment giving full scope to the powers of imagination, it came forward wrapt in the most tremendous colouring.

When the agitation of his frame, however, had somewhat subsided, he again drew near, and, lifting the massy knocker, was going to strike, when the gate yielded to the impulse, being left a little open, a circumstance which its sable covering, and the momentary light of heaven, had not before given him an opportunity of perceiving. He now, therefore, entered the outer ballium, and was slowly and cautiously proceeding, when a deep groan, as from one in acute pain, struck his ear, and the lightning, at that instant, glancing across him, he beheld the ground moistened with blood, and two of his servants stretched dead at his feet. A sight so shocking, fixed him for some moments to the spot, but the groan being repeated, he started, and advanced to

49

the place whence it issued, when a voice, whose tones he well recollected as those of an old and faithful domestic, in tremulous accents implored his mercy. Henry, to the infinite joy of the poor man, immediately discovered himself, and, impatient to learn the cause of events so horrible, urged him to an explanation. Faint, however, with the loss of blood, racked with pain, and overwhelmed with the most tumultuous sensations on recognising his beloved master, he was unable to articulate a word, but grasping Henry's hand, as he stooped to assist him, he pressed it with convulsive energy, and, uttering a deep sigh, reclined upon his master, and expired.

The most acute anguish now seized the unhappy Henry, who called down the bitterest imprecations on the author of his misfortunes; but conscious that all now depended upon his personal activity, and tortured with anxiety for those he held most dear, he once more endeavoured to proceed, for the darkness was so profound, that, except when the lightning streamed, not a single object could be discerned. From his knowledge of the place, however, he contrived to pass into the inner ballium, and then soon reaching the keep, entered his great hall, which he found completely deserted, not a single being returning his repeated calls; yet at intervals he thought he could distinguish low groans, which seemed to issue from a considerable distance. Crossing the hall he now ascended the winding staircase, and, having attained the gallery, perceived a light which glimmered through the crevice at the bottom of a door, and making the castle again re-echo with the names of Adeline and Clara, was at last answered by the shrill tones of the women, who, with rapture almost too great for utterance, had now, for the first time, recollected his voice. Rushing to the door, therefore, he made every exertion to open it, but the lock being strong and massy, it resisted, for some time, his utmost efforts, though assisted by those within. At length, however, it did yield, and, the next moment, Clara Fitzowen was in his arms; but in vain did he look round for Adeline, and dreading even the result of inquiry, sank into a chair, silent, and racked with anxiety and disappointment; a few minutes, however, gave him the information he apprehended, for her mother, in an agony of distress, which drew tears from all present, soon accounted for the loss of her beloved child.

It appeared from her relation that, about the dusk of the evening, a party of armed men, their features concealed in masks, had surprised the castle, a circumstance of easy occurrence when no hostile attempt was suspected, and entering the great hall, where the females were then assembled, seized upon Adeline, and were forcing her away, when some of the servants interfered, and a severe struggle took place, but which, as the ruffians were prepared for opposition, soon terminated in their favour. They then bound the men they had subdued, and threw them into the dungeon of the keep, and compelling the women, and their servants, to go up stairs, locked them in an inner room, though with a light, and carried off Adeline in triumph.

This event, though it had frequently occurred to the mind of Henry since his approach to the castle, yet now that it was fully ascertained, occasioned him as much distress as if it had not been for a moment apprehended. As soon, however, as the violence of his emotion had, in some degree, abated, he accused Walleran as the author of the atrocious deed, and proposed an immediate expedition to, and attack upon, his castle; then presently recollecting the dreadful scenes he had witnessed at the great gate, he requested an explanation of his sister; but Clara being totally ignorant of the circumstances he alluded to, he lighted a torch, and descended to release his servants from their dungeon, which he effected through the medium of a private passage, the principal entrance being left too well secured for their efforts to overcome. He found several of them wounded, but so rejoiced at seeing their master again, that for some minutes they completely forgot their situation and sufferings. Many, however, were still absent; and he learnt that whilst those who had been confined were still contending with the villains, a party of their fellow servants had gone round to secure the great gate, but of their fate they knew nothing. Henry now requesting those who were able to follow him, procured some more torches, and issued forth to search the outer ballium. Here weltering in their blood were found slain the two men whom he had seen by the glare of the lightning, and, a little further, his old steward, who had expired in his arms. Close by the gate, also wounded, and on the ground, they discovered the porter and his assistant; these, on receiving some refreshment, and due attention to their injuries, speedily revived, and had soon strength enough to inform Henry, that when the struggle commenced in the great hall, they had flown to the support of their friends, but perceiving it would be vain to continue the contest without better arms, they, with three or four others, separated to procure them, and to secure the great gate and barbican, which, in their hurry and alarm they had left open and unguarded. Hither, however, they had not arrived many moments before the ruffians, having subdued opposition in the hall, approached with the unhappy Adeline, whose prayers and entreaties were in vain addressed to beings who knew no touch of pity. A severe engagement now took place, but the numbers proving very unequal, and themselves and their companions shortly either wounded or slain, the villains, with their helpless charge, passed on, nor could it be ascertained in what direction they travelled. The porter, however, it seems, had sufficient strength remaining to crawl to the lodge, where seizing the black mantle, the omen of disaster, he had just power to suspend it on the gate, and then dropt exhausted by its side. This he did, with a view to alarm any passenger, or pilgrim, who might in the morning be journeying that way, and induce him to inquiry, and the offer of assistance.

The thunder had by this time passed off; twilight began to dawn, and Henry, notwithstanding the fatigues of the preceding day, determined to push forward immediately to the castle of Walleran, in hopes of taking him by surprise. Accordingly, arming those of his servants who had not been injured in the previous contest, and entrusting the wounded to the care of the women, he clothed himself in mail, and mounting a fresh steed, reached the magnificent halls of Walleran in little more than an hour. Here, however, to his great disappointment, he learnt, that Walleran had not returned from the chase, but that about two hours after noon, a man, who to them was a stranger, and mounted on a horse bathed in foam, had arrived to say, that the Earl would not revisit his castle for some weeks, but refused to give them any information with regard to his present place of residence.

Henry, oppressed in body and mind, now slowly returned to Ruydvellin, pondering on the plan he should pursue; and on his arrival at the castle, hastened to consult his sister, and the mother of his Adeline.

II

What is this so wither'd, and so wild in its attire;
That looks not like an inhabitant o' the earth,
And yet is on 't? -   SHAKESPEARE

Though no present intelligence could be obtained relative to the abode of Walleran, yet as it was most probable that where he was, there Adeline would be found, Henry determined, with the concurrence of his family, to spare no effort in detecting his residence. After a few hours' rest, therefore, he armed himself completely, and bidding adieu to his disconsolate friends, to whom, assuming a cheerful tone, he promised the speedy restoration of Adeline, he mounted his favourite roan, and issued from the great gate, whilst the sun, now verging towards noon, smote full upon his plumed casque.

Not willing, however, to alarm the neighbouring country, where his person and accoutrements would be known wherever he should stop for inquiry, and secrecy being likewise necessary toward the completion of his views, he carefully concealed his features beneath his visor, assumed unusual arms, took a different device, and no

53

retinue whatever, resolved, should he find Walleran surrounded by his myrmidons, to hasten back to Ruydvellin, and collecting his faithful followers, return and attack him in full force, placing no confidence in his honour, should a single combat ensue, when thus supported by banditti. That no time might be lost in the pursuit, he dismissed two of his confidential servants on different routes, and under similar precautions.

These measures being taken, Henry carried his researches through the neighbouring seats, and made every inquiry that could lead to detection, but in vain; striking further into the country, therefore, he unexpectedly came into very wild scenery, and it was with difficulty he could procure the most homely provision in a tract so thinly inhabited, and where a shepherd's hut, or the cottage of a peasant, proved his only places of rest. Some weeks had thus passed, when toward the sunset of a very fine day, after having traversed a lone and unfrequented part, he arrived at the edge of a thick and dark forest; the sky became suddenly overcast, and it began to rain; the thunder rolled at a distance, and sheets of livid lightning flashed across the heath. Overcome with fatigue and hunger, he rode impatiently along the border of the forest, in hopes of discovering an entrance, but none was to be found. At length, just as he was about to dismount with an intention of breaking the fence, he discerned, as he thought, something moving upon the heath, and upon advancing towards it, it proved to be an old woman gathering peat, and who, overtaken by the storm, was hurrying home as fast as her infirm limbs could carry her. The sight of a human creature filled the heart of Fitzowen with joy, and, hastily riding up, he inquired how far he had deviated from the right road, and where he could procure a night's lodging. The old woman now slowly lifting up her palsied head, discovered a set of features which could scarcely be called human, her eyes were red, piercing and distorted, and rolling horribly, glanced upon every object but the person by whom she was addressed, and, at intervals, they emitted a fiery disagreeable light; her hair, of a dirty gray, hung matted in large masses upon her shoulders, and a few thin portions rushed abrupt and horizontally from the upper part of her forehead, which was much wrinkled, and of a parchment hue; her cheeks were hollow, withered, and red with a quantity of acrid rheum; her nose was large, prominent, and sharp; her lips thin, skinny, and livid; her few teeth black; and her chin long and peaked, with a number of bushy hairs depending from its extremity; her nails also were acute, crooked, and bent over her fingers; and her garments, ragged and fluttering in the wind, displayed every possible variety of colour. Henry was a little daunted: but, the old woman having mentioned a dwelling at some distance, and offering to lead the way, the pleasure received from this piece of intelligence effaced the former impression, and, alighting from his horse, he laid hold of the bridle, and they slowly moved over the heath.

The storm had now ceased, and the moon rising gave presage of a fine night, just as this singular conductor, taking a sudden turn, plunged into the wood by a path, narrow and almost choked up with a quantity of brier and thorn. The trees were thick, and, save a few glimpses of the moon, which, now and then, poured light on the uncouth features of his companion, all was dark and dismal; the heart of Fitzowen misgave him; neither spoke; and he pursued his guide merely by the noise she made in hurrying through the bushes, which was done with a celerity totally inconsistent with her former decrepitude. At length the path grew wider, and a faint blue light, which came from a building at some distance, glimmered before them; they now left the wood, and issued upon a rocky and uneven piece of ground, whilst the moon, struggling through a cloud, cast a doubtful and uncertain light, and the old woman, with a leer which made the very hair of Fitzowen stand on end, told him that the dwelling was at hand. It was so; for a Gothic castle, placed on a considerable elevation, now came in view; it was a large massy structure, much decayed, and some parts of it in a totally ruinous condition; a portion, however, of the keep, or great tower, was still entire, as was also the entrance to the court or enclosure, preserved probably by the ivy, whose fibres crept round with solicitous care. Large fragments of the ruin were scattered about, covered with moss and half sunk in the ground, and a number of old elm trees, through whose foliage the wind sighed with a sullen and melancholy sound, dropped a deep and settled gloom, that scarce permitted the moon to stream by fits upon the building. Fitzowen drew near, ardent curiosity mingled with awe dilated his bosom, and he inwardly congratulated himself upon so singular an adventure, when turning round to question his companion, a glimpse of the moon poured full upon his eye so horrid a contexture of feature, so wild and preternatural a combination, that, smote with terror and unable to move, a cold sweat trickled from every pore, and immediately this infernal being seizing him by the arm, and hurrying him over the draw-bridge to the great entrance of the keep, the portcullis fell with a tremendous sound, and the astonished youth, starting as it were from a trance, drew his sword in act to destroy his treacherous guide, when instantly a horrible and infernal laugh burst from her, and in a moment the whole castle was in an uproar, peal after peal issuing from every quarter, till at length growing faint they died away, and a dead silence ensued.

Fitzowen, who, during this strange tumult, had collected all his scattered powers, now looked round him with determined resolution; his terrible companion had disappeared, and the moon shining full upon the portcullis convinced him that any escape that way was impracticable; the wind sighed through the elms, and the scared owl, uttering his discordant note, broke from his nest, and, sweeping through the vale beneath, sought for more secure repose. Having reasoned himself, therefore, into a state of cool fortitude, and bent up every power to the appalling enterprise, our Adventurer entered the great tower, from a loop-hole near the summit of which a dim twinkling light could be just discerned. He extended his sword before him, for it was dark, and proceeded carefully to search around, in hopes, either of discovering some aperture which might lead to the vestibule, or staircase, or of wreaking his vengeance on the wretch who had thus decoyed him. All was still as death, but as he strode over the floor, a dull, hollow sound issued from beneath, and rendered him apprehensive of falling through into some dismal vault, from which he might never be able to extricate himself. In this situation, dreading the effect of each light footstep, a sound, as of many people whispering, struck his ear; he bent forward, listening with eager attention, and as it seemed to proceed from a little distance only before him, he determined to follow it; he did so, and instantly fell through the mouldering pavement, whilst at the same time, peals of horrid laughter again burst, with reiterated clamour, from every chamber of the castle.

Fitzowen rose with considerable difficulty, and much stunned with the fall, although, fortunately, the spot he had dropped upon was covered with a quantity of damp and soft earth, which gave way to his weight. He now found himself in a large vault, arched in the Gothic manner, and supported by eight massy pillars, down whose sides the damp moisture ran in cold and heavy drops, the moon shining with great lustre through three iron grated windows, which, although rusty with age, were strong enough to resist his utmost efforts, and having in vain tried to force them, he now looked around for his sword, which, during the fall, had started from his grasp, and in searching the ground with his fingers, he laid hold of, and drew forth, the fresh bones of an enormous skeleton; he started back with horror; a cold wind brushed violently along the surface of the vault, and a ponderous iron door, slowly grating on its hinges, opened at one corner, and disclosed to his wondering eye a broken staircase, down whose steps a blue and faint light flashed by fits, like the lightning of a summer's eve.

Appalled by these dreadful prodigies, Fitzowen felt, in spite of all his resolution, a cold and death-like chill pervade his frame, and kneeling down, he prayed fervently to that Power without whose mandate no being is let loose upon another, and feeling himself more calm and resolved, he

57

again began to search for his sword, when a moon-beam, falling on the blade, at once restored it to its owner.

Having thus resumed his wonted fortitude and resolution, he held a parley with himself, and perceiving no way by which he could escape, boldly resolved to brave all the terrors of the staircase, and, once more recommending himself to his Maker, began to ascend. The light still flashed, enabling him to climb those parts which were broken or decayed. He had proceeded in this manner a considerable way, mounting, as he supposed, to the summit of the keep, when suddenly a shrill and agonizing shriek issued from the upper part of it, and something rudely brushing down grasped him with tremendous strength; in a moment he became motionless and cold as ice, and felt himself hurried back by some irresistible being; but, just as he had reached the vault, a spectre of so dreadful a shape stalked by within it, that, straining every muscle, he sprang from the deadly grasp: the iron door rushed in thunder upon its hinges, and a deep hollow groan resounded from beneath. No sooner had the door closed, than yelling screams, and sounds which almost suspended the very pulse of life, issued from the vault, as if a troop of hellish furies, with their chains untied, were dashing them in frenzy, and howling to the uproar. Henry stood fixed in horror, a deadly fear ran through every vein, and the throbbing of his heart oppressed him. The tumult, however, at length subsiding, he recovered some portion of strength, and immediately making use of it to convey himself as far as possible from the iron door, presently reached his former elevation on the staircase, which, after ascending a few more steps, terminated in a winding gallery.

The light, which had hitherto flashed incessantly, now disappeared, and he was left in almost total darkness, except when, now and then, the moon threw a few cool rays through some shattered loop-hole, heightening the horror of the scene. He felt reluctant to proceed, and looked back with apprehension lest some yelling fiend should again plunge him into the vault. A mournful wind howled through the apartments of the castle, and listening, he thought he heard the iron door grate upon its hinges; he started with terror, the sweat stood in big drops upon his forehead, and he rushed forward with desperate despair, till having turned a corner of the gallery, a taper, burning with a faint light, gleamed through a narrow dark passage; approaching the spot whence it streamed, he perceived it arose from an extensive room, the folding doors of which were wide open: he entered; a small taper in a massy silver candlestick stood upon a table in the middle of the room, but gave so inconsiderable an illumination, that one end was wrapped in palpable darkness, and the other scarcely broken in upon by a dim light that glimmered through a large ramified window covered with thick ivy. An arm-chair, shattered and damp with age, was placed near the table, and the remains of a recent fire were still visible in the grate. The wainscot of black oak, had formerly been hung with tapestry, and several portions still clung to those parts which were near the fire; they possessed some vivacity of tint, and, with much gilding yet apparent on the chimney-piece, and several mouldering reliques of costly frames and paintings, gave indisputable evidence of the ancient grandeur of the place. Henry closed the folding doors, and, taking the taper, was about to survey the room, when a half-stifled groan from the dark end of it smote cold upon his heart, at the same time the sound as of something falling with a dead weight, echoed through the room, and a bell tolled deep and hollow from the tower above. He replaced the taper, the flame of which was agitated; now quivering, sunk, now streaming, flamed aloft, and as the last pale portion died away, the scarce distinguished form of some terrific being floated slowly by, and again another dreadful groan ran deepening through the gloom and the bell swung solemn from the keep. Henry stood for some time incapable of motion; at length summoning all his fortitude, he advanced with his sword extended to the darkest part of the room: instantly burst forth in fierce irradiations a blue sulphureous splendour, and the mangled body of a man distorted with the agony of

59

death, his every fibre racked with convulsion, his beard and hair stiff and matted with blood, his mouth open, and his eyes protruding from their sockets, rushed upon his maddening senses; he started, uttering a wild shriek, and, hurrying he knew not whither, burst through the folding doors.

Darkness again spread her sable pall over the unfortunate Fitzowen, and he strode along the narrow passage with a feeble and a faltering step. His intellect shook, and overwhelmed by the late appalling objects, had not yet recovered any degree of recollection; and he wandered, as in a dream, a confused train of horrible ideas passing unconnected through his mind; at length, however, memory resumed her function, resumed it but to daunt him with harrowing suggestions; the direful horrors of the room behind, and of the vault below, were still present to his eyes, and, as a man whom hellish fiends had frightened, he stood trembling, pale and staring wild. All was now once more silent and dark, and he determined to wait in this spot the dawn of day, but a few minutes had scarce elapsed, when the iron door screaming on its hinges, bellowed through the murmuring ruin. Henry nearly fainted at the sound, which, pausing for some time, again swelled upon the wind, and at last died away in shrill melancholy shrieks; again all was silent, and again the same fearful noise struck terror to his soul. Whilst his mind was thus agitated with horror and apprehension, a feeble light streaming from behind, accompanied with a soft, quick, and hollow tread, convinced him that something was pursuing, and struck with wildering fear, he rushed unconscious down the steps; the vault received him, and its portals swinging to their close, sounded as the sentence of death. A dun fetid vapour filled the place, in the centre of which arose a faint and bickering flame. Fitzowen approached, and beheld a corse suspended over it by the neck, whilst the flame flashing through the vault, gleamed on a throng of hideous and ghastly features that came forward through the smoke. With the desperate valour of a man who sees destruction before him, he ran furiously

60

forward; a universal shriek burst forth, and the fire, rising with tenfold brilliance, placed full in view the dreadful form of his infernal guide, dilated into horror itself; her face was pale as death, her eyes were wide open, dead, and fixed, a horrible grin sate upon her features, her lips black and tumid were drawn back, disclosing a set of large blue teeth, and her hair, standing stiffly erect, was of a withered red.

Fitzowen felt his blood freeze within him; his limbs became enervated, and at this moment, when resistance on his part appeared almost impossible, a door bursting open at the extremity of the vault, in rushed the form of Walleran, who wielding a battle-axe, aimed a blow at Henry, that, situated as he then was, and rendered torpid through the influence of preternatural agency, he conceived would be effectual for his destruction. In this, however, he was, fatally for himself, mistaken, for no sooner was he perceived, than the effect of the enchantment ceased; indignation swelling at the heart of Henry, impelled the lingering fluid, his cheek flushed with the crimson tide, his limbs recovered their elasticity and tone, and avoiding with active vigour the death that was intended him, he sheathed his falchion in the breast of his opponent, who, having wasted his impetuous strength upon the air, had thus exposed himself to instant ruin.

III

...........................Fairy Elves
Whose midnight revels by a forest side,
Or fountain, some belated peasant sees,
Or dreams he sees, while over head the moon
Sits arbitress, and nearer to the earth
Wheels her pale course, they on their mirth and
dance
Intent, with jocund music charm his ear;
At once with joy and fear his heart rebounds.
MILTON

Walleran dropt lifeless on the ground, and the dreadful appearances in the vault, the fire, and all its apparatus, immediately vanished, whilst loud howlings and lamentations were heard at a distance in the air. A profound silence, however, now ensued throughout the castle, and Henry, by the light of the moon, as it streamed through the grated window, beheld at his feet the bleeding corse of his antagonist. Starting from the contemplation of his fallen enemy, he resolved to explore the ruins in search of Adeline, of whose concealment in some part of the building, he entertained not the smallest doubt, and apprehensive now of little opposition, he once more attempted those stairs, in ascending which he had formerly encountered so many terrors. He reached the gallery without any interruption, and passing through the folding doors into the apartment already described, discovered at one end, and on the very spot where he had beheld the tremendous vision of the agonizing wretch, a narrow, winding, and arched passage, and which, taking a circular direction, probably passed into the opposite portion of the great tower. Here he entered, but had not proceeded far before the sound as of soft and very distant music reached his ear; and shortly afterward was distinctly heard the murmur of falling water. Sounds such as these, and in such a place, greatly surprised him, and hastening forward to ascertain from what quarter they originated, he found himself suddenly immersed in a very cold and damp vapour, whose density was such, that for a short time it totally suffocated the smallest ray of light; in a few minutes, however, it began in some measure to clear away, accompanied with a whispering noise, whilst vast eddies and gusts of thin vapour passed him with a whirling motion. He now perceived himself in a kind of large cavern whose sides were of unhewn stone, and from the roof were pendent numbers of beautiful stalactites, from whose points fell, at intervals, with a tinkling sound, large drops of water, whilst the dying notes of distant harps, the gurgling of vapour, formed a harmony so singular, yet so soothing, that when united to the surrounding chill and torpid atmosphere, seemed calculated to inspire the most profound repose. Fitzowen now advanced a little further into the cavity, and, through the chasms of the ever fluctuating mist, discerned, hanging from the centre of the roof, a vast globe, which emitted rays of the palest hue, and which, in passing through the turbid vapour, shed a kind of twilight.

Whilst pondering on the purport of this very peculiar scene, he felt a heaviness, and a tendency to sleep creep upon him, accompanied with an indistinctness and confusion of intellect; at this instant, however, a mass of vapour rushing by him, the light gleamed more steadily, and he beheld in an excavation of the adjacent wall, and recumbent on a couch, what he conceived to be a human body. Curiosity was now so powerfully excited, as completely to expel the approaching torpor, and drawing nearer the object of his attention, he could hear the deep breathings of a person in profound sleep; the next moment he could perceive the garments of female attire, and in the succeeding instant hung with rapture and astonishment over the well-known features of his beloved Adeline. The globe shed a silvery and preternatural whiteness over her form, and the rose had left her cheek; she lay with her head reclined upon her hand, and the utmost tranquillity sate upon her countenance, though, now and then, a deep-drawn sigh would indicate the tissue of idea.

Henry stood, for some moments, rivetted to the spot, then starting from his reverie, he wound his arms about her beauteous frame, and impressed upon her lips a glowing kiss - she awoke, and instantly a tremendous tempest burst upon them, loud thunder shook the earth, and a whirlwind, rushing through the pile, tore it from its foundations.

The lovers recovering from a trance, which the conflict of the elements had occasioned, found themselves seated on some mossy turf, and around them the soft, the sweet and tranquil scenery of a summer's moon-light night. Enraptured with this sudden and unexpected change, they rose gently off the ground; over their heads towered a large and majestic oak, at whose foot they believed some kind and compassionate being had placed them. Delight and gratitude dilated their hearts, and advancing from beneath the tree, whose gigantic branches spread a large extent of shade, a vale, beautiful and romantic, through which ran a clear and deep stream, came full in view; they walked to the edge of the water; the moon shone with mellow lustre on its surface, and its banks, fringed with shrubs, breathed a perfume more delicate than the odours of the east. On one side, the ground, covered with a vivid, soft, and downy verdure, stretched for a considerable extent to the borders of a large forest, which, sweeping round, finally closed up the valley; on the other, it was broken into abrupt and rocky masses swarded with moss, and from whose clefts grew thick and spreading trees, the roots of which, washed by many a fall of water, hung bare and matted from their craggy beds.

Henry and his Adeline forgot in this delicious vale all their former sufferings, and giving up their minds to the pleasing influence of curiosity and wonder, they determined to explore the place by tracing the windings of the stream. Scarcely had they entered upon this plan, when music of the most ravishing sweetness filled the air, sometimes it seemed to float along the valley, sometimes it stole along the surface of the water, now it died away among the woods, and now, with deep and mellow symphony, it swelled upon the gale. Fixed in astonishment, they scarce ventured to breathe, every sense, save that of hearing, seemed absorbed; and when the last faint warblings melted on the air, they started from the spot, solicitous to know from what being those more than human strains had parted; but nothing appeared in view; the moon, full and unclouded, shone with unusual lustre; and filled with hope, they again pursued the windings of the water, which, conducting to the narrowest part of the valley, continued their course through the wood. This they entered by a path smooth, but narrow and perplexed, where, although its branches were so numerous that no preference could be given, or any direct route long persisted in, yet every turn presented something to amuse, something to sharpen the edge of research. The beauty of the trees, through whose interstices the moon gleamed in the most picturesque manner, the glimpses of the water, and the notes of the nightingale, who now began to fill the valley with her song, were more than sufficient to take off the sense of fatigue, and they wandered on, still eager to explore, still ardent for further discovery.

The wood now became more thick and obscure, and at length almost dark, when, the path taking suddenly an oblique direction, they found themselves on the edge of a circular lawn, whose tint and softness were beyond compare, and which seemed to have been lightly brushed by fairy feet. A number of fine old trees, around whose boles crept the ivy and the woodbine, rose at irregular distances, here they mingled into groves, and there, separate and emulous of each other, vied in spiral elegance, or magnitude of form. The water which had been for some time concealed, now murmured through a thousand beds, and visiting each little flower, added vigour to its vegetation, and poignancy to its fragrance. Along the edges of the wood, and beneath the shadows of the trees, an innumerable host of glow-worms lighted their innocuous fires, lustrous as the gems of Golconda; and, desirous yet longer to enjoy the scene, they went forward with light footsteps on the lawn; all was calm, and, except the breeze of night, that sighed soft and sweetly through the world of leaves, a perfect silence prevailed. Not many minutes, however, had elapsed, before the same enchanting music, to which they had listened with so much rapture in the vale, again arrested their attention, and presently they discovered on the border of the lawn, just rising above the wood, and floating on the bosom of the air, a being of the most delicate form; from his shoulders streamed a tunic of tenderest blue, his wings and feet were clothed in downy silver, and in his grasp he had a wand white as the mountain-snow. He rose swiftly in the air, his brilliance became excessive from the lunar rays, his song echoed through the vault of night, but having quickly diminished to

65

the size and appearance of the evening star, it died away, and the next moment he was lost in ether. The lovers still fixed their view on that part of the heavens where the vision had disappeared, and shortly had the pleasure of again seeing the star-like radiance, which in an instant unfolded itself into the full and fine dimensions of the beauteous being, who, having collected dew from the cold vales of Saturn, now descended rapidly towards the earth, and waving his wand as he passed athwart the woods, a number of like form and garb flew round him, and all alighting on the lawn, separated at equal distances on its circumference, and then shaking their wings, which spread a perfume through the air, burst into one general song.

Henry and Adeline, who, apprehensive of being discovered, had retreated within the shadow of some mossy oaks, now waited with eager expectation the event of so singular a scene. In a few moments a bevy of elegant nymphs, dancing two by two, issued from the wood on the right, and an equal number of warlike knights, accompanied by a band of minstrels, from that on the left. The knights were clothed in green; on their bosoms shone a plate of burnished steel, and in their hands they grasped a golden targe, and lance of beamy lustre. The nymphs, whose form and symmetry were beyond the youthful poet's dream, were dressed in robes of white, their zones were azure dropt with diamonds, and their light brown hair decked with roses, hung in ample ringlets. So quick, so light and airy, was their motion, that the turf, the flowers, shrunk not beneath the gentle pressure, and each smiling on her favourite knight, he flung his brilliant arms aside, and mingled in the dance.

Whilst they thus flew in rapid measures over the lawn, the lovers, forgetting their situation, and impatient to salute the assembly, involuntarily stept forward, and instantaneously, a shrill and hollow gust of wind murmured through the woods, the moon dipt into a cloud, and the knights, the nymphs, and aerial spirits, vanished from the view, leaving the astonished pair to repent at leisure their precipitate intrusion; scarce, however, had they time to

66

determine what plan they should pursue, when a gleam of light flashed suddenly along the horizon, and the beauteous being whom they first beheld in the air, stood before them; he waved his snow-white wand, and pointing to the wood, which now appeared sparkling with a thousand fires, moved gently on. Henry and his amiable companion felt an irresistible impulse which compelled them to follow, and having penetrated the wood, they perceived many bright rays of light, which darting like the beams of the sun through every part of it, most beautifully illumined the shafts of the trees. As they advanced forward, the radiance became more intense, and converged towards a centre, and the fairy being turning quickly round, commanded them to kneel down, and having squeezed the juice of an herb into their eyes, bade then now proceed, but that no mortal eye, unless its powers of vision were adapted to the scene, could endure the glory that would shortly burst upon them. Scarcely had he uttered these words when they entered an amphitheatre; in its centre was a throne of ivory inlaid with sapphires, on which sate a female form of exquisite beauty, a plain coronet of gold obliquely crossed her flowing hair, and her robe of white satin hung negligent in ample folds. Around her stood five-and-twenty nymphs clothed in white and gold, and holding lighted tapers; beyond these were fifty of the aerial beings, their wings of downy silver stretched for flight, and each a burning taper in his hand; and lastly, on the circumference of the amphitheatre, shone one hundred knights in mail of tempered steel; in one hand they shook aloft a targe of massy diamond, and in the other flashed a taper. So excessive was the reflection, that the targes had the lustre of an hundred suns, and, when shaken, sent forth streams of vivid lightning: from the gold, the silver, and the sapphires, rushed a flood of tinted light, that mingling, threw upon the eye a series of revolving hues.

Henry and Adeline, impressed with awe, with wonder and delight, fell prostrate on the ground, whilst the fairy spirit, advancing, knelt and presented to the queen a crystal vase. She rose, she waved her hand, and smiling, bade them to approach. "Gentle strangers," she exclaimed, "let not fear appal your hearts, for to them whom courage, truth, and piety have distinguished, our friendship and our love are given. Spirits of the blest we are, our sweet employment to befriend the wretched and the weary, to lull the torture of anguish, and the horror of despair. Ah! never shall the tear of innocence, or the plaint of sorrow, the pang of injured merit, or the sigh of hopeless love, implore our aid in vain. Upon the moon-beam do we float, and, light as air, pervade the habitations of men: and hearken, O favoured mortals! I tell you spirits pure from vice are present to your inmost thoughts; when terror, and when madness, when spectres, and when death surrounded you, our influence put to flight the ministers of darkness; we placed you in the moon-light vale, and now upon your heads we pour the planetary dew: go, happy pair! from Hecate's dread agents we have freed you, from wildering fear and gloomy superstition." ——

She ended, and the lovers, impatient to express their gratitude, were about to speak, when suddenly the light turned pale, and died away, the spirits fled, and music soft and sweet was heard remotely in the air. They started, and, in place of the refulgent scene of magic, beheld a public road, Fitzowen's horse cropping the grass which grew upon its edge, and a village at a little distance, on whose spire the rising sun had shed his earliest beams.

SAMUEL TAYLOR COLERIDGE (1772-1834) made his first significant contribution to fantastic literature in "The Rime of the Ancient Mariner", the first item in the book of *Lyrical Ballads* which he issued with William Wordsworth in 1798. The collection was a significant departure from the habits and modes of eighteenth century poetry and became a key document of the English Romantic Movement. Coleridge had been taking laudanum for some time for medicinal reasons, and eventually because he became heavily addicted to it. His most famous poems were written under its influence, including the phantasmagoric account of unnatural lust "Christabel" (1816), which he never finished, and the celebrated "Kubla Khan" (1816) whose ornate exoticism struck a new note in English poetry.

Under the influence of the German transcendentalist philosophers Coleridge developed his own philosophical theory of art, based in a novel theory of the imagination. This theory distinguishes between the "primary imagination", which filters and organises sensory perception, and the "secondary imagination", which interprets and creates, but imagines the two working in harness to unify experience and render it meaningful. It makes a further distinction between this unifying imagination and "fancy", whose function is to elaborate and decorate particular imaginative products. The theory was never fully extrapolated, although a fragmentary version of it appears in *Biographia Literaria* (1817); it was in those pages that he made use of the notion of the reader's "willing suspension of disbelief for that moment, which constitutes poetic faith". It was also Coleridge who first posed (in *Anima Poetae*, 1816) a question which has remained at the heart of fantasy fiction ever since, extrapolated in dozens of stories: "If a man could pass through Paradise in a dream, and have a flower presented to him as a pledge that his soul had really been there, and if he found that flower in his hand when he woke - Aye, and what then?"

KUBLA KHAN

by Samuel Taylor Coleridge

In Xanadu did Kubla Khan
A stately pleasure-dome decree:
Where Alph, the sacred river, ran
Through caverns measureless to man
     Down to a sunless sea.
So twice five miles of fertile ground
With walls and towers were girdled round:
And there were gardens bright with sinuous rills,
Where blossomed many an incense-bearing tree;
And here were forests as ancient as the hills,
Enfolding sunny spots of greenery.

But oh! that deep romantic chasm which slanted
Down the green hill athwart a cedarn cover!
A savage place! as holy and enchanted
As e'er beneath a waning moon was haunted
By woman wailing for her demon-lover!
And from this chasm, with ceaseless turmoil seething,
As if this earth in fast thick pants were breathing,
A mighty fountain momently was forced:
Amid whose swift half-intermitted burst
Huge fragments vaulted like rebounding hail,
Or chaffy grain beneath the thresher's flail:
And' mid these dancing rocks at once and ever
It flung up momently the sacred river.
Five miles meandering with a mazy motion
Through wood and dale the sacred river ran,
Then reached the caverns measureless to man,
And sank in tumult to a lifeless ocean:
And 'mid this tumult Kubla heard from far
Ancestral voices prophesying war!
     The shadow of the dome of pleasure
     Floated midway on the waves;

Where was heard the mingled measure
From the fountain and the caves.
It was a miracle of rare device,
A sunny pleasure-dome with caves of ice!

A damsel with a dulcimer
In a vision once I saw:
It was an Abyssinian maid,
And on her dulcimer she played,
Singing of Mount Abora.
Could I revive within me
Her symphony and song,
To such a deep delight 'twould win me,
That with music loud and long,
I would build that dome in air,
That sunny dome! those caves of ice!
And all who heard should see them there,
And all should cry, Beware! Beware!
His flashing eyes, his floating hair!
Weave a circle round him thrice,
And close your eyes with holy dread,
For he on honey-dew hath fed,
And drunk the milk of Paradise.

JOHN KEATS (1795-1821) died young but nevertheless established himself as a central figure of the British Romantic Movement, and was considered by many to be the leading poet of his day. His poems aim to employ the alchemy of art to transmute sensation, thought and emotion into Beauty. He drew extensively on classical and folkloristic sources for his themes, habitually using the supernatural as a part of his allegorical apparatus. His best poems were issued in a collection published in 1820; they include "Isabella; or the Pot of Basil", based on a gruesome vignette from Boccaccio's *Decameron*; " Lamia", borrowed from Philostratus *via* Burton's *Anatomy of Melancholy*; "The Eve of St. Agnes", which redevelops a Medieval legend; and "La Belle Dame Sans Merci", a blend of chivalric romance and the more sinister legends featuring the Queen of Faerie.

Elaborate and eccentric homage to Keats' unique status within the history of fantasy has recently been paid by a group of novels in which he features as a character as well as an inspiration: *The Stress of Her Regard* by Tim Powers and *Hyperion* and *The Fall of Hyperion* by Dan Simmons; the latter novels are named after the two attempts which Keats made - but never brought to perfection - to produce a literary masterpiece allegorising his ideas about the nature and virtue of art.

LAMIA

by John Keats

Part I

Upon a time, before the faery broods
Drove Nymph and Satyr from the prosperous woods,
Before king Oberon's bright diadem,
Sceptre, and mantle, clasp'd with dewy gem,
Frighted away the Dryads and the Fauns
From rushes green, and brakes, and cowslip'd lawns,
The ever-smitten Hermes empty left
His golden throne, bent warm on amorous theft:
From high Olympus had he stolen light,
On this side of Jove's clouds, to escape the sight
Of his great summoner, and made retreat
Into a forest on the shores of Crete.
For somewhere in that sacred island dwelt
A nymph, to whom all hoofed Satyrs knelt;
At whose white feet the languid Tritons poured
Pearls, while on land they wither'd and adored.
Fast by the springs where she to bathe was wont,
And in those meads where sometime she might haunt,
Were strewn rich gifts, unknown to any Muse,
Though Fancy's casket were unlock'd to choose.
Ah, what a world of love was at her feet!
So Hermes thought, and a celestial heat
Burnt from his winged heels to either ear,
That from a whiteness, as the lilly clear,
Blush'd into roses 'mid his golden hair,
Fallen in jealous curls about his shoulders bare.

From vale to vale, from wood to wood, he flew,
Breathing upon the flowers his passion new,
And wound with many a river to its head,
To find where this sweet nymph prepar'd her secret bed:
In vain; the sweet nymph might nowhere be found,

And so he rested, on the lonely ground,
Pensive, and full of painful jealousies
Of the Wood-Gods, and even the very trees.
There as he stood, he heard a mournful voice,
Such as once heard, in gentle heart, destroys
All pain but pity: thus the lone voice spake:
"When from this wreathed tomb shall I awake!
When move in a sweet body fit for life,
And love, and pleasure, and the ruddy strife
Of hearts and lips! Ah, miserable me!"
The God, dove-footed, glided silently
Round bush and tree, soft-brushing, in his speed,
The taller grasses and full-flowering weed,
Until he found a palpitating snake,
Bright, and cirque-couchant in a dusky brake.

She was a gordian shape of dazzling hue,
Vermilion -spotted, golden, green, and blue;
Striped like a zebra, freckled like a pard,
Eyed like a peacock, and all crimson barr'd;
And full of silver moons, that, as she breathed,
Dissolv'd, or brighter shone, or interwreathed
Their lustres with the gloomier tapestries-
So rainbow-sided, touch'd with miseries,
She seem'd, at once, some penanced lady elf,
Some demon's mistress, or the demon's self.
Upon her crest she wore a wannish fire
Sprinkled with stars, like Ariadne's tiar:
Her head was serpent, but ah, bitter-sweet!
She had a woman's mouth with all its pearls complete:
And for her eyes: what could such eyes do there
But weep, and weep, that they were born so fair?
As Proserpine still weeps for her Sicilian air.
Her throat was serpent, but the words she spake
Came, as through bubbling honey, for Love's sake,
And thus; while Hermes on his pinions lay,
Like a stoop'd falcon ere he takes his prey.

"Fair Hermes, crown'd with feathers, fluttering light,
I had a splendid dream of thee last night:
I saw thee sitting on a throne of gold,
Among the Gods, upon Olympus old,
The only sad one; for thou didst not hear
The soft, lute-finger'd Muses chaunting clear,
Nor even Apollo when he sang alone,
Deaf to his throbbing throat's long, long melodious moan.
I dreamt I saw thee, robed in purple flakes,
Break amorous through the clouds, as morning breaks,
And, swiftly as a bright Phoebean dart,
Strike for the Cretan isle; and here thou art!
Too gentle Hermes, has thou found the maid?"
Whereat the star of Lethe not delay'd
His rosy eloquence, and thus inquired:
"Thou smooth-lipp'd serpent, surely high inspired!
Thou beauteous wreath, with melancholy eyes,
Possess whatever bliss thou canst devise,
Telling me only where my nymph is fled,-
Where she doth breathe!" "Bright planet, thou has said,"
Return'd the snake, "but seal with oaths, fair God!"
"I swear," said Hermes, "by my serpent rod,
And by thine eyes, and by thy starry crown!"
Light flew his earnest words, among the blossoms blown.
Then thus again the brilliance feminine:
"Too frail of heart! for this lost nymph of thine,
Free as the air, invisibly, she strays
About these thornless wilds; her pleasant days
She tastes unseen; unseen her nimble feet
Leave traces in the grass and flowers sweet;
From weary tendrils, and bow'd branches green,
She plucks the fruit unseen, she bathes unseen:
And by my power is her beauty veil'd
To keep it unaffronted, unassail'd
By the love-glances of unlovely eyes,
Of Satyrs, Fauns, and blear'd Silenus' sighs.
Pale grew her immortality, for woe
Of all these lovers, and she grieved so

I took compassion on her, bade her steep
Her hair in weird syrops, that would keep
Her loveliness invisible, yet free
To wander as she loves, in liberty.
Thou shalt behold her, Hermes, thou alone,
If thou wilt, as thou swearest, grant my boon!"
Then, once again, the charmed God began
An oath, and through the serpent's ears it ran
Warm, tremulous, devout, psalterian.
Ravish'd, she lifted her Circean head,
Blush'd a live damask, and swift-lisping said,
"I was a woman, let me have once more
A woman's shape, and charming as before.
I love a youth of Corinth - O the bliss!
Give me my woman's form, and place me where he is.
Stoop, Hermes, let me breathe upon thy brow,
And thou shalt see thy sweet nymph even now."
The God on half-shut feathers sank serene,
She breath'd upon his eyes, and swift was seen
Of both the guarded nymph near-smiling on the green.
It was no dream; or say a dream it was,
Real are the dreams of Gods, and smoothly pass
Their pleasures in a long immortal dream.
One warm, flush'd moment, hovering, it might seem
Dash'd by the wood-nymph's beauty, so he burn'd;
Then, lighting on the printless verdure, turn'd
To the swoon'd serpent, and with languid arm,
Delicate, put to proof the lythe Caducean charm.
So done, upon the nymph his eyes he bent
Full of adoring tears and blandishment,
And towards her stept: she, like a moon in wane,
Faded before him, cower'd, nor could restrain
Her fearful sobs, self-folding like a flower
That faints into itself at evening hour:
But the God fostering her chilled hand,
She felt the warmth, her eyelids open'd bland,
And, like new flowers at morning song of bees,
Bloom'd, and gave up her honey to the lees.

Into the green-recessed woods they flew;
Nor grew they pale, as mortal lovers do.

Left to herself, the serpent now began
To change; her elfin blood in madness ran,
Her mouth foam'd, and the grass, therewith besprent,
Wither'd at dew so sweet and virulent;
Her eyes in torture fix'd, and anguish drear,
Hot, glaz'd, and wide, with lid - lashes all sear,
Flash'd phosphor & sharp sparks, without one cooling tear.
The colours all inflam'd throughout her train,
She writh'd about, convuls'd with scarlet pain:
A deep volcanian yellow took the place
Of all her milder-mooned body's grace,
And, as the lava ravishes the mead,
Spoilt all her silver mail, and golden brede;
Made gloom of all her frecklings, streaks and bars,
Eclips'd her crescents, and lick'd up her stars:
So that, in moments few, she was undrest
Of all her sapphires, greens, and amethyst,
And rubious-argent: of all these bereft,
Nothing but pain and ugliness were left.
Still shone her crown; that vanish'd, also she
Melted and disappear'd as suddenly;
And in the air, her new voice luting soft,
Cried, "Lycius! gentle Lycius!" Borne aloft
With the bright mists about the mountains hoar
These words dissolv'd: Crete's forests heard no more.

Whither fled Lamia, now a lady bright,
A full-born beauty new and exquisite?
She fled into that valley they pass o'er
Who go to Corinth from Cenchreas' shore;
And rested at the foot of those wild hills,
The rugged founts of the Peraean rills,
And of that other ridge whose barren back
Stretches, with all its mist and cloudy rack,
South-westward to Cleone. There she stood

About a young bird's flutter from a wood,
Fair, on a sloping green of mossy tread,
By a clear pool, wherein she passioned
To see herself escap'd from so sore ills,
While her robes flaunted with the daffodils.

Ah, happy Lycius! - for she was a maid
More beautiful than ever twisted braid,
Or sigh'd, or blush'd, or on spring-flowered lea
Spread a green kirtle to the minstrelsy:
A virgin purest lipp'd, yet in the lore
Of love deep learned to the red heart's core:
Not one hour old, yet of sciential brain
To unperplex bliss from its neighbour pain;
Define their pettish limits, and estrange
Their points of contact, and swift counterchange;
Intrigue with the specious chaos, and dispart
Its most ambiguous atoms with sure art;
As though in Cupid's college she had spent
Sweet days a lovely graduate, still unshent,
And kept his rosy terms in idle languishment.

Why this fair creature chose so faerily
By the wayside to linger, we shall see;
But first 'tis fit to tell how she could muse
And dream, when in the serpent prison-house,
Of all she list, strange or magnificent:
How, ever, where she will'd, her spirit went;
Whether to faint Elysium, or where
Down through tress-lifting waves the Nereids fair
Wind into Thetis' bower by many a pearly stair;
Or where God Bacchus drains his cups divine,
Stretch'd out, at ease, beneath a glutinous pine;
Or where in Pluto's gardens palatine
Mulciber's columns gleam in far piazzian line.
And sometimes into cities she would send
Her dream, with feast and rioting to blend;
And once, while among mortals dreaming thus,

She saw the young Corinthian Lycius
Charioting foremost in the envious race,
Like a young Jove with calm uneager face,
And fell into a swooning love of him.
Now on the moth-time of that evening dim
He would return that way, as well she knew,
To Corinth from the shore; for freshly blew
The eastern soft wind, and his galley now
Grated the quaystones with her brazen prow
In port Cenchreas, from Egina isle
Fresh anchor'd; whither he had been awhile
To sacrifice to Jove, whose temple there
Waits with high marble doors for blood and incense rare.
Jove heard his vows, and better'd his desire;
For by some freakful chance he made retire
From his companions, and set forth to walk,
Perhaps grown wearied of their Corinth talk:
Over the solitary hills he fared,
Thoughtless at first, but ere eve's star appeared
His phantasy was lost, where reason fades,
In the calm'd twilight of Platonic shades.
Lamia beheld him coming, near, more near -
Close to her passing, in indifference drear,
His silent sandals swept the mossy green;
So neighbour'd to him, and yet so unseen
She stood: he pass'd, shut up in mysteries,
His mind wrapp'd like his mantle, while her eyes
Follow'd his steps, and her neck regal white
Turn'd-syllabling thus, "Ah, Lycius bright,
And will you leave me on the hills alone?
Lycius, look back! and be some pity shown."
He did; not with cold wonder fearingly,
But Orpheus-like at an Eurydice;
For so delicious were the words she sung,
It seem'd he had lov'd them a whole summer long:
And soon his eyes had drunk her beauty up,
Leaving no drop in the bewildering cup,
And still the cup was full, - while he, afraid

Lest she should vanish ere his lip had paid
Due adoration, thus began to adore;
Her soft look growing coy, she saw his chain so sure:
"Leave thee alone! Look back! Ah, Goddess, see
Whether my eyes can ever turn from thee!
For pity do not this sad heart belie-
Even as thou vanishest so shall I die.
Stay! though a Naiad of the rivers, stay!
To thy far wishes will thy streams obey:
Stay! though the greenest woods be thy domain,
Alone they can drink up the morning rain;
Though a descended Pleiad, will not one
Of thine harmonious sisters keep in tune
Thy spheres, and as thy silver proxy shine?
So sweetly to these ravish'd ears of mine
Came thy sweet greeting, that if thou shouldst fade
Thy memory will waste me to a shade:-
For pity do not melt!" - "If I should stay,"
Said Lamia, "here, upon this floor of clay,
And pain my steps upon these flowers too rough,
What canst thou say or do of charm enough
To dull the nice remembrance of my home?
Thou canst not ask me with thee here to roam
Over these hills and vales, where no joy is, -
Empty of immortality and bliss!
Thou art a scholar, Lycius, and must know
That finer spirits cannot breathe below
In human climes, and live: Alas! poor youth,
What taste of purer air hast thou to soothe
My essence? What serener palaces,
Where I may all my many senses please,
And by mysterious sleights a hundred thirsts appease?
It cannot be - Adieu! "So said, she rose
Tiptoe with white arms spread. He, sick to lose
The amorous promise of her lone complain,
Swoon'd, murmuring of love, and pale with pain.
The cruel lady, without any show
Of sorrow for her tender favourite's woe,

But rather, if her eyes could brighter be,
With brighter eyes and slow amenity,
Put her new lips to his, and gave afresh
The life she had so tangled in her mesh:
And as he from one trance was wakening
Into another, she began to sing,
Happy in beauty, life, and love, and everything,
A song of love, too sweet for earthly lyres,
While, like held breath, the stars drew in their panting fires.
And then she whisper'd in such trembling tone,
As those who, safe together met alone
For the first time through many anguish'd days,
Use other speech than looks; bidding him raise
His drooping head, and clear his soul of doubt,
For that she was a woman, and without
Any more subtle fluid in her veins
Than throbbing blood, and that the self-same pains
Inhabited her frail-strung heart as his.
And next she wonder'd how his eyes could miss
Her face so long in Corinth, where, she said,
She dwelt but half retir'd, and there had led
Days happy as the gold coin could invent
Without the aid of love; yet in content
Till she saw him, as once she pass'd him by,
Where 'gainst a column he lent thoughtfully
At Venus' temple porch, 'mid baskets heap'd
Of amorous herbs and flowers, newly reap'd
Late on that eve, as 'twas the night before
The Adonian feast; whereof she saw no more,
But wept alone those days, for why should she adore?
Lycius from death awoke into amaze,
To see her still, and singing so sweet lays;
Then from amaze into delight he fell
To hear her whisper woman's lore so well;
And every word she spake entic'd him on
To unperplex'd delight and pleasure known.
Let the mad poets say whate'er they please
Of the sweets of Faeries, Peris, Goddesses,

81

There is not such a treat among them all,
Haunters of cavern, lake, and waterfall,
As a real woman, lineal indeed
From Pyrrha's pebbles or old Adam's seed.
Thus gentle Lamia judg'd, and judg'd aright,
That Lycius could not love in half a fright,
So threw the goddess off, and won his heart
More pleasantly by playing woman's part,
With no more awe than what her beauty gave,
That, while it smote, still guaranteed to save.
Lycius to all made eloquent reply,
Marrying to every word a twinborn sigh;
And last, pointing to Corinth, ask'd her sweet.
If 'twas too far that night for her soft feet.
The way was short, for Lamia's eagerness
Made, by a spell, the triple league decrease
To a few paces; not at all surmised
By blinded Lycius, so in her comprized.
They pass'd the city gates, he knew not how,
So noiseless, and he never thought to know.

As men talk in a dream, so Corinth all,
Throughout her palaces imperial,
And all her populous streets and temples lewd,
Mutter'd, like tempest in the distance brew'd,
To the wide-spreaded night above her towers.
Men, women, rich and poor, in the cool hours,
Shuffled their sandals o'er the pavement white,
Companion'd or alone; while many a light
Flared, here and there, from wealthy festivals,
And threw their moving shadows on the walls,
Or found them cluster'd in the corniced shade
Of some arch'd temple door, or dusky colonnade.

Muffling his face, of greeting friends in fear,
Her fingers he press'd hard, as one came near
With curl'd gray beard, sharp eyes, and smooth bald crown,
Slow-stepp'd, and robed in philosophic gown:

82

Lycius shrank closer, as they met and past,
Into his mantle, adding wings to haste,
While hurried Lamia trembled: "Ah," said he,
"Why do you shudder, love, so ruefully?
Why does your tender palm dissolve in dew?" -
"I'm wearied," said fair Lamia: "tell me who
Is that old man? I cannot bring to mind
His features:- Lycius! wherefore did you blind
Yourself from his quick eyes?" Lycius replied,
" 'Tis Apollonius sage, my trusty guide
And good instructor; but to-night he seems
The ghost of folly haunting my sweet dreams."

While yet he spake they had arrived before
A pillar'd porch, with lofty portal door,
Where hung a silver lamp, whose phosphor glow
Reflected in the slabbed steps below,
Mild as a star in water; for so new,
And so unsullied was the marble's hue,
So through the crystal polish, liquid fine,
Ran the dark veins, that none but feet divine
Could e'er have touch'd there. Sounds Aeolian
Breath'd from the hinges, as the ample span
Of the wide doors disclos'd a place unknown
Some time to any, but those two alone,
And a few Persian mutes, who that same year
Were seen about the markets: none knew where
They could inhabit; the most curious
Were foil'd, who watch'd to trace them to their house:
And but the flitter-winged verse must tell,
For truth's sake, what woe afterwards befel,
'Twould humour many a heart to leave them thus,
Shut from the busy world of more incredulous.

PART II

Love in a hut, with water and a crust,

83

Is - Love, forgive us! - cinders, ashes, dust;
Love in a palace is perhaps at last
More grievous torment than a hermit's fast:-
That is a doubtful tale from faery land,
Hard for the non-elect to understand.
Had Lycius liv'd to hand his story down,
He might have given the moral a fresh frown,
Or clench'd it quite: but too short was their bliss
To breed distrust and hate, that make the soft voice hiss.
Beside, there, nightly, with terrific glare,
Love, jealous grown of so complete a pair,
Hover'd and buzz'd his wings, with fearful roar,
Above the lintel of their chamber door,
And down the passage cast a glow upon the floor.

For all this came a ruin: side by side
They were enthroned, in the even tide,
Upon a couch, near to a curtaining
Whose airy texture, from a golden string,
Floated into the room, and let appear
Unveil'd the summer heaven, blue and clear,
Betwixt two marble shafts:- there they reposed,
Where use had made it sweet, with eyelids closed,
Saving a tythe which love still open kept,
That they might see each other while they almost slept;
When from the slope side of a suburb hill,
Deafening the swallow's twitter, came a thrill
Of trumpets - Lycius started - the sounds fled,
But left a thought, a buzzing in his head.
For the first time, since first he harbour'd in
That purple-lined palace of sweet sin,
His spirit pass'd beyond its golden bourn
Into the noisy world almost forsworn.
The lady, ever watchful, penetrant,
Saw this with pain, so arguing a want
Of something more, more than her empery
Of joys; and she began to moan and sigh
Because he mused beyond her, knowing well

84

That but a moment's thought is passion's passing bell.
"Why do you sigh, fair creature?" whisper'd he:
"Why do you think?" return'd she tenderly:
"You have deserted me; - where am I now?
Not in your heart while care weighs on your brow:
No, no, you have dismiss'd me; and I go
From your breast houseless: aye, it must be so."
He answer'd, bending to her open eyes,
Where he was mirror'd small in paradise,
"My silver planet, both of eve and morn!
Why will you plead yourself so sad forlorn,
While I am striving how to fill my heart
With deeper crimson, and a double smart?
How to entangle, trammel up and snare
Your soul in mine, and labyrinth you there
Like the hid scent in an unbudded rose?
Aye, a sweet kiss - you see your mighty woes.
My thoughts! shall I unveil them? Listen then!
What mortal hath a prize, that other men
May be confounded and abash'd withal,
But lets it sometimes pace abroad majestical,
And triumph, as in thee I should rejoice
Amid the hoarse alarm of Corinth's voice.
Let my foes choke, and my friends shout afar,
While through the thronged streets your bridal car
Wheels round its dazzling spokes. " The lady's check
Trembled; she nothing said, but, pale and meek,
Arose and knelt before him, wept a rain
Of sorrows at his words; at last with pain
Beseeching him, the while his hand she wrung,
To change his purpose. He thereat was stung,
Perverse, with stronger fancy to reclaim
Her wild and timid nature to his aim:
Besides, for all his love, in self despite,
Against his better self, he took delight
Luxurious in her sorrows, soft and new.
His passion, cruel grown, took on a hue
Fierce and sanguineous as 'twas possible

In one whose brow had no dark veins to swell.
Fine was the mitigated fury, like
Apollo's presence when in act to strike
The serpent - Ha, the serpent! certes, she
Was none. She burnt, she lov'd the tyranny,
And, all subdued, consented to the hour
When to the bridal he should lead his paramour.
Whispering in midnight silence, said the youth,
"Sure some sweet name thou hast, though, by my truth,
I have not ask'd it, ever thinking thee
Not mortal, but of heavenly progeny,
As still I do. Hast any mortal name,
Fit appellation for this dazzling frame?
Or friends or kinsfolk on the citied earth,
To share our marriage feast and nuptial mirth?"
"I have no friends," said Lamia, "no, not one;
My presence in wide Corinth hardly known:
My parents' bones are in their dusty urns
Sepulchred, where no kindled incense burns,
Seeing all their luckless race are dead, save me,
And I neglect the holy rite for thee.
Even as you list invite your many guests;
But if, as now it seems, your vision rests
With any pleasure on me, do not bid
Old Apollonius - from him keep me hid."
Lycius, perplex'd at words so blind and blank,
Made close inquiry; from whose touch she shrank,
Feigning a sleep; and he to the dull shade
Of deep sleep in a moment was betray'd.

It was the custom then to bring away
The bride from home at blushing shut of day,
Veil'd, in a chariot, heralded along
By strewn flowers, torches, and a marriage song,
With other pageants: but this fair unknown
Had not a friend. So being left alone,
- Lycius was gone to summon all his kin -
And knowing surely she could never win

His foolish heart from its mad pompousness,
She set herself, high-thoughted, how to dress
The misery in fit magnificence.
She did so, but 'tis doubtful how and whence
Came, and who were her subtle servitors.
About the halls, and to and from the doors,
There was a noise of wings, till in short space
The glowing banquet-room shone with wide-arched grace
A haunting music, sole perhaps and lone
Supportress of the faery-roof, made moan
Throughout, as fearful the whole charm might fade.
Fresh carved cedar, mimicking a glade
Of palm and plantain, met from either side,
High in the midst, in honour of the bride:
Two palms and then two plantains, and so on,
From either side their stems branch'd one to one
All down the aisled place; and beneath all
There ran a stream of lamps straight on from wall to wall.
So canopied, lay an untasted feast
Teeming with odours. Lamia, regal drest,
Silently paced about, and as she went,
In pale contented sort of discontent,
Mission'd her viewless servants to enrich
The fretted splendour of each nook and niche.
Between the tree-stems, marbled plain at first,
Came jasper pannels; then, anon, there burst
Forth creeping imagery of slighter trees,
And with the larger wove in small intricacies.
Approving all, she faded at self-will,
And shut the chamber up, close, hush'd and still,
Complete and ready for the revels rude,
When dreadful guests would come to spoil her solitude.

The day appear'd, and all the gossip rout.
O senseless Lycius! Madman! wherefore flout
The silent-blessing fate, warm cloister'd hours,
And show to common eyes these secret bowers?
The herd approach'd; each guest, with busy brain,

Arriving at the portal, gaz'd amain,
And enter'd marveling: for they knew the street,
Remember'd it from childhood all complete
Without a gap, yet ne'er before had seen
That royal porch, that high-built fair demesne;
So in they hurried all, maz'd, curious and keen:
Save one, who look'd thereon with eye severe,
And with calm-planted steps walk'd in austere;
'Twas Apollonius: something too he laugh'd,
As though some knotty problem, that had daft
His patient thought, had now begun to thaw,
And solve and melt:- 'twas just as he foresaw.

He met within the murmurous vestibule
His young disciple. " 'Tis no common rule,
Lycius," said he, "for uninvited guest
To force himself upon you, and infest
With an unbidden presence the bright throng
Of younger friends; yet must I do this wrong,
And you forgive me." Lycius blush'd, and led
The old man through the inner doors broad-spread;
With reconciling words and courteous mien
Turning into sweet milk the sophist's spleen.

Of wealthy lustre was the banquet-room,
Fill'd with pervading brilliance and perfume:
Before each lucid pannel fuming stood
A censer fed with myrrh and spiced wood,
Each by a sacred tripod held aloft,
Whose slender feet wide-swerv'd upon the soft
Wool-woofed carpets: fifty wreaths of smoke
From fifty censers their light voyage took
To the high roof, still mimick'd as they rose
Along the mirror'd walls by twin-clouds odorous.
Twelve sphered tables, by silk seats insphered,
High as the level of a man's breast rear'd
On libbard's paws, upheld the heavy gold
Of cups and goblets, and the store thrice told

Of Ceres' horn, and, in huge vessels, wine
Come from the gloomy tun with merry shine.
Thus loaded with a feast the tables stood,
Each shrining in the midst the image of a God.

When in an antichamber every guest
Had felt the cold full sponge to pleasure press'd,
By minist'ring slaves, upon his hands and feet,
And fragrant oils with ceremony meet
Pour'd on his hair, they all mov'd to the feast
In white robes, and themselves in order placed
Around the silken couches, wondering
Whence all this mighty cost and blaze of wealth could spring.

Soft went the music the soft air along,
While fluent Greek a vowel'd undersong
Kept up among the guests, discoursing low
At first, for scarcely was the wine at flow;
But when the happy vintage touch'd their brains,
Louder they talk, and louder come the strains
Of powerful instruments:- the gorgeous dyes,
The space, the splendour of the draperies,
The roof of awful richness, nectarous cheer,
Beautiful slaves, and Lamia's self, appear,
Now, when the wine has done its rosy deed,
And every soul from human trammels freed,
No more so strange; for merry wine, sweet wine,
Will make Elysian shades not too fair, too divine.
Soon was God Bacchus at meridian height;
Flush'd were their cheeks, and bright eyes double bright:
Garlands of every green, and every scent
From vales deflower'd, or forest-trees branch-rent,
In baskets of bright osier'd gold were brought
High as the handles heap'd, to suit the thought
Of every guest; that each, as he did please,
Might fancy-fit his brows, silk-pillow'd at his ease.

What wreath for Lamia? What for Lycius?

What for the sage, old Apollonius?
Upon her aching forehead be there hung
The leaves of willow and of adder's tongue;
And for the youth, quick, let us strip for him
The thyrsus, that his watching eyes may swim
Into forgetfulness; and, for the sage,
Let spear-grass and the spiteful thistle wage
War on his temples. Do not all charms fly
At the mere touch of cold philosophy?
There was an awful rainbow once in heaven:
We know her woof, her texture; she is given
In the dull catalogue of common things.
Philosophy will clip an Angel's wings,
Conquer all mysteries by rule and line,
Empty the haunted air, and gnomed mine-
Unweave a rainbow, as it erewhile made
The tender-person'd Lamia melt into a shade.

By her glad Lycius sitting, in chief place,
Scarce saw in all the room another face,
Till, checking his love trance, a cup he took
Full brimm'd, and opposite sent forth a look
'Cross the broad table , to beseech a glance
From his old teacher's wrinkled countenance,
And pledge him. The bald-head philosopher
Had fix'd his eye, without a twinkle or stir,
Full on the alarmed beauty of the bride,
Brow-beating her fair form, and troubling her sweet pride
Lycius then press'd her hand, with devout touch,
As pale it lay upon the rosy couch:
'Twas icy, and the cold ran through his veins;
Then sudden it grew hot, and all the pains
Of an unnatural heat shot to his heart.
"Lamia, what means this? Wherefore dost thou start?
Know'st thou that man?" Poor Lamia answer'd not.
He gaz'd into her eyes, and not a jot
Own'd they the lovelorn piteous appeal:
More, more he gaz'd: his human senses reel:

90

Some hungry spell that loveliness absorbs;
There was no recognition in those orbs.
"Lamia!" he cried - and no soft-toned reply.
The many heard, and the loud revelry
Grew hush; the stately music no more breathes;
The myrtle sicken'd in a thousand wreaths.
By faint degrees, voice, lute, and pleasure ceased;
A deadly silence step by step increased,
Until it seem'd a horrid presence there,
And not a man but felt the terror in his hair.
"Lamia!" he shriek'd; and nothing but the shriek
With its sad echo did the silence break.
"Begone, foul dream!" he cried, gazing again
In the bride's face, where now no azure vein
Wander'd on fair-spaced temples; no soft bloom
Misted the cheek; no passion to illume
The deep-recessed vision:- all was blight;
Lamia, no longer fair, there sat a deadly white.
"Shut, shut those juggling eyes, thou ruthless man!
Turn them aside, wretch! or the righteous ban
Of all the Gods, whose dreadful images
Here represent their shadowy presences,
May pierce them on the sudden with the thorn
Of painful blindness, leaving thee forlorn,
In trembling dotage to the feeblest fright
Of conscience, for their long offended might,
For all thine impious proud-heart sophistries,
Unlawful magic, and enticing lies.
Corinthians! look upon that grey-beard wretch!
Mark how, possess'd, his lashless eyelids stretch
Around his demon eyes! Corinthians, see!
My sweet bride withers at their potency."
"Fool!" said the sophist, in an under-tone
Gruff with contempt; which a death-nighing moan
From Lycius answer'd, as heart-struck and lost,
He sank supine beside the aching ghost.
"Fool! Fool!" repeated he, while his eyes still
Relented not, nor mov'd; "from every ill

Of life have I preserv'd thee to this day,
And shall I see thee made a serpent's prey?"
Then Lamia breath'd death breath; the sophist's eye,
Like a sharp spear, went through her utterly,
Keen, cruel, perceant, stinging: she, as well
As her weak hand could any meaning tell,
Motion'd him to be silent; vainly so,
He look'd and look'd again a level - No!
"A serpent!" echoed he; no sooner said,
Than with a frightful scream she vanished:
And Lycius' arms were empty of delight,
As were his limbs of life, from that same night.
On the high couch he lay! - his friends came round -
Supported him - no pulse or breath they found,
And in its marriage robe the heavy body wound.

EDWARD BULWER-LYTTON (1803-1873), who eventually became the first Baron Lytton of Knebworth, was for a while the best-selling Victorian novelist. His novels wore many and various, but he is today best-remembered for the much-filmed *The Last Days of Pompeii* (1834) and for his classic haunted house story "The Haunted and the Haunters" (1859; also know as "The House and the Brain"). In later years he involved himself with the occult fads of the day; although it is difficult to ascertain how credulous he was he wrote two notable occult romances, *Zanoni* (1842) and *A Strange Story* (1861), and produced a curious quasi-Utopian fantasy in *The Coming Race* (1871; initially issued anonymously) in which the inhabitants of a secret Underworld have achieved complete mastery of their environment by harnessing the omnipotent occult force *vril*.

Many of Lytton's earliest works appeared in *The New Monthly Magazine*, whose editor he was for twenty months in 1832-1833. He wrote several allegorical fantasies for the magazine, including "The Nymph of the Lurlei Berg"; others can be found, with a number of essays, in *The Student* (1835). He also serialised his satirical fantasy novel modelled on Alain René le Sage's *The Devil on Two Sticks* (1707), *Asmodeus at Large* (1833). More allegorical tales are embedded in *The Pilgrim of the Rhine* (1834), which is a highly eccentric combination of travel book and fairy romance.

Like Coleridge before him Lytton was strongly infected by the aesthetic theories of the German Romantic philosophers, and he became an enthusiastic champion of a theory of art which exalted the supernatural and derided conventional realism, claiming that literary works require some kind of metaphysical framework if they are to be deemed whole and complete. Whether these theories (laid out in a series of articles in *Blackwood's* in mid-century) functioned as an inspiration to others it is difficult to judge, but Lytton was an important defender of fantastic elements in literature in a period when the more fashionable view derided their use.

THE NYMPH OF THE LURLEI BERG - A TALE

by Edward Bulwer-Lytton

> O Syrens, beware of a fair young Knight,
> He loves and he rides away.

A group of armed men were sitting cheerlessly round a naked and ill-furnished board in one of those rugged castles that overhang the Rhine - they looked at the empty bowl, and they looked at the untempting platter - then they shrugged their shoulders, and looked foolishly at each other. A young Knight, of a better presence than the rest, stalked gloomily into the hall.

"Well, comrades," said he, pausing in the centre of the room, and leaning on his sword, "I grieve to entertain ye no better - my father's gold is long gone - it bought your services while it lasted, and with these services, I, Rupert the Fearnought, won this castle from its Lord - levied tolls on the river - plundered the Burgesses of Bingen - and played the chieftain as nobly as a robber may. But alas! wealth flies - luck deserts us - we can no longer extract a doit from traveller or citizen. We must separate."

The armed men muttered something unintelligible - then they looked again at the dishes - then they shook their heads very dismally, and Rupert the Fearnought continued -

"For my part I love every thing wealth purchases - I cannot live in poverty, and when you have all gone, I propose to drown myself in the Rhine."

The armed men shouted out very noisily their notions on the folly of such a project of relief; but Rupert sank on a stone seat, folded his arms, and scarcely listened to them.

"Ah, if one could get some of the wealth that lies in the Rhine!" said an old marauder, " that would be worth diving for!"

"There cannot be much gold among the fishes I fancy," growled out another marauder, as he played with his dagger.

"Thou art a fool," quoth the old man; "gold there is, for

94

I heard my father say so, and it may be won too by a handsome man, if he be brave enough.":

Rupert lifted his head - " And how?" said he.

"The Water Spirits have the key to the treasure, and he who wins their love, may perhaps win their gold."

Rupert rose and took the old robber aside; they conversed long and secretly, and Rupert, returning to the hall, called for the last hogshead of wine the cellar contained.

"Comrades," said he, as he quaffed off a bumper, "Comrades, pledge to my safe return; I shall leave ye for a single month, since one element can yield no more, to try the beings of another; I may perish - I may return not. Tarry for me, therefore, but the time I have mentioned, if ye then see me not, depart in peace. Meanwhile, ye may manage to starve on, and if the worst comes to the worst, ye can eat one another."

So saying, the young spendthrift (by birth a Knight, by necessity a Robber, and by name and nature, Rupert the Fearnought) threw down the cup, and walking forth from the hall, left his companions to digest his last words with what appetite they might.

Among the Spirits of the Water, none were like Lurline; she was gentle as the gentlest breeze that floats from the realms of Spring over the bosom of the Rhine, and wherever at night she glided along the waves, there the beams of the love-star lingered, and lit up her path with their tenderest ray. Her eyes were of the softest azure of a southern heaven, and her hair like its setting sun. But above all her charms was the melody of her voice, and often when she sat upon the Lurlei Rock by the lonely moonlight, and sent her wild song above the silent waters, the nightingale paused from her wail to listen, and the winds crept humbled round her feet, as at a Sorcerer's spell.

One night as she thus sat, and poured forth her charmed strains, she saw a boat put from the opposite shore, and as it approached nearer and nearer towards her, she perceived it was guided by one solitary mariner; the moonlight rested upon his upward face, and it was the face of manhood's first dawn - beautiful, yet stern, and daring in its beauty - the light curls, surmounted by a plumed semi-casque, danced above a brow that was already marked by thought; and something keen and proud in the mien and air of the stranger, designated one who had learnt to act no less than to meditate. The Water Spirit paused as he approached, and gazed admiringly upon the fairest form that had ever yet chanced upon her solitude; she noted that the stranger too kept his eyes fixed upon her, and steered his boat to the rock on which she sat. And the shoals then as now were fraught with danger, but she laid her spell upon the wave and upon the rock, and the boat glided securely over them, - and the bold stranger was within but a few paces of her seat, when she forbade the waters to admit his nearer approach. The stranger stood erect in the boat, as it rocked tremulously to and fro, and still gazing upon the Water Nymph, he said -

"Who art thou, O beautiful maiden ! and whence is thine art? Night after night I have kept watch among the wild rocks that tenanted the sacred Goar, and listened enamoured to thy lay. Never before on earth was such minstrelsy heard. Art thou a daughter of the river? and dost thou - as the greybeards say - lure us to destruction? Behold, I render myself up to thee! Sweet is Death if it cradle me in thine arms! Welcome the whirlpool, if it entomb me in thy home!"

"Thou art bold, young mortal," - said the Water Spirit, with trembling tones, for she felt already the power of Love. "And wherefore say thy tribe such harsh legends of my song? Who ever perished by my art? Do I not rather allay the wind and smooth the mirror of the waves? Return to thine home safely and in peace, and vindicate, when thou hearest it maligned, the name of the Water Spirit of the Rhine."

"Return!" - said the Stranger haughtily - " never, until I have touched thee - knelt to thee - felt that thy beauty is not a dream. Even now my heart bounds as I gaze on thee! Even now I feel that thou *shalt* be mine! Behold! I trust

96

myself to thine element! I fear nothing but the loss of thee!"

So saying the young man leapt into the water, and in a minute more he knelt by the side of Lurline.

It was the stillest hour of night; the stars were motionless in the heavens: the moonlight lay hushed on the rippling tide:- from cliff to vale, no living thing was visible, save them, the Spirit and her human wooer.

"Oh!" - said he, passionately, - "never did I believe that thy voice was aught but some bodily music from another world; - in madness, and without hope, I tracked its sound homeward, and I have found *thee*. I touch thee! - thou livest! - the blood flows in thy form! thou art as woman, but more lovely! Take me to thy blue caverns and be my bride!"

As a dream from the sleeper, as a vapour from the valley, Lurline glided from the arms of the stranger, and sunk into the waters; the wave closed over her, but, beneath its surface, he saw her form gliding along to the more shadowy depths; he saw, and plunged into the waves!

The morning came, and the boat still tossed by the Lurlei Berg - without a hand to steer it. The Rhine rolled bright to the dewy sun, but the stranger had returned not to its shores.

The cavern of the Water Spirit stretches in many chambers beneath the courses of the river, and in its inmost recess - several days after the stranger's disappearance - Lurline sat during the summer noon; but not alone. Love lighted up those everlasting spars, and even beneath the waters and beneath the earth held his temple and his throne.

"And tell me, my stranger bridegroom," - said Lurline, as the stranger lay at her feet, listening to the dash of the waters against the cavern - " tell me of what country and parentage art thou? Art thou one of the many chiefs whose castles frown from the opposite cliffs? - or a wanderer from some distant land? What is thy mortal name?"

"Men call me Rupert the Fearnought," - answered the stranger. "A penniless chief am I, and a cheerless castle do

97

I hold; my sword is my heritage; - and as for gold, the gold which my Sire bequeathed me, alas! on the land, beautiful Lurline, there are many more ways of getting rid of such dross than in thy peaceful dominions beneath the river. Yet, Lurline," - and the countenance of Rupert became more anxious and more earnest -" Is it not true that the Spirits of thy race hoard vast treasures of gems and buried gold within their caves? Do ye not gather all that the wind and tempest have sunk beneath the waves in your rocky coffers? And have ye not the power to endow a mortal with the forgotten wealth of ages?"

"Ah, yes!" - answered the enamoured Water Spirit. "These chambers contain enough of such idle treasures, dull and useless, my beloved, to those who love."

"Eh - em!" - quoth the mortal - "what thou sayest has certainly a great deal of truth in it; but - but just to pass away the next hour or two - suppose thou showest me, dearest Lurline, some of these curiosities of thine. Certes I am childishly fond of looking at coins and jewels."

"As thou wilt, my stranger," answer Lurline, and, rising, she led the way through the basalt arches that swept in long defiles through her palace, singing with the light heart of contented love to the waves that dashed around. The stranger followed wondering - but not fearing - with his hand every now and then, as they made some abrupt turning, mechanically wandering to his sword, and his long plume waving lightly to the rushing air, that at times with a hollow roar swept through their mighty prison. At length the Water Spirit came to a door, before which lay an enormous shell, and, as the stranger looked admiringly upon its gigantic size, a monstrous face gradually rose from the aperture of the shell, and with glaring eyes and glistening teeth gloated out upon the mortal.

Three steps backward did Rupert the Fearnought make, and three times did he cross himself with unwonted devotion, and very irreverently, and not in exact keeping with the ceremony, blurted he forth a northern seafarer's oath. Then outflashed his sword; and he asked Lurline if he

98

were to prepare against a foe. The Water Spirit smiled, and murmuring some words in a language unknown to Rupert, the monster slowly wound itself from the cavities of the shell; and, carrying the shell itself upon its back, crept with a long hiss and a trailing slime from the door, circuitously approaching Rupert the Fearnought by the rear. "*Christe beate!* " ejaculated the lover, veering round with extreme celerity, and presenting the point of the sword to the monster, "What singular shell-fish there are at the bottom of the Rhine!" Then, gazing more attentively on the monster, he perceived that it was in the shape of a dragon, substituting only the shell for wings.

"The dragon-race," said the Water Spirit, "are the guardians of all treasure, whether in the water or in the land. And deep in the very centre of the earth, the hugest of the tribe lies coiled around the load-stone of the world."

The door now opened. They entered a vast vault. Heavens! how wondrous was the treasure that greeted the Fearnought's eyes! All the various wrecks that, from the earliest ages of the world, had enriched the Rhine or its tributary streams, contributed their burthen to this mighty treasury: there was the first rude coin ever known in the North, cumbrous and massive, teaching betimes the moral that money is inseparable from the embarrassment of taking care of it. There were Roman vases and jewels in abundance; rings, and chains, and great necklaces of pearl: there, too, were immense fragments of silver that, from time to time, had been washed into the river, and hurried down into this universal recipient. And, looking up, the Fearnought saw that the only roof above was the waters, which rolled black and sullenly overhead, but were prevented either by a magic charm, or the wonderful resistance of the pent air, from penetrating farther. But wild, and loud, and hoarse was the roar above, and the Water Spirit told him, that they were then below the Gewirre or Whirlpool which howls along the bank opposite to the Lurlei Berg.

"I see," - quoth the bold stranger, as he grasped at a

99

heap of jewels, - " that wherever there is treasure below the surface, there is peril above!"

" Rather say," - answered the Water Spirit - "that the whirlpool betokens the vexation and strife which are the guardians and parents of riches."

The Fearnought made no answer; but he filled his garments with the most costly gems he could find, in order, doubtless, to examine them more attentively at his leisure.

And that evening as his head lay upon the lap of the Water Spirit, and she played with his wreathy hair, Rupert said, "Ah, Lurline! ah, that thou wouldst accompany me to the land. Thou knowest not in these caves (certainly pretty in their way, but, thou must confess, placed in a prodigiously dull neighbourhood); - thou knowest not, I say, dear Lurline, how charming a life it is to live in a beautiful castle on the land." And with that Rupert began to paint in the most eloquent terms the mode of existence then most approvedly in fashion. He dwelt with a singular flow of words on the pleasures of the chase: he dressed the water-nymph in green - mounted her on a snow-white courser - supposed her the admiration of all who flocked through the green wood to behold her. Then he painted the gorgeous banquet, the Lords and Dames that, glittering in jewels and cloth of gold, would fill the hall over which Lurline should preside - all confessing her beauty, and obedient to her sway; harps were for ever to sound her praises; Minstrels to sing and Knights to contest for it; and, above all, he, Rupert himself, was to be eternally at her feet -" Not, dearest Love," (added he, gently rubbing his knees,) "on these rocky stones, but upon the softest velvets - or, at least, upon the greenest mosses."

The Water Spirit was moved, for the love of change and the dream of Ambition can pierce even below the deepest beds of the stream; and the voice of Flattery is more persuasive than were the melodies of the Syren herself.

By degrees she allowed herself to participate in Rupert's desire for land; and, as she most tenderly loved him, his evident and growing ennui, his long silences, and his frequent yawns, made her anxious to meet his wishes, and fearful lest otherwise he should grow utterly wearied of her society. It was settled then that they should go to the land.

"But, oh my beloved," said Rupert the Fearnought, "I am but a poor and mortgaged Knight, and in my hall the winds whistle through dismantled casements, and over a wineless board. Shall I not go first to the shore, and with some of the baubles thou keepest all uselessly below, refit my castle among yonder vine-clad mountains, so that it shall be a worthy tenement for the Daughter of the Rhine? then I shall hasten back for thee, and we will be wedded with all the pomp that befits thy station."

The poor Water Spirit, having lived at the bottom of the Rhine all her life, was not so well read in the world as might have been expected from a singer of her celebrity. She yielded to the proposition of Rupert; and that very night the moon beheld the beautiful Lurline assisting Rupert to fill his boat (that lay still by the feet of the Lurlei Berg) with all the largest jewels in her treasury. Rupert filled and filled till he began to fear the boat would hold no more without sinking; and then, reluctantly ceasing, he seized the oars, and every now and then kissing his hand at Lurline with a melancholy expression of fondness, he rowed away to the town of St. Goar.

As soon as he had moored his boat in a little creek, overshadowed at that time by thick brambles, he sprang lightly on land, and seizing a hunting-horn that he wore round his neck, sounded a long blast. Five times was that blast echoed from the rock of the Lurlei Berg by the sympathising Dwarf who dwelt there, and who, wiser than Lurline, knew that her mortal lover had parted from her for ever. Rupert started in dismay, but soon recovered his native daring. "Come fiend, sprite or dragon," said he, "I will not give back the treasure I have won!" He looked defyingly to the stream, but no shape rose from its depths - the moonlight slept on the water - all was still, and without sign of life, as the echo died mournfully away. He looked wistfully to the land, and now crashing through the boughs came the

101

armed tread of men - plumes waved - corslets glittered, and Rupert the Fearnought was surrounded by his marauding comrades. He stood with one foot on his boat, and pointed exultingly to the treasure. "Behold," he cried, to the old robber who had suggested the emprize, "I have redeemed my pledge, and plundered the coffer of the Spirits of the Deep!"

Then loud broke the robbers' voices over the still stream, and mailed hands grasped the heavy gems, and fierce eyes gloated on their splendour.

"And how didst' thou win the treasure? - with thy good sword, we'll warrant," cried the robbers.

"Nay," answered Rupert, "there is a weapon more dangerous to female, whether spirit or flesh, than the sword - a soft tongue and flattering words! - Away; take each what he can carry, - and away, I say, to our castle!"

Days and weeks rolled on but the Mortal returned not to the Maiden of the Waters; and night after night Lurline sat alone on the moonlight rock, and mourned for her love in such wild and melancholy strains, as now at times the fisherman starts to hear. The Dwarf of the Lurlei Berg sometimes put forth his shagged head, from the little door in his rock, and sought to solace her with wise aphorisms on human inconstancy; but the soft Lurline was not the more consoled by his wisdom, and still not the less she clung to the vain hope that Rupert the Flatterer would return.

And Rupert said to his comrades, as they quaffed the wine, and carved the meat at his castle board -

"I hear there is a maiden in the castle of Lörchausen, amidst the valleys, on the other side the Rhine, fair to see, and rich to wed. She shall be the Bride of the Fearnought."

The robbers shouted at the proposal, and the next day, in their sheenest armour, they accompanied their beautiful chief in his wooing to the Lady of Lörchausen. But Rupert took care not to cross by the Lurlei Berg; for Fearnought as he was, he thought a defrauded dragon and a betrayed sprite were hard odds for a mortal chief. They arrived at the castle, and Rupert wooed with the same flattery and the same success as before. But as one female generally avenges

102

the wrongs of another, so Rupert was caught by the arts he practised, and loved no less ardently than he was loved. The Chief of Lörchausen consented to the wedding, and the next week he promised to bring the bride and her dowry to the Fearnought's castle.

"But, ah! dearest Unna," said Rupert to his betrothed, "take heed as you pass the river that your bark steer not by the Lurlei Berg, for *there* lurks a dragon ever athirst for beauty and for gold; and he lashes with his tail the waters when such voyagers as thou pass, and whirls the vessel down into his cave below."

The beautiful Unna was terrified, and promised assent to so reasonable a request.

Rupert and his comrade returned home, and set the old castle in order for the coming of the bride.

The morning broke bright and clear - the birds sang out - the green vines waved merrily on the breeze - and the sunlight danced gaily upon the bosom of the Rhine. Rupert and his comrades stood ranged by the rocky land that borders St. Goar to welcome the bride. And now they heard the trumpets sounding far away, and looking down the river they saw the feudal streamers of Lörchausen glittering on the tide, as the sail from which they waved cut its way along the waters.

Then the Dwarf of the Lurlei Berg, startled by the noise of the trumpets, peeped peevishly out of his little door, and he saw the vessel on the wave, and Rupert on the land; and at once he knew, as he was a wise dwarf, what was to happen. "Ho, ho!" said he to himself, "not so fast, my young gallant: I have long wanted to marry, myself. What if I get your bride, and what if my good friend the Dragon comfort himself for your fraud by a snap at her dowry - Lurline my cousin shall be avenged!" So with that the dwarf slipped into the water, and running along the cavern, came up to the Dragon quite out of breath. The monster trailed himself hastily out of his shell. "And what now, Master Dwarf," quoth he, very angrily; "no thoroughfare here, I assure you!" "Pooh," said the Dwarf, "are you so stupid that you do not want to be avenged upon the insolent mortal who robbed your treasury, and deserted your mistress. Behold! he stands on the rocks of Goar, about to receive a bride, who sails along with a dowry, that shall swell thy exhausted coffers; behold! I say, I will marry the lady, and thou shalt have the dower."

Then the dragon was exceedingly pleased - "And how shall it be managed?" said he, rubbing his claws with delight.

"Lock thy door, Master Dragon," answered the Dwarf, "and go up to the Gewirre above thee, and lash the waters with thy tail, so that no boat may approach."

The Dragon promised to obey, and away went the Dwarf to Lurline. He found her sitting listlessly in her crystal chamber, her long hair drooping over her face, and her eyes bent on the rocky floor, heavy with tears.

"Arouse thee, cousin," said the Dwarf, "thy lover may be regained. Behold he sails along the Rhine with a bride he is about to marry; and if thou wilt ascend the surface of the water, and sing, with thy sweetest voice, the melodies he loves, doubtless he will not have the heart to resist thee, and thou shalt yet gain the Faithless from his bride."

Lurline started wildly from her seat; she followed the Dwarf up to the Lurlei Berg, and seated herself on a ledge in the rock. The Dwarf pointed out to her in the boat the glittering casque and nodding plumes of the Lord of Lörchausen. "Behold thy lover!" said he, "but the helmet hides his face. See he sits by the bride - he whispers her - he presses her hand. Sing now thy sweetest song, I beseech thee."

"But who are they on the opposite bank?" asked the Water Spirit.

"Thy lover's vassals only," answered the Dwarf

"Be cheered, child! " said the Chief of Lörchausen. "See how the day smiles on us - thy bridegroom waits thee yonder - even now I see him towering above his comrades."

"Oh! my father, my heart sinks with fear!" murmured Unna; "and behold the frightful Lurlei Berg frowns upon us.

Thou knowest how Rupert cautioned us to avoid it."

"And did we not, my child, because of that caution, embark yonder at the mouth of the *Wisperbach*? Even now our vessel glides towards the opposite shore, and nears not the mountain thy weak heart dreadest."

At that moment, a wild and most beautiful music broke tremulously along the waves; and they saw, sitting on the Lurlei Berg, a shape fairer than the shapes of the Children of Earth. "Hither," she sang, "hither, oh! gallant bark! Behold here is thy haven, and thy respite from the waters and the winds. Smooth is the surface of the tide around, and the rock hollows its bosom to receive thee. Hither, oh! nuptial band! The bridals are prepared. Here shall the betrothed gain the bridegroom, and the bridegroom welcome the bride!"

The boatmen paused, entranced with the air, the oars fell from their hands - the boat glided on towards the rock.

Rupert in dismay and terror heard the strain and recognized afar the silvery beauty of the Water Spirit. "Beware," he shouted - "beware - this way steer the vessel, nor let it near to the Lurlei Berg."

Then the Dwarf laughed within himself, and he took up the sound ere it fell, and five times across the water, louder far than the bridegroom's voice, was repeated "Near to the Lurlei Berg."

At this time by the Gewirre opposite, the Dragon writhed his vast folds, and fierce and perilous whirled the waters round.

"See, my child," said the Chief of Lörchausen, "how the whirlpool foams and eddies on the opposite shore - wisely hath Sir Rupert dismissed superstition in the presence of real danger; and yon fair figure is doubtless stationed by his command to direct us how to steer from the whirlpool."

"Oh, no, no, my father!" cried Unna, clinging to his arm. "No, yon shape is but the false aspect of a fiend - I beseech you to put off from the Rock - see, we near - we near - its base!"

"Hark - hear ye not five voices telling us to near it!"

answered the Chief; and he motioned to the rowers, who required no command to avoid the roar of the Gewirre.

"Death!" cried Rupert, stamping fiercely on the ground; "they heed me not!" - and he shouted again "Hither, for dear life's sake, hither!" And again, five times drowning his voice, came the echo from the Lurlei Berg, "For dear life's sake, hither!"

"Yes, hither!" sang once more the Water Spirit - "hither, O gallant bark! - as the brooklet to the river - as the bird to the sunny vine - flies the heart to the welcome of love!"

"Thou art avenged!" shouted the Dwarf, as he now stood visible and hideous on the Rock. "Lurline, thou art avenged!"

And from the opposite shore, the straining eyes of Rupert beheld the boat strike suddenly among the shoals - and lo, in the smoothest waves it reeled once, and vanished beneath for ever! An eddy - a rush - and the Rhine flowed on without a sign of man upon its waves. "Lost, lost!" cried Rupert, clasping his hands, and five times from the Lurlei Berg echoed "Lost!"

And Rupert the Fearnought left his treasures and his castle, and the ruins still moulder to the nightly winds: and he sought the Sea-kings of the North; they fitted out a ship for the brave stranger, and he sailed on a distant cruise. And his name was a name of dread by the shores on which the fierce beak of his war-bark descended. And the bards rang it forth to their Runic harps over the blood-red wine. But at length they heard of his deeds no more - they traced not his whereabouts - a sudden silence enwrapt him - his vessel had gone forth on a long voyage - it never returned, nor was heard of more. But still the undying Water Spirit mourns in her lonely caves - and still she fondly believes that the Wanderer will yet return. Often she sits, when the night is hushed, and the stars watch over the sleep of Earth, upon her desolate rock, and pours forth her melancholy strains. And yet the fishermen believe that she strives by her song to lure every raft and vessel that seems, to the deluded eyes of her passion, one which may contain her lover!

And still, too, when the Huntsman's horn sounds over the water - five times is the sound echoed from the Rock - the Dwarf himself may ever and anon be seen, in the new moon, walking on the heights of the Lurlei Berg, with a female form in an antique dress, devoutly believed to be the Lady of Lörchausen, - who, defrauded of a Knight, has reconciled herself to marriage with a Dwarf!

As to the moral of the tale, I am in doubt whether it is meant as a caution to heiresses or to singers; if the former, it is to be feared that the moral is not very efficacious, seeing that no less than three persons of that description have met with Ruperts within the last fortnight; but if to the latter, as is my own private opinion, it will be an encouragement to moralists ever after. Warned by the fate of their sister syren, those ladies take the most conscientious precautions, that, though they may sometimes be *deserted*, they should never at least be *impoverished,* by their lovers!

BENJAMIN DISRAELI (1804-1881) was a successful novelist before he embarked upon the political career which culminated in his elevation to leader of the Tory party and his election as prime minister; he was subsequently awarded a life peerage. He wrote several satirical fantasies in the early part of his career, beginning with *The Voyage of Captain Popanilla* (1828), which followed the adventures of an innocent youth from the Isle of Fantaisie in the civilised land of Vraibleusia. "The Infernal Marriage" (1832) is a classical fantasy which sarcastically retells the story of Proserpine in much the same way that "Ixion in Heaven" (first published in Bulwer-Lytton's *New Monthly Magazine* in 1832-33) retells another Greek myth. His novel *Alroy* (1833) is a more earnest romance of Jewish history with some supernatural embellishments.

Britain lost a fine fantasy writer when Disraeli decided to embark upon his real-life adventure among the Olympians; the remarkable fact that he fared better than Popanilla, Persephone or Ixion serves to reminds us that the real world can, on very rare occasions, be more rewarding than imaginary ones.

"Ixion in Heaven" inspired an even more sarcastic burlesque, "Endymion; or, A family Party on Olympus" (1842) by William Aytoun (1813-65). Aytoun was the son-in-law of John Wilson, who was for many years the guiding light of *Blackwood's Magazine* (in the invented persona of "Christopher North"); Aytoun was a satirist of some note, who achieved brief celebrity when he published the verse play *Firmilian* (1854), which passed into obscurity along with the "Spasmodic school" of poets whose pretensions it mocked and whose fate it helped to seal.

IXION IN HEAVEN

by Benjamin Disraeli

' Ixion, King of Thessaly, famous for its horses, married Dia, daughter of Deioneus, who, in consequence of his son-in-law's non-fulfilment of his engagements, stole away some of the monarch's steeds. Ixion concealed his resentment under the mask of friendship. He invited his father-in-law to a feast at Larissa, the capital of his kingdom; and when Deioneus arrived according to his appointment, he threw him into a pit which he had previously filled with burning coals. This treachery so irritated the neighbouring princes, that all of them refused to perform the usual ceremony by which a man was then purified of murder, and Ixion was shunned and despised by all mankind. Jupiter had compassion upon him, carried him to heaven, and introduced him to the Father of the Gods. Such a favour, which ought to have awakened gratitude in Ixion, only served to inflame his bad passions; he became enamoured of Juno, and attempted to seduce her. Juno was willing to gratify the passion of Ixion, though, according to others,' &c. - *Classical Dictionary,* art. *'Ixion'.*

PART I

The thunder groaned, the wind howled, the rain fell in hissing torrents, impenetrable darkness covered the earth.

A blue and forky flash darted a momentary light over the landscape. A Doric temple rose in the centre of a small and verdant plain, surrounded on all sides by green and hanging woods.

"Jove is my only friend," exclaimed a wanderer, as he muffled himself up in his mantle; "and were it not for the porch of his temple, this night, methinks, would complete the work of my loving wife and my dutiful subjects."

The thunder died away, the wind sank into silence, the rain ceased, and the parting clouds exhibited the glittering crescent of the young moon. A sonorous and majestic voice sounded from the skies:-

"Who art thou that has no other friend than Jove"

"One whom all mankind unite in calling a wretch."

"Art thou a philospher?"

"If philosophy be endurance. But for the rest, I was sometime a king, and am now a scatterling."

"How do they call thee?"

"Ixion of Thessaly."

"Ixion of Thessaly! I thought he was a happy man. I heard that he was just married."

"Father of Gods and men! for I deem thee such, Thessaly is not Olympus. Conjugal felicity is only the portion of the Immortals!"

"Hem! What! was Dia jealous, which is common; or false, which is commoner; or both, which is commonest?"

"It may be neither. We quarrelled about nothing. Where there is little sympathy, or too much, the splitting of a straw is plot enough for a domestic tragedy. I was careless, her friends stigmatised me as callous; she cold, her friends styled her magnanimous. Public opinion was all on her side, merely because I did not choose that the world should interfere between me and my wife. Dia took the world's advice upon every point, and the world decided that she always acted rightly. However, life is life, either in a palace or a cave. I am glad you ordered it to leave off thundering."

"A cool dog this. And Dia left thee?"

"No I left her."

"What, craven?"

"Not exactly. The truth is ......'tis a long story. I was over head and ears in debt."

"Ah! that accounts for everything. Nothing so harassing as a want of money! But what lucky fellows you Mortals are with your *post-obits!* We Immortals are deprived of this resource. I was obliged to get up a rebellion against my father, because he kept me so short, and could not die."

"You could have married for money. I did."

"I had no opportunity, there was so little female society

110

in those days. When I came out, there were no heiresses except the Parcae, confirmed old maids; and no very rich dowager, except my grandmother, old Terra."

"Just the thing; the older the better. However, I married Dia, the daughter of Deioneus, with a prodigious portion: but after the ceremony the old gentleman would not fulfil his part of the contract without my giving up my stud. Can you conceive anything more unreasonable? I smothered my resentment at the time; for the truth is, my tradesmen all renewed my credit on the strength of the match, and so we went on very well for a year, but at last they began to smell a rat, and grew importunate. I entreated Dia to interfere; but she was a paragon of daughters, and always took the side of her father. If she had only been dutiful to her husband, she would have been a perfect woman. At last I invited Deioneus to the Larissa races, with the intention of conciliating him. The unprincipled old man bought the horse that I had backed, and by which I intended to have redeemed my fortunes, and withdrew it. My book was ruined. I dissembled my rage. I dug a pit in our garden, and filled it with burning coals. As my father-in-law and myself were taking a stroll after dinner, the worthy Deioneus fell in, merely by accident. Dia proclaimed me the murderer of her father, and, as a satisfaction to her wounded feelings, earnestly requested her subjects to decapitate her husband. She certainly was the best of daughters. There was no withstanding public opinion, an infuriated rabble, and a magnanimous wife at the same time. They surrounded my palace: I cut my way through the greasy-capped multitude, sword in hand, and gained a neighbouring Court, where I solicited my brother princes to purify me from the supposed murder. If I had only murdered a subject, they would have supported me against the people; but Deioneus being a crowned head, like themselves, they declared they would not countenance so immoral a being as his son-in-law. And so, at length, after much wandering, and shunned by all my species, I am here, Jove, in much higher society than I ever expected to mingle"

111

"Well, thou art a frank dog, and in a sufficiently severe scrape. The Gods must have pity on those for whom men have none. It is evident that Earth is too hot for thee at present, so I think thou hadst better come and stay a few weeks with us in Heaven."

"Take my thanks for hecatombs, great Jove. Thou art, indeed, a God!"

"I hardly know whether our life will suit you. We dine at sunset; for Apollo is so much engaged that he cannot join us sooner, and no dinner goes off well without him. In the morning you are your own master, and must find amusement where you can. Diana will show you some tolerable sport. Do you shoot?"

"No arrow surer. Fear not for me, Aegiochus: I am always at home. But how am I to get to you?"

"I will send Mercury; he is the best travelling companion in the world. What ho! my Eagle!"

The clouds joined, and darkness again fell over the earth.

II

"So! tread softly. Don't be nervous. Are you sick?"

"A little nausea; 'tis nothing."

"The novelty of the motion. The best thing is a beefsteak. We will stop at Taurus and take one."

"You have been a great traveller, Mercury?"

"I have seen the world."

"Ah! a wondrous spectacle. I long to travel"

"The same thing over and over again. Little novelty and much change. I am wearied with exertion, and if I could get a pension would retire."

"And yet travel brings wisdom."

"It cures us of care. Seeing much we feel little, and learn how very petty are all those great affairs which cost us such anxiety."

"I feel that already myself. Floating in this blue aether, what the devil is my wife to me, and her dirty earth! My

112

persecuting enemies seem so many pismires; and as for my debts, which have occasioned me so many brooding moments, honour and infamy, credit and beggary, seem to me alike ridiculous."

"Your mind is opening, Ixion. You will soon be a man of the world. To the left, and keep clear of that star."

"Who lives there?"

"The Fates know, not I. Some low people who are trying to shine into notice. 'Tis a parvenu planet, and only sprung into space within this century. We do not visit them."

"Poor devils! I feel hungry."

"All right. We shall get into Heaven by the first dinner bolt. You cannot arrive at a strange house at a better moment. We shall just have time to dress. I would not spoil my appetite by luncheon. Jupiter keeps a capital cook."

"I have heard of Nectar and Ambrosia."

"Poh! nobody touches them. They are regular old-fashioned celestial food, and merely put upon the side-table. Nothing goes down in Heaven now but infernal cookery. We took our *chef* from Proserpine."

"Were you ever in Hell?"

"Several times. 'Tis the fashion now among the Olympians to pass the winter there."

"Is this the season in Heaven?"

"Yes; you are lucky. Olympus is quite full."

"It was kind of Jupiter to invite me."

"Ay! he has his good points. And, no doubt, he has taken a liking to you, which is all very well. But be upon your guard. He has no heart, and is as capricious as he is tyrannical."

"Gods cannot be more unkind to me than men have been."

"All those who have suffered think they have seen the worst. A great mistake. However, you are now in the high road to preferment, so we will not be dull. There are some good fellows enough amongst us. You will like old Neptune."

"Is he there now?"

"Yes, he generally passes his summer with us. There

113

is little stirring in the ocean at that season."

"I am anxious to see Mars."

"Oh! a brute, more a bully than a hero. Not at all in the best set. These mustachioed gentry are by no means the rage at present in Olympus. The women are all literary now, and Minerva has quite eclipsed Venus. Apollo is our hero. You must read his last work."

"I hate reading."

"So do I. I have no time, and seldom do anything in that way but glance at a newspaper. Study and action will not combine."

"I supposed I shall find the Goddesses very proud?"

"You will find them as you find women below, of different dispositions with the same object. Venus is a flirt; Minerva a prude, who fancies she has a correct taste and a strong mind; and Juno a politician. As for the rest, faint heart never won fair lady, take a friendly hint, and do not be alarmed."

"I fear nothing. My mind mounts with my fortunes. We are above the clouds. They form beneath us a vast and snowy region, dim and irregular, as I have sometimes seen them clustering upon the horizon's ridge at sunset, like a raging sea stilled by some sudden supernatural frost and frozen into form! How bright the air above us, and how delicate its fragrant breath! I scarcely breathe, and yet my pulses beat like my first youth. I hardly feel my being. A splendour falls upon your presence. You seem, indeed, a God! Am I so glorious? This, this is Heaven!"

III

The travellers landed on a vast flight of sparkling steps of lapis-lazuli. Ascending, they entered beautiful gardens; winding walks that yielded to the feet, and accelerated your passage by their rebounding pressure; fragrant shrubs covered with dazzling flowers, the fleeting tints of which changed every moment; groups of tall trees, with strange birds of brilliant and variegated plumage,

114

singing and reposing in their sheeny foliage, and fountains of perfumes.

Before them rose an illimitable and golden palace, with high spreading domes of pearl, and long windows of crystal. Around the huge portal of ruby was ranged a company of winged genii, who smile on Mercury as he passed them with his charge.

"The father of Gods and men is dressing," said the son of Maia. "I shall attend his toilet and inform him of your arrival. These are your rooms. Dinner will be ready in half an hour. I will call for you as I go down. You can be formally presented in the evening. At that time, inspired by liqueurs and his matchless band of wind instruments, you will agree with the world that Aegiochus is the most finished God in existence."

IV

"Now, Ixion, are you ready?"

"Even so. What says Jove?"

"He smiled, but said nothing. He was trying on a new robe. By this time he is seated. Hark! the thunder. Come on!"

They entered a cupolaed hall. Seats of ivory and gold were ranged round a circular table of cedar, inlaid with the campaigns against the Titans, in silver exquisitely worked, a nuptial present of Vulcan. The service of gold plate threw all ideas of the King of Thessaly as to Royal magnificence into the darkest shade. The enormous plateau represented the constellations. Ixion viewed the father of Gods and men with great interest, who, however, did not notice him. He acknowledged the majesty of that countenance whose nod shook Olympus. Majestically robust and luxuriantly lusty, his tapering waist was evidently immortal, for it defied Time, and his splendid auburn curls, parted on his forehead with celestial precision, descended over cheeks glowing with the purple radiancy of perpetual manhood.

The haughty Juno was seated on his left hand and

Ceres on his right. For the rest of the company there was Neptune, Latona, Minerva, and Apollo, and when Mercury and Ixion had taken their places, one seat was still vacant.

"Where is Diana?" inquired Jupiter, with a frown.

" My sister is hunting," said Apollo.

"She is always too late for dinner," said Jupiter. "No habit is less Goddess-like."

"Godlike pursuits cannot be expected to induce Goddess-like manners," said Juno, with a sneer.

"I have no doubt Diana will be here directly," said Latona, mildly.

Jupiter seemed pacified, and at that instant the absent guest returned.

"Good sport, Di?" inquired Neptune.

"Very fair, uncle. Mamma," continued the sister of Apollo, addressing herself to Juno, who she ever thus styled when she wished to conciliate her, " I have brought you a new peacock."

Juno was fond of pets, and was conciliated by the present.

"Bacchus made a great noise about this wine, Mercury," said Jupiter, "but I think with little cause. What think you?"

"It pleases me, but I am fatigued, and then all wine is agreeable."

"You have had a long journey," replied the Thunderer. "Ixion, I am glad to see you in Heaven."

"Your Majesty arrived to-day?" inquired Minerva, to whom the King of Thessaly sat next.

"Within this hour."

"You must leave off talking of Time now," said Minerva, with a severe smile. "Pray is there anything new in Greece?"

"I have not been at all in society lately."

"No new editions of Homer? I admire him exceedingly."

"All about Greece interests me," said Apollo, who, although handsome, was a somewhat melancholy lack-a-daisical looking personage, with his shirt collar thrown open,

116

and his long curls theatrically arranged. "All about Greece interests me. I always consider Greece my peculiar property. My best poems were written at Delphi. I travelled in Greece when I was young. I cnvy mankind."

"Indeed!" said Ixion.

"Yes: they at least can look forward to a termination of the ennui of existence, but for us Celestials there is no prospect. Say what they likc, Immortality is a bore."

"You eat nothing, Apollo," said Ceres.

"Nor drink, " said Neptune.

"To eat, to drink, what is it but to live; and what is life but death, if death be that which all men deem it, a thing insufferable, and to be shunned. I refresh myself now only with soda-water and biscuits. Ganymede, bring some."

Now, although the *cuisine* of Olympus was considered perfect, the forlorn poet had unfortunately fixed upon the only two articles which were not comprised in its cellar or larder. In Heaven, there was neither soda-water nor biscuits. A great confusion consequently ensued; but at length the bard, whose love of fame was only equalled by his horror of getting fat, consoled himself with a swan stuffed with truffles, and a bottle of strong Tenedos wine.

"What do you think of Homer?" inquired Minerva of Apollo. "Is he not delightful?"

"If you think so."

"Nay, I am desirous of your opinion"

"Then you should not have given me yours, for your taste is too fine for me to dare to differ with it."

"I have suspected, for some time, that you are rather a heretic."

"Why, the truth is" replied Apollo, playing with his rings, "I do not think much of Homer. Homer was not esteemed in his own age, and our contemporaries are generally our best judges. The fact is, there are very few people who are qualified to decide upon matters of taste. A certain set, for certain reasons, resolve to cry up a certain writer, and the great mass soon join in. All is cant. And the present admiration of Homer is not less so. They say I have

117

borrowed a great deal from him. The truth is, I never read Homer since I was a child, and I thought of him then what I think of him now, a writer of some wild irregular power, totally deficient in taste. Depend upon it, our contemporaries are our best judges, and his contemporaries decided that Homer was nothing. A great poet cannot be kept down. Look at my case. Marsyas said of my first volume that it was pretty good poetry for a God, and in answer I wrote a satire, and flayed Marsyas alive. But what is poetry, and what is criticism, and what is life? Air. And what is Air? Do you know? I don't. All is mystery, and all is gloom, and ever and anon from out the clouds a star breaks forth, and glitters, and that star is Poetry."

"Splendid!" exclaimed Minerva.

"I do not exactly understand you," said Neptune.

"Have you heard from Proserpine, lately?" inquired Jupiter of Ceres.

"Yesterday," said the domestic mother. "They talk of soon joining us. But Pluto is at present so busy, owing to the amazing quantity of wars going on now, that I am almost afraid he will scarcely be able to accompany her."

Juno exchanged a telegraphic nod with Ceres. The Goddesses rose, and retired.

"Come, old boy," said Jupiter to Ixion, instantly throwing off all his chivalric majesty, "I drink your welcome in a magnum of Maraschino. Damn your poetry, Apollo, and Mercury give us one of your good stories."

V

"Well ! what do you think of him ?" asked Juno.

"He appears to have a fine mind," said Minerva.

"Poh ! he has very fine eyes," said Juno.

"He seems a very nice, quiet young gentleman," said Ceres.

"I have no doubt he is very amiable," said Latona.

"He must have felt very strange," said Diana.

118

Hercules arrived with his bride Hebe; soon after the Graces dropped in, the most delightful personages in the world for a *soirée*, so useful and ready for anything. Afterwards came a few of the Muses, Thalia, Melpomene, and Terpsichore, famous for a charade or a proverb. Jupiter liked to be amused in the evening. Bacchus also came, but finding that the Gods had not yet left their wine, retired to pay them a previous visit.

V11

Ganymede announced coffee in the saloon of Juno. Jupiter was in superb good humour. He was amused by his mortal guest. He had condescended to tell one of his best stories in his best style, about Leda, not too scandalous, but gay.

"Those were bright days," said Neptune.

"We can remember," said the Thunderer, with a twinkling eye. "These youths have fallen upon duller times. There are no fine women now. Ixion, I drink to the health of your wife."

"With all my heart, and may we never be nearer than we are at present."

"Good ! i'faith, Apollo, your arm. Now for the ladies. La, la, la, la! la, la, la, la !"

VIII

The Thunderer entered the saloon of Juno with that bow which no God could rival; all rose, and the King of Heaven seated himself between Ceres and Latona. The melancholy Apollo stood apart, and was soon carried off by Minerva to an assembly at the house of Mnemosyne. Mercury chatted with the Graces, and Bacchus with Diana. The three Muses favoured the company with singing, and the Queen of Heaven approached Ixion.

"Does your Majesty dance ?" she haughtily inquired.

"On earth; I have few accomplishments even there, and none in Heaven."

"You have led a strange life ! I have heard of your adventures."

"A king who has lost his crown may generally gain at least experience."

"Your courage is firm."

"I have felt too much to care for much. Yesterday I was a vagabond exposed to every pitiless storm, and now I am the guest of Jove. While there is life there is hope, and he who laughs at Destiny will gain Fortune. I would go through the past again to enjoy the present, and feel that after all, I am my wife's debtor, since, through her conduct, I can gaze upon you."

"No great spectacle. If that be all, I wish you better fortune."

"I desire no greater"

"You are moderate."

"I am perhaps more unreasonable than you imagine."

"Indeed!"

Their eyes met; the dark orbs of the Thessalian did not quail before the flashing vision of the Goddess. Juno grew pale. Juno turned away.

PART II

"Others say it was only a cloud."

I

Mercury and Ganymede were each lolling on an opposite couch in the antechamber of Olympus.

"It is wonderful," said the son of Maia, yawning.

"It is incredible," rejoined the cup-bearer of Jove, stretching his legs.

"A miserable mortal!" exclaimed the God, elevating his eyebrows.

"A vile Thessalian!" said the beautiful Phrygian, shrugging his shoulders.

"Not three days back an outcast among his own wretched species !"

"And now commanding everybody in Heaven"

"He shall not command me, though," said Mercury.

"Will he not ?" replied Ganymede. " Why, what do you think ? only last night; hark ! here he comes."

The companions jumped up from their couches; a light laugh was heard. The cedar portal was flung open, and Ixion lounged in, habited in a loose morning robe, and kicking before him one of his slippers.

"Ah !" exclaimed the King of Thessaly, "the very fellows I wanted to see ! Ganymede, bring me some nectar; and Mercury, run and tell Jove that I shall not dine at home today."

The messenger and the page exchanged looks of indignant consternation.

"Well ! what are you waiting for ?" continued Ixion, looking round from the mirror in which he was arranging his locks. The messenger and the page disappeared.

"So ! this is Heaven," exclaimed the husband of Dia, flinging himself upon one of the couches; "and a very pleasant place too. These worthy Immortals required their minds to be opened, and I trust I have effectually performed the necessary operation. They wanted to keep me down with their dull old-fashioned celestial airs, but I fancy I have given them change for their talent. To make your way in Heaven you must command. These exclusives sink under the audacious invention of an aspiring mind. Jove himself is really a fine old fellow, with some notions too. I am a prime favourite, and no one is greater authority with Aegiochus on all subjects, from the character of the fair sex or the pedigree of a courser, down to the cut of a robe or the flavour of a dish. Thanks, Ganymede," continued the Thessalian, as he took the goblet from his returning attendant.

"I drink to your *bonnes fortunes*. Splendid ! This nectar makes me feel quite immortal. By-the-bye, I hear sweet sounds. Who is in the Hall of Music ?"

"The Goddesses, royal sir, practise a new air of Euterpe, the words by Apollo. 'Tis pretty, and will doubtless be very popular, for it is all about moonlight and the misery of existence."

"I warrant it."

"You have a taste for poetry yourself?" inquired Ganymede.

"Not the least," replied Ixion.

"Apollo," continued the heavenly page, "is a great genius, though Marsyas said that he never would be a poet because he was a god, and had no heart. But do you think, sir, that a poet does indeed need a heart ?"

"I really cannot say. I know my wife always said I had a bad heart and worse head; but what she meant, upon my honour I never could understand."

"Minerva will ask you to write in her album."

"Will she indeed ! I am sorry to hear it , for I can scarcely scrawl my signature. I should think that Jove himself cared little for all this nonsense."

"Jove loves an epigram. He does not esteem Apollo's works at all. Jove is of the classical school, and admires satire, provided there be no allusions to gods and kings."

"Of course; I quite agree with him. I remember we had a confounded poet at Larissa who proved my family lived before the deluge, and asked me for a pension. I refused him, and then he wrote an epigram asserting that I sprang from the veritable stones thrown by Deucalion and Pyrrha at the re-peopling of the earth, and retained all the properties of my ancestors."

"Ha, ha ! Hark ! there's a thunderbolt ! I must run to Jove."

"And I will look in on the musicians. This way, I think?"

"Up the ruby staircase, turn to your right, down the amethyst gallery. Farewell !"

122

"Good bye; a lively lad that !"

II

The King of Thessaly entered the Hall of Music with its golden walls and crystal dome. The Queen of Heaven was reclining in an easy chair, cutting out peacocks in small sheets of note paper. Minerva was making a pencil observation on a manuscript copy of the song: Apollo listened with deference to her laudatory criticisms. Another divine dame, standing by the side of Euterpe, who was seated by the harp, looked up as Ixion entered. The wild liquid glance of her soft but radiant countenance denoted the famed Goddess of Beauty

Juno just acknowledged the entrance of Ixion by a slight and haughty inclination of the head, and then resumed her employment. Minerva asked him his opinion of her amendment, of which he greatly approved. Apollo greeted him with a melancholy smile, and congratulated him on being mortal. Venus complimented him on his visit to Olympus, and expressed the pleasure that she experienced in making his acquaintance.

"What do you think of Heaven?" inquired Venus, in a soft still voice, and with a smile like summer lightning.

"I never found it so enchanting as at this moment," replied Ixion.

"A little dull? For myself, I pass my time chiefly at Cnidos: you must come and visit me there. 'Tis the most charming place in the world. 'Tis said, you know, that our onions are like other people's roses. We will take care of you, if your wife comes."

"No fear of that. She always remains at home and piques herself on her domestic virtues, which means pickling, and quarrelling with her husband."

"Ah! I see you are a droll. Very good indeed. Well, for my part, I like a watering-place existence. Cnidos, Paphos, Cythera; you will usually find me at one of these places. I like the easy distraction of a career without any visible

123

result. At these fascinating spots your gloomy race, to whom, by-the-bye, I am exceedingly partial, appear emancipated from the wearing fetters of their regular, dull, orderly, methodical, moral, political, toiling existence. I pride myself upon being the Goddess of Watering-places. You really must pay me a visit at Cnidos."

"Such an invitation requires no repetition. And Cnidos is your favourite spot ?"

"Why, it was so; but of late it has become so inundated with invalid Asiatics and valetudinarian Persians, that the simultaneous influx of the handsome heroes who swarm in from the islands to look after their daughters, scarcely compensates for the annoying presence of their yellow faces and shaking limbs. No, I think, on the whole, Paphos is my favourite."

"I have heard of its magnificent luxury."

"Oh! 'tis lovely! Quite my idea of country life. Not a single tree! When Cyprus is very hot, you run to Paphos for a sea-breeze, and are sure to meet every one whose presence is in the least desirable. All the bores remain behind, as if by instinct."

"I remember when we married, we talked of passing the honeymoon at Cythera, but Dia would have her waiting-maid and a bandbox stuffed between us in the chariot, so I got sulky after the first stage, and returned by myself."

"You were quite right. I hate bandboxes: they are always in the way. You would have liked Cythera if you had been in the least in love. High rocks and green knolls, bowery woods, winding walks, and delicious sunsets. I have not been there much of late," continued the Goddess, looking somewhat sad and serious, "since: but I will not talk sentiment to Ixion."

"Do you think, then, I am insensible?"

"Yes."

"Perhaps you are right. We mortals grow callous."

"So I have heard. How very odd!" So saying , the Goddess glided away and saluted Mars, who at that moment entered the hall. Ixion was presented to the military hero, who looked fierce and bowed stiffly. The King of Thessaly turned upon his heel. Minerva opened her album, and invited him to inscribe a stanza.

"Goddess of Wisdom," replied the King, " unless you inspire me, the virgin page must remain pure as thyself. I can scarcely sign a decree."

"Is it Ixion of Thessaly who says this; one who has seen so much, and, if I am not mistaken, has felt and thought so much? I can easily conceive why such a mind may desire to veil its movements from the common herd, but pray concede to Minerva the gratifying compliment of assuring her that she is the exception for whom this rule has been established."

"I seem to listen to the inspired music of an oracle. Give me a pen."

"Here is one, plucked from a sacred owl."

"So! I write. There! Will it do?"

Minerva read the inscription:-

I HAVE SEEN THE WORLD, AND MORE THAN THE WORLD: I HAVE STUDIED THE HEART OF MAN, AND NOW I CONSORT WITH IMMORTALS. THE FRUIT OF MY TREE OF KNOWLEDGE IS PLUCKED, AND IT IS THIS, *'ADVENTURES ARE TO THE ADVENTUROUS'* *Written in the Album of Minerva, by Ixion in Heaven.*

" 'Tis brief," said the Goddess, with a musing air, "but full of meaning. You have a daring soul and pregnant mind."

"I have dared much: what I may produce we have yet to see."

"I must to Jove," said Minerva, "to council. We shall meet again. Farewell, Ixion."

"Farewell, Glaucopis."

The King of Thessaly stood away from the remaining guests, and leant with folded arms and pensive brow against a wreathed column. Mars listened to Venus with an air of deep devotion. Euterpe played an inspiring accompaniment to their conversation. The Queen of Heaven seemed

125

engrossed in the creation of her paper peacocks.

Ixion advanced and seated himself on a couch, near Juno. His manner was divested of that reckless bearing and careless coolness by which it was in general distinguished. He was, perhaps, even a little embarrassed. His ready tongue deserted him. At length he spoke.

"Has your Majesty ever heard of the peacock of the Queen of Mesopotamia?"

"No," replied Juno, with stately reserve; and then she added with an air of indifferent curiosity, "Is it in any way remarkable?"

"Its breast is of silver, its wings of gold, its eyes of carbuncle, its claws of amethyst."

"And its tail?" eagerly inquired Juno.

"That is a secret," replied Ixion. "The tail is the most wonderful part of all."

"Oh! tell me, pray tell me!"

"I forget."

"No, no, no; it is impossible!" exclaimed the animated Juno. "Provoking mortal!" continued the Goddess. "Let me entreat you; tell me immediately."

"There is a reason which prevents me."

"What can it be? How very odd! What reason can it possibly be? Now tell me; as a particular, a personal favour, I request you, do tell me."

"What! The tail or the reason? The tail is wonderful, but the reason is much more so. I can only tell one. Now choose."

"What provoking things these human beings are! The tail is wonderful, but the reason is much more so. Well then, the reason; no, the tail. Stop, now, as a particular favour, pray tell me both. What can the tail be made of and what can the reason be? I am literally dying of curiosity."

"Your Majesty has cut out that peacock wrong," remarked Ixion. "It is more like one of Minerva's owls."

"Who care about paper peacocks, when the Queen of Mesopotamia has got such a miracle!" exclaimed Juno; and she tore the labours of the morning to pieces, and threw

126

away the fragments with vexation. "Now tell me instantly; if you have the slightest regard for me, tell me instantly. What was the tail made of?"

"And do you not wish to hear the reason?"

"That afterwards. Now! I am all ears." At this moment Ganymede entered, and whispered to the Goddess, who rose in evident vexation, and retired to the presence of Jove.

III

The King of Thessaly quitted the Hall of Music. Moody, yet not uninfluenced by a degree of wild excitement, he wandered forth into the gardens of Olympus. He came to a beautiful green retreat surrounded by enormous cedars, so vast that it seemed they must have been coeval with the creation; so fresh and brilliant, you would have deemed them wet with the dew of their first spring. The turf, softer than down, and exhaling, as you pressed it, an exquisite perfume, invited him to recline himself upon this natural couch. He threw himself upon the aromatic herbage, and leaning on his arm, fell into a deep reverie.

Hours flew away; the sunshiny glades that opened in the distance had softened into shade.

"Ixion, how do you do? " inquired a voice, wild, sweet, and thrilling as a bird. The King of Thessaly started and looked up with the distracted air of a man roused from a dream, or from complacent meditation over some strange, sweet secret. His cheek was flushed, his dark eyes flashed fire; his brow trembled, his dishevelled hair played in the fitful breeze. The King of Thessaly looked up, and beheld a most beautiful youth.

Apparently, he had attained about the age of puberty. His stature, however, was rather tall for his age, but exquisitely moulded and proportioned. Very fair, his somewhat round cheeks were tinted with a rich but delicate glow, like the rose of twilight, and lighted by dimples that twinkled like stars. His large and deep-blue eyes sparkled

127

with exultation, and an air of ill-suppressed mockery quivered round his pouting lips. His light auburn hair, braided off his white forehead, clustered in massy curls on each side of his face, and fell in sunny torrents down his neck. And from the back of the beautiful youth there fluttered forth two wings, the tremulous plumage of which seemed to have been bathed in a sunset: so various, so radiant, and so novel were its shifting and wondrous tints; purple, and crimson, and gold; streaks of azure, dashes of orange and glossy black; now a single feather, whiter than light, and sparkling like the frost, stars of emerald and carbuncle, and then the prismatic blaze of an enormous brilliant! A quiver hung at the side of the beautiful youth, and he leant upon a bow.

"Oh! god, for god thou must be!" at length exclaimed Ixion. " Do I behold the bright divinity of Love?"

"I am indeed Cupid," replied the youth; "and am curious to know what Ixion is thinking about."

"Thought is often bolder than speech."

"Oracular, though a mortal! You need not be afraid to trust me. My aid I am sure you must need. Who ever was found in a reverie on the green turf, under the shade of spreading trees, without requiring the assistance of Cupid? Come! be frank, who is the heroine? Some love-sick nymph deserted on the far earth; or worse, some treacherous mistress, whose frailty is more easily forgotten than her charms? 'Tis a miserable situation, no doubt. It cannot be your wife?"

"Assuredly not," replied Ixion, with energy.

"Another man's?"

"No."

"What! an obdurate maiden?"

Ixion shook his head.

"It must be a widow, then," continued Cupid. "Who ever heard before of such a piece of work about a widow!"

"Have pity upon me, dread Cupid!" exclaimed the King of Thessaly, rising suddenly from the ground, and falling on his knee before the God. "Thou art the universal friend of

128

man, and all nations alike throw their incense on thy altars. Thy divine discrimination has not deceived thee. I *am* in love; desperately, madly, fatally enamoured. The object of my passion is neither my own wife nor another man's. In spite of all they have said and sworn, I am a moral member of society. She is neither a maid nor a widow. She is - "

"What? what?" exclaimed the impatient deity.

"A Goddess!" replied the King.

"Wheugh!" whistled Cupid. "What! has my mischievous mother been indulging you with an innocent flirtation?"

"Yes; but it produced no effect upon me."

"You have a stout heart, then. Perhaps you have been reading poetry with Minerva, and are caught in one of her Platonic man-traps."

"She set one, but I broke away."

"You have a stout leg, then. But where are you, where are you? Is it Hebe? It can hardly be Diana, she is so cold. Is it a Muse, or is it one of the Graces?"

Ixion again shook his head.

"Come, my dear fellow," said Cupid, quite in a confidential tone, "you have told enough to make further reserve mere affectation. Ease you heart at once, and if I can assist you, depend upon my exertions."

"Beneficent God!" exclaimed Ixion, "if I ever return to Larissa, the brightest temple in Greece shall hail thee for its inspiring deity. I address thee with all the confiding frankness of a devoted votary. Know, then, the heroine of my reverie was no less a personage than the Queen of Heaven herself!"

"Juno! by all that is sacred!" shouted Cupid.

"I am here," responded a voice of majestic melody. The stately form of the Queen of Heaven advanced from a neighbouring bower. Ixion stood with his eyes fixed upon the ground, with a throbbing heart and burning cheeks. Juno stood motionless, pale and astounded. The God of Love burst into excessive laughter.

"A pretty pair," he exclaimed, fluttering between both,

and laughing in their faces. "Truly a pretty pair. Well! I see I am in your way. Good bye!" And so saying , the God pulled a couple of arrows from his quiver, and with the rapidity of lightning shot one in the respective breasts of the Queen of Heaven and the King of Thessaly.

IV

The amethystine twilight of Olympus died away. The stars blazed with tints of every hue. Ixion and Juno returned to the palace. She leant upon his arm; her eyes were fixed upon the ground; they were in sight of the gorgeous pile, and yet she had not spoken. Ixion, too, was silent, and gazed with abstraction upon the glowing sky.

Suddenly, when within a hundred yards of the portal, Juno stopped, and looking up into the face of Ixion with an irresistible smile, she said, "I am sure you cannot now refuse to tell me what the Queen of Mesopotamia's peacock's tail was made of!"

"It is impossible now," said Ixion. "Know, then beautiful Goddess, that the tail of the Queen of Mesopotamia's peacock's tail was made of some plumage she had stolen from the wings of Cupid"

"And what was the reason that prevented you from telling me before?"

"Because, beautiful Juno, I am the most discreet of men, and respect the secret of a lady, however trifling."

"I am glad to hear that," replied Juno, and they re-entered the palace.

V

Mercury met Juno and Ixion in the gallery leading to the grand banqueting hall.

"I was looking for you," said the God, shaking his head. "Jove is in a sublime rage. Dinner has been ready this hour."

The King of Thessaly and the Queen of Heaven exchanged a glance and entered the saloon. Jove looked up with a brow of thunder, but did not condescend to send forth a single flash of anger. Jove looked up and Jove looked down. All Olympus trembled as the father of Gods and men resumed his soup. The rest of the guests seemed nervous and reserved, except Cupid, who said immediately to Juno, "Your majesty has been detained? "

"I fell asleep in a bower reading Apollo's last poem," replied Juno. "I am lucky, however, in finding a companion in my negligence. Ixion, where have you been?"

"Take a glass of nectar, Juno," said Cupid, with eyes twinkling with mischief; "and perhaps Ixion will join us."

This was the most solemn banquet ever celebrated in Olympus. Every one seemed out of humour or out of spirits. Jupiter spoke only in monosyllables of suppressed rage, that sounded like distant thunder.

Apollo whispered to Minerva. Mercury never opened his lips, but occasionally exchanged significant glances with Ganymede. Mars compensated, by his attentions to Venus, for his want of conversation. Cupid employed himself in asking disagreeable questions. At length the Goddesses retired. Mercury exerted himself to amuse Jove, but the Thunderer scarcely deigned to smile at his best stories. Mars picked his teeth, Apollo played with his rings, Ixion was buried in a profound reverie.

VI

It was a great relief to all when Ganymede summoned them to the presence of their late companions.

"I have written a comment upon your inscription," said Minerva to Ixion, " and am anxious for your opinion of it."

"I am a wretched critic," said the King, breaking away from her. Juno smiled upon him in the distance.

"Ixion," said Venus, as he passed by, "come and talk to me."

The bold Thessalian blushed, he stammered out an unmeaning excuse, he quitted the astonished but good-natured Goddess, and seated himself by Juno, and as he

131

seated himself his moody brow seemed suddenly illumined with brilliant light.

"Is it so?" said Venus

"Hem! " said Minerva

"Ha, ha! " said Cupid.

Jupiter played piquette with Mercury.

"Everything goes wrong to-day," said the King of Heaven; "cards wretched, and kept waiting for dinner, and by - a mortal!"

"Your Majesty must not be surprised," said the good-natured Mercury, with whom Ixion was no favourite. "Your Majesty must not be very much surprised at the conduct of this creature. Considering what he is, and where he is, I am only astonished that his head is not more turned than it appears to be. A man, a thing made of mud, and in Heaven! Only think, sire! Is it not enough to inflame the brain of any child of clay? To be sure, keeping your Majesty from dinner is little short of celestial high treason. I hardly expected that, indeed. To order me about, to treat Ganymede as his own lackey, and, in short, to command the whole household; all this might be expected from such a person in such a situation, but I confess I did think he had some little respect left for your Majesty."

"And he does order you about, eh?" inquired Jove. "I have the spades."

"Oh! 'tis quite ludicrous," responded the son of Maia. "Your Majesty would not expect from me the offices that this upstart daily requires."

"Eternal destiny! is't possible? That is my trick. And Ganymede, too?"

"Oh! quite shocking, I assure you, sire," said the beautiful cupbearer, leaning over the chair of Jove with all the easy insolence of a privileged favourite. "Really sire, if Ixion is to go on in the way he does, either he or I must quit."

"Is it possible?" exclaimed Jupiter. "But I can believe anything of a man who keeps me waiting for dinner. Two and three make five."

"It is Juno that encourages him so," said Ganymede.

"Does she encourage him?" inquired Jove.

"Everybody notices it," protested Ganymede.

"It is indeed a little noticed," observed Mercury.

"What business has such a fellow to speak to Juno?" exclaimed Jove. "A mere mortal, a mere miserable mortal! You have the point. How I have been deceived in this fellow! Who ever could have supposed that, after all my generosity to him, he would ever have kept me waiting for dinner?"

"He was walking with Juno," said Ganymede. "It was all a sham about their having met by accident. Cupid saw them."

"Ha!" said Jupiter, turning pale; "you don't say so! Repiqued, as I am a God. That is mine. Where is the Queen?"

"Talking to Ixion, sire," said Mercury. "Oh, I beg your pardon, sire; I did not know you meant the queen of diamonds."

"Never mind. I am repiqued, and I have been kept waiting for dinner. Accursed be this day! Is Ixion really talking to Juno? We will not endure this."

VII

"Where is Juno?" demanded Jupiter.

"I am sure I cannot say," said Venus, with a smile.

"I am sure I do not know," said Minerva, with a sneer.

"Where is Ixion?" said Cupid, laughing outright.

"Mercury, Ganymede, find the Queen of Heaven instantly," thundered the father of Gods and men.

The celestial messenger and the heavenly page flew away out of different doors. There was a terrible, an immortal silence. Sublime rage lowered on the brow of Jove like a storm upon the mountain-top. Minerva seated herself at the card-table and played at Patience. Venus and Cupid tittered in the background. Shortly returned the envoys, Mercury looking solemn, Ganymede malignant.

"Well?" inquired Jove; and all Olympus trembled at the monosyllable.

133

Mercury shook his head.

"Her Majesty has been walking on the terrace with the King of Thessaly," replied Ganymede.

"Where is she now, sir?" demanded Jupiter.

Mercury shrugged his shoulders.

"Her Majesty is resting herself in the pavilion of Cupid, with the King of Thessaly," replied Ganymede.

"Confusion!" exclaimed the father of Gods and men; and he rose and seized a candle from the table, scattering the cards in all directions. Every one present, Minerva and Venus, and Mars and Apollo, and Mercury and Ganymede, and the Muses, and the Graces, and all the winged Genii - each seized a candle; rifling the chandeliers, each followed Jove.

"This way," said Mercury.

"This way," said Ganymede.

"This way, this way!" echoed the celestial crowd.

"Mischief!" cried Cupid; "I must save my victims."

They were all upon the terrace. The father of Gods and men, though both in a passion and a hurry, moved with dignity. It was, as customary in Heaven, a clear and starry night; but this eve Diana was indisposed, or otherwise engaged, and there was no moonlight. They were in sight of the pavilion.

"What are you?" inquired Cupid of one of the Genii, who accidentally extinguished his candle.

"I am a Cloud," answered the winged Genius.

"A Cloud! Just the thing. Now do me a shrewd turn, and Cupid is ever your debtor. Fly, fly, pretty Cloud, and encompass yon pavilion with your form. Away! ask no questions; swift as my word."

"I declare there is a fog," said Venus.

"An evening mist in Heaven! " said Minerva.

"Where is Nox?" said Jove. "Everything goes wrong. Who ever heard of a mist in Heaven?"

"My candle is out," said Apollo.

"And mine, too," said Mars.

"And mine, and mine, and mine," said Mercury and

134

Ganymede, and the Muses and the Graces.

"All the candles are out!" said Cupid; " a regular fog. I cannot even see the pavilion: it must be hereabouts, though, said the God to himself. "So, so; I should be at home in my own pavilion, and am tolerably accustomed to stealing about in the dark. There is a step; and here, surely, is the lock. The door opens, but the Cloud enters before me. Juno, Juno," whispered the God of Love, " we are all here. Be contented to escape, like many other innocent dames, with your reputation only under a cloud: it will soon disperse; and lo! the heaven is clearing."

"It must have been the heat of our flambeaux" said Venus; "for see, the mist is vanished; here is the pavilion."

Ganymede ran forward, and dashed open the door. Ixion was alone.

"Seize him!" said Jove.

"Juno is not here," said Mercury, with an air of blended congratulation and disappointment.

"Never mind," said Jove; "seize him! He kept me waiting for dinner."

"Is this your hospitality, Aegiochus?" exclaimed Ixion, in a tone of bullying innocence. "I shall defend myself."

"Seize him, seize him!" exclaimed Jupiter, "What! do you all falter? Are you afraid of a mortal?"

"And a Thessalian?" added Ganymede.
No one advanced.

"Send for Hercules," said Jove.

"I will fetch him in an instant," said Ganymede.

"I protest," said the King of Thessaly, "against this violation of the most sacred rights."

"The marriage tie?" said Mercury.

"The dinner-hour?" said Jove.

"It is no use talking sentiment to Ixion," said Venus; "all mortals are callous."

"Adventures are to the adventurous," said Minerva.

"Here is Hercules! here is Hercules!"

"Seize him!" said Jove; "seize that man."
In vain the mortal struggled with the irresistible demi-god.

135

"Shall I fetch your thunderbolt, Jove?" inquired Ganymede.

"Anything short of eternal punishment is unworthy of a God," answered Jupiter, with great dignity. "Apollo, bring me a wheel of your chariot."

"What shall I do tomorrow morning?" inquired the God of Light.

"Order an eclipse," replied Jove. "Bind the insolent wretch to the wheel; hurl him to Hades; its motion shall be perpetual."

"What am I to bind him with?" inquired Hercules.

"The girdle of Venus," replied the Thunderer.

"What is all this?" inquired Juno, advancing, pale and agitated.

"Come along; you shall see," answered Jupiter. "Follow me, follow me."

They all followed the leader, all the Gods, all the Genii; in the midst, the brawny husband of Hebe bearing Ixion aloft, bound to the fatal wheel. They reached the terrace; they descended the sparkling steps of lapis-lazuli. Hercules held his burthen on high, ready, at a nod, to plunge the hapless but presumptuous mortal through space into Hades. The heavenly group surrounded him, and peeped over the starry abyss. It was a fine moral, and demonstrated the usual infelicity that attends unequal connections.

"Celestial despot!" said Ixion.

In a moment all sounds were hushed, as they listened to the last words of the unrivalled victim. Juno, in despair, leant upon the respective arms of Venus and Minerva.

"Celestial despot!" said Ixion, "I defy the immortal ingenuity of thy cruelty. My memory must be as eternal as thy torture: that will support me."

136

CHARLES DICKENS (1812-1870) was the most influential champion of fantastic fiction in nineteenth century Britain, although his support was compromised by the opinion that fantasy should be allowed free rein only in its proper place. As an editor, of *Household Words* and *All the Year Round* , Dickens used a good deal of fantastic fiction, but saved most of it for the special Christmas numbers. His own fantasies are either anecdotal tales or novellas issued as "Christmas Books". Several comic fantasies are incorporated into *The Posthumous Papers of the Pickwick Club* (1836-37), including "The Story of the Goblins Who Stole a Sexton", which imports the moral message later to be more elaborately developed in *A Christmas Carol* (1843).

Dickens was ambitious for his Christmas Book fantasies, but they fell victim to an irreconcilable conflict of format and ambition. *The Chimes* (1844) was intended to "strike a great blow for the poor" by spelling out the requirements for psychological survival in the face of economic misfortune, but it made its middle-class readers far too uneasy, and they much preferred the cosy sentimentality of *The Cricket on The Hearth* (1845). *The Haunted Man and The Ghost's Bargain* (1848) plumbs murkier moral depths in a cautionary tale of a catastrophic infection which obliterates pain by spreading emotional and moral anaesthesia, but it too proved too discomfiting for an audience expecting light entertainment.

A Christmas Carol still reminds us, year in and year out, of the power which fantasy has to affect reality. Our contemporary ideas regarding the proper way to celebrate Christmas are mostly a product of that book, and the way in which its moral message has been converted by degrees into a species of crass commercial cant far more hypocritical than anything Dickens could ever have imagined provides a strikingly ironic example of a message commonly to be found in fantasies: the consequences of fantastic interventions *never* live up to the optimistic expectations of those who invoke them.

THE STORY OF
THE GOBLINS WHO
STOLE A SEXTON

by Charles Dickens

In an old abbey town, down in this part of the country, a long, long, while ago - so long, that the story must be a true one, because our great-grandfathers implicitly believed it - there officiated as sexton and grave-digger in the churchyard, one Gabriel Grub. It by no means follows that because a man is a sexton, and constantly surrounded by the emblems of mortality, therefore he should be a morose and melancholy man; your undertakers are the merriest fellows in the world; and I once had the honour of being on intimate terms with a mute, who in private life, and off duty, was as comical and jocose a little fellow as ever chirped out a devil-may-care song, without a hitch in his memory, or drained off the contents of a good stiff glass without stopping for breath. But, notwithstanding these precedents to the contrary, Gabriel Grub was an ill-conditioned, cross-grained, surly fellow - a morose and lonely man, who consorted with nobody but himself, and an old wicker bottle which fitted into his large deep waistcoat pocket - and who eyed each merry face, as it passed him by, with such a deep scowl of malice and ill-humour, as it was difficult to meet, without feeling something the worse for.

A little before twilight, one Christmas Eve, Gabriel shouldered his spade, lighted his lantern, and betook himself towards the old churchyard; for he had got a grave to finish by next morning, and, feeling very low, he thought it might raise his spirits, perhaps, if he went on with his work at once. As he went his way, up the ancient street, he saw the cheerful light of the blazing fires gleam through the old casements, and heard the loud laughter and the cheerful shouts of those who were assembled around them; he marked the bustling preparations for next day's cheer, and smelt the numerous savoury odours consequent thereupon, as they steamed up from the kitchen windows in clouds. All this was gall and wormwood to the heart of Gabriel Grub; and when groups of children bounded out of the houses, tripped across the road and were met, before they could knock at the opposite door, by half a dozen curly-headed little rascals who crowded round them as they flocked upstairs to spend the evening in their Christmas games, Gabriel smiled grimly, and clutched the handle of his spade with a firmer grasp, as he thought of measles, scarlet-fever, thrush, whooping-cough, and a good many other sources of consolation besides.

In this happy frame of mind, Gabriel strode along: returning a short, sullen growl to the good-humoured greetings of such of his neighbours as now and then passed him: until he turned into the dark lane which led to the churchyard. Now, Gabriel had been looking forward to reaching the dark lane, because it was, generally speaking, a nice, gloomy, mournful place, into which the townspeople did not much care to go, except in broad daylight, and when the sun was shining; consequently, he was not a little indignant to hear a young urchin roaring out some jolly song about a merry Christmas, in this very sanctuary, which had been called Coffin Lane ever since the days of the old abbey, and the time of the shaven headed monks. As Gabriel walked on, and the voice drew nearer, he found it proceeded from a small boy, who was hurrying along, to join one of the little parties in the old street, and who, partly to keep himself company, and partly to prepare himself for the occasion, was shouting out the song at the highest pitch of his lungs. So Gabriel waited until the boy came up, and then dodged him into a corner, and rapped him over the head with his lantern five or six times, to teach him to modulate his voice. And as the boy hurried away with his hand to his head, singing quite a different sort of tune, Gabriel Grub chuckled very heartily to himself, and entered the churchyard, locking the gate behind him.

He took off his coat, put down his lantern, and getting into the unfinished grave, worked at it for an hour or so,

139

with right good will. But the earth was hardened with the frost, and it was no very easy matter to break it up, and shovel it out; and although there was a moon, it was a very young one, and shed little light upon the grave, which was in the shadow of the church. At any other time, these obstacles would have made Gabriel Grub very moody and miserable, but he was so well pleased with having stopped the small boy's singing, that he took little heed of the scanty progress he had made, and looked down into the grave, when he had finished work for the night, with grim satisfaction: murmuring as he gathered up his things:

"Brave lodgings for one, brave lodgings for one,
A few feet of cold earth, when life is done;
A stone at the head, a stone at the feet
A rich, juicy meal for the worms to eat;
Rank grass over head, and damp clay around,
Brave lodgings for one, these, in holy ground!"

"Ho! Ho!" laughed Gabriel Grub, as he sat himself down on a flat tombstone which was a favourite resting-place of his; and drew forth his wicker bottle. "A coffin at Christmas! A Christmas Box. Ho! ho! ho!"

"Ho! ho! ho!" repeated a voice which sounded close behind him.

Gabriel paused, in some alarm, in the act of raising the wicker bottle to his lips: and looked round. The bottom of the oldest grave about him, was not more still and quiet, than the churchyard in the pale moonlight. The cold hoar frost glistened on the tombstones, and sparkled like rows of gems, among the stone carvings of the old church. The snow lay hard and crisp upon the ground; and spread over the thickly-strewn mounds of earth so white and smooth a cover that it seemed as if corpses lay there, hidden only by their winding sheets. Not the faintest rustle broke the profound tranquillity of the solemn scene. Sound itself appeared to be frozen up, all was so cold and still.

"It was the echoes," said Gabriel Grub, raising the

bottle to his lips again.

"It was *not*," said a deep voice.

Gabriel started up, and stood rooted to the spot with astonishment and terror; for his eyes rested on a form that made his blood run cold.

Seated on an upright tombstone, close to him, was a strange unearthly figure, whom Gabriel felt at once, was no being of this world. His long fantastic legs which might have reached the ground, were cocked up, and crossed after a quaint, fantastic fashion; his sinewy arms were bare; and his hands rested on his knees. On his short round body, he wore a close covering, ornamented with small slashes; a short cloak dangled at his back; the collar was cut into curious peaks, which served the goblin in lieu of ruff or neckerchief; and his shoes curled at his toes into long points. On his head, he wore a broad-brimmed sugar-loaf hat, garnished with a single feather. The hat was covered with the white frost; and the goblin looked as if he had sat on the same tombstone very comfortably, for two or three hundred years. He was sitting perfectly still; his tongue was put out, as if in derision; and he was grinning at Gabriel Grub with such a grin as only a goblin could call up.

"It was *not* the echoes," said the goblin

Gabriel Grub was paralysed, and could make no reply.

"What do you do here on Christmas Eve?" said the goblin sternly.

"I came to dig a grave, sir," stammered Gabriel Grub.

"What man wanders among graves and churchyards on such a night as this?" cried the goblin

"Gabriel Grub! Gabriel Grub!" screamed a wild chorus of voices that seemed to fill the churchyard. Gabriel looked fearfully round - nothing was to be seen.

"What have you got in that bottle?" said the goblin.

"Hollands, sir," replied the sexton, trembling more than ever; for he had bought it of the smugglers, and he thought that perhaps his questioner might be in the excise department of the goblins.

"Who drinks Hollands alone, and in a churchyard, on

141

such a night as this?" said the goblin.

"Gabriel Grub! Gabriel Grub!" exclaimed the wild voices again.

The goblin leered maliciously at the terrified sexton, and then raising his voice, exclaimed: "And who, then, is our fair and lawful prize?"

To this enquiry the invisible chorus replied, in a strain that sounded like the voices of many choristers singing to the mighty swell of the old church organ - a strain that seemed borne to the sexton's ears upon a wild wind, and to die away as it passed onward; but the burden of the reply was still the same, "Gabriel Grub! Gabriel Grub!"

The goblin grinned a broader grin than before, as he said, "Well Gabriel, what do you say to this?"

The sexton gasped for breath.

"What do you think of this, Gabriel?" said the goblin, kicking up his feet in the air on either side of the tombstone, and looking at the turned-up points with as much complacency as if he had been contemplating the most fashionable pair of Wellingtons in all Bond Street.

"It's - it's - very curious sir," replied the sexton, half dead with fright; "very curious, and very pretty, but I think I'll go back and finish my work, sir, if you please."

"Work!" said the goblin, "what work?"

"The grave, sir; making the grave," stammered the sexton.

"Oh, the grave, eh?" said the goblin. "Who makes graves at a time when all other men are merry, and takes a pleasure in it?"

Again the mysterious voices replied, "Gabriel Grub! Gabriel Grub!"

"I'm afraid my friends want you, Gabriel," said the goblin, thrusting his tongue further into his cheek than ever - and a most astonishing tongue it was -" I'm afraid my friends want you, Gabriel," said the goblin.

"Under favour, sir," replied the horror-stricken sexton, "I don't think they can, sir; they don't know me, sir; I don't think the gentlemen have ever seen me, sir."

"Oh yes they have," replied the goblin; "we know the man with the sulky face and grim scowl, that came down the street tonight, throwing his evil looks at the children, and grasping his burying spade the tighter. We know the man who struck the boy in the envious malice of his heart, because the boy could be merry, and he could not. We know him, we know him."

Here the goblin gave a loud shrill laugh, which the echoes returned twenty-fold: and throwing his legs up in the air, stood upon his head, or rather upon the very point of his sugar-loaf hat, on the narrow edge of the tombstone: whence he threw a somerset with extraordinary agility, right to the sexton's feet, at which he planted himself in the attitude in which tailors generally sit upon the shop-board.

"I - I - am afraid I must leave you, sir," said the sexton, making an effort to move.

"Leave us!" said the goblin, "Gabriel Grub going to leave us. Ho! ho! ho!"

As the goblin laughed, the sexton observed, for one instant, a brilliant illumination within the windows of the church, as if the whole building were lighted up; it disappeared, the organ pealed forth a lively air, and whole troops of goblins, the very counterpart of the first one, poured into the churchyard, and began playing at leap-frog with the tombstones: never stopping for an instant to take breath, but 'overing' the highest among them, one after the other, with the most marvellous dexterity. The first goblin was a most astonishing leaper, and none of the others could come near him; even in the extremity of his terror the sexton could not help observing, that while his friends were content to leap over the common-sized gravestones, the first one took the family vaults, iron railings and all, with as much ease as if they had been so many street-posts.

At last the game reached to a most exciting pitch; the organ played quicker and quicker; and the goblins leaped faster and faster: coiling themselves up, rolling head over heels upon the ground, and bounding over the tombstones like footballs. The sexton's brain whirled round with the rapidity of the motion he beheld, and his legs reeled beneath him, as the spirits flew before his eyes: when the goblin king, suddenly darting towards him, laid his hand upon his collar, and sank with him through the earth.

When Gabriel Grub had had time to fetch his breath, which the rapidity of his descent had for the moment taken away, he found himself in what appeared to be a large cavern, surrounded on all sides by crowds of goblins, ugly and grim; in the centre of the room, on an elevated seat, was stationed his friend of the churchyard; and close beside him stood Gabriel Grub himself, without power of motion.

"Cold tonight," said the king of the goblins, "very cold. A glass of something warm, here!"

At this command, half a dozen officious goblins, with a perpetual smile upon their faces, whom Gabriel Grub imagined to be courtiers, on that account, hastily disappeared, and presently returned with a goblet of liquid fire, which they presented to the king.

"Ah!" cried the goblin, whose cheeks and throat were transparent, as he tossed down the flame, "This warms one, indeed! Bring a bumper of the same, for Mr Grub."

It was in vain for the unfortunate sexton to protest that he was not in the habit of taking anything warm at night; one of the goblins held him while another poured the blazing liquid down his throat; the whole assembly screeched with laughter as he coughed and choked, and wiped away the tears which gushed plentifully from his eyes, after swallowing the burning draught.

"And now," said the king, fantastically poking the taper corner of his sugar-loaf hat into the sexton's eyes, and thereby occasioning him the most exquisite pain: "And now, show the man of misery and gloom, a few of the pictures from our own great storehouse!"

As the goblin said this, a thick cloud which obscured the remoter end of the cavern, rolled gradually away, and disclosed, apparently at a great distance, a small and scantily furnished, but neat and clean apartment. A crowd of little children were gathered round a bright fire, clinging to their mother's gown, and gambolling around her chair. The mother occasionally rose, and drew aside the window-curtain, as if to look for some expected object: a frugal meal was placed near the fire. A knock was heard at the door: the mother opened it, and the children crowded round her, and clapped their hands for joy, as their father entered. He was wet and weary, and shook the snow from his garments, as the children crowded round him, and seizing his cloak, hat, stick and gloves, with busy zeal, ran with them from the room. Then, as he sat down to his meal before the fire, the children climbed about his knee, and the mother sat by his side, and all seemed happiness and comfort.

But a change came upon the view, almost imperceptibly. The scene was altered to a small bedroom, where the fairest and youngest child lay dying; the roses had fled from his cheek, and the light from his eye; and even as the sexton looked upon him with an interest he had never felt or known before, he died. His young brothers and sisters crowded round his little bed, and seized his tiny hand, so cold and heavy; but they shrunk back from its touch, and looked with awe on his infant face; for calm and tranquil as it was, and sleeping in rest and peace as the beautiful child seemed to be, they saw that he was dead, and they knew that he was an Angel looking down upon, and blessing them, from a bright and happy Heaven.

Again the light cloud passed across the picture, and again the subject changed. The father and mother were old and helpless now, and the number of those about them was diminished more than half; but content and cheerfulness sat on every face, and beamed in every eye, as they crowded round the fireside, and told and listened to old stories of earlier and bygone days. Slowly and peacefully, the father sank into the grave, and soon after, the sharer of all his cares and troubles followed him to a place of rest. The few, who yet survived them, knelt by their tomb, and watered the green turf which covered it, with their tears; then rose, and turned away: sadly and mournfully, but not with bitter cries, or despairing lamentations, for they knew that they should one day meet again; and once more they mixed with the busy world, and their content and cheerfulness was restored. The cloud settled upon the picture and concealed it from the sexton's view.

"What do you think of *that*?" said the goblin, turning his large face towards Gabriel Grub.

Gabriel murmured out something about its being very pretty, and looked somewhat ashamed, as the goblin bent his fiery eyes upon him.

"*You* a miserable man! " said the goblin, in a tone of excessive contempt. "You!" He appeared disposed to add more, but indignation choked his utterance, so he lifted up one of his very pliable legs, and flourishing it above his head a little, to insure his aim, administered a good sound kick to Gabriel Grub; immediately after which, all the goblins in waiting, crowded round the wretched sexton, and kicked him without mercy: according to the established and invariable custom of courtiers upon the earth, who kick whom royalty kicks, and hug whom royalty hugs.

"Show him some more!" said the king of the goblins.

At these words, the cloud was dispelled, and a rich and beautiful landscape was disclosed to view - there is just such another, to this day, within half a mile of the old abbey town. The sun shone from out the clear blue sky, the water sparkled beneath his rays, and the trees looked greener, and the flowers more gay, beneath his cheering influence. The water rippled on, with a pleasant sound; the trees rustled in the light wind that murmured among their leaves; the birds sang upon the boughs; and the lark carolled on high her welcome to the morning. Yes, it was morning; the bright, balmy morning of summer; the minutest leaf, the smallest blade of grass, was instinct with life. The ant crept forth to her daily toil, the butterfly fluttered and basked in the warm rays of the sun; myriads of insects spread their transparent wings, and revelled in their brief but happy existence. Man walked forth, elated with the scene; and all was brightness and splendour.

"*You* a miserable man!" said the king of the goblins, in a more contemptuous tone than before. And again the king of the goblins gave his leg a flourish; again it descended on the shoulders of the sexton; and again the attendant goblins imitated the example of their chief.

Many a time the cloud went and came, and many a lesson it taught to Gabriel Grub, who, although his shoulders smarted with pain from the frequent applications of the goblins' feet, looked on with an interest that nothing could diminish. He saw that men who worked hard, and earned their scanty bread with lives of labour, were cheerful and happy; and that to the most ignorant, the sweet face of nature was a never-failing source of cheerfulness and joy. He saw those who have been delicately nurtured, and tenderly brought up, cheerful under privations, and superior to suffering that would have crushed many of a rougher grain, because they bore within their own bosoms the materials of happiness, contentment, and peace. He saw that women, the tenderest and most fragile of all God's creatures, were the oftenest superior to sorrow, adversity, and distress; and he saw that it was because they bore, in their own hearts, an inexhaustible well-spring of affection and devotion. Above all, he saw that men like himself, who snarled at the mirth and cheerfulness of others, were the foulest weeds on the fair surface of the earth; and setting all the good of the world against the evil, he came to the conclusion that it was a very decent and respectable sort of world after all. No sooner had he formed it, than the cloud which closed over the last picture, seemed to settle on his senses, and lull him to repose. One by one, the goblins faded from his sight; and as the last one disappeared, he sunk to sleep.

The day had broken when Gabriel Grub awoke, and found himself lying, at full length on the flat gravestone in the churchyard, with the wicker bottle lying empty by his side, and his coat, spade, and lantern, all well whitened by the last night's frost, scattered on the ground. The stone on which he had first seen the goblin seated, stood bolt upright before him, and the grave at which he had worked, the night before, was not far off. At first, he began to doubt the reality of his adventures, but the acute pain in his shoulders when he attempted to rise, assured him that the kicking of the goblins was certainly not ideal. He was staggered again, by observing no traces of footsteps in the snow on which the goblins had played at leap-frog with the gravestones, but he speedily accounted for this circumstance when he remembered that, being spirits, they would leave no visible impression behind them. So, Gabriel Grub got on his feet as well as he could, for the pain in his back; and brushing the frost off his coat, put it on, and turned his face towards the town.

But he was an altered man, and he could not bear the thought of returning to a place where his repentance would be scoffed at, and his reformation disbelieved. He hesitated for a few moments; and then turned away to wander where he might, and seek his bread elsewhere.

The lantern, the spade, and the wicker bottle, were found, that day, in the churchyard. There were a great many speculations about the sexton's fate, at first, but it was speedily determined that he had been carried away by the goblins; and there were not wanting some very credible witnesses who had distinctly seen him whisked through the air on the back of a chestnut horse blind of one eye, with the hind-quarters of a lion, and the tail of a bear. At length all this was devoutly believed; and the new sexton used to exhibit to the curious, for a trifling emolument, a good-sized piece of the church weathercock which had been accidentally picked up by himself in the churchyard, a year or two afterwards.

Unfortunately, these stories were somewhat disturbed by the unlooked-for re-appearance of Gabriel Grub himself, some ten years afterwards, a ragged, contented, rheumatic old man. He told his story to the clergyman, and also to the mayor; and in course of time it began to be received, as a matter of history, in which form it has continued down to this very day. The believers in the weathercock tale, having misplaced their confidence once, were not easily prevailed upon to part with it again, so they looked as wise as they could, shrugged their shoulders, touched their foreheads, and murmured something about Gabriel Grub having drunk all the Hollands, and then fallen asleep on the flat tombstone; and they affected to explain what he supposed he had witnessed in the goblin's cavern, by saying that he had seen the world, and grown wiser. But this opinion, which was by no means a popular one at any time, gradually died off; and be the matter how it may, as Gabriel Grub was afflicted with rheumatism to the end of his days, this story has at least one moral, if it teach no better one - and that is, that if a man turn sulky and drink by himself at Christmas time, he may make up his mind to be not a bit the better for it: let the spirits be never so good, or let them be even as many degrees beyond proof, as those which Gabriel Grub saw in the goblin's cavern.

JOHN STERLING (1806-1844) wrote a notable series of pieces for *Blackwood's* entitled "Legendary Lore", which culminated in the serial novel "The Onyx Ring" (1838-39); this was revised by Sterling with a view to book publication but he died before making such an arrangement and the revised version eventually appeared in his posthumously assembled *Essays and Tales* (1848). Several earlier fantasy stories appeared in the *Atheneum* while he was its editor and co-proprietor in 1828-29, and a few more are strewn about the text of his novel *Arthur Coningsby* (1833).

Sterling would surely have become one of the leading writers of his day had he not died so young, and he might well have become the most important nineteenth century fantasy writer; his prose fantasies are more various and more adventurous than any other contemporary work. They include "The Last of the Giants" (1828), whose title is self-explanatory; "Zamor" (1828), about a cautionary vision experienced by Alexander the Great; "Cydon" (1829), about a Greek athlete persuaded by a spirit to embark on a quest to find the cave of Prometheus; "The Substitute for Apollo" (1833), a neat classical allegory; and "The Palace of Morgana" (1837), a uniquely delicate prose poem. "A Chronicle of England" (1840) was his last story.

Sterling is almost forgotten today, despite the fact that the biographical sketch by Julius Hare which introduced *Essays and Tales* so annoyed Sterling's friend Thomas Carlyle that Carlyle was moved to write a book-length biography by way of correction. It is a great pity that "The Onyx Ring", an intense and deeply personal moral fantasy in which an unhappy young man is enabled by the eponymous object temporarily to assume the identities of several of his seemingly-more-fortunate friends (including a thinly-disguised version of Carlyle), was never published in volume form.

A CHRONICLE OF ENGLAND

by John Sterling

Hark! above the Sea of Things
How the uncouth mermaid sings:
Wisdom's Pearl doth often dwell
Closed in Fancy's rainbow shell.

"Sister," said the little one to her companion, "dost thou remember aught of this fair bay, these soft white sands, and yonder woody rocks?"

"Nay," replied the other, who was somewhat taller, and with a fuller yet sweet voice, "I knew not that I had ever been here before. And yet it seems not altogether new, but like a vision seen in dreams. The sea ripples on the sand with a sound which I feel as friendly and not unknown. Those purple shapes that rise out of the distant blue, and float past over the surface like the shadows of clouds, do not fill me with the terror which haunts me when I look on vast and strange appearances."

"To me," said the little one, "they look only somewhat more distinct than the marks which I have so often watched upon the sea."

"Oh! far brighter are they in colour, far more peculiar and more various in their forms. My heart beats while I look at them. There are ships and horses, living figures, bearded, crowned, armed, and some bear banners and some books, and softer shapes, waving and glistening with plumes, veils, and garlands. Ah! now 'tis gone."

"Rightly art thou called the Daughter of the Sea, and art indeed our own Sea-Child. Here in this bay did I and my sisters, in this land of Faëry, first find our nursling of another race."

"Was this then my first name among you, beloved friends? The bay is so beautiful, that, even in your land of Faëry, I have seen no spot where it were better to open one's

151

eyes upon the light."

"Yes, here did our Sea-Child first meet our gaze. I and a troop of my sisters were singing on the shore our ancient Song of Pearls, and watching the sun, which, while we sang, and while it went down, changed the sands its beams fell on into gold, and the foam that rippled to the shore into silver. We had often watched it before; and we knew that, if without ceasing our song we gathered the gold sands and silver foam while the sun was on them, into the shells that lay about, they would continue in their changed state. Left till sunset, they returned to what they were, and we had only the sands and foam. We thought the sport so pleasant, that we had carried it on for some minutes, and even amused ourselves with scattering the shining dust over each other's hair, when I saw something floating between us and the sun. We all looked; and soon it drifted near us, and was entangled in the web of sea-weed that waves in the tide round this black single rock. A large sea-eagle at the moment stooped to seize the prize. But I wished myself there before it; and one bound carried me farther than a long stone's-throw of our dark enemies the mountaineers. Thus the eagle in his descent struck only the waters with his talons, and flew off again screaming to the clouds, while I brought what I had won to my sisters."

"Dear one!" said the Sea-Child, "I guess what it was." And she kissed the airy face of her companion with her own, which seemed rather of rose-leaves, and the other only of coloured vapour.

"Yes," said she, "my own Sea-Child, there was a small basket of palm-leaf lined with the down of the phoenix; and in this the baby lay asleep. Beautiful it was indeed, but far unlike the beauty of my sisters. We cared no more for gold or silver dust, or rippling waves, or the rays of the setting sun. We even hushed our song, and bent over our nursling, and took her to be our own. Thus was it that our Sea-Child came to our Faëryland."

The Sea-Child bent to embrace her friend; for she was somewhat taller than the elfin sprite. They could not hold

152

each other in their arms; for one was gleaming air, and the other human substance. But the fairy hung round the child, as the reflection of a figure in bright water round one who bathes at the same spot of the same transparent pool. To the phantom it was more delightful than to rest and breathe upon a bank of flowers: to the mortal it seemed as if she was encompassed by a soft warm air, full of the odours of opening carnations and of ripe fruits.

"Let us sit here," said the Sea-Child, "and look around us, and discourse."

She placed herself on a mossy stone at the foot of a green birch-tree; and the fairy sat on the extremity of one of the sprays, which hung beside her companion's face, and which hardly bent a hair's-breadth with her weight. By one hand she held to a leaf above her, and with the other touched the dark-brown locks that streamed round the mortal head. The child sat, and looked down, and seemed to think, till the fairy said, "Why art thou sad? Of what art thou musing?"

The child blushed, and stooped her head, and at last looked up confusedly and said: "I never before felt so strongly the difference between me and you, who call me sister. Here, while we sit together on the spot where I was first wafted to your hands, it seems to me strange, - so strange! - that ye should have adopted me for your own, and not thrown me back into the waters, or left me a prey to the mountaineers, from whom ye have so long protected me."

"Strange!" said the other, "how strange? We could do no otherwise than we did. I know not how it is, that our Sea-Child often speaks as if it were possible to do aught else than what one wishes. We felt we loved you: we saw that, in that pretty but solid mortal frame, there was a breath and beauty like our own, though also something akin to those huge enemies, who, but for our cunning, would swiftly have devoured thee."

"I too never thought of it in former years; but now, when I believe I am really capable of loving you, when I more want to be loved, and to find nothing dividing me from you, it seems so unnatural, so horrible, that I should be altogether

153

unlike you. You are all of sunbeams and bright hues, and are soft like dewy gossamers; and I, - my limbs, through which no ray can pass, my head, that crushes the flowers I rest it on, as if it had been a head carved in stone! - Oh, sister! I am wretched at the thought. I touched the wing of a butterfly only yesterday with my finger; and I could perceive it shrink and shiver with pain. My touch had bruised its wing; and I thought I could see it ache, as it flew frightened away."

She burst into tears; and these were the first that ever were shed in Faëryland. But there they could not flow long; and she soon shook them from her eyes, and looked up smiling and said: "There thou see'st, dear sister, how unfit I am to live with such as thee. Better perhaps had I met my natural fate, and been destroyed on my first arrival by thy monstrous foes, or by the eagle from which thou didst save me."

"Strange would it have been, if we had not had wit enough to disappoint that big, brutal race!"

"I never could well understand why it was that they hated either you or me."

"They could not do otherwise being what they are, - thou what thou art, - and we the sprites thou knowest us. Curious is the tale, and long to tell, of all that has happened betwixt them and us."

"How came ye to have such dreadful inhabitants in your isle of Faëry?"

"Ah! that I know not. They and we seem to belong to it by the same necessity. Before thou camest we had no measure of time; which we now reckon, as thou knowest, by thy years, not by ours. Till then our existence was like what thou describest thy dreams to be. It is in watching thee, that we have learned to mark how thy fancies and wishes and actions rise and succeed one another, as the sun and moon, the stars and clouds travel and change. And even now I hardly feel, as thou appearest to do, what is meant by to-day, yesterday, and to-morrow. Of times and years therefore I can tell thee little. We grow not old, nor cease to be young. Nor

154

can we say of each other, as we can of thee, - thou art such a one, and none else. We discern differences of sunshine and shade, of land and sea, of wind and calm; but all of us feel alike under the same circumstances, and have no fixed peculiarity of being, such as that which makes thee so different from us. I know not whether it was I, or some other of my sisters, who visited this field and shore yesterday, and the day before danced in the showering drops of the white waterfall yonder up the valley. Each of us feels as all do, and all as each. I love thee not more than do my sisters, nor they more than I. Of our past life I only know, that we seemed always to have been in this our own land, and to have been happy here. The flowers fill us with odours, the sky with warmth; the dews bathe us in delight; the moonbeams wind us in a ring with filmy threads when we dance upon the sands; and, when the woods murmur above us, we have a thrill of quiet joy, which belongs not to me more than to another, but is the common bliss of all. Of all times have the mountains and deep ravines and bare and rocky uplands of our isle been the abode of a fierce and ugly race of giants, whom we have been accustomed to call our brothers, and to believe them allied with us by nature, though between us there has ever been a mortal enmity."

"Often, often," said the Sea-Child, "have I thought how much happier we should be, had there been no giants in the land."

"I know not," replied the fairy, "how that might be. Much is the vexation that they cause us; but it is said that our race is inseparable from theirs, and that, if they were altogether destroyed, we also must perish. Never, till we had thee among us, did their enmity seem very dangerous, difficult as it often was to avoid their injuries. Always, as now, when the shadows of the storm-cloud swept from the hills over our plains, when the dark mist rolled out of the ravines down to our sunny meadows, the shaggy and huge creatures strode forth from their caves and forests, leaning on their pine clubs, shouting and growling, defacing our green and flowery sward with their weighty tramp, and scaring us away before them. When, as it has happened, some of us were trodden beneath their feet, or dashed below their swinging clubs, a faint shriek, a sudden blaze burst from under the blow; and all of us, lurking beneath the waterfalls, clinging amid the hidden nooks of flowers, or shrunken into sparry grottoes in the rocks, felt stricken and agonized, although none of us could cease to live. All round this bay, and others larger and more broken of our shore, the giant horde of our brothers would sit upon the cliffs and crags, looking themselves like prodigious rocks, and, with the rain and storm about them, and the sea-foam dashing up against their knees, would wash their dark beards in the brine, and seem to laugh aloud at the sound of the tempest. But when calm and sunshine were about to return, they always sprang from their places on the shore, and, like one of those herds of wild bulls that they chase before them, hurried back with dizzy bellowings, and rush of limbs and clubs, into their dark mountains. Sometimes indeed they were more malicious, and sought more resolutely to do us mischief. I have known them tear asunder the jaws of one of their hill-torrents, so as to pour the waters suddenly on our fields and valleys. Sometimes too we have seen them standing upon the mountains, with their figures marked against the sky, plying great stems of trees around a mass of snow and ice, till, loosened at last, it rolled down mile after mile, crashing through wood and stream. Thus our warm bright haunts were buried under a frozen heap of ruins, while the laughter of the mountain-monsters rang through the air, above the roar of the falling mass. But often we had our revenge. Once, when the storms had gathered fiercely on those far hills, and rushed in rainy gusts and black fogs down every gully, and opened at last over the green vale and sunny bay, our brothers hurried in tumult from their own region, their swinish ears tossing in the dark folds of their locks and beards, and, with mouths like wolves, drinking in the tempest as they ran. They rioted and triumphed on the shore, while the wind whistled loudly round them; and they played with the billows which tumbled on the beach, as I have seen you play with lambs in the green fields. We peeped from the grottoes where we had hidden ourselves, and saw them catch some round black heaps out of the waters, like skins of animals full of liquid. These they threw at each other, till at last one burst, and covered the giant whom it had struck with a red stain. On this there was a loud shout: they flung the skins about no more, but caught them tenderly in their arms, lifted them to their mouths, bit them open and drained the contents. This increased their tumult and grim joy; and they turned to the meadow, and began to wrestle and leap and tear down the young trees, and disport themselves, till one by one they sank upon the turf in sleep. The storm was clearing off: we ventured from our hiding-places, and looked upon the hairy dismal shapes, that lay scattered and heaped like brown rocks overgrown with weeds and moss. Suddenly we all looked at each other, and determined what to do. We pierced through the crevices of our grottoes, till we reached a fount of sunny fire. This we drew upwards by our singing to follow us, and led it in a channel over the grass, till it formed a stream of diamond light, dividing this field from the mountains, and encircling the whole host of giants. The warm sunshine at the same time began to play on them. They felt the soft sweet flowery air of our lower land; our songs sounded in their bristled ears; and they began to toss, roll, snort, and endeavoured to rise and escape to their dark hills. But this was not so easy now. They could not pass the bright pure stream. The sunshine, in which we revelled, weakened them so much that they could not rise and stand, but staggered on their knees, fell upon their hands and faces, and seemed to dissolve away, like their own ice-crags when flung with all their clay and withered herbage down into our warm lakes and dells. We thought there was now a chance of seeing our enemies, who were also our brothers, for ever destroyed. We began to deliberate whether we also should necessarily perish with them, when we heard a sudden gust of wind and flash of rain; another storm broke from the mountains; a torrent of snow-water quenched our diamond flame. The giants stood up, bold, wild, and strong as ever, leaped, roared, and swung their clubs, and, with the friendly tempest playing round them, stormed back into the depths of their own mountain world."

"Could ye not," said the Sea-Child, "have always taken refuge from them in the lower garden, where I have been with you?"

"We did not know it till thou wert among us, and should perhaps never have ventured thither, had we not been driven to distress by the hatred of the giants for thee. When we had thee for our nursling and sister, their attempts were no longer bursts of violence that passed away. They seemed always lying in wait to discover and to destroy thee. Had we not known a strain of music, of power when sung to frighten them away, thou, dear Sea-Child, wouldst long ere this have been taken from us. When they came rushing down in the wind and darkness, and sought for thee in every thicket, and every hollow tree, and under each of those large pink shells which we often made thy bed, they sang and shouted together such words as these:

> Lump and thump, and rattling clatter,
> These the brawny brothers love;
> While the lightnings flash and shatter,
> While the winds the forest tatter,
> We too spatter, stamp, and batter,
> Whirling our clubs at whate'er's above.

But we too had our song; and never could these grim wild beasts resist the spell, when we sang together with soft voice,

> The giant is strong; but the fairy is wise:
> And the clouds cannot wither the stars in the skies.

"Oh! well I remember," said her companion, "with what delight I first heard you sing that song. I fancied that, if I could only listen long enough to it, I should become as airy and gentle as ye are, and no longer be encumbered with this

158

dark solid flesh. We were in that green chamber in the midst of red rocks, where the pines spread over the brinks of the precipices far above the mossy floor we sat on; and the vines hung their branches down the stony walls from the pine-boughs which they cling to on the summit, and drop their clusters into the smooth stream, with its floating water-lilies, which traverses the spot. There, dear sisters, were ye sporting, climbing up the vine-trails, and throwing yourselves headlong down, or launching over the quick ripples of the stream. Ye had laid me on a bed of harebells; and I looked up with half-shut eyes. I saw your sparkling hosts pass to and fro up the cliff, through the straggling beams of sunshine; when something blacker than the pine-boughs on the summit appeared in the deepest of their shade. Long tangled locks, and two fierce round eyes, and a mouth with huge protruding lip, came on and peered over, till the monster spied me, and gave a yell. I saw a crag, with two young pine-trees growing on it, toppling before the thrust of his hand, and at the moment of falling to crush me. Then suddenly came your cry and song. A sheet of water, thinner than a rose-leaf, and transparent as the starry sky, rose from the stream, and seemed to form an arch above me. There was in it a perpetual trembling and eddying of the brightest colours; and I saw the forms of thousands of my sisters, floating, circling, wavering up and down in the liquid light. All seemed joining in the song, -

The giant is strong; but the fairy is wise:
And the clouds cannot wither the stars in the skies.

The crag fell, but shattered not my crystal vault, down the side of which it rolled into the stream; and the giant, with a roar of rage, fell after it, and stung by the warm air, and pierced through and through by the music, and writhing in the bright stream, half melted, half was broken like a lump of ice, and darkened the water, while he flowed away in it."

"It was the frequency of such attempts however," said

159

the fairy, "which drove us to take refuge in the regions of our friends, the dwarfs. We found too that we had no longer the mere risk of being surprised by our enemies in the sudden descent of storm and mists, and through the opportunities of thick and gloomy lurking-places near our sunlit haunts. They had discovered a secret, by which they could at will darken and deface our whole kingdom, and blight all its sweet flowers and fruitage. There is somewhere, in the centre of their mountains, in the midst of desolate rocks, a black ravine. The upper end of it is enclosed by an enormous crag, which turns as on a pivot, and is the door of an immeasurable cave. The giants, hating our Sea-Child, and determined to drive her from the land, heaved with their pine-stem clubs at this great block of stone, until they had forced it open. Thence, so long as they had strength to hold it thus, a thick and chilling mist boiled out, poured down the glens and mountains, and stifled all our island. When they were so wearied with the huge weight that they could endure no longer, the rock swung to again and closed the opening; but not until the work was done for that time, and the land made well nigh uninhabitable to thee and us. Then in the fearful gloom the giants rushed abroad, howling and trampling over high and low; and many were the devices we were compelled to use in order to preserve thee from their fury. We scattered the golden sea-sand, which had been transmuted by the sunbeams, over the softest greensward, and watered it with the dew shaken from musk-roses; and it grew up into a golden trelliswork, with large twining leaves of embossed gold, and fruits like bunches of stars. When thou hadst been sprinkled with the same dew, and so hushed into charmed sleep, we laid thee beneath the bowery roof, and kept watch around thee. The giants could not approach this spot; for it threw off the darkness, and burnt in the midst of storm and fog with an incessant light. But still we were obliged to be perpetually on our guard; and we shivered and pined in the desolation of our beautiful empire. At last we resolved to try our fortunes in a new region. When we had lulled thee into deep slumber, we all glided down the waterfall that pours out of the lake of lilies, and sank with it deep into the ground. We were here in the kingdom of the dwarfs.

"The little people showed us as much friendship, as the giants had ever displayed of enmity. Their great hall had a thousand columns, each of a different metal, and with a capital of a different precious stone. The roof was opal, and the floor lapis-lazuli. In the centre stood a pillar, which seemed cut off at half its height. On it sat a dwarf, rather smaller than the others, but broad and strong. His dark and twisted face looked like a little copy of one of the giants; but his clear blue eyes were as beautiful as ours, or as thine, my Sea-Child. He sat with his arms folded, and his legs hung down and swinging. His head was turned to one side, and rather upwards; and on the tip of his nose spun perpetually a little golden circle, with a golden pin run through it, on which it seemed to dance unweariedly, turning round and round for ever, smooth and swift as an eddy in a stream. In its whirl the little circle gave out large flakes of white fire, which formed a wheel of widening rings above the head of the dwarf, flashing off on all sides between the capitals of the pillars, and lighting the whole hall. The queer cunning look, with which the dwarf's blue eyes glanced up at the small spinner, as if it were alive, and answering his glances with its own, amused us much.

"The dwarfs, when we entered, were all placed round on ranges of seats rising above one another. Every seat was like a small pile of round plates of gold, each of them, as we afterwards found, having a head on it with some strange figures. These plates, the dwarfs told us, were all talismans, which would one day make the owners lords of the world. At the head of the hall, under a canopy of state, sat the king of the dwarfs, who looked wonderfully old and wise, with two eyes of ruby, and a long crystal tooth growing out of one side of his mouth, and a beard of gold-wire falling below his feet and twirled on the floor, going three times round the throne.

" ' What seek ye?" said the King; and his words did not come out of his lips, but from a little hole in the top of his

161

crystal tooth.

" ' Help! necromancer.'

" ' It belongeth rightly to the helpful, and shall not be denied you. What bring ye?'

" ' A young Sea-child.'

" ' It is in the youngest that the oldest may see hope. She is welcome. What fear ye?'

" ' The rage of the tall giants.'

" ' We are deeper than they are high. I can protect you against them.'

"He rose up and walked before us; and his golden beard streamed behind over both his shoulders, and seemed to be a stately cloth woven with figures for us to walk on. There was darkness round us; and we advanced upon this shining path, following the dwarf, till suddenly he disappeared, and we found ourselves in the garden which thou hast dwelt in with us. Thou rememberest the still and glistening loveliness of the place; and of the moon that lighted it, and the sweet moonflowers that filled its glades, I need not speak. But thou knowest not what wise instruction the old dwarf king was wont to give us, while thou wert sleeping under the myrtle shade.

" ' Mourn not,' he would say, ' fair sisters, that ye are driven from your upper land of life into this lower garden of peace.

" ' All things are but as they must be; and, were they otherwise, they would not be the things they are.

" ' Each worketh for itself, and doeth and knoweth all it can, save in so far as other things oppose it, which are also accomplishing their due tasks.

" ' Each is but a portion of the whole, and vainly seeketh to be aught but that which the whole willeth it to be.

" ' All, - that is, dwarfs, and giants, and fairies, and the world that holds them, - subsist in successions of strife, and, while they seem struggling to destroy each other, exert, as alone it is possible for them to do, the energies of their own being.

" ' All rise out of death to life; and many are the

semblances of death which still accompany their life at its highest. They grow into harmony only by discord with themselves and others, and, while they labour to escape the common lot, rebound painfully from the walls which they strive against idly.

" 'The giant disturbeth, the fairy brighteneth, the dwarf enricheth the world. Each doeth well in his own work. But therein often must he thwart and cross the work of another.

" 'I am oldest, I am wisest of workers in the world. I was at the birth of things; and what hath been I know well: but what is future I know not yet, nor can read whether there shall be a new birth of all that may bring death to me.'

"Thus did the old King teach us a sad yet melodious contentment, that seemed suited to that visionary garden. This quiet state however was not to last, nor the wisdom of the dwarfs to secure them happiness. We longed for our upper world of daylight and freedom; and thou seemedst rather dreaming than awake. Yet thou beamedst ever fairer and fairer, and didst grow in stature and in loveliness. Thus was it that thou wert the occasion of our first difference with the dwarfs. Their King, so old, so wise, looked on thee ever with more joy and sadness; and at last he told us that he would fain have thee for his queen, to abide with him always in that secret lunar empire. Us too the other dwarfs appeared to love more than we wished; and we found that we must either leave their dominions, or consent to inhabit them for ever. We spake to the old King, and said, that for thee it would be a woeful doom to see our native Faëry land no more; and we entreated him of his goodness and wisdom to enable us to dwell there without further peril. Ruby tears fell from his ruby eyes upon his golden beard as he turned away; and the faces of all Dwarfland were darkened.

"No long space seemed to have passed, before we were summoned again to the great hall, while thou wert left sleeping in the moon-garden. The King was on his throne; the dwarfs were seated round. But, instead of the pillars we had seen before, the metals now had all become transparent;

and in the midst of each stood one of our enemies, the giants, with one heavy hand hung down, and clenched, as if in pain, and the other raised above his head, and sustaining the capital of the column. The small gold plate with its gold pin still spun incessantly on the nose; the blue eyes still watched it cunningly; the flakes of fire streamed off and flew between the pillars, and scorched the faces and brown-red shoulders of the giants. Our enemies grinned and writhed when they saw us, but seemed unable to utter any sound. The dwarfs also did not speak; but the King rose and moved before us. His beard fell over his shoulders, and formed a path on which we walked. We proceeded on and on, till the Dwarfland seemed changing, and daylight fell faintly upon us. The King grew more and more like the stones and trees around; and at last, we knew not how, instead of his figure before us, there was only a cleft in the rock, nearly of the same shape. The golden beard was now a track of golden sands, such as we had often seen before, with the bright sunshine falling on it. We were again in our own world of Faëry. But oh, dear Sea-Child! I cannot say the grief that smote us when we missed thee. We wailed and drooped; and even the delights of our land could do nothing to console us, till we found thee sleeping in a grotto of diamond and emerald, which recalled the treasures of the dwarfs to us. Even now we were not happy; for we remembered a prophecy of the old man, that, though he might restore us to our home, and rescue us from the giants, short would be our enjoyment of thee whom we had refused him."

The companions embraced anew; and the fairy hung round her friend like a rainbow on a smooth green hill. The fairies now poured in on all sides, singing and exulting in their own land, though not without a thought of grief from the dwarf's prophecy. The sun was hanging over the sea, and gilding the shore; and they looked at the bright waters, and marked the spot where they had first discerned the Sea-Child's swimming cradle. Lo! there was again a speck. A floating shape appeared, and came nearer and nearer. It looked a living thing. Soon it touched the shore; and they saw a figure like that of the Sea-Child, but taller and stronger and bolder, and in a stately dress. The fairies said in their hearts, It is a man! Them he seemed not to see, but only her. She was frightened, but with a mixture of gladness at his appearance, and was trembling and nigh to sink, when he took her in his arms, and spake to her of hope and joy.

"I am come from distant lands upon this strange adventure, warned in dreams, and by aërial voices, and by ancient lays, that here I should find my bride, and the queen of my new dominions."

He too was beautiful, and of a sweet voice; and she heard him with more fear than pain. When she looked around, she no longer saw the fairies near. There were gleams floating over the landscape, and quivering in the woods, and a song of sweet sorrow, so sweet, that, as it died away, it left the sense of an eternal peace.

Thus did the land of England receive its first inhabitants. Ever since has it been favoured by the fairies; the dwarfs have enriched it secretly; and the giants have upbourne its foundations upon their hands, and done it huge though sullen service.

DINAH MARIA MULOCK (1826-1887) who signed herself MRS. CRAIK following her marriage, wrote several fairy romances for children, of which the best is *Alice Learmont* (1852) - a story more carefully and sensitively rooted in Scottish folklore than most contemporary works of its kind. Her fantasies for adults, including the tale below, were brought together in the collection *Avillion and Other Tales* (1853), and subsequently reprinted in *Romantic Tales* (1859); they include two novellas: "Avillion", a visionary fantasy about the Isle of the Blest, in which Ulysses and King Arthur make brief appearances; and "The Self-Seer", a curious didactic fantasy in which two friends exchange places with their spirit *doppelgängers*.

The frequent intrusion of pietistic homilies into her work marks Mrs. Craik out as one of the most Victorian of all the Victorian lady novelists, and testifies to her unease in dealing with the vocabulary of ideas typical of fantasy (which is, of course, drawn almost entirely from pagan sources). Like Dickens, she never introduced fantasy elements into her novels, but her fascination with fantasy motifs is evident in her shorter works.

EROTION

A Tale of Ancient Greece

by Mrs. Craik

Chapter I

In the early days of Greece, when the gods yet spoke with men, before the oracles were silent in the groves of Dodona, and while the nymphs and dryads still lingered by wood and fountain, there was in Taurica a temple consecrated to Diana. Night and day in the sanctuary the virgin priestesses of the goddess kept vigil round her statue. Men said that this treasure was not the work of human hands, but had fallen from heaven. The elders of the generation well remembered that when the temple was finished, the priesthood who mourned over the yet vacant shrine of the goddess, had one night left it in moonlight solitude, and lo! next morning a beautiful statue of the divinity was in its place. How such glorious loveliness could have sprung to life from the cold marble, unless by an immortal touch, no one could imagine, but all worshipped the form as a token direct from heaven that their piety had been accepted. Not many days after, at the very foot of the statue, died a pale youth, whom no one knew, save that he had haunted the temple for months. Some kind hand gave him a tomb, and his name was never spoken; the worshippers worshipped, and no man dreamed that their idol was only divine in that it came from the hand of an unknown, but heaven-born and immortal genius.

This old tale was now forgotten, but far and wide spread the fame and renown of the shrine. Pilgrims came from all lands to kneel before the statue which was believed to have fallen from heaven, and brought back to their distant homes wondrous tales of its divine loveliness. Men spoke with reverence of the oracle of Diana Taurica, and the white

167

pinnacles of the temple were looked upon from afar with enthusiastic adoration. But after a time these worshippers from foreign lands came no more. It was whispered that one of the pretended devotees had offered sacrilege to the goddess, and that Diana had exacted a fearful expiation. The real secret was never breathed; but for years after, many strangers who entered the temple were seen no more on earth. Still the white-robed priestesses encircled the flower-crowned shrine, and the statue of the goddess shone in imperishable beauty.

It was the yearly festival of Diana Taurica, and the temple was filled with the music of choral hymns, and the odours of incense-laden sacrifices. Throughout the long summer day the goddess was worshipped in her character of huntress. No longer hovering silently in the dim light of the temple, the virgin priestesses laid aside their white garments for a sylvan dress, and rushed to the open woods, where the day was spent in wild joy, and sports such as befitted the nymphs of Diana. Upon these revels no unhallowed eye dared look; such intrusion was instantly punished with death.

But when twilight drew on, began the worship of Cynthia, the goddess of the night. As the full moon arose, there was heard from the temple a hymn, sweet yet plaintive, and solemn withal. Through the deserted streets wound the maiden train, led by the high-priestess. Then came the initiated, who had long been devoted to the service of the temple, and afterwards walked the young novices, crowned with poppy-garlands, and chanting hymns in the still and solemn moonlight. Last of all came the young maidens of the city, who alone were permitted to witness and share in the solemnities.

These ceremonies ended with the twilight. When night came, the mysterious rites of Diana Triformis were celebrated. There, in her character of Queen of the land of silence and death, Hecate was propitiated; but how, or by what unearthly ceremonies, was known to none except the

168

higher order of the priesthood. The golden curtains of the inner sanctuary were drawn, and nothing was heard or seen by those who waited without, crouching with veiled faces, or lying prostrate on the marble floor. These chosen worshippers were all young girls, some hardly past childhood; self-dedicated, or else vowed by their parents to the service of Diana. Many of them were beautiful; some with the pure, pale statue-like features of their clime; others with dazzling golden locks, and cheeks like rose-leaves. One of them - she was fairest of all - knelt motionless, not in fear, but with her head uplifted in an ecstatic enthusiasm that dilated her child-like face, until it wore an almost divine aspect. One of the elder novices drew near, and looked at her, saying in a whisper, as if she trembled at the sound of her own voice:-

"Erotion, how is it with thee?"

Erotion moved not nor answered.

"Hush! Phrene, speak not to her," said another maiden, fearfully. "Seest thou not that the power of the goddess is upon her?" And the young girls stole away from their companion, whose wild eyes were fixed on vacancy, as if beholding what was invisible to all the rest.

"Diana the mighty has called her," whispered Phrene; "she was never like one of us."

"And none know whence she came, for she was brought up from a babe in the temple, an orphan, and homeless," said the violet-eyed Cydippe.

"It is the goddess's will, doubtless, that the lot this night should fall upon her," murmured Leuconoe; and then a heavy silence gathered over all the maidens, for they trembled at the fearful ordeal which one of them, they knew not who, must go through in that long, lonely vigil, before the statue of Diana Triformis.

At last, from the dead stillness which pervaded the sanctuary, arose a faint melody, like the wind passing over the strings of a harp; clouds of incense rolled in fragrant wreaths from above the golden screen, filling the temple with luxurious perfume, that steeped every sense with its intoxicating power. Then the curtains were lifted, and, with her long black garments sweeping the ground, came forth the high-priestess, the chosen of Diana - Iphigenia, daughter of Agamemnon.

Beautiful was she, as when she was led to the sacrifice at Aulis - but it was the beauty of a marble statue. There was no trace of life in her face, except in the dark, unfathomable eyes,

"Orb within orb, deeper than sleep or death."

Her black robes moved without a sound, and her unbound hair twined like a golden serpent round her white arms, which were folded on her breast. As she advanced, the young novices moved aside, all but the still-kneeling Erotion, who remained immovable. The high-priestess looked upon the child, and touched her with a light finger. A shiver came over her frame, she lifted her eyes, and glanced round wildly, like one awaking from a trance.

"Arise, my daughter," said Iphigenia, in a voice that sounded sweet, and yet solemn; and the maiden rose up, and crept silently to her companions.

And now the golden urn was brought forth, that the fatal lot might be drawn, which appointed one of the young novices to the awful vigil. Each year one of the band was thus chosen, who, after this initiation, was received into the order of priestesses, or else was banished the temple, and never more seen by human eye. That the ordeal was terrible, all knew well, for many a frail creature had been found in the gray light of morning, dead on the marble pavement; while those who passed through that fearful night, never again recovered the sweet smiling face of youth. But what the trial was none could tell, for each novice took a solemn vow never to reveal it. No marvel was it that many a bright cheek grew pale, and many a lip quivered with fear, as the maidens advanced one by one to the urn.

The lot fell upon Erotion. Then rose up the wild chorus of the priestesses, as they closed round the chosen

170

one of Diana, the pale, silent child, who stood without word or movement while they took away her novice's tunic, and robed her in a long garment of white wool, placing on her head the consecrated poppy-wreath, sacred to the goddess.

"Dost thou fear?" said the high-priestess, as the young girl bent at her feet, ere entering the sanctuary. "Dost thou fear, my daughter?"

"I have no fear," murmured Erotion; and there was indeed no terror on that fair young face, but an expression of mingled awe and rapture.

Iphigenia laid her hands on the child's head -

"The goddess calls, and must be obeyed. Go, and be thou fortunate; for the influence of her whose name is unutterable is upon thee."

The child arose - the golden curtains were lifted - they closed upon her, and the awful vigil was begun.

Chapter II

There was dead silence in the temple; the lamps burned dimly on the altar, and threw long shadows on the wall; everywhere else the darkness seemed like a visible presence - a gloom that could be felt, gathering around, and taking wild and horrible shapes, the more horrible because they were undefined. Beneath the veiled statue of the goddess crouched Erotion; her large dark eyes were not drooping, but fixed steadfastly on the image - her head was not buried in her robe, but raised fearlessly. Still there was no sound, no movement - the statue moved not under its drapery; there was no presence in the temple save that of night and darkness, and these had no terrors to the heart of the lonely child.

By degrees it seemed as if the poppies which bound her hair were piercing with their dreamy influence unto her brain. Her eye-lids closed, her cheek fell upon her hand, and a delicious numbness, which was scarcely sleep, absorbed the senses of Erotion. Gradually the veiled image upon which she looked appeared to move underneath its drapery;

171

the marble dissolved into folds that took the appearance of mist, and two strangely-beautiful eyes gleamed from out that vapoury shroud. The child felt them upon her, looking into her very soul, and binding her with a spell of stillness, so that she could not turn away from that mysterious gaze. At last words came to her trembling lips, and Erotion said -

"What wouldst thou, O goddess? Behold, I am here. Art thou she whose name I may not utter?"

An answer came - it was not from the animated statue, but a voice, an "airy tongue," like that which poets hear in the wind, in the rustling of the trees, in the stirring of the grass. So faint was it, that whence it came Erotion knew not; but to her opened ears it was distinct and intelligible.

"I am the spirit whom mankind worship under the name of Diana, the spirit of purity, existing in heaven, on earth, and in the land of the dead. I have no form, but men give me such shape, and ascribe to me such symbols, as are easiest of comprehension to the human mind. What is purer than the moon in heaven, or the life of a woodland virgin on earth? But these are only personifications of my being. Mankind invest me with a nature half human, half divine; they build me temples and shrines, yet I am everywhere - a spiritual essence, needing neither prayers nor sacrifices."

As the voice spoke, boldness and clearness came to the young maiden's soul; every cloud of fear and mortal weakness was swept away; her intellect expanded, and the child of fourteen years felt and apprehended as a woman, nay, as an angel.

"Yet, O spirit," said Erotion, "thou sufferest us to worship thee as a goddess!"

"Because man's piety clings so closely to outward forms; yet those whom I choose know me as I am - therefore have I chosen thee, Erotion."

"Can the divine thus regard the human?" said the child.

"Look by thy side, and thou shalt know."

Erotion turned, and lo! on either hand there stood beside her two forms, of stature far above mortal height.

One seemed a spirit of light, with floating garments, woven as it were of sunbeams; the other, dark, gloomy, and half concealed by an ebon mantle, that veiled the face and form. The child looked in wonder, but, even while she beheld, the phantoms melted into air.

"These are thy good and evil genii," said the invisible voice; "they were with thee at thy birth, and will follow thee until death. It is they who inspire thee with thoughts holy or sinful, sweet or bitter; who produce all those strange and warring impulses which rule thy life. They have power over thee, but not over thy destiny, except so far as it is under thine own control, according as thou listenest to one or other of these guardian spirits."

"I see! I feel!" cried the child. "I dreamed of this before - now I know it. Life is a mystery indeed!" and Erotion's voice sank, solemn and trembling. "Tell me, what is death?"

No answer came; but a touch, light as that of summer air, pressed Erotion's lips and eyes. Immediately the lips drooped; she beheld no more the sanctuary or the image, but a dim haze, through which myriads of shapes, some horrible, some lovely, were visible, like bright floating spectres, that glide before the eyes ere slumber comes on. Faintly in the child's ear came aërial music, sweeter than she had ever before heard, even in dreams; her breathing ceased, and yet it was no pain; her limbs relaxed, and a frozen calm came over them. A voice, which she knew was that of the spirit, whispered, "Erotion, this is death;" and then she felt no more.

The child awoke as out of a long sleep, and found herself wandering on what seemed a desolate shore. Before, in the distance, lay the dim and gloomy sea: behind, clouds shut out the view. Those who reached that shore might no more look behind. The child glanced fearfully round her, but could see nothing except the lonely shore, and the terrible, waveless sea, that looked as though no living thing had ever stirred upon or beneath its waters. Erotion wrung her hands, but lo! palm met palm as air meets air - they were nought but outward semblance. She lifted her voice to cry aloud, but no sound echoed in the stillness of that fearful place. She glided over the shore, but her feet felt not the sands over which they passed, and left no prints behind. Again Erotion's lips strove to utter a sound; all was still; but an answer came - a voice, which the child knew well, murmured -

"Fear not, Erotion; I am here. I rule in the land of silence as upon earth. Come with me, and thou shalt cross the ocean which separates life from eternity."

Impelled by an invisible power, Erotion reached the margin of that dark sea. It neither ebbed nor flowed; no light waves danced upon its surface, which was of one unvaried dusky hue, as if an eternal thunder-cloud hung over it, and was reflected in its mysterious depths. Only one slender thread of brightness, answering to the milky way across the night-heaven, made a pathway over it. The child stood trembling on its verge.

"Erotion, place thy foot on the ocean without fear," said the voice at her side.

Erotion did so, and it yielded not. Swiftly she glided along the silver line, with a motion like that which is felt in dreams, when we seem borne through the air invisibly. The desolate shore grew dim as the child sped on; the clouds furled off from the sky; the sea beneath her feet grew pellucid and blue, and melodious with dancing ripples. On, on, until in the dim horizon arose a golden cloud, which gradually formed itself into a land, beautiful as Paradise. Erotion beheld vales, and purple hills, trees, fountains and rivers; among which flitted, like fire-flies on eastern nights, bright and lovely forms, transparent as vapours, and yet bearing mortal semblance. As her feet touched the golden strand, she heard glorious music; she strove to join in the heavenly melody, and strains came from her lips, so sweet, so divine, that her soul was ravished with the angelic harmony.

"Thou hast passed through the Ocean of Death," said the voice which still accompanied her; "thou art now in the land of immortality."

And never, save in dreams, did mortal behold a land so

glorious. It was most like those landscapes we trace sometimes in the sky, where snowy hills, and purple valleys, and silver streams, seemed formed in the clouds of sunset, vanishing as soon as formed. But here there was no night to dim the never-fading view; for though like earth, as, in its glorified beauty, it sprang from the hand of the Fashioner, still it was not earth.

The child's spirit lifted its airy hands in rapture; and then glided toward the green plain that sloped to the sea, the unseen voice leading. Thus she passed, until she came nearer to those beautiful shadows which were flitting about on every side. Human they seemed, but it was humanity exalted into perfect beauty.

"Who are these shapes that I see?" asked the child.

"They are the spirits of the dead," answered the guiding voice. "Thou seest that each bears the face and form which it wore on earth; yet they are only shadows, for the soul is of itself impalpable. They enjoy perfect bliss; and those delights which the spirit felt while in its clay-vestures, are theirs now unalloyed - love in its essence, knowledge, wisdom, genius, every sensation in which the body had no share; and those who on earth most cherished these spiritual pleasures, enjoy them highest now."

"And oh!" said Erotion, "if those are the souls of the wise and holy dead, where are those of the unrighteous?"

A soft sigh, like the closing of a flower at sunset, was heard by the child, and the voice answered sadly -

"We may not speak of them; they are not here - they sleep".

Without another word, Erotion glided on until she came to a green recess, golden-wove with sunbeam threads, that made a fairy network through the trees. There, hymning glorious poetry, such as never earthly bard conceived, reclined a shadow which seemed a youth. His face - and it was the same which had grown pale and sunken in life - now shone with divine beauty; the golden hair waved, and the sweet eyes looked as they did on earth.

"I lived - I suffered - I died!" cried the poet in his song;

175

"And yet men knew me not. I brought with me fire from heaven, and it was not seen; yet I cherished it in my bosom - it warmed and cheered me, and I was happy."

The child drew near, and her spirit stood face to face with the poet's soul. Erotion spoke, for she felt no fear -

"And yet thou didst die unknown, and hast left behind no immortal name?"

"Not so," said the shadow; "for men sing my songs. I live again in their hearts, though they never heard my name. Age after age they will think my thoughts, repeat my words, hold me as a dear friend, and honour me as a great teacher. This is the only immortality on earth."

And as the child turned she heard from another celestial bower the echoing of the same song. There stood another soul, like the poet's in radiance; and lo! wherever the shadow turned its beaming eyes, lovely pictures appeared in air; the artist had now no need of the frail hand which lay mingled with earth's dust, to embody his divine conception.

"Genius is the only immortality!" echoed the shadow. "I laboured, I perished, and no man heeded; yet it is nought to me now; I am blessed. No friendly foot hovers near my grave, but I am not forgotten even on earth. Do not men bow down before my work? - do not they call it divine? - my glorious ideal! - do they not adore it, thinking it came from the finger of a god? and yet the hand that made it is now a heap of dust. But the work remains, and I live still in the creation of my genius."

Erotion knew not the form of the spirit which thus spake; but her awakened soul told her that she beheld the youth who had given to the temple of Diana Taurica its goddess - and died.

Onward went the spirit of the child, through meadows and valleys thick with imperishable flowers - over streams that sang ever their own sweet melodies-amidst woods whose leaves knew no withering; and still the invisible voice followed. At last Erotion came where the sunshine grew less bright, the flowers less beautiful, while a thin silver mist, like twilight vapours, obscured the view. Through it there floated shadows like the rest, but less brilliant, while on each face rested a pensive sweetness that was almost sad. Again a question rose to the child's lips, but ere it was uttered the voice answered -

"These are they who have once erred, suffered, and repented on earth. They are happy, yet there still remains a faint shade of sadness - the memory of the past - until every sorrow which their error caused to others on earth shall have passed away."

As the voice ceased, one of the spirits glided towards the child. It bore the semblance of a fair woman: the face was pale, but oh, how heavenly sweet! Erotion had seen it in her dreams; it had looked down upon her from among the stars in her night-watches. She had not known it then, save as a sweet fancy; but now her senses were all unclouded, and the child felt that she was near the spirit of her mother, whom on earth she had never beheld. The shadow approached : soft arms clasped Erotion - sweet kisses were upon her eyelids; for death cannot change love, least of all the love of a mother.

"Has death freed thee, too, oh, my daughter!" whispered the spirit, and bright pearls - they were not tears now - shone in the celestial eyes; "then soon shall all trace of suffering caused by me be swept from earth, and I shall be entirely blessed."

"Art thou not so now?" said the child.

Again that mournful look rested on the face of the spirit.

"I sinned - I broke the solemn vows of a priestess for earthly love - I carried a deceitful heart to the holy shrine; yet I paid in death a fearful atonement - more fearful still was the thought of thee. Cruel was the mercy that delayed the punishment until thy birth, to make it only more bitter. But ere death came, I met it with a calm and penitent heart, and it wafted me to rest and peace. Here I await thee - and one more. The day is now come."

"Not yet, not yet!" uttered the mysterious voice, and Erotion felt herself borne away as on the wings of a summer breeze into a lovely glade. There spirits, diviner and more beautiful in shape than any she had yet beheld, were floating over the grass, or listening to ethereal music. They were crowned with stars, and bore golden palm-branches, and their brightness was such, that the child veiled her eyes from the sight. But they came near and lifted her in their dazzling arms, while their song rose loud and triumphant-

"We are blessed, we are blessed! we died joyfully for what was dearest to us on earth; we feared not the lonely shore nor the gloomy sea, and we enjoy a rapturous immortality. O spirit! loosed from the earth bonds for a time, behold thy destiny - thou shalt be one of us - rejoice, rejoice! Such a death is sweet - sweet as a babe's slumber - such an immortality is unspeakably glorious. Erotion, fulfil thy destiny, and come to us."

The child seemed to fall from that divine embrace, down, down through mists and darkness unfathomable - time and space, myriads of ages, and millions of leagues appeared to gather behind her, until some soft touch was laid upon her eyes and lips, and Erotion awoke from her trance.

She lay on the floor of the sanctuary; the sacred lamp was nearly extinguished, and the gray morning twilight rested on the veiled statue of Diana Taurica, which stood immovable in its white shroud.

Chapter III

Never more after that night did the vowed one of Diana look or speak as a child. Erotion was not sad, but none ever heard from her lips the light-hearted laughter of girlhood. Her eyes were of a dreamy depth, and had a strange, mysterious look, as if her soul saw without the aid of mere bodily organs. She walked through the world as though she beheld it not; shut up in herself, her outward life seemed mechanical, while her inner mind was ever brooding over things beyond earth. Men looked upon her as one on whom the spirit of the goddess had fallen; the few words which dropped from her lips were held as oracles; no eye followed her - no power controlled her. Wrapped in her priestess' veil,

178

the young maiden passed from the temple to the city, from the city to the sylvan forest, or the lone sea-shore, and no one stayed her. She passed, like a spirit of purity and beauty; wild, untutored men looked and turned aside in reverence, as if Diana herself were among them; children beheld with wonder one who was like themselves, and yet so unlike. But one and all regarded Erotion as the chosen of the goddess.

As months and years gathered over the head of the maiden, the strange spell which had overshadowed her childhood seemed to grow stronger. Even the vowed novices thought of their own beauty in girlish vanity, and talked of the world outside the temple walls; but no such feelings ever disturbed Erotion's unworldly nature. Beautiful she was, but it was the beauty of an angel, not of a woman; no eye could look upon her and mingle her idea with that of earthly love.

In the long summer days, Erotion went out in the forest; there, in the deepest glades, she wandered alone. Sometimes children who were suffered to run wild in the woods, came home and told of a strange and lovely face which they had seen gleaming through the trees, and mothers remembered that it was a place haunted by Dryad and Oread, and thought it no marvel that such should love to look upon beauteous infancy. Often, too, the wayfaring peasant heard, above the melody of hidden waters, a sweet and mysterious voice, and said it was the Naiad singing beside her fountain.

But more than the green plains and the woody recesses, did the young priestess love the sea-shore. A spell for which she could not account drew her ever to the margin of that dark sea, now called the Euxine, on whose shore the city stood. Its gloomy billows, its wild coast, its frowning rocks, had for her an inexplicable charm; it might be that they recalled the memory of her wondrous dream in the temple, if dream indeed it were, which seemed so real. In the splendour of noon, in the dusky eve, in storm and in calm, Erotion haunted the shore and watched the sea.

179

Mariners from afar saw her white garments floating on high cliffs and in sand-bound caves, which hitherto only the sea-bird had visited, and told strange tales of ocean nymphs and coral-crowned Nereids.

In this solitude, Erotion pondered on her destiny; the winds and ever-murmuring waves were her teachers and companions; they seemed to speak to her as the invisible voice had done in her dream, of things great and wonderful - of the marvels of nature - of the life of the soul - of poetry, genius, and all-pervading love. Often she thought of her own strange and lonely life - of her mysterious birth, and again she felt the embrace of the spirit who had called her "child," and whose mystic words she had heard in the vision. Then Erotion's thoughts turned from the dark and unexplained past to the future, still more vague and shadowy; and amidst all these musings came pealing the farewell chant which she had last heard in the land of immortality - "Erotion, Erotion, fulfil thy destiny, and come!"

It was on one of those evenings when the glories of the setting sun might truly bring to a Greek imagination the idea of Hyperion in his golden chariot, or of Tithonus the bridegroom sinking into the wavy arms of Thetis - that Erotion wandered along by the sea-shore. She watched the sun in his cloud-pavilion, and thought that an orb so glorious was a fit dwelling for a god. She remembered the legends of the priestesses concerning the elder race of gods - of Hyperion the Titan, whose throne was in the sun, and before whose giant beauty even that of the young Apollo grew dim; how that he and his brethren had been overthrown by a mightier power than even their own, and that Olympian Jove was now worshipped by mankind. And then came across the memory of the inspired maiden the words which she had listened to from the voice, that even these were shadows, and that the gods of Olympus were but personifications of the various powers of nature, or of holy sentiments, thus made tangible objects of worship for the darkened mind of man.

Absorbed in thoughts like these, Erotion saw not that black clouds had gathered over the fair evening sky, that the waves were rising, and the whirlwind was heard in the air. The sea-birds shrieked, and flew to the crevices of the rocks, against which dashed the billows thundering and heavily Nearer came the tempest, bearing destruction on its wings, as if the powers of earth, heaven, and sea were at warfare, and were mingled together in deadly confusion. Through all this fearful contest went the maiden, her long black hair tossed by the winds, her garments torn, her feet bleeding, and leaving their red traces over the sand, until she came to a little cave she knew. She stood at its entrance, and the struggling moonbeam that glimmered through the edge of a black cloud, lighting up her form, made her seem like a wandering ghost by the side of the gloomy river of Tartarus.

As she stood and looked into the thick darkness of the cave, a man's voice, hoarse with terror, sounded from within-

"Iole! Iole! art though come to visit me? Has no tomb yet received thy clay, that thou must wander here as an avenging spirit? Iole! Iole! depart, and let me die!"

And the cry became a shriek of horror as Erotion drew nigh, and bent over the speaker - a gray-haired man, whose foreign garments, covered with sea-weed, and bruised limbs, bespoke him a shipwrecked stranger, driven thither by the storm.

"Fear me not," said the sweet voice of Erotion; "I am no spirit, but a woman, a priestess of the temple which is nigh here, the temple of Diana Taurica."

A cry such as only the wildest agony forces from man's lips, was uttered by the stranger -

"Diana Taurica - a priestess!" he shrieked. "Oh, ye gods, am I then here? It is no dream; thou art indeed Iole. Tortured spirit, pardon! I knew not of thy vows! I knew not that to love thee was a sin. Spirit of Iole, pardon!"

Erotion shuddered as she listened to these ravings.

"Stranger, I am not called Iole; I am Erotion, and never until now did mine eyes behold thee. Tell me who thou art, and why thou speakest thus wildly?"

"I am Tisamenes of Crete," answered the stranger, in a calmer voice. "Seventeen years ago, the fatal wrath of the sea-gods threw me on this coast. I saw, wooed, and won a fair virgin, named Iole; I knew not her birth or fortunes, save that she loved me - oh, too well! Maiden, like thee she was a priestess of Diana. Her punishment was death. She betrayed me not; I escaped. Traitor that I was, who dared not die with Iole! But she was revenged; night and day the furies haunt me; and she too, O maiden - she stands and looks like thee - like thee; with her marble features, her dark floating hair, her mournful eyes. Off, off! look not at me with those eyes - they are the eyes of Iole!"

As Erotion listened, her stature dilated, and wild excitement shone in her countenance. She lifted up her arms in the moonlight, which grew broader and brighter as the storm passed away, and cried -

"O great Diana, pardon! The will of the gods be done." Then she turned to the stranger, and said, in tones low and tremulous - "I never beheld father or mother. I was born in the temple sixteen years ago. They told me my mother was a priestess, who sinned and died; but I knew not her name till now. O stranger! O *father!* let me kiss thy garment's hem, for I am surely Iole's child."

Chapter IV

Throughout the moonlight summer's night which succeeded the tempest, the father and daughter sat together in the cave. Erotion bound up the bruised limbs of the shipwrecked man with her priestess's veil; she dipped her long tresses in the cool water, and laid them on his brow; she called him by the sweet name which her lips had never uttered before - "Father, dear father!" and the madness passed away from the soul of Tisamenes of Crete. He sat with his daughter's hand in his, looking into her calm sweet face, in which the wild enthusiasm of the vowed and inspired priestess had given place to an expression of tenderness and human love.

"Now thou lookest like Iole," he would say: "not the fearful vision for which I first mistook thee, but like Iole in the days of our early love. I knew not but that the

182

murderers destroyed the babe with the mother. The gods be praised, that through sorrow, shipwreck, and pain, I have found mine own child - the child of the dead Iole. I will stay here, I will never leave thee, Erotion, since that is thy name - but I can only call thee my daughter, my sweet daughter. We will not be parted more."

As the morning dawned, Tisamenes tried to raise himself from the floor of the cave.

"I am faint, my child," he said, feebly, - "faint from hunger. Take me with thee to the city, where I may find food."

Erotion turned away and wept.

"Oh, my father!" she said, " I thought not of this in my joy; the gods have pity upon us! Dost thou not know that for these sixteen years, as an atonement for thy - oh, not thy sin, my father; never will my lips utter such word against thee; - but that since then, all strangers whom the sea casts on our shore are sacrificed to the vengeance of the goddess. Thou wilt be murdered; and I, how shall I save thee?"

"Is it even so? " murmured Tisamenes. "Then the fates have brought me hither, that the same hands which shed Iole's blood may be imbrued in mine. I am content, since I have found thee, Erotion. Let me die."

"Thou shalt not die, my father!" cried Erotion, in a voice of shrill agony, which startled the very birds that the first beams of daylight had awakened from their cavern-nook. They flew over the heads of father and daughter, uttering discordant screams.

Tisamenes buried his face in his robe, and spoke no more; but Erotion, after a thoughtful silence, said quickly and decisively -

"My father, thou must stay here. It is bright morning; I will go in search of food - not to the temple - let them think I have perished in the storm. If no man will give me food, I will beg; is it not for thee? Lie here in peace, my father; I will come again - thou shalt not die."

And Erotion, wrapping around her the fragments of her white robe, with her young face, no longer hidden by her

183

priestess's veil, now pale, now glowing with shame, as curious eyes were cast upon its beauty, passed through solitary and devious ways into the city. She heard a wailing from the temple, and saw a band of the sacred attendants come from the shore, with half-extinguished torches. As they passed her hiding-place, they talked, with low tones, of the lost priestess; of how, amidst the conflict of the elements, Diana had carried away her own. Then Erotion sprang up where she had nestled beside a vine-dresser's cottage, tore the rich bunches of grapes that hung beside her, and sped away like a hunted deer.

Ere long, Erotion was beside her almost dying father, with his head on her knee, placing between his parched lips the cooling fruit, and weeping over him with a fullness of joy that was utterly regardless of future sorrow.

"We will stay here, my father," she said, "until thou art recovered, and then, in the dead of night, we will go far away to the wild forest - I know it well. I will seek fruits for thee, and we will live with the birds and the flowers, and never know sorrow more."

Tisamenes lifted up his eyes; he was helpless as a child.

"I will go anywhere with thee, my daughter. The gods have surely pardoned my sin, since they have sent thee to me, Erotion."

As he spoke, a shadow darkened the mouth of the cave, and before them stood, stern, cold, and silent as a figure of stone, Iphigenia, the high-priestess of the temple. Not a word passed between her lips, as she looked on the father and daughter clinging to each other in mute despair. She waved her hand, and the cave was filled with the armed guards of Thoas the King. It was too late. Tisamenes was surrounded; rude hands untwined his daughter's clinging arms; he was borne away; Erotion was left lying on the floor of the cavern, cold and speechless. The servants of the temple advanced to seize her, but Iphigenia stayed them.

"Touch her not!" said the stern tones of the daughter of Agamemnon; "she is the inspired of Diana. Shall I doom to death a child because she would fain preserve a father - I, who willingly had died for mine?"

The attendants silently departed, and the high-priestess was alone with Erotion.

"Arise, my daughter," said Iphigenia, lifting the maiden up by the cold, powerless hand - "arise, and come with me."

Erotion arose, and without a sigh or tear, as passively as one of those moving, golden statues with which, as Homer sings, the artificer-god supported his steps, the maiden followed the high-priestess to the temple.

Tisamenes was doomed: no power, no prayers could save the man who had done sacrilege to the shrine of Diana. His blood must be added to that of many a guiltless stranger which had been shed in vain atonement, until fate brought the rightful victim thither. So reasoned the kingly and priestly devotees, and night and day, until the day of sacrifice came, thankful libations were poured upon the shrine, and paeans were chanted in joy that the rightful sacrifice was come. Tisamenes lay in his prison, awaiting the time, calm, if not happy. Erotion, whose wild eyes gleamed with a yet wilder inspiration, so that none dared look upon her or stay her feet: Erotion went hither and thither at her own will, flitting about like a phantom - now in the city, now at the shrine, and then in the very prison where the captive lay. Sometimes she would look upon her father with eyes of fearful calmness, and then weep over him in frantic despair, repeating the agonized cry which had first rung in the fatal cave, "My father, my father, thou shalt not die!"

At last a sudden purpose seemed to give her strength and firmness. Some days before the yearly festival of Diana, whose midnight rites were to be crowned with a human sacrifice - the death of Tisamenes - Erotion, alone and unaided, passed from the prison doors to the palace of Thoas. The barbarian King of Taurica sat among his counsellors, when he was told that a maiden craved audience. In the midst of a throng of savage men the virgin priestess passed,

185

until she stood like a vision of light before the throne of the King, and preferred her request - the prayer of a child for a father's life.

"King," she cried - all listening, for was she not the priestess Erotion, the chosen of Diana? "Remember, the very memory of the crime has passed away from earth: she who sinned was punished - oh, how sorely: and oceans of innocent blood have since then wiped out the stain. The goddess requires no more. O Thoas, be merciful!" and through the streaming hair the face of Erotion, beautiful as that of Venus herself, was lifted up to the monarch, as she knelt at the foot of the throne.

Alcinous, the son of Thoas, arose and knelt beside her.

"O King, O father, be merciful! hear the child who pleads for a father." Erotion turned towards the youth her lovely face in thankfulness, and again repeated, "Be merciful." But Thoas would not hear. Then the maiden rose up from her knees; her whole countenance was changed - she was no longer the weeping girl, but the inspired priestess, who, with gleaming eyes and uplifted arms, poured forth her dreaded denunciations.

"Since thou hearest not prayers, tyrant, hear the words of one in whom the spirit of the divinity speaks. How darest thou defile the pure shrine of Diana with human blood? How darest thou make her whom the goddess saved at Aulis, the high-priestess of a rite as murderous as that to which she herself was once doomed? Hear, O King! I see in the dim future the end of all this - I see the victim saved - the shrine deserted - the sacred statue borne away - the fane dishonoured; and all this shall surely be seen by thine own eyes likewise, if thou dost not hearken unto me."

A dead silence pervaded the assembly. Thoas looked on the maiden whose passionate prophecies had struck terror into all hearts, and he quailed beneath her heroic gaze.

"Priestess," he said, and his tone was like a suppliant, not a king, "take off thy curse; thy father's blood shall not be on my hands. He shall depart to a far country; and may he, and such as he, never more come nigh the shrine of Diana Taurica!"

Without a word of acknowledgment, but with the air of

186

one who had discharged a prophetic mission, Erotion glided from the presence-chamber. Many eyes followed her retreating form, so graceful in its youthful dignity; but the longest and most lingering gaze was that of the young and noble warrior, Alcinous.

Chapter V

It was once again the high festival in honour of Diana Taurica. The young novices, the priestesses, even Iphigenia herself, had donned their green tunics, and were celebrating in the forest the rites of the huntress-queen. Green leaves danced, and sunbeams glimmered among the trees, through glades where Pan might have piped to the Hamadryads, or Silenus presided at the revels of the young Bacchus and the Fauns. The virgins of the temple felt the beauty of the spot, and songs of delight rose up from the lonely wood.

Erotion was among the band; but her heart was too full to sympathize with their joyous sports: she seemed weighed down by excess of happiness, and sought to be alone, to realize the blissful certainty that her father would not die.

The King had pledged his royal word that the horrible sacrifice should not take place; that at midnight the prisoner should be conveyed to the sea-shore, placed in a boat, and left to the mercy of the same ocean deities, who had wafted him to Taurica. More than this Erotion dared not implore - but she feared little the wrath of the waters, compared to that terrible doom which had seemed hanging over Tisamenes. Her heart was no longer oppressed - this new and beloved tie had weaned her thoughts from those imaginings which had haunted her from childhood, causing her to be looked upon as one inspired. Earthly affections had sprung up within her young bosom; she clung to life, for the world was no more solitary ; she forgot even her mysterious dream in the devotion of filial love.

Erotion quitted her companions, and wandered to a

lonely and quiet dell, which no human foot save her own had ever entered: only the hind came hither with her fawns, and the nightingale broke the stillness with her music. As Erotion entered, she heard her name breathed in tones low and tender as those which wooed Ariadne on the shore of Naxos. She turned, and beside her stood a youth, so beautiful in face, so graceful in form, that Apollo when keeping the flocks of Admetus was not fairer. It was Alcinous, the prince of Taurica.

Grateful tears came to the eyes of Erotion, as she remembered how he had knelt before his father's throne, and joined his prayer to hers; and then she trembled - for even to the King's son it was death to be found in the sacred wood.

"I bless thee - I will ever remember thee, gentle and noble prince," cried Erotion; "but stay not here."

He heard her words as if understanding them not; but gazed on her as if it were a deity whom he beheld.

"Erotion - beautiful Erotion - hast thou ever seen a shadow following thy footsteps day after day, haunting thee in the temple, in the forest, to the very prison-doors - and knewest not that it was I? Erotion, I say not that I love thee - I worship thee, I adore thee - I kneel before thee now as thou dost kneel before thy goddess. I would die for thee, and yet I dare not ask of thee one answering word - Erotion, I dare not say, 'Love me!' "

The young girl listened to these new and strange words, as if she heard them in a dream: no blush dyed her cheek, no maidenly shame bent her head.

"Why sayest thou that I love thee not?" she answered, calmly; "I love all that is good and beautiful on earth: the birds, the trees - why should I not love thee? Thou, too, didst entreat for my father, whom I love best of all."

Alcinous looked at her, and saw that in that pure and heavenly mind there was no trace of a love like that which consumed him. He dashed himself on the ground at her feet, and cried in passionate tones -

"Erotion, this is not love like mine for thee; thou must love me - me only - as thy mother loved thy father. Thou

188

must leave all for my sake, as I for thine - home, father, country. Oh, maiden, this is love."

She turned on him her calm, soft eyes, and said -

"Alcinous, the love of which thou speakest, is not for me. I am a priestess - I have never felt thus. Rise, dear prince, and talk no more of such love. Do not grieve," she continued, in sweet and compassionate tones, as Alcinous lifted from the grass his face, bedewed with burning tears. "Do no grieve - I pity thee - I love thee with the only love I can give; but I am vowed to heaven and to my father - he is saved, and I am happy."

Again the youth burst forth impetuously -

"Erotion, dost thou believe that false oath? - Thy father *must* perish - his freedom is but a stratagem - no power can save him from death."

The young priestess grew cold as marble, but she stood immovable before her lover. He went on rapidly -

"Tisamenes must die - a subtle and lingering poison will be administered in the farewell cup of Chian wine; then pretended liberty will be given to him, when already bound in the iron fetters of slow but certain death."

"Is there no hope?" said Erotion, in a tone so deadly calm, that it was terrible to hear.

"None; for the guards are sworn to see that the poison-cup has been drained before the prisoner is set free."

A light from the setting sun illumined the face of Erotion. It became radiant with joy, until it was all but divine. Alcinous saw it not: with bowed head he pursued his vows and prayers -

"Erotion, thou wilt be left alone - thy father will die; oh, let me be thy comforter - let me teach thee to love as I love thee. Come, my beloved."

"Not yet - not yet," murmured Erotion, in a strangely altered voice; "the goddess must be obeyed; I see it now - I hear the mystic song - it is destiny. Yes, Alcinous, I come."

Wild with rapturous joy, Alcinous pressed her hand to his lips, his breast, his brow, and then vanished through the trees, as the singing train of priestesses was heard approaching nearer.

When the moon had risen, and the choral hymn to Cynthia was yet pealing through the city, Erotion came to the gate of the prison where Tisamenes of Crete, now freed from the chains which had bound his limbs, waited for the blessed time of liberty. His daughter stood beside him, and kissed his hands, his robe, with a rapturous expression of joy.

"The hour is almost come, my father," she cried, "and thou wilt be free. We shall depart hence, I and thou; far over the sea we will sail together. Ay," she continued, "this night I shall cross it - the wild, wild sea - the desert shore - I remember all."

And then a shivering came over the maiden, and her words sank in broken murmurings.

"Thou art not afraid, my child," said Tisamenes, "not even of the gloomy ocean, when I am with thee."

"No, no," hastily cried Erotion; "I think but of thee - I am happy, most happy, O my father."

As she spoke, her eyes glanced anxiously round the prison, and rested on a goblet of carved wood, filled to the brim with Chian wine.

"I thirst, I thirst, my father," said Erotion, in low tones, as her head drooped upon his shoulder; "I have been on a weary journey in the forest this day; wilt thou give me to drink?"

Tisamenes placed the cup in his daughter's hand.

"The gods have been good to us this day; it is meet we should acknowledge their benefits," she said. "O thou, whom we worship as Diana Triformis, accept the offering I bring thee now - a libation not unworthy of thee." And lifting upwards her calm eyes, Erotion poured on the floor of the dungeon a few drops from the goblet; then putting it to her lips she drained it to the dregs.

"My father, my father," she cried, throwing herself on the breast of Tisamenes, as the guard of Thoas entered. "The will of Diana is accomplished; thou art indeed saved!"

Chapter VI

Beneath the silence of the midnight moon, a boat put off from the shore of Taurica. In it were only an old man and a girl, Tisamenes of Crete and his daughter. The little vessel had scarcely spread its hoary wings, when a dark figure sprang from behind a rock, and plunging into the sea, pursued the boat. Soon from the waves that revelled around its prow, rose the head of Alcinous; his golden locks dripping with brine, and his eyes eagerly fixed where Erotion sat, silent and calm, by her father's side. Tisamenes drew the youth into the boat.

"Thou wouldst leave me, then, Erotion," Alcinous cried, passionately, "but it shall not be so. I will follow thee wherever thou goest, whether thou lovest me or not - through life, unto death."

"Be it so, Alcinous," replied the young priestess in her own low tones. She took his hand, pressed it softly in hers, and then turned again to her father.

Hour after hour the three floated over the ocean, which lay sleeping in the moonlight, nor suffered one angry wave to rise on its bosom, to bring fear or danger to the fugitives. Erotion half reclined in her father's arms, while Alcinous lay crouched at her feet, never turning his eyes from her, except to look anxiously and mournfully at Tisamenes of Crete. Erotion spoke little; was it only the moonlight that made her countenance appear at times so deadly pale? Alcinous thought so, but the expression it wore was so divine that a feeling of awe crept over him, stilling even the passionate emotions of his love. At times he fancied the cold sea-breeze made her whole frame tremble; now and then he saw her lips quiver; she would clasp her father's hand with an agonized movement, and be calm again.

The moon sank, and the night grew dark. A heavy sleep, which Alcinous thought was the forerunner of death, fell upon Tisamenes. The youth hardly dared to breathe, lest he should bring anguish to her he loved so well. Anxiously did he watch for the first streak of dawn, and, as it appeared, a

191

cold wandering hand touched his lips, thrilling his inmost frame.

It was too dark to see Erotion's face; but her voice sounded faint and quivering.

"Alcinous, my father sleeps; tell him all is well with me. It was I who drank of the doomed cup: I have fulfilled my destiny; he is saved!"

A light sigh, a faint movement, were all that Alcinous distinguished: the little cold hand still lay on his cheek - sealing up all horror and anguish in an awful peace. Ere long the broad sunbeam glided over the water, and rested on the sleepers; one wrapped in the calm slumber of weariness after toil; the other - ay, she lay sleeping also, but it was eternal rest.

As Alcinous looked, he saw what seemed a white dove rise in the air. Whence it came he knew not; it hovered awhile over the vessel, then spread its dazzling wings to the sun, and departed. The youth watched it as it flew over the brightening sea, over the lovely shore to which they were safely drifting, over the blue mountains higher and higher, until he saw it no more. Then Alcinous knew that it was the spirit of the beautiful, the self-devoted one whom the gods had loved and taken away - that it was the soul of Erotion.

ALFRED TENNYSON (1809-1892) was the third writer included in these pages to be elevated to the peerage. He was one of the leading poets of the Victorian era, and in 1850 he succeeded Wordsworth as poet laureate. The poems in his early collections of 1830 and 1833 were replete with classical and folkloristic imagery; the latter included "The Lady of Shallott" and "The Lotus-Eaters". In 1842 he issued a selection of these older works together with some previously unpublished items, including "Morte d'Arthur".

"Morte D'Arthur" ultimately became the seed of the *Idylls of the King*, which was first issued in segments between 1859 and 1885; the whole sequence was published in its final form in 1891. Though not as wide-ranging as Malory's *Morte D'Arthur*, the *Idylls* present the entire life-story of Arthur and the history of Lancelot, as well as a wealth of detail concerning minor characters. Tennyson's became the definitive nineteenth century version of the group of legends, and it embodies a thoroughly Victorian attitude to the adultery of Guenevere (who is made to grovel on the floor while Arthur denounces her at length, before eventually offering his forgiveness).

Some of Tennyson's contemporaries disliked the *Idylls* intensely and thought them inferior work (although they sold very well indeed), but some modern critics have found in them a daringly original symbolic vision of impending apocalypse. However they are evaluated, though, the *Idylls* remain one of the most significant lenses through which modern eyes perceive the substance of Arthurian legend, and Tennyson's work in this vein consequently has a highly significant place in the evolution of British fantasy.

MORTE D'ARTHUR

by Alfred Lord Tennyson

So all day long the noise of battle roll'd
Among the mountains by the winter sea;
Until King Arthur's table, man by man,
Had fall'n in Lyonnesse about their Lord,
King Arthur: then, because his wound was deep,
The bold Sir Bedivere uplifted him,
Sir Bedivere, the last of all his knights,
And bore him to a chapel nigh the field,
A broken chancel with a broken cross,
That stood on a dark strait of barren land.
On one side lay the Ocean, and on one
Lay a great water, and the moon was full.
Then spake King Arthur to Sir Bedivere:
"The sequel of to-day unsolders all
The goodliest fellowship of famous knights
Whereof this world holds record. Such a sleep
They sleep - the men I loved. I think that we
Shall never more, at any future time,
Delight our souls with talk of knightly deeds,
Walking about the gardens and the halls
Of Camelot, as in the days that were.
I perish by this people which I made, -
Tho' Merlin sware that I should come again
To rule once more - but let what will be, be,
I am so deeply smitten thro' the helm
That without help I cannot last till morn.
Thou therefore take my brand Excalibur,
Which was my pride: for thou rememberest how
In those old days, one summer noon, an arm
Rose up from out the bosom of the lake,
Clothed in white samite, mystic, wonderful,
Holding the sword - and how I row'd across
And took it, and have worn it, like a king

And, wheresoever I am sung or told
In aftertime, this also shall be known:
But now delay not: take Excalibur,
And fling him far into the middle mere:
Watch what thou seeëst, and lightly bring me word."
To him replied the bold Sir Bedivere:
"It is not meet, Sir King, to leave thee thus,
Aidless, alone, and smitten thro' the helm.
A little thing may harm a wounded man.
Yet I thy hest will all perform at full,
Watch what I see, and lightly bring thee word."
So saying, from the ruin'd shrine he stept.
And in the moon athwart the place of tombs,
Where lay the mighty bones of ancient men,
Old knights, and over them the sea-wind sang
Shrill, chill, with flakes of foam. He, stepping down
By zig-zag paths, and juts of pointed rock,
Came on the shining levels of the lake.
There drew he forth the brand Excalibur,
And o'er him, drawing it, the winter moon,
Brightening the skirts of a long cloud, ran forth
And sparkled keen with frost against the hilt:
For all the haft twinkled with diamond sparks,
Myriads of topaz-lights, and jacinth-work
Of subtlest jewellery. He gazed so long
That both his eyes were dazzled, as he stood,
This way and that dividing the swift mind.
In act to throw: but at the last it seem'd
Better to leave Excalibur conceal'd
There in the many-knotted waterflags,
That whistled stiff and dry about the marge.
So strode he back slow to the wounded King.
Then spake King Arthur to Sir Bedivere:
"Hast thou perform'd my mission which I gave?
What is it thou has seen? or what has heard?"
And answer made the bold Sir Bedivere:
"I heard the ripple washing in the reeds,
And the wild water lapping on the crag."

To whom replied King Arthur, faint and pale:
"Thou hast betray'd thy nature and thy name,
Not rendering true answer, as beseem'd
Thy fëalty, nor like a noble knight:
For surer sign had follow'd, either hand,
Or voice, or else a motion of the mere,
This is a shameful thing for men to lie.
Yet now, I charge thee, quickly go again
As thou art lief and dear, and do the thing
I bad thee, watch, and lightly bring me word."
Then went Sir Bedivere the second time
Across the ridge, and paced beside the mere,
Counting the dewy pebbles, fix'd in thought;
But when he saw the wonder of the hilt,
How curiously and strangely chased, he smote
His palms together, and he cried aloud,
"And if indeed I cast the brand away,
Surely a precious thing, one worthy note,
Should thus be lost for ever from the earth,
Which might have pleased the eyes of many men.
What good should follow this, if this were done?
What harm, undone? deep harm to disobey,
Seeing obedience is the bond of rule.
Were it well to obey then, if a king demand
An act unprofitable, against himself?
The King is sick, and knows not what he does.
What record, or what relic of my lord
Should be to aftertime, but empty breath
And rumours of a doubt? but were this kept,
Stored in some treasure-house of mighty kings,
Some one might show it at a joust of arms,
Saying, "King Arthur's sword, Excalibur,
Wrought by the lonely maiden of the Lake.
Nine years she wrought it, sitting in the deeps
Upon the hidden bases of the hills."
So might some old man speak in the aftertime
So all the people, winning reverence.
But now much honour and much fame were lost."

So spake he, clouded with his own conceit,
And hid Excalibur the second time,
And so strode back slow to the wounded King.
Then spoke King Arthur, breathing heavily:
"What is it thou hast seen? or what hast heard?"
And answer made the bold Sir Bedivere:
"I heard the water lapping on the crag,
And the long ripple washing in the reeds."
To whom replied King Arthur, much in wrath:
"Ah, miserable and unkind, untrue.
Unknightly, traitor-hearted! Woe is me!
Authority forgets a dying king,
Laid widow'd of the power in his eye
That bow'd the will. I see thee what thou art,
For thou, the latest-left of all my knights,
In whom should meet the offices of all,
Thou wouldst betray me for the precious hilt;
Either from lust of gold, or like a girl
Valuing the giddy pleasure of the eyes.
Yet, for a man may fail in duty twice,
And the third time may prosper, get thee hence:
But, if thou spare to fling Excalibur,
I will arise and slay thee with my hands."
Then quickly rose Sir Bedivere, and ran,
And, leaping down the ridges lightly, plunged
Among the bulrush-beds, and clutch'd the sword,
And strongly wheel'd and threw it. The great brand
Made lightnings in the splendour of the moon,
And flashing round and round, and whirl'd in an arch,
Shot like a streamer of the northern morn,
Seen where the moving isles of winter shock
By night, with noises of the northern sea.
So flash'd and fell the brand Excalibur:
But ere he dipt the surface, rose an arm
Clothed in white samite, mystic, wonderful,
And caught him by the hilt, and brandish'd him
Three times, and drew him under in the mere.
And lightly went the other to the King.

Then spoke King Arthur, drawing thicker breath:
"Now see I by thine eyes that this is done.
Speak out: what is it thou has heard, or seen ?"
And answer made the bold Sir Bedivere:
"Sir King, I closed mine eyelids, lest the gems
Should blind my purpose, for I never saw,
Nor shall see, here or elsewhere, till I die,
Not tho' I live three lives of mortal men,
So great a miracle as yonder hilt.
Then with both hands I flung him, wheeling him;
But when I look'd again, behold an arm,
Clothed in white samite, mystic, wonderful,
That caught him by the hilt, and brandish'd him
Three times, and drew him under in the mere."
And answer made King Arthur, breathing hard:
"My end draws nigh; 'tis time that I were gone.
Make broad thy shoulders to receive my weight,
And bear me to the margin; yet I fear
My wound hath taken cold, and I shall die."
So saying, from the pavement he half rose,
Slowly, with pain, reclining on his arm,
And looking wistfully with wide blue eyes
As in a picture. Him Sir Bedivere
Remorsefully regarded thro' his tears,
And would have spoken, but he found not words,
Then took with care, and kneeling on one knee,
O'er both his shoulders drew the languid hands,
And rising bore him thro' the place of tombs.
But, as he walk'd, King Arthur panted hard,
Like one that feels a nightmare on his bed
When all the house is mute. So sigh'd the King,
Muttering and murmuring at his ear, "Quick, quick!
I fear it is too late, and I shall die."
But the other swiftly strode from ridge to ridge,
Clothed with his breath, and looking,as he walk'd,
Larger than human on the frozen hills.
He heard the deep behind him, and a cry
Before. His own thought drove him like a goad.

Dry clash'd his harness in the icy caves
And barren chasms, and all to left and right
The bare black cliff clang'd round him, as he based
His feet on juts of slippery crag that rang
Sharp-smitten with the dint of armed heels-
And on a sudden, lo! the level lake,
And the long glories of the winter moon.
Then saw they how there hove a dusky barge,
Dark as a funeral scarf from stem to stern,
Beneath them; and descending they were ware
That all the decks were dense with stately forms
Black-stoled, black-hooded, like a dream - by these
Three Queens with crowns of gold - and from them rose
A cry that shiver'd to the tingling stars,
And, as it were one voice, an agony
Of lamentation, like a wind, that shrills
All night in a waste land, where no one comes,
Or hath come, since the making of the world.
Then murmur'd Arthur, "Place me in the barge,"
And to the barge they came. There those three Queens
Put forth their hands, and took the King, and wept.
But she, that rose the tallest of them all
And fairest, laid his head upon her lap,
And loos'd the shattered casque, and chafed his hands,
And call'd him by his name, complaining loud,
And dropping bitter tears against his brow
Striped with dark blood: for all his face was white
And colourless, and like the wither'd moon
Smote by the fresh beam of the springing east;
And all his greaves and cuisses dash'd with drops
Of onset; and the light and lustrous curls -
That made his forehead like a rising sun
High from the dais-throne - were parch'd with dust;
Or, clotted into points and hanging loose,
Mix'd with the knightly growth that fringed his lips.
So like a shatter'd column lay the King;
Not like that Arthur who, with lance in rest,
From spur to plume a star of tournament,

Shot thro' the lists at Camelot, and charged
Before the eyes of ladies and of kings.
Then loudly cried the bold Sir Bedivere,
"Ah! my Lord Arthur, whither shall I go?
Where shall I hide my forehead and my eyes?
For now I see the true old times are dead,
When every morning brought a noble chance,
And every chance brought out a noble knight.
Such times have been not since the light that led
The holy Elders with the gift of myrrh.
But now the whole ROUND TABLE is dissolved
Which was an image of the mighty world;
And I, the last, go forth companionless,
And the days darken round me, and the years,
Among new men, strange faces, other minds."
And slowly answered Arthur from the barge:
"The old order changeth, yielding place to new,
And God fulfils Himself in many ways,
Lest one good custom should corrupt the world.
Comfort thyself: what comfort is in me?
I have lived my life, and that which I have done
May He within Himself make pure! but thou
If thou shouldst never see my face again,
Pray for my soul. More things are wrought by prayer
Than this world dreams of. Wherefore, let thy voice
Rise like a fountain for me night and day.
For what are men better than sheep or goats
That nourish a blind life within the brain,
If, knowing God, they lift not hands of prayer
Both for themselves and those who call them friend?
For so the whole round earth is every way
Bound by gold chains about the feet of God.
But now farewell. I am going a long way
With these thou seeëst - if indeed I go -
(For all my mind is clouded with a doubt)
To the island-valley of Avilion;
Where falls not hail, or rain, or any snow,
Nor ever wind blows loudly; but it lies

Deep-meadow'd, happy, fair with orchard-lawns
And bowery hollows crown'd with summer sea,
Where I will heal me of my grievous wound."
So said he, and the barge with oar and sail
Moved from the brink, like some full-breasted swan
That, fluting a wild carol ere her death,
Ruffles her pure cold plume, and takes the flood
With swarthy webs. Long stood Sir Bedivere
Revolving many memories, till the hull
Look'd one black dot against the verge of dawn,
And on the mere the wailing died away.

      Here ended Hall, and our last light, that long
Had wink'd and threaten'd darkness, flared and fell·
At which the Parson, sent to sleep with sound,
And waked with silence, grunted "Good!" but we
Sat rapt: it was the tone with which he read -
Perhaps some modern touches here and there
Redeem'd it from the charge of nothingness -
Or else we loved the man and prized his work;
I know not: but we sitting, as I said,
The cock crew loud; as at that time of year
The lusty bird takes every hour for dawn:
Then Francis, muttering, like a man ill-used,
"There now - that's nothing!" drew a little back,
And drove his heel into the smoulder'd log,
That sent a blast of sparkles up the flue:
And so to bed; where yet in sleep I seem'd
To sail with Arthur under looming shores,
Point after point; till on to dawn, when dreams
Begin to feel the truth and stir of day,
To me, methought, who waited with a crowd,
There came a bark that, blowing forward, bore
King Arthur, like a modern gentleman
Of stateliest port; and all the people cried,
"Arthur is come again: he cannot die."
Then those that stood upon the hills behind
Repeated - "Come again, and thrice as fair;"

And, further inland, voices echoed - "Come
With all good things, and war shall be no more."
At this a hundred bells began to peal,
That with the sound I woke, and heard indeed
The clear church-bells ring in the Christmas morn.

LEWIS CARROLL was the pseudonym used by the Reverend Charles Lutwidge Dodgson (1832-1898) on *Alice's Adventures in Wonderland* (1865) and its sequel *Through the Looking Glass and What Alice Found There* (1872), the two classic works of Victorian children's fantasy. Dodgson used his expertise in logical sophistry and his fondness for tricky wordplay to devastating effect in these two stories, whose adult readers cannot have realised how deftly they mocked and subverted the rigidities of the Victorian world-view in producing a phantasmagorically-disguised account of its follies.

The Hunting of the Snark (1876) is equally fine, but perhaps even Dodgson did not know quite what he had accomplished or how, because he seemed to lose the knack entirely afterwards. The overlong and unutterably tedious fairy romance contained in *Sylvie and Bruno* (1889) and *Sylvie and Bruno Concluded* (1893) tries to be constructive instead of anarchic, and the abysmal magnitude of its failure is startling.

"The Walking Stick of Destiny " is one of the earliest stories that Dodgson wrote, but it already demonstrates his predilection for linguistic and logical tomfoolery; it was rescued from a manuscript version penned in 1850 or thereabouts for posthumous publication in 1932.

203

THE WALKING STICK OF DESTINY

By Lewis Carroll

Chapter I

The Baron was pacing his tapestried chamber two mortal hours ere sunrise. Ever and anon he would pause at the open casement, and gaze from its giddy height on the ground beneath. Then a stern smile would light up his gloomy brow and muttering to himself in smothered accents, " 'twill do" he would again resume his lonely march.

Uprose the glorious sun, and illumined the darkened world with the light of day: still was the haughty Baron pacing his chamber, albeit his step was hastier and more impatient than before, and more than once he stood motionless, listening anxiously and eagerly, then turned with a disappointed air upon his heel, while a darker shade passed over his brow. Suddenly the trumpet which hung at the castle gate gave forth a shrill blast: the Baron heard it, and savagely beating his breast with both his clenched fists, he murmured in bitter tone "the time draws nigh, I must nerve myself for action." Then, throwing himself into an easy chair, he hastily drank off the contents of a large goblet of wine which stood on the table, and in vain attempted to assume an air of indifference. The door was suddenly thrown open and in a loud voice an attendant announced "Signor Blowski!"

"Be seated! Signor! you are early this morn, and Alonzo! ho! fetch a cup of wine for the Signor! spice it well, boy! ha! ha! ha!" and the Baron laughed loud and boisterously, but the laugh was forced and hollow, and died quickly away. Meanwhile the stranger, who had not uttered a syllable, carefully divested himself of his hat and gloves, and seated himself opposite to the Baron, then having quietly waited till the Baron's laughter had subsided, he commenced in a harsh grating tone, "The Baron Muggzwig greets you, and sends you this"; why did a sudden paleness overspread the Baron Slogdod's features? why did his fingers tremble, so that he could scarcely open the letter? for one moment he glanced at it, and then raising his head, "Taste the wine, Signor," he said in strangely altered tone, "regale yourself, I pray," handing him one of the goblets which had just been brought in.

The Signor received it with a smile, put his lips to it, and then quietly changing goblets with the Baron without his perceiving it, swallowed half the contents at a draught. At that moment Baron Slogdod looked up, watched him for a moment as he drank, and smiled the smile of a wolf.

For full ten minutes there was a dead silence through the apartment, and then the Baron closed the letter, and raised his face: their eyes met: the Signor had many a time faced a savage tiger at bay without flinching, but now he involuntarily turned away his eyes. Then did the Baron speak in calm and measured tone: "You know, I presume, the contents of this letter?" the Signor bowed, "and you await an answer?" "I do". "*This*, then, is my answer," shouted the Baron, rushing upon him, and in another moment he had precipitated him from the open window. He gazed after him for a few seconds as he fell, and then tearing up the letter which lay on the table into innumerable pieces, he scattered them to the wind.

Chapter II

"One! two! three!" The magician set down the bottle, and sank exhausted into a seat: "Nine weary hours," he sighed, as he wiped his smoking brow, "nine weary hours have I been toiling, and only got to the eight-hundred and thirty-second ingredient! a-well! I verily believe Martin Wagner hath ordered three drops of everything on the face of this earth in his prescription. However, there are only a hundred and sixty-eight ingredients more to put in - 'twill soon be done - then comes the seething - and then - " He was checked in his soliloquy by a low timid rap outside: " 'Tis Blowski's knock," muttered the old man, as he slowly undid the bars

205

and fastenings of the door, "I marvel what brings *him* here at this late hour. He is a bird of evil omen: I do mistrust his vulture face. - Why! how now, Signor?" he cried, starting back in surprise as his visitor entered, "where got you that black eye? and verily your face is bruised like any rainbow! who has insulted you? or rather, " he muttered in an undertone, "whom have you been insulting, for that were the more likely of the two."

"Never mind my face, good father, " hastily answered Blowski, "I only tripped up, coming home last night in the dark, that's all, I do assure you. But I am now come on other business - I want advice - or rather I should say I want your opinion - on a difficult question - suppose a man was to - suppose two men - suppose there were two men, A and B -" "suppose! suppose!" contemptuously muttered the magician, "and suppose these men, good father, that is A, was to bring B a letter, then we'll suppose A read the letter, that is B, and then B tried - I mean A tried - to poison B - I mean A - and then suppose" - "My son," here interposed the old man, "is this a general case you are putting? Methinks you state it in a marvellously confused manner." "Of *course* it's a general case," savagely answered Blowski, "and if you'd just listen instead of interrupting, methinks you'd understand it better!" "Proceed, my son," mildly replied the other.

"And then suppose A - that is B - threw A out of the window - or rather," he added in conclusion, being himself by this time a little confused, "or rather I should have said the other way." The old man rubbed his beard, and mused for some time: "Aye, aye," he said at length, "I see, A - B - so so - B poisons A - " "No! no! " cried the signor, "B *tries* to poison A, he didn't really do it, I changed the - I mean," he hastily added, turning crimson as he spoke, "you're to *suppose* that he doesn't really do it." "Aye!" continued the magician, "it's all clear *now* - B - A - to be sure - but what has all this to do with your cut face?" he suddenly asked. "Nothing whatever," stammered Blowski, "I've told you once that I cut my face by a fall from my horse -" "Ah! well! let's see," repeated the other in a low voice, "tripped up in the dark -

206

fell from his horse - hm! hm! - yes, my lad, *you're* in for it - I should say," he continued in a louder voice, "it were better - but troth I know not yet what the question is." "Why, what had B better do," said the signor. "But who is B?" inquired the magician, "standeth B for Blowski?" "No," was the reply, "I meant A." "Oh!" returned he, "*now* I perceive - but verily I must have time to consider it, so adieu, fair sir," and, opening the door he abruptly showed his visitor out: "And now," said he to himself, "for the mixture - let me see - three drops of - yes, yes, my lad, *you're* in for it."

Chapter III

It had struck twelve o'clock two minutes and a quarter. The Baron's footman hastily seized a large goblet, and gasped with terror as he filled it with hot, spiced wine.
" 'Tis past the hour, 'tis past," he groaned in anguish, "and surely I shall now get the red hot poker the Baron hath so often promised me, oh! woe is me! would that I had prepared the Baron's lunch before!" and, without pausing a second he grasped in one hand the steaming goblet and flew along the lofty passages with the speed of a race horse. In less time than we take to relate it he reached the Baron's apartment, opened the door, and - remained standing on tiptoe, not daring to move one way or the other, petrified with utter astonishment. "Now then! donkey!" roared the Baron, "why stand you there staring your eyes out like a great toad in a fit of apoplexy?" (the Baron was remarkably choice in his similes:) "what's the matter with you? speak out! can't you?"

The unfortunate domestic made a desperate effort to speak, and managed at length to get out the words "Noble Sir!" "Very good! that's a very good beginning!" said the Baron in a rather pacified tone for he liked being called 'noble', "go ahead! don't be all day about it!" "Noble Sir!" stammered the alarmed man, "where - where - ever - is - the stranger?" "*Gone!*" said the Baron sternly and emphatically, pointing unconsciously his thumb over his right shoulder, "gone! he had other visits to pay, so he *condescended* to go and pay them - but where's my wine?" he abruptly asked, and his attendant was only too glad to place the goblet in his hands, and get out of the room.

The Baron drained the goblet at a draught, and then walked to the window: his late victim was no longer to be seen, but the Baron, gazing on the spot where he had fallen muttered to himself with a stern smile, "Methinks I see a dint in the ground." At that moment a mysterious looking figure passed by, and the Baron, as he looked after him, could not help thinking, "I wonder who that is!" Long time he gazed after his retreating footsteps, and still the only thought which rose to his mind was "I do wonder who that is!"

Chapter IV

Down went the western sun, and darkness was already stealing over the earth when for the second time that day the trumpet which hung at the Baron's gate was blown. Once more did the weary domestic ascend to his master's apartment, but this time it was a stranger whom he ushered in, "Mr Milton Smith!" The Baron hastily rose from his seat at the unwonted name, and advanced to meet his visitor.

"Greetings fair, noble sir," commenced the illustrious visitor, in a pompous tone and with a toss of the head, "it betided me to hear of your name and abode, and I made high resolve to visit and behold you ere night!" "Well, fair sir, I hope you are satisfied with the sight," interrupted the Baron, wishing to cut short a conversation he neither understood nor liked. "It rejoiceth me," was the reply, "nay, so much so that I could wish to prolong the pleasure, for there is a Life and Truth in those tones which recall to me scenes of earlier days - " "Does it indeed?" said the Baron, considerably puzzled. "Ay soothly," returned the other; "and now I bethink me," walking to the window, "it was the country likewise I did desire to look upon; 'tis fine, is't not?" "It's a very fine country," replied the Baron, adding internally, "and I wish

208

you were well out of it!"

The stranger stood some minutes gazing out of the window, and then said, suddenly turning to the Baron, "You must know, fair sir, that I am a poet!" "Really?" replied he, "and pray what's that?" Mr Milton Smith made no reply, but continued his observations, "Perceive you, mine host, the enthusiastic halo which encircles yon tranquil mead?" "The quickset hedge, you mean," remarked the Baron rather contemptuously, as he walked up to the window. "My mind," continued his guest, "feels alway a bounding - and a longing - for - what is True and Fair in Nature, and - and - see you not the gorgeous rusticity - I mean sublimity, which is wafted over, and as it were intermingled with the verdure - that is, you know, the grass?" " Intermingled with the grass? oh! you mean the buttercups?" said the other, "yes, they've a very pretty effect." "Pardon me," replied Mr Milton Smith, "I meant not that, but- but I could almost poetise thereon!

'Lovely meadow, thou whose fragrance
Beams beneath the azure sky,

"Where repose the lowly -" "Vagrants," suggested the Baron: "Vagrants!" repeated the poet, staring with astonishment, "Yes, vagrants, gipsies you know," coolly replied his host, "there are very often some sleeping down in the meadow." The inspired one shrugged his shoulders, and went on.

"Where repose the lowly violets," "Violets doesn't rhyme half as well as vagrants," argued the Baron. "Can't help that," was the reply:

"Murmuring gently" - "oh my eye!" said the Baron, finishing the line for him, "so there's one stanza done, and now I must wish you good night; you're welcome to a bed, so, when you've done poetising, ring the bell, and the servant will show you where to sleep." "Thanks," replied the poet, as the Baron left the room.

"Murmuring gently with a sigh - Ah! *that's* all right," he continued when the door was shut, and leaning out of the window he gave a low whistle. The mysterious figure in a cloak immediately emerged from the bushes and said in a whisper, "All right?" "*All right*," returned the poet, "I've sent the old covey to sleep with some poetry, by the bye I nearly forgot that stanza you taught me, I got into *such* a fix! However the coast is clear now, so look sharp." The figure then produced a rope ladder from under his cloak, which the poet proceeded to draw up.

Chapter V

READER! dare you enter once more the cave of the great Magician? If your heart be not bold, abstain: close these pages: read no more. High in air suspended hung the withered forms of two black cats; between was an owl, resting on a self-supported hideous viper.

The spiders were crawling on the long grey hair of the great Astrologer, as he wrote with letters of gold an awful spell on the magic scroll which hung from the deadly viper's mouth. A strange figure like an animated potatoe with arms and legs hovered over the mystic scroll, and appeared to be reading the words upside down. Hark!

A shrill scream rolled round the cave, echoing from side to side till it died in the massive roof. Horror! yet did not the Magician's heart quail, albeit his little finger shook slightly thrice, and one of his grey hairs stood out straight from his head, erect with terror: there was one other that would have followed its example, but a spider was hanging on it, and it could not.

A flash of mystic light, black as the darkest ebony, now pervades the place, and in its momentary gleam the owl is seen to wink once. Dread omen! Did its supporting viper hiss? Ah no! that would be *too* terrible! In the deep dead silence which followed this thrilling event, a solitary sneeze was distinctly heard from the left-hand cat. Distinct, and now the Magician *did* tremble. "Gloomy spirits of the vasty deep!" he murmured in faltering tone, as his aged limbs seemed about to sink beneath him, "I did not call for ye: why come ye?" He spoke, and the potatoe answered, in hollow tone: "Thou didst!" then all was silence.

The magician recoiled in terror. What ! bearded by a potatoe! never! He smote his aged breast in anguish, and then collecting strength to speak, he shouted, "Speak but the word again, and on the spot I'll boil thee!" There was an ominous pause, long, vague, and mysterious. What is about to happen? The potatoe sobbed audibly, and its thick showering tears were heard falling heavily down on the rocky floor. Then slow, clear, and terrible came the awful words: "Gobno strodgol slok slabolgo!" and then in a low hissing whisper " 'tis time!"

"Mystery! mystery!" groaned the horrified Astrologer, "The Russian war cry! oh Slogdod! Slogdod! what hast thou done?" He stood expectant, tremulous; but no sound met his anxious ear; nothing but the ceaseless dribble of the far-off waterfall. At length a voice said "now!" and at the word the right-hand cat fell with a heavy thump to the earth. Then an Awful Form was seen, dimly looming through the darkness: it prepared to speak, but a universal cry of "corkscrews!" resounded through the cave, three voices cried "yes!" at the same moment, and it was light. Dazzling light, so that the Magician shuddering closed his eyes, and said, "It is a dream, oh that I could wake!" He looked up, and cave, Form, cats, everything were gone; nothing remained before him but the magic scroll and pen, a stick of red sealing wax, and a lighted wax taper.

"August potatoe!" he muttered, "I obey your potent voice." Then sealing up the mystic roll, he summoned a courier, and dispatched it: "Haste for thy life, post! haste! haste! for thy life post! haste!" were the last words the frightened man heard dinned in his ears as he galloped off.

Then with a heavy sigh the great magician turned back into the gloomy cave, murmuring in a hollow tone, "Now for the toad!"

Chapter VI

"HUSH!" The Baron slumbers! two men with stealthy steps are removing his strong-box. It is very heavy, and their knees tremble, partly with the weight, partly with fear. He snores and they both start: the box rattles, not a moment is to be lost, they hasten from the room. It was very, very hard to get the box out of the window but they did it at last, though not without making noise enough to waken ten ordinary sleepers: the Baron, luckily for them, was an *extra*ordinary sleeper.

At a safe distance from the castle they set down the box, and proceeded to force off the lid. Four mortal hours did Mr Milton Smith and his mysterious companion labour thereat: at sunrise it flew off with a noise louder than the explosion of fifty powder-magazines, which was heard for miles and miles around. The Baron sprang from his couch at the sound, and full furiously did he ring his bell: up rushed the terrified domestic, and tremblingly related when he got down stairs again, how "his Honour was wisibly frustrated, and pitched the poker at him more than ordinary savage-like!" But to return to our two adventurers: as soon as they recovered from the swoon into which the explosion had thrown them, they proceeded to examine the contents of the box. Mr M. Smith drew a long breath, and ejaculated, "Well! I never!" "Well! you never!" angrily repeated the other, "what's the good of going on like that? just tell us what's in the box, and don't make such an ass of yourself!" "My dear fellow! " interposed the poet, "I give you my honour -" "I wouldn't give twopence for your honour," retorted his friend, savagely tearing up the grass by handfuls, "give me what's in the box, that's a deal more valuable." "Well but you won't hear me out, I was just going to tell you; there's nothing whatever in the box but a walking-stick! and that's a fact; if you won't believe me, come and look yourself!" "You don't say so!" shouted his companion, springing to his feet, his laziness gone in a moment, "*surely* there's more than that!" "I tell you there isn't!" replied the poet rather sulkily, as he

212

stretched himself on the grass.

The other one however turned the box over, and examined it on all sides before he would be convinced, and then carelessly twirling the stick on his forefinger he began: "I suppose it's no use taking *this* to Baron Muggzwig? it'll be no sort of use." "Well, I don't know!" was the somewhat hesitating reply, "it might be as well - you see he didn't say what he expected -" "*I* know that, you donkey!" interrupted the other impatiently, "but I don't suppose he expected a walking-stick! if that had been all, do you think he'd have given us ten dollars a piece to do the job?" "I'm sure I can't say," muttered the poet: "Well! do as you please then!" said his companion angrily, and flinging the walking-stick at him as he spoke he walked hastily away.

Never had he of the hat and cloak thrown away such a good opportunity of making his fortune! At twelve o'clock that day a visitor was announced to Baron Muggzwig, and our poet entering placed the walking-stick in his hands. The Baron's eyes flashed with joy, and hastily placing a large purse of gold in his hand he said, "Adieu for the present, my dear friend! you shall hear from me again!" and then he carefully locked up the stick muttering, "nothing is now wanting but the toad!"

Chapter VII

The Baron Muggzwig was fat. Far be it from the humble author of these pages to insinuate that his fatness exceeded the bounds of proportion, or the manly beauty of the human figure, but he certainly was fat, and of that fact there is not the shadow of a doubt. It may perhaps have been owing to this fatness of body that a certain thickness and obtuseness of intellect was at times perceptible in the noble Baron. In his ordinary conversation he was, to say the least of it, misty and obscure, but after dinner or when at all excited his language certainly verged on the incomprehensible. This was perhaps owing to his liberal use of the parenthesis without any definite pause to mark the different clauses of the sentence. He used to consider his arguments unanswerable, and they certainly were so perplexing, and generally reduced his hearers to such a state of bewilderment and stupefaction, that few ever ventured to attempt an answer to them.

He usually however compensated in length for what his speeches wanted in clearness, and it was owing to this cause that his visitors, on the morning we are speaking of had to blow the trumpet at the gate three times before they were admitted, as the footman was at that moment undergoing a lecture from his master, supposed to have reference to the yesterday's dinner, but which, owing to a slight admixture of extraneous matter in the discourse, left on the footman's mind a confused impression that his master had been partly scolding him for not keeping a stricter watch on the fishing trade, partly setting forth his own private views on the management of railway shares, and partly finding fault with the bad arrangement of financial affairs in the moon.

In this state of mind it is not surprising that his first answer to their question, "Is the Baron at home?" should be, "The fish, sir, was the cook's affair, I had nothing whatsumdever to do with it," which on reflection he immediately afterwards corrected to, "the trains was late, so it was unpossible as the wine could come sooner." "The man is surely mad or drunk!" angrily exclaimed one of the strangers, no other than the mysterious man in a cloak: "Not so," was the reply in gentle voice, as the great magician stepped forward, "but let me interrogate him - ho! fellow!" he continued in a louder tone, "is thy master at home?" The man gazed at him for a moment like one in a dream, and then suddenly recollecting himself he replied, "I begs pardon, gentleman, the Baron *is* at home: would you please to walk in?" and with these words he ushered them up stairs.

On entering the room they made a low obeisance, and the Baron starting from his seat exclaimed with singular rapidity, "And even if you have called on behalf of Slogdod that infatuated wretch and I'm sure I've often told him -"

"We have called," gravely interrupted the Magician, "to ascertain whether -" "Yes," continued the excited Baron,"scores of times aye scores of times I have and you may believe me or not as you like for though - " "To ascertain," persisted the Magician, "whether you have in your possession, and if so -" "But yet" broke in Muggzwig, "he always would and as he used to say if - " " And if so," shouted the man in a cloak despairing of the Magician ever getting through the sentence, "to know what you would like to be done with regard to Signor Blowski." So saying, they retired a few steps, and waited for the Baron's reply, and their host, without further delay delivered the following remarkable speech: "And though I have no wish to provoke the enmity which considering the provocations I have received and really if you reckon them up they are more than any mortal man let alone a Baron for the family temper has been known for years to be beyond nay the royal family themselves will hardly boast of considering too that he has so long a time kept which I shouldn't have found out only that rascal Blowski said and how he could bring himself to tell all those lies I can't think for I have always considered him quite honest and of course wishing if possible to prove him innocent and the walking-stick since it is absolutely necessary in such matters and begging your pardon I consider the toad and all that humbug but that's between you and me and even when I had sent for it by two of my bandits and one of them bringing it to me yesterday for which I gave him a purse of gold and I hope he was grateful for it and though the employment of bandits is at all times and particularly in this case if you consider the but even on account of some civilities he showed me though I daresay there was something and by-the-bye perhaps that was the reason he pitched himself I mean him out of the window for -" here he paused, seeing that his visitors in despair had left the room. Now, Reader, prepare yourself for the last chapter.

All was silence. The Baron Slogdod was seated in the hall of his ancestors, in his chair of state, but his countenance wore not its usual expression of calm content: there was an uncomfortable restlessness about him which betokened a mind ill at ease, for why? closely packed in the hall around, so densely wedged together as to resemble one vast living ocean without a gap or hollow, were seated seven thousand human beings: all eyes were bent upon him, each breath was held in eager expectation, and he felt, he felt in his inmost heart, though he vainly endeavoured to conceal his uneasiness under a forced and unnatural smile, that something awful was about to happen. Reader! if your nerves are not adamant, turn not this page!

Before the Baron's seat there stood a table: what sat thereon? well knew the trembling crowds, as with blanched cheek and tottering knees they gazed upon it, and shrank from it even while they gazed: ugly, deformed, ghastly and hideous it sat, with large dull eyes, and bloated cheeks, the magic toad!

All feared and loathed it, save the Baron only, who rousing himself at intervals from his gloomy meditations, would raise his toe, and give it a sportive kick, of which it took not the smallest notice. *He* feared it not, no, deeper terrors possessed *his* mind, and clouded his brow with anxious thought.

Beneath the table was crouched a quivering mass, so abject and grovelling as scarce to bear the form of humanity: none regarded, and none pitied it.

Then outspake the Magician: "The man I accuse, if man indeed he be, is - Blowski!" At the word, the shrunken form arose, and displayed to the horrified assembly the well-known vulture face: he opened his mouth to speak, but no sound issued from his pale and trembling lips ...a solemn stillness settled on all around... the Magician raised the walking-stick of destiny, and in thrilling accents pronounced the fatal words: "Recreant vagabond! misguided reprobate!

216

receive thy due deserts!" ... Silently he sank to the earth...all was dark for a moment, ... returning light revealed to their gaze...a heap of mashed potatoe...a globular form faintly loomed through the darkness, and howled once audibly, then all was still. Reader, our tale is told.

WILLIAM MORRIS (1834-1896) was the most prolific British fantasy writer of the nineteenth century, and the fact that he produced the first full-length Secondary World fantasy, *The Wood Beyond the World* (1894), has moved him to a central position in the tradition in the eyes of commentators like Lin Carter.   Morris met Burne-Jones, Rossetti and Swinburne while he was at Oxford, and there became a member of the Pre-Raphaelite Brotherhood; he subsequently became a devout socialist . He helped to found the *Oxford and Cambridge Magazine* in 1856 and most of his early writings appeared there, including poems later reprinted in *The Defence of Guenevere and Other Poems* (1858) and several prose romances, including "A Dream" and the strange allegorical novella "The Hollow Land".

Morris's verse epics include the classical fantasies *The Life and Death of Jason* (1867) and *The Earthly Paradise* (1868).   He became greatly enamoured with the Icelandic sagas, which he imitated in *The Story of Sigurd the Volsung and the Fall of the Niblungs* (1876). *A Dream of John Ball* (1888) is a historical fantasy; *The House of the Wolfings* (1888) and *The Roots of the Mountains* (1889) are pseudo-sagas. His later fantastic romances were issued by his own Kelmscott Press between 1891 and 1897. The last two, *The Water of the Wondrous Isles* (1897) and the unfinished *The Sundering Flood* (1897) were dictated in the months before his death and are somewhat rough-hewn, but *The Story of the Glittering Plain* (1891) is a highly original re-casting of the story of Orpheus, and the long allegory *The Well at the World's End* (1896) is also interesting.   *Child Christopher and Goldilind the Fair* (1895) re-casts the legend of Havelock the Dane.

None of these works were as successful in their own day as Morris's Utopian romance *News from Nowhere* (1890) - one of several replies in kind to Edward Bellamy's hugely successful *Looking Backward, 2000-1887* (1888) - but the fashionability of contemporary Secondary World fantasy has helped to redeem their reputation and bring them back into print.

218

A DREAM

By William Morris

I dreamed once, that four men sat by the winter fire talking and telling tales, in a house that the wind howled round.

And one of them, the eldest, said: "When I was a boy, before you came to this land, that bar of red sand rock, which makes a fall in our river, had only just been formed; for it used to stand above the river in a great cliff, tunnelled by a cave about midway between the green-growing grass and the green-flowing river; and it fell one night, when you had not yet come to this land, no, nor your fathers.

"Now, concerning this cliff, or pike rather (for it was a tall slip of rock and not part of a range), many strange tales were told; and my father used to say, that in his time many would have explored that cave, either from covetousness (expecting to find gold therein), or from that love of wonders which most young men have, but fear kept them back. Within the memory of man, however, some had entered, and, so men said, were never seen on earth again; but my father said that the tales told concerning such, very far from deterring him (then quite a youth) from the quest of this cavern, made him all the more earnestly long to go; so that one day in his fear, my grandfather, to prevent him, stabbed him in the shoulder, so that he was obliged to keep his bed for long; and somehow he never went, and died at last without ever having seen the inside of the cavern.

"My father told me many wondrous tales about the place, whereof for a long time I have been able to remember nothing; yet, by some means or another, a certain story has grown up in my heart, which I will tell you something of: a story which no living creature ever told me, though I do not remember the time when I knew it not. Yes, I will tell you some of it, not all perhaps, but as much as I am allowed to tell."

219

The man stopped and pondered awhile, leaning over the fire where the flames slept under the caked coal: he was an old man, and his hair was quite white. He spoke again presently. "And I have fancied sometimes, that in some way, how I know not, I am mixed up with the strange story I am going to tell you". Again he ceased, and gazed at the fire, bending his head down till his beard touched his knees; then, rousing himself, said in a changed voice (for he had been speaking dreamily hitherto): "That strange-looking old house that you all know, with the limes and yew-trees before it, and the double line of very old yew-trees leading up from the gateway-tower to the porch - you know how no one will live there now because it is so eerie, and how even that bold bad lord that would come there, with his turbulent followers, was driven out in shame and disgrace by invisible agency. Well, in times past there dwelt in that house an old grey man, who was lord of that estate, his only daughter, and a young man, a kind of distant cousin of the house, whom the lord had brought up from a boy, as he was the orphan of a kinsman who had fallen in combat in his quarrel. Now, as the young knight and the young lady were both beautiful and brave, and loved beauty and good things ardently, it was natural enough that they should discover as they grew up that they were in love with one another; and afterwards, as they went on loving one another, it was, alas! not unnatural that they should sometimes have half-quarrels, very few and far between indeed, and slight to lookers-on, even while they lasted, but nevertheless intensely bitter and unhappy to the principal parties thereto. I suppose their love then, whatever it has grown to since, was not so all-absorbing as to merge all differences of opinion and feeling, for again there were such differences then. So, upon a time it happened, just when a great war had arisen , and Lawrence (for that was the knight's name) was sitting and thinking of war, and his departure from home; sitting there in a very grave, almost a stern mood, that Ella, his betrothed, came in, gay and sprightly, in a humour that Lawrence often enough could little understand, and this time liked less than ever, yet the bare sight of her made him yearn for her full heart, which he was not to have yet; so he caught her by the hand, and tried to draw her down to him, but she let her hand lie loose in his, and did not answer the pressure in which his heart flowed to hers; then he arose and stood before her, face to face, but she drew back a little, yet he kissed her on the mouth and said, though a rising in his throat almost choked his voice, "Ella, are you sorry I am going?" "Yea," she said, "and nay, for you will shout my name among the swordflashes, and you will fight for me." "Yes," he said, "for love and duty, dearest." "For duty? ah! I think, Lawrence, if it were not for me, you would stay at home and watch the clouds, or sit under the linden-trees singing dismal love ditties of your own making, dear knight: truly, if you turn out a great warrior, I too shall live in fame, for I am certainly the making of your desire to fight." He let drop his hands from her shoulders, where he had laid them, and said, with a faint flush over his face, "You wrong me, Ella, for, though I have never wished to fight for the mere love of fighting, and though," (and here again he flushed a little) "and though I am not, I well know, so free of the fear of death as a good man would be, yet for this duty's sake, which is really a higher love, Ella, love of God, I trust I would risk life, nay honour, even if not willingly, yet cheerfully at least." "Still duty, duty," she said; "you lay, Lawrence, as many people do, most stress on the point where you are weakest; moreover, those knights who in time past have done wild, mad things merely at their ladies' word, scarcely did so for duty; for they owed their lives to their country surely, to the cause of good, and should not have risked them for a whim, and yet you praised them the other day." "Did I?" said Lawrence; "well, and in a way they were much to be praised, for even blind love and obedience is well; but reasonable love, reasonable obedience is so far better as to be almost a different thing; yet, I think, if the knights did well partly, the ladies did altogether ill: for if they had faith in their lovers, and did this merely from a mad longing to see them do "noble" deeds, then had they but little faith in God, Who can, and at His good pleasure does give time and opportunity to every man, if he will but watch for it, to serve Him with reasonable service, and gain love and all noble things in greater measure thereby: but if these ladies did as they did, that they might prove their knights, then surely did they lack faith both in God and man. I do not think that two friends even could live together on such terms but for lovers - ah! Ella, Ella, why do you look so at me? on this day, almost the last, we shall be together for long; Ella, your face is changed, your eyes - O Christ! help her and me, help her, good Lord." "Lawrence," she said, speaking quickly and in jerks, "dare you, for my sake, sleep this night in the cavern of the red pike? for I say to you that, faithful or not, I doubt your courage." But she was startled when she saw him, and how the fiery blood rushed up to his forehead, then sank to his heart again, and his face became as pale as the face of a dead man: he looked at her and said, "Yes, Ella, I will go now; for what matter where I go?" He turned and moved toward the door; he was almost gone, when that evil spirit left her, and she cried out aloud, passionately, eagerly: "Lawrence, Lawrence, come back once more, if only to strike me dead with your knightly sword." He hesitated, wavered, turned, and in another moment she was lying in his arms weeping into his hair.

" 'And yet, Ella, the spoken word, the thought of our hearts cannot be recalled, I must go, and go this night too, only promise one thing.' 'Dearest what? you are always right!' 'Love, you must promise that if I come not again by to-morrow at moonrise, you will go to the red pike, and, having entered the cavern, go where God leads you, and seek me, and never leave that quest, even if it end not but with death.' 'Lawrence how your heart beats! poor heart! are you afraid that I shall hesitate to promise to perform that which is the only thing I could do? I know I am not worthy to be with you, yet I must be with you in body or soul, or body and soul will die.' They sat silent, and the birds sang in the garden of lilies beyond; then said Ella again; 'Moreover, let us pray God to give us longer life, so that if our natural lives are short for the accomplishment of this quest, we may have more, yea, even many more lives.' 'He will, my Ella,' said Lawrence, 'and I think, nay, I am sure that our wish will be granted; and I, too, will add a prayer, but will ask it

222

very humbly, namely, that he will give me another chance or more to fight in his cause, another life to live instead of this failure.' 'Let us pray too that we may meet, however long the time be before our meeting,' she said: so they knelt down and prayed, hand fast locked in hand meantime; and afterwards they sat in that chamber facing the east, hard by the garden of lilies; and the sun fell from his noontide light gradually, lengthening the shadows, and when he sank below the sky-line all the sky was faint, tender, crimson on a ground of blue; the crimson faded too, and the moon began to rise, but when her golden rim first showed over the wooded hills, Lawrence arose; they kissed one long trembling kiss, and then he went and armed himself; and their lips did not meet again after that, for such a long, long time, so many weary years; for he had said: 'Ella, watch me from the porch, but touch me not again at this time; only, when the moon shows level with the lily-heads, go into the porch and watch me from thence.'

"And he was gone; - you might have heard her heart beating while the moon very slowly rose, till it shone through the rose-covered trellises, level with the lily-heads; then she went to the porch and stood there, -

"And she saw him walking down toward the gateway tower, clad in his mail coat, with a bright, crestless helmet on his head, and his trenchant sword newly grinded, girt to his side; and she watched him going between the yew-trees, which began to throw shadows from the shining of the harvest moon. She stood there in the porch, and round by the corners of the eaves of it looked down towards her and the inside of the porch two serpent-dragons, carved in stone; and on their scales, and about their leering eyes, grew the yellow lichen; she shuddered as she saw them stare at her, and drew closer toward the half-open door; she, standing there, clothed in white from her throat till over her feet, altogether ungirdled; and her long yellow hair, without plait or band, fell down behind and lay along her shoulders, quietly, because the night was without wind, and she too was now standing scarcely moving a muscle.

"She gazed down the line of the yew-trees, and watched how, as he went for the most part with a firm step, he yet shrank somewhat from the shadows of the yews; his long brown hair flowing downward, swayed with him as he walked; and the golden threads interwoven with it, as the fashion was with the warriors in those days, sparkled out from among it now and then; and the faint, far-off moonlight lit up the waves of his mail coat; he walked fast, and was disappearing in the shadows of the trees near the moat, but turned before he was quite lost in them, and waved his ungauntletted hand; then she heard the challenge of the warder, the falling of the drawbridge, the swing of the heavy wicket-gate on its hinges; and, into the brightening lights, and deepening shadows of the moonlight he went from her sight; and she left the porch and went to the chapel, all that night praying earnestly there.

"But he came not back again all the next day, and Ella wandered about that house pale, and fretting her heart away; so when night came and the moon, she arrayed herself in that same raiment that she had worn on the night before, and went toward the river and the red pike.

"The broad moon shone right over it by the time she came to the river; the pike rose up from the other side, and she thought at first that she would have to go back again, cross over the bridge, and so get to it; but, glancing down on the river just as she turned, she saw a little boat fairly gilt and painted, and with a long slender paddle in it, lying on the water, stretching out its silken painter as the stream drew it downwards, she entered it, and taking the paddle made for the other side; the moon meanwhile turning the eddies to silver over the dark green water: she landed beneath the shadow of that great pile of sandstone, where the grass grew green, and the flowers sprang fair right up to the foot of the bare barren rock; it was cut in many steps till it reached the cave, which was overhung by creepers and matted grass; the stream swept the boat downwards, and Ella, her heart beating so as almost to stop her breath, mounted the steps slowly, slowly. She reached at last the platform below the cave, and turning, gave a long gaze at the moonlit country; 'her last,' she said; then she moved, and the cave hid her as the water of the warm seas close over the pearl-diver.

"Just so the night before had it hidden Lawrence. And they never came back, they two: - never, the people say. I wonder what their love has grown to now; ah! they love, I know, but cannot find each other yet: I wonder also if they ever will."

So spoke Hugh the white-haired. But he who sat over against him, a soldier as it seemed, black-bearded, with wild grey eyes that his great brows hung over far; he, while the others sat still, awed by some vague sense of spirits being very near them; this man, Giles, cried out "Never? old Hugh, it is not so. - Speak! I cannot tell you how it happened, but I know it was not so, not so: - speak quick, Hugh! tell us all, all!"

"Wait a little, my son, wait," said Hugh; "the people indeed said they never came back again at all, but I, but I - Ah! the time is long past over." So he was silent, and sank his head on his breast, though his old thin lips moved, as if he talked softly to himself, and the light of past days flickered in his eyes.

Meanwhile Giles sat with his hands clasped finger over finger, tightly, "till the knuckles whitened;" his lips were pressed firmly together; his breast heaved as though it would burst, as though it must be rid of its secret. Suddenly he sprang up, and in a voice that was a solemn chant, began: "In full daylight, long ago, on a slumberously-wrathful, thunderous afternoon of summer"; - then across his chant ran the old man's shrill voice: " On an October day, packed close with heavy-lying mist, which was more than mere autumn mist" : - the solemn stately chanting dropped, the shrill voice went on; Giles sank down again, and Hugh standing there swaying to and fro to the measured ringing of his own shrill voice, his long beard moving with him, said: -

"On such a day, warm, and stifling so that one could scarcely breathe even down by the sea-shore, I went from bed to bed in the hospital of the pest-laden city with my soothing draughts and medicines. And there went with me a holy woman, her face pale with much watching; yet I think even without those same desolate lonely watchings her face would still have been pale. She was not beautiful, her face being somewhat peevish-looking; apt, she seemed, to be made angry by trifles, and, even on her errand of mercy, she spoke roughly to those she tended: - no, she was not beautiful, yet I could not help gazing at her, for her eyes were very beautiful and looked out from her ugly face as a fair maiden might look from a grim prison between the window-bars of it.

"So, going through that hospital, I came to a bed at last, whereon lay one who had not been struck down by fever or plague, but had been smitten through the body with a sword by certain robbers, so that he had narrowly escaped death. Huge of frame, with stern suffering face he lay there; and I came to him, and asked him of his hurt, and how he fared, while the day grew slowly toward even, in that pest-chamber looking toward the west; the sister came to him soon and knelt down by his bed-side to tend him.

"O Christ! As the sun went down on that dim misty day, the clouds and the thickly-packed mist cleared off, to let him shine on us, on that chamber of woes and bitter unpurifying tears; and the sunlight wrapped those two, the sick man and the ministering woman, shone on them - changed, changed utterly. Good Lord! How was I struck dumb, nay, almost blinded by that change; for there - yes there, while no man but I wondered; there, instead of the unloving nurse, knelt a wonderfully beautiful maiden, clothed all in white, and with long golden hair down her back. Tenderly she gazed at the wounded man, as her hands were put about his head, lifting it up from the pillow but a very little; and he no longer the grim, strong wounded man, but fair, and in the first bloom of youth; a bright polished helmet crowned his head, a mail coat flowed over his breast, and his hair streamed down long from his head, while from among it here and there shone out threads of gold.

226

"So they spake thus in a quiet tone: 'Body and soul together again, Ella, love; how long will it be now before the last time of all?' 'Long,' she said, 'but the years pass; talk no more, dearest, but let us think only, for the time is short, and our bodies call up memories, change love to better even than it was in the old time.'

"Silence so, while you might count a hundred, then with a great sigh: 'Farewell, Ella, for long,' - 'Farewell, Lawrence,' and the sun sank, all was as before.

"But I stood at the foot of the bed pondering, till the sister coming to me, said: 'Master Physician, this is no time for dreaming; act - the patients are waiting, the fell sickness grows worse in this hot close air; feel' - (and she swung open the casement), 'the outer air is no fresher than the air inside; the wind blows dead towards the west, coming from the stagnant marshes; the sea is like a stagnant pool too, you can scarce hear the sound of the long, low surge breaking.' I turned from her and went up to the sick man, and said: 'Sir Knight, in spite of all the sickness about you, you yourself better strangely, and another month will see you with your sword girt to your side again.' 'Thanks, kind master Hugh,' he said, but impatiently, as if his mind were on other things, and he turned in his bed away from me restlessly.

"And till late that night I ministered to the sick in that hospital; but when I went away, I walked down to the sea, and paced there to and fro over the hard sand: and the moon showed bloody with the hot mist, which the sea would not take on its bosom, though the dull east wind blew it onward continually. I walked there pondering till a noise from over the sea made me turn and look that way; what was that coming over the sea? Laus Deo! the WEST WIND: Hurrah! I feel the joy I felt then over again now, in all its intensity. How came it over the sea? first, far out to sea, so that it was only just visible under the red-gleaming moon-light, far out to sea, while the mists above grew troubled, and wavered, a long level bar of white; it grew nearer quickly, it rushed on toward me fearfully fast, it gathered form, strange, misty, intricate form - the ravelled foam of the green sea; then oh!

hurrah! I was wrapped in it, - the cold salt spray - drenched with it, blinded by it, and when I could see again, I saw the great green waves rising, nodding and breaking, all coming on together; and over them from wave to wave leaped the joyous WEST WIND; and the mist and the plague clouds were sweeping back eastward in wild swirls; and right away were they swept at last, till they brooded over the face of the dismal stagnant meres, many miles away from our fair city, and there they pondered wrathfully on their defeat.

"But somehow my life changed from the time when I beheld the two lovers, and I grew old quickly." He ceased; then after a short silence said again; "And that was long ago, very long ago, I know not when it happened."

So he sank back again, and for a while no one spoke; till Giles said at last:

"Once in full daylight I saw a vision, while I was waking, while the eyes of men were upon me: long ago on the afternoon of a thunderous summer day, I sat alone in my fair garden near the city; for on that day a mighty reward was to be given to the brave man who had saved us all, leading us so mightily in that battle a few days back; now the very queen, the lady of the land, whom all men reverenced almost as the Virgin Mother, so kind and good and beautiful she was, was to crown him with flowers and gird a sword about him; after the 'Te Deum' had been sung for the victory, and almost all the city were at that time either in the Church, or hard by it, or else were by the hill that was near the river where the crowning was to be: but I sat alone in the garden of my house as I said; sat grieving for the loss of my brave brother, who was slain by my side in that same fight.

"I sat beneath an elm-tree; and as I sat and pondered on that still, windless day, I heard suddenly a breath of air rustle through the boughs of the elm. I looked up, and my heart almost stopped beating, I knew not why, as I watched the path of that breeze over the bowing lilies and the rushes by the fountain; but when I looked to the place whence the breeze had come, I became all at once aware of an appearance that told me why my heart stopped beating. Ah!

there they were, those two whom before I had but seen in dreams by night, now before my waking eyes in broad daylight. One, a knight (for so, he seemed), with long hair mingled with golden threads, flowing over his mail coat, and a bright crestless helmet on his head, his face sad-looking, but calm; and by his side, but not touching him, walked a wondrously fair maiden, clad in white, her eyelids just shadowing her blue eyes: her arms and hands seeming to float along with her as she moved on quickly, yet very softly; great rest on them both, though sorrow gleamed through it.

"When they came opposite to where I stood, these two stopped for a while, being in nowise shadowy, as I have heard men say ghosts are, but clear and distinct. They stopped close by me, as I stood motionless, unable to pray; they turned to each other, face to face, and the maiden said,'Love, for this our last true meeting before the end of all, we need a witness; let this man, softened by sorrow, even as we are, go with us.'

"I never heard such music as her words were; though I used to wonder when I was young whether the angels in heaven sung better than the choristers sang in our church, and though, even then the sound of the triumphant hymn came up to me in a breath of wind, and floated round me, making dreams, in that moment of awe and great dread, of the old long-past days in that old church, of her who lay under the pavement of it; whose sweet voice once, once long ago, once only to me - yet I shall see her again." He became silent as he said this, and no man cared to break in upon his thoughts, seeing the choking movement in his throat, the fierce clenching of hand and foot, the stiffening of the muscles all over him; but soon, with an upward jerk of his head, he threw back the long elf locks that had fallen over his eyes while his head was bent down, and went on as before:

"The knight passed his hand across his brow, as if to clear away some mist that had gathered there, and said, in a deep murmurous voice, 'Why the last time, dearest, why the last time? Know you not how long a time remains yet? the old man came last night to the ivory house and told me it would be a hundred years, ay, more, before the happy end.' 'So long,' she said; 'so long; ah! love, what things words are; yet this is the last time; alas! alas! for the weary years! my words, my sin!' 'O love, it is very terrible,' he said; ' I could almost weep, old though I am, and grown cold with dwelling in the ivory house: O, Ella, if you only knew how cold it is there, in the starry nights when the north wind is stirring; and there is no fair colour there, naught but the white ivory, with one narrow line of gleaming gold over every window, and a fathom's-breadth of burnished gold behind the throne. Ella, it was scarce well done of you to send me to the ivory house.' 'Is it so cold, love?' she said, 'I knew it not; forgive me! but as to the matter of a witness, some one we must have, and why not this man?' 'Rather old Hugh,' he said, 'or Cuthbert, his father; they have both been witnesses before.' 'Cuthbert,' said the maiden solemnly, 'has been dead twenty years; Hugh died last night.' " (Now, as Giles said these words, carelessly, as though not heeding them particularly, a cold sickening shudder ran through the other two men, but he noted it not and went on.) " ' This man then be it, ' said the knight, and therewith they turned again, and moved on side by side as before; nor said they any word to me, and yet I could not help following them, and we three moved on together, and soon I saw that my nature was changed, and that I was invisible for the time, for, though the sun was high, I cast no shadow, neither did any man that we past notice us, as we made toward the hill by the riverside.

"And by the time we came there the queen was sitting at the top of it, under a throne of purple and gold, with a great band of knights gloriously armed on either side of her; and their many banners floated over them. Then I felt that those two had left me, and that my own right visible nature was returned; yet still did I feel strange, and as if I belonged not wholly to this earth. And I heard one say, in a low voice to his fellow, ' See, Sir Giles is here after all; yet, how came he here, and why is he not in armour among the noble knights yonder, he who fought so well? How wild he looks too!' 'Poor knight,' said the other, ' he is distraught with the loss of of his brother; let him be; and see, here comes the noble stranger knight, our deliverer.' As he spoke, we heard a great sound of trumpets, and therewithal a long line of knights on foot wound up the hill towards the throne, and the queen rose up, and the people shouted; and, at the end of all the procession went slowly and majestically the stranger knight; a man of noble presence he was, calm, and graceful to look on; grandly he went amid the gleaming of their golden armour; himself clad in the rent mail and tattered surcoat he had worn on the battle-day; bareheaded, too; for, in that fierce fight, in the thickest of it, just where he rallied our men, one smote off his helmet, and another, coming from behind would have slain him, but that my lance bit into his breast.

"So, when they had come within twenty paces of the throne, the rest halted, and he went up by himself toward the queen; and she, taking the golden hilted sword in her left hand, with her right hand caught him by the wrist, when he would have knelt to her, and held him so, tremblingly, and cried out, 'No, no, thou noblest of all knights, kneel not to me: have we not heard of thee even before thou camest hither? how many widows bless thee, how many orphans pray for thee, how many happy ones that would be widows and orphans but for thee, sing to their children, sing to their sisters, of thy flashing sword, and the heart that guides it! And now, O noble one! thou has done the very noblest deed of all, for thou hast kept grown men from weeping shameful tears! Oh truly! the greatest I can do for thee is very little; yet, see this sword, golden hilted, and the stones flash out from it,' (then she hung it round him) 'and see this wreath of lilies and roses for thy head; lilies no whiter than thy pure heart, roses no tenderer than thy true love; and here, before all these my subjects, I fold thee, noblest, in my arms, so, so.' Ay, truly it was strange enough! those two were together again; not the queen and the stranger knight, but the young-seeming knight and the maiden I had seen in the garden. To my eyes they clung together there; though they say, that to

231

the eyes of all else, it was but for a moment that the queen held both his hands in hers; to me also, amid the shouting of the multitude, came an undercurrent of happy song: 'Oh! truly, very truly, my noblest, a hundred years will not be long after this.' 'Hush! Ella, dearest, for talking makes the times speed; think only.'

"Pressed closed to each other, as I saw it, their bosoms heaved - but I looked away - alas! when I looked again, I saw naught but the stately stranger knight, descending, hand in hand, with the queen, flushed with joy and triumph, and the people scattering flowers before them.

"And that was long ago, very long ago." So he ceased; then Osric, one of the two younger men, who had been sitting in awe-struck silence all this time, said, with eyes that dared not meet Giles's, in a terrified half whisper, as though he meant not to speak, "How long?" Giles turned round and looked him full in the face, till he dragged his eyes up to his own, then said, "More than a hundred years ago."

"So they all sat silent, listening to the roar of the south-west wind; and it blew the windows so, that they rocked in their frames.

"Then suddenly, as they sat thus, came a knock at the door of the house; so Hugh bowed his head to Osric, to signify that he should go and open the door; so he arose, trembling, and went.

"And as he opened the door the wind blew hard against him, and blew something white against his face, then blew it away again, and his face was blanched, even to his lips; but he plucking up heart of grace, looked out, and there he saw, standing with her face upturned in speech to him, a wonderfully beautiful woman, clothed from her throat till over her feet in long white raiment, ungirt, unbroidered, and with a long veil, that was thrown off from her face, and hung from her head, streaming out in the blast of the wind; which veil was what had struck against his face: beneath her veil her golden hair streamed out too, and with the veil, so that it touched his face now and then. She was very fair, but she did not look young either, because of her statue-like

232

features. She spoke to him slowly and queenly; 'I pray you give me shelter in your house for an hour, that I may rest, and so go on my journey again.' He was too much terrified to answer in words, and so only bowed his head; and she swept past him in stately wise to the room where the others sat, and he followed her, trembling.

"A cold shiver ran through the other men when she entered and bowed low to them, and they turned deadly pale, but dared not move; and there she sat while they gazed at her, sitting there and wondering at her beauty, which seemed to grow every minute; though she was plainly not young, oh no, but rather very, very old, who could say how old? there she sat, and her long, long hair swept down in one curve from her head, and just touched the floor. Her face had the tokens of a deep sorrow on it, ah! a mighty sorrow, yet not so mighty as that it might mar her ineffable loveliness; that sorrow-mark seemed to gather too, and at last the gloriously-slow music of her words flowed from her lips: 'Friends, has one with the appearance of a youth come here lately; one with long brown hair, interwoven with threads of gold, flowing down from out of his polished steel helmet; with dark blue eyes and high white forehead, and mail coat over his breast, where the light and shadow lie in waves as he moves; have you seen such an one, very beautiful?'

"Then withal as they shook their heads fearfully in answer, a great sigh rose up from her heart, and she said: 'Then must I go away again presently, and yet I thought it was the last night of all.'

"And so she sat awhile with her head resting on her hand; after, she arose as if about to go, and turned her glorious head round to thank the master of the house; and they, strangely enough, though they were terrified at her presence, were yet grieved when they saw that she was going.

"Just then the wind rose higher than ever before, yet through the roar of it they could all hear plainly a knocking at the door again; so the lady stopped when she heard it, and, turning, looked full in the face of Herman the youngest, who thereupon, being constrained by that look, rose and went to the door; and as before with Osric, so now the wind blew strong against him; and it blew into his face, so as to blind him, tresses of soft brown hair mingled with glittering threads of gold; and blinded so, he heard some one ask him musically, solemnly, if a lady with golden hair and white raiment was in that house; so Herman, not answering in words, because of his awe and fear, merely bowed his head; then he was ware of some one in bright armour passing him, for the gleam of it was all about him, for as yet he could not see clearly, being blinded by the hair that had floated about him.

"But presently he followed him into the room, and there stood such an one as the lady had described; the wavering flame of the light gleamed from his polished helmet, touched the golden threads that mingled with his hair, ran along the rings of his mail.

"They stood opposite to each other for a little, he and the lady, as if they were somewhat shy of each other after their parting of a hundred years, in spite of the love which they had for each other; at last he made one step, and took off his gleaming helmet, laid it down softly, then spread abroad his arms, and she came to him, and they were clasped together, her head lying on his shoulder; and the four men gazed, quite awe-struck.

"And as they gazed, the bells of the church began to ring, for it was New-Year's-eve; and still they clung together, and the bells rang on, and the old year died.

"And there beneath the eyes of those four men the lovers slowly faded away into a heap of snow-white ashes. Then the four men kneeled down and prayed, and the next day they went to the priest, and told him all that had happened.

"So the people took those ashes and buried them in their church, in a marble tomb, and above it they caused to be carved their figures lying with clasped hands; and on the sides of it the history of the cave in the red pike.

"And in my dream I saw the moon shining on the

tomb, throwing fair colours on it from the painted glass; till a sound of music rose, deepened, and fainted; then I awoke".

> "No memory labours longer from the deep
> Gold mines of thought to lift the hidden ore
> That glimpses, moving up, than I from sleep
> To gather and tell o'er
> Each little sound and sight."

GEORGE MACDONALD (1824-1905) is, with William Morris, one of the two central figures in the development of Victorian fantasy. He was a clergyman for some years but resigned his ministry in 1851 because he could not help holding certain heretical views; his literary works can easily be seen as an attempt to explore and come to terms with these heresies. Most of his novels are non-supernatural, but some - like *Thomas Wingfold, Curate* (1876), which has a character whose spiritual troubles lead him to believe that he is the Wandering Jew - have allegorical intrusions. He was for a while the editor of the children's periodical *Good Words for the Young*, in which capacity he first began to produce moralistic fairy tales for children; several of his works in this vein are interpolated in *Adela Cathcart* (1864) and others were collected in *Dealings with the Fairies* (1867).

MacDonald's first fantastic novel was an extended allegorical fairy tale, *Phantastes: A Faerie Romance for Men and Women* (1858), quite without precedent in prose fiction, which was in the fullness of time to be a powerful influence on C. S. Lewis. The tale below is included in it as a story encountered by the hero in the course of his travels.

The allegorical discourse contained in *Phantastes* is further extrapolated in other works, including several children's stories. This added depth of meaning helps to give such stories as "The Golden Key", "The Carasoyn" and "The History of Photogen and Nycteris" (also known as "The Day Boy and the Night Girl") a place among the most interesting Victorian children's fantasies, alongside *Alice in Wonderland*. (MacDonald knew Dodgson, and read *Alice* in an early manuscript version - he may have been instrumental in persuading Dodgson to publish it.) MacDonald's longer works for children, all of which have allegorical undertones, are *At the Back of the North Wind* (1871), *The Princess and the Goblin* (1872), *The Wise Woman* (1875), and *The Princess and Curdie* (1883).

MacDonald's later fantasy novels for adults were *The Portent* (1864), a feverish account of a man accursed; and

Lilith (1895), an allegory whose peculiarity and ultimate lack of coherence reveal that MacDonald's painful doubts were unresolved to the bitter end. A ten-volume set of *Works of Fancy and Imagination* issued in 1871 includes almost all the fantasies MacDonald wrote before that date.

MacDonald developed his own theory of the Imagination - influenced like Coleridge's, by the German Romantics - in his essay "The Imagination its Functions and Culture" (1867), reprinted in *Orts* (1882).

THE WOMAN IN THE MIRROR

By George MacDonald

Cosmo von Wehrstahl was a student at the University of Prague. Though of a noble family, he was poor, and prided himself upon the independence that poverty gives; for what will not a man pride himself upon, when he cannot get rid of it? A favourite with his fellow students, he yet had no companions; and none of them had ever crossed the threshold of his lodging in the top of one of the highest houses in the old town. Indeed, the secret of much of that complaisance which recommended him to his fellows, was the thought of his unknown retreat, whither in the evening he could betake himself and indulge undisturbed in his own studies and reveries. These studies, besides those subjects necessary to his course at the University, embraced some less commonly known and approved; for in a secret drawer lay the works of Albertus Magnus and Cornelius Agrippa, along with others less read and more abstruse. As yet, however, he had followed these researches only from curiosity, and had turned them to no practical purpose.

His lodging consisted of one large low-ceiled room, singularly bare of furniture; for besides a couple of wooden chairs, a couch which served for dreaming on both by day and night, and a great press of black oak, there was very little in the room that could be called furniture. But curious instruments were heaped in the corners; and in one stood a skeleton, half-leaning against the wall, half-supported by a string about its neck. One of its hands, all of fingers, rested on the heavy pommel of a great sword that stood beside it. Various weapons were scattered about over the floor. The walls were utterly bare of adornment; for the few strange things, such as a large dried bat with wings dispread, the skin of a porcupine, and a stuffed sea-mouse, could hardly be reckoned as such. But although his fancy delighted in vagaries like these, he indulged his imagination with far different fare. His mind had never yet been filled with an absorbing passion; but it lay like a still twilight open to any wind, whether the low breath that wafts but odours, or the storm that bows the great trees till they strain and creak. He saw everything as through a rose-coloured glass. When he looked from his window on the street below, not a maiden passed but she moved as in a story, and drew his thoughts after her till she disappeared in the vista. When he walked in the streets, he always felt as if reading a tale, into which he sought to weave every face of interest that went by; and every sweet voice swept his soul as with the wing of a passing angel. He was in fact a poet without words; the more absorbed and endangered, that the springing waters were dammed back into his soul, where, finding no utterance, they grew, and swelled, and undermined. He used to lie on his hard couch, and read a tale or a poem, till the book dropped from his hand; but he dreamed on, he knew not whether awake or asleep, until the opposite roof grew upon his sense and turned golden in the sunrise. Then he arose too; and the impulses of vigorous youth kept him ever active, either in study or in sport, until again the close of the day left him free; and the world of night, which had lain drowned in the cataract of the day, rose up in his soul, with all its stars, and dim-seen phantom shapes. But this could hardly last long. Some one form must sooner or later step within the charmed circle, enter the house of life, and compel the bewildered magician to kneel and worship.

One afternoon, towards dusk, he was wandering dreamily in one of the principal streets, when a fellow student roused him by a slap on the shoulder, and asked him to accompany him into a little back alley to look at some old armour which he had taken a fancy to possess. Cosmo was considered an authority in every matter pertaining to arms, ancient or modern. In the use of weapons, none of the students could come near him; and his practical acquaintance with some had principally contributed to establish his authority in reference to all. He accompanied him willingly. They entered a narrow alley, and thence a dirty little court, where a low arched door admitted them into a heterogeneous assemblage of everything musty, and dusty, and old, that could well be imagined. His verdict on the armour was satisfactory, and his companion at once concluded the purchase. As they were leaving the place, Cosmo's eye was attracted by an old mirror of an elliptical shape, which leaned against the wall, covered with dust. Around it was some curious carving, which he could see but very indistinctly by the glimmering light which the owner of the shop carried in his hand. It was this carving that attracted his attention; at least so it appeared to him. He left the place, however, with his friend, taking no further notice of it. They walked together to the main street, where they parted and took opposite directions.

No sooner was Cosmo left alone, than the thought of the curious old mirror returned to him. A strong desire to see it more plainly arose within him, and he directed his steps once more towards the shop. The owner opened the door when he knocked, as if he had expected him. He was a little, old, withered man, with a hooked nose, and burning eyes constantly in a slow restless motion, and looking here and there as if after something that eluded them. Pretending to examine several other articles, Cosmo at last approached the mirror, and requested to have it taken down.

"Take it down yourself, master; I cannot reach it," said the old man.

Cosmo took it down carefully, when he saw that the carving was indeed delicate and costly, being both of admirable design and execution; containing withal many devices which seemed to embody some meaning to which he had no clue. This, naturally, in one of his tastes and temperament, increased the interest he felt in the old mirror; so much, indeed, that he now longed to possess it, in order to study its frame at his leisure. He pretended, however, to want it only for use; and saying he feared the plate could be of little service, as it was rather old, he brushed away a little of the dust from its face, expecting to see a dull reflection within. His surprise was great when he found the reflection brilliant, revealing a glass not only

240

uninjured by age, but wondrously clear and perfect (should the whole correspond to this part) even for one newly from the hands of the maker. He asked carelessly what the owner wanted for the thing. The old man replied by mentioning a sum of money far beyond the reach of poor Cosmo, who proceeded to replace the mirror where it had stood before.

"You think the price too high?" said the old man.

"I do not know that it is too much for you to ask," replied Cosmo; "but it is far too much for me to give."

The old man held up his light towards Cosmo's face.

"I like your look," said he.

Cosmo could not return the compliment. In fact, now he looked closely at him for the first time, he felt a kind of repugnance to him, mingled with a strange feeling of doubt whether a man or a woman stood before him.

"What is your name?" he continued.

"Cosmo von Wehrstahl."

"Ah, ah! I thought as much. I see your father in you. I knew your father very well, young sir. I dare say in some odd corners of my house, you might find some old things with his crest and cipher upon them still. Well, I like you: you shall have the mirror at the fourth part of what I asked for it; but upon one condition."

"What is that?" said Cosmo; for, although the price was still a great deal for him to give, he could just manage it; and the desire to possess the mirror had increased to an altogether unaccountable degree, since it had seemed beyond his reach.

"That if you should ever want to get rid of it again, you will let me have the first offer."

"Certainly," replied Cosmo, with a smile; adding, "a moderate condition indeed."

"On your honour?" insisted the seller.

"On my honour," said the buyer; and the bargain was concluded.

"I will carry it home for you," said the old man, as Cosmo took it in his hands.

"No, no; I will carry it myself," said he; for he had a

241

peculiar dislike to revealing his residence to any one, and more especially to this person, to whom he felt every moment a greater antipathy.

"Just as you please," said the old creature, and muttered to himself as he held his light at the door to show him out of the court: "Sold for the sixth time! I wonder what will be the upshot of it this time. I should think my lady had enough of it by now!"

Cosmo carried his prize carefully home. But all the way he had an uncomfortable feeling that he was watched and dogged. Repeatedly he looked about, but saw nothing to justify his suspicions. Indeed, the streets were too crowded and too ill lighted to expose very readily a careful spy, if such there should be at his heels. He reached his lodgings in safety, and leaned his purchase against the wall, rather relieved, strong as he was, to be rid of its weight; then, lighting his pipe, threw himself on the couch, and was soon lapt in the folds of one of his haunting dreams.

He returned home earlier than usual the next day, and fixed the mirror to the wall, over the hearth, at one end of this long room. He then carefully wiped away the dust from its face, and, clear as the water of a sunny spring, the mirror shone out from beneath the envious covering. But his interest was chiefly occupied with the curious carving of the frame. This he cleaned as well as he could with a brush; and then he proceeded to a minute examination of its various parts, in the hope of discovering some index to the intention of the carver. In this, however, he was unsuccessful; and, at length, pausing with some weariness and disappointment, he gazed vacantly for a few moments into the depth of the reflected room. But ere long he said, half aloud: "What a strange thing a mirror is! and what a wondrous affinity exists between it and a man's imagination! For this room of mine, as I beheld it in the glass, is the same, and yet not the same. It is not the mere representation of the room I live in, but it looks just as if I were reading about it in a story I like. All its commonness has disappeared. The mirror has lifted it out of the region of fact into the realm of art; and the very representing of it to me has clothed with interest that which was otherwise hard and bare; just as one sees with delight upon the stage the representation of a character from which one would escape in life as from something unendurably wearisome. But is it not rather that art rescues nature from the weary and sated regards of our senses, and the degrading injustice of our anxious everyday life, and, appealing to the imagination, which dwells apart, reveals Nature in some degree as she really is, and as she represents herself to the eye of the child, whose everyday life, fearless and unambitious, meets the true import of the wonder-teeming world around him, and rejoices therein without questioning? That skeleton, now - I almost fear it, standing there so still, with eyes only for the unseen, like a watch-tower looking across all the waste of this busy world into the quiet regions of rest beyond. And yet I know every bone and every joint in it as well as my own fist. And that old battle-axe looks as if any moment it might be caught up by a mailed hand, and, borne forth by the mighty arm, go crashing through casque, and skull, and brain, invading the Unknown with yet another bewildered ghost. I should like to live in *that* room if I could only get into it."

Scarcely had the half-moulded words floated from him, as he stood gazing into the mirror, when, striking him as with a flash of amazement that fixed him in his posture, noiseless and unannounced, glided suddenly through the door into the reflected room, with stately motion, yet reluctant and faltering step, the graceful form of a woman, clothed all in white. Her back only was visible as she walked slowly up to the couch in the further end of the room, on which she had laid herself wearily, turning towards him a face of unutterable loveliness, in which suffering, and dislike, and a sense of compulsion, strangely mingled with the beauty. He stood without the power of motion for some moments, with his eyes irrecoverably fixed upon her; and even after he was conscious of the ability to move, he could not summon up courage to turn and look on her, face to face, in the veritable chamber in which he stood. At length, with a sudden effort, in which the exercise of the will was so pure, that it seemed involuntary, he turned his face to the couch. It was vacant. In bewilderment, mingled with terror, he turned again to the mirror: there, on the reflected couch, lay the exquisite lady-form. She lay with closed eyes, whence two large tears were just welling from beneath the veiling lids; still as death, save for the convulsive motion of her bosom.

Cosmo himself could not have described what he felt. His emotions were of a kind that destroyed consciousness, and could never be clearly recalled. He could not help standing yet by the mirror, and keeping his eyes fixed on the lady, though he was painfully aware of his rudeness, and feared every moment that she would open hers, and meet his fixed regard. But he was, ere long, a little relieved; for, after a while, her eyelids slowly rose, and her eyes remained uncovered, but unemployed for a time; and when, at length, they began to wander about the room, as if languidly seeking to make some acquaintance with her environment, they were never directed towards him: it seemed nothing but what was in the mirror could affect her vision; and, therefore, if she saw him at all, it could only be his back, which, of necessity, was turned towards her in the glass. The two figures in the mirror could not meet face to face, except he turned and looked at her, present in his room; and, as she was not there, he concluded that if he were to turn towards the part in his room corresponding to that in which she lay, his reflection would either be invisible to her altogether, or at least it must appear to her to gaze vacantly towards her, and no meeting of the eyes would produce the impression of spiritual proximity. By-and-by her eyes fell upon the skeleton, and he saw her shudder and close them. She did not open them again, but signs of repugnance continued evident on her countenance. Cosmo would have removed the obnoxious thing at once, but he feared to discompose her yet more by the assertion of his presence which the act would involve. So he stood and watched her. The eyelids yet shrouded the eyes, as a costly case the jewel within; the troubled expression gradually faded from the countenance, leaving only a faint sorrow behind; the features settled into an unchanging expression of rest; and by these signs, and the slow regular motion of her breathing, Cosmo knew she slept. He could now gaze on her without embarrassment. He saw that her figure, dressed in the simplest robe of white, was worthy of her face; and so harmonious, that either the delicately moulded foot, or any figure of the equally delicate hand, was an index to the whole. As she lay, her whole form manifested the relaxation of perfect repose. He gazed till he was weary, and at last seated himself near the new-found shrine, and mechanically took up a book, like one who watches by a sick-bed. But his eyes gathered no thoughts from the page before him. His intellect had been stunned by the bold contradiction, to its face, of all its experience, and now lay passive, without assertion, or speculation, or even conscious astonishment; while his imagination sent one wild dream of blessedness after another coursing through his soul. How long he sat he knew not; but at length he roused himself, rose, and, trembling in every portion of his frame, looked again into the mirror. She was gone. The mirror reflected faithfully what his room presented, and nothing more. It stood there like a golden setting whence the central jewel has been stolen away - like a night-sky without the glory of its stars. She had carried with her all the strangeness of the reflected room. It had sunk to the level of the one without. But when the first pangs of his disappointment had passed, Cosmo began to comfort himself with the hope that she might return, perhaps the next evening, at the same hour. Resolving that if she did, she should not at least be scared by the hateful skeleton, he removed that and several other articles of questionable appearance into a recess by the side of the hearth, whence they could not possibly cast any reflection into the mirror; and having made his poor room as tidy as he could, sought the solace of the open sky and of a night wind that had begun to blow, for he could not rest where he was. When he returned, somewhat composed, he

245

could hardly prevail with himself to lie down on his bed; for he could not help feeling as if she had lain upon it; and for him to lie there would now be something like sacrilege. However, weariness prevailed; and laying himself on the couch, dressed as he was, he slept till day.

With a beating heart, beating till he could hardly breathe, he stood in dumb hope before the mirror, on the following evening. Again the reflected room shone as through a purple vapour in the gathering twilight. Everything seemed waiting like himself for a coming splendour to glorify its poor earthliness with the presence of a heavenly joy. And just as the room vibrated with the strokes of the neighbouring church bells, announcing the hour of six, in glided the pale beauty, and again laid herself on the couch. Poor Cosmo nearly lost his senses with delight. She was there once more! Her eyes sought the corner where the skeleton had stood, and a faint gleam of satisfaction crossed her face, apparently at seeing it empty. She looked suffering still, but there was less of discomfort expressed in her countenance than there had been the night before. She took more notice of the things about her, and seemed to gaze with some curiosity on the strange apparatus standing here and there in her room. At length, however, drowsiness seemed to overtake her, and again she fell asleep. Resolved not to lose sight of her this time, Cosmo watched the sleeping form. Her slumber was so deep and absorbing that a fascinating repose seemed to pass contagiously from her to him as he gazed upon her; and he started as if from a dream when the lady moved, and, without opening her eyes, rose, and passed from the room with the gait of a somnambulist.

Cosmo was now in a state of extravagant delight. Most men have a secret treasure somewhere. The miser has his golden hoard; the virtuoso his pet ring; the student his rare book; the poet his favourite haunt; the lover his secret drawer; but Cosmo had a mirror with a lovely lady in it. And now that he knew by the skeleton, that she was affected by the things around her, he had a new object in life: he would turn the bare chamber in the mirror into a room such as no lady need disdain to call her own. This he could effect only by furnishing and adorning his. And Cosmo was poor. Yet he possessed accomplishments that could be turned to account; although, hitherto, he had preferred living on his slender allowance, to increasing his means by what his pride considered unworthy of his rank. He was the best swordsman in the University; and now he offered to give lessons in fencing and similar exercises, to such as chose to pay him well for the trouble. His proposal was heard with surprise by the students; but it was eagerly accepted by many; and soon his instructions were not confined to the richer students, but were anxiously sought by many of the young nobility of Prague and its neighbourhood. So that very soon he had a good deal of money at his command. The first thing he did was to remove his apparatus and oddities into a closet in the room. Then he placed his bed and a few other necessaries on each side of the hearth, and parted them from the rest of the room by two screens of Indian fabric. Then he put an elegant couch for the lady to lie upon, in the corner where his bed had formerly stood; and, by degrees, every day adding some article of luxury, converted it, at length, into a rich boudoir.

Every night, about the same time, the lady entered. The first time she saw the new couch, she started with a half smile; then her face grew very sad, the tears came to her eyes, and she laid herself upon the couch, and pressed her face into the silken cushions, as if to hide from everything. She took notice of each addition and each change as the work proceeded; and a look of acknowledgment, as if she knew that some one was ministering to her, and was grateful for it, mingled with the constant look of suffering. At length, after she had lain down as usual one evening, her eyes fell upon some paintings with which Cosmo had just finished adorning the walls. She rose, and to his great delight, walked across the room, and proceeded to examine them carefully, testifying much pleasure in her looks as she did so. But again the sorrowful, tearful expression returned, and again she buried her face in the pillows of her couch.

247

Gradually, however, her countenance had grown more composed; much of the suffering manifest on her first appearance had vanished, and a kind of quiet, hopeful expression had taken its place; which, however, frequently gave way to an anxious, troubled look mingled with something of sympathetic pity.

Meantime, how fared Cosmo? As might be expected in one of his temperament, his interest had blossomed into love, and his love - shall I call it *ripened* , or - *withered* into passion. But, alas! he loved a shadow. He could not come near her, could not speak to her, could not hear a sound from those sweet lips, to which his longing eyes would cling like bees to their honey-founts. Ever and anon he sang to himself:

"I shall die for love of the maiden,"

and ever he looked again, and died not, though his heart seemed ready to break with intensity of life and longing. And the more he did for her, the more he loved her; and he hoped that, although she never appeared to see him, yet she was pleased to think that one unknown would give his life to her. He tried to comfort himself over his separation from her, by thinking that perhaps some day she would see him and make signs to him, and that would satisfy him; "for," thought he, " is not this all that a loving soul can do to enter into communion with another? Nay, how many who love never come nearer than to behold each other as in a mirror; seem to know and yet never know the inward life; never enter the other soul; and part at last, with but the vaguest notion of the universe on the borders of which they have been hovering for years? If I could but speak to her, and knew that she heard me, I should be satisfied." Once he contemplated painting a picture on the wall, which should, of necessity, convey to the lady a thought of himself; but, though he had some skill with the pencil, he found his hand tremble so much when he began the attempt, that he was forced to give it up.

"Who lives, he dies; who dies, he is alive."

One evening, as he stood gazing on his treasure, he thought he saw a faint expression of self-consciousness on her countenance, as if she surmised that passionate eyes were fixed upon her. This grew; till at last the red blood rose over her neck, and cheek, and brow. Cosmo's longing to approach her became almost delirious. This night she was dressed in an evening costume, resplendent with diamonds. This could add nothing to her beauty, but it presented it in a new aspect; enabled her loveliness to make a new manifestation of itself in a new embodiment. For essential beauty is infinite; and, as the soul of Nature needs an endless succession of varied forms to embody her loveliness, countless faces of beauty springing forth, not any two the same, at any one of her heart-throbs; so the individual form needs an infinite change of its environments, to enable it to uncover all the phases of its loveliness. Diamonds glittered from amidst her hair, half hidden in its luxuriance, like stars through dark rain clouds; and the bracelets on her white arms flashed all the colours of a rainbow of lightnings, as she lifted her snowy hands to cover her burning face. But her beauty shone down all its adornments. "If I might have but one of her foot to kiss," thought Cosmo "I should be content." Alas! he deceived himself, for passion is never content. Nor did he know that there are *two* ways out of her enchanted house. But, suddenly, as if the pang had been driven into his heart from without, revealing itself first in pain, and afterwards in definite form, the thought darted into his mind, "She has a lover somewhere. Remembered words of his bring the colour on her face now. I am nowhere to her. She lives in another world all day, and all night, after she leaves me. Why does she come and make me love her, till I, a strong man, am too faint to look upon her more?" He looked again, and her face was pale as a lily. A sorrowful compassion seemed to rebuke the glitter of the restless jewels, and the slow tears rose in her eyes. She left her room

249

sooner this evening than was her wont. Cosmo remained alone, with a feeling as if his bosom had been suddenly left empty and hollow, and the weight of the whole world was crushing in its walls. The next evening, for the first time since she began to come, she came not.

And now Cosmo was in wretched plight. Since the thought of a rival had occurred to him, he could not rest for a moment. More than ever he longed to see the lady face to face. He persuaded himself that if he but knew the worst he would be satisfied; for then he could abandon Prague, and find that relief in constant motion, which is the hope of all active minds when invaded by distress. Meantime he waited with unspeakable anxiety for the next night, hoping she would return; but she did not appear. And now he fell really ill. Rallied by his fellow students on his wretched looks, he ceased to attend the lectures. His engagements were neglected. He cared for nothing. The sky, with the great sun in it, was to him a heartless, burning desert. The men and women in the streets were mere puppets, without motives in themselves, or interest to him. He saw them all as on the everchanging field of a *camera obscura*. She - she alone and altogether - was his universe, his well of life, his incarnate good. For six evenings she came not. Let his absorbing passion, and the slow fever that was consuming his brain, be his excuse for the resolution which he had taken and begun to execute, before that time had expired.

Reasoning with himself, that it must be by some enchantment connected with the mirror, that the form of the lady was to be seen in it, he determined to attempt to turn to account what he had hitherto studied principally from curiosity. "For", said he to himself, "if a spell can force her presence in that glass (and she came unwillingly at first), may not a stronger spell, such as I know, especially with the aid of her half-presence in the mirror, if ever she appears again, compel her living form to come to me here? If I do her wrong, let love be my excuse. I want only to know my doom from her own lips." He never doubted, all the time, that she was a real earthly woman; or rather, that there was a woman, who, somehow or other, threw this reflection of her form into the magic mirror.

He opened his secret drawer, took out his books of magic, lighted his lamp, and read and made notes from midnight till three in the morning, for three successive nights. Then he replaced his books; and the next night went out in quest of the materials necessary for the conjuration. These were not easy to find; for; in love-charms and all incantations of this nature, ingredients are employed scarcely fit to be mentioned, and for the thought even of which, in connection with her, he could only excuse himself on the score of his bitter need. At length he succeeded in procuring all he required; and on the seventh evening from that on which she had last appeared, he found himself prepared for the exercise of unlawful and tyrannical power.

He cleared the centre of the room; stooped and drew a circle of red on the floor, around the spot where he stood; wrote in the four quarters mystical signs, and numbers which were all powers of seven or nine; examined the whole ring carefully, to see that no smallest break had occurred in the circumference; and then rose from his bending posture. As he rose, the church clock struck seven; and, just as she had appeared the first time, reluctant, slow, and stately, glided in the lady. Cosmo, trembled; and when turning, she revealed a countenance worn and wan, as with sickness or inward trouble, he grew faint, and felt as if he dared not proceed. But as he gazed on the face and form, which now possessed his whole soul, to the exclusion of all other joys and griefs, the longing to speak to her, to know that she heard him, to hear from her one word in return, became so unendurable, that he suddenly and hastily resumed his preparations. Stepping carefully from the circle, he put a small brazier into its centre. He then set fire to its contents of charcoal, and while it burned up, opened his window and seated himself, waiting, beside it.

It was a sultry evening. The air was full of thunder. A sense of luxurious depression filled the brain. The sky seemed to have grown heavy, and to compress the air

251

beneath it. A kind of purplish tinge pervaded the atmosphere, and through the open window came the scents of the distant fields, which all the vapours of the city could not quench. Soon the charcoal glowed. Cosmo sprinkled upon it the incense and other substances which he had compounded, and, stepping within the circle, turned his face from the brazier and towards the mirror. Then, fixing his eyes upon the face of the lady, he began with a trembling voice to repeat a powerful incantation. He had not gone far, before the lady grew pale; and then, like a returning wave, the blood washed all its banks with its crimson tide, and she hid her face in her hands. Then he passed to a conjuration stronger yet. The lady rose and walked uneasily to and fro in her room. Another spell; and she seemed seeking with her eyes for some object on which they wished to rest. At length it seemed as if she suddenly espied him; for her eyes fixed themselves full and wide upon his, and she drew gradually, and somewhat unwillingly, close to her side of the mirror, just as if his eyes had fascinated her. Cosmo had never seen her so near before. Now at least, eyes met eyes; but he could not quite understand the expression of hers. They were full of tender entreaty, but there was something more that he could not interpret. Though his heart seemed to labour in his throat, he would allow no delight or agitation to turn him from his task. Looking still in her face, he passed on to the mightiest charm he knew. Suddenly the lady turned and walked out of the door of her reflected chamber. A moment after she entered his room with veritable presence; and, forgetting all his precautions, he sprang from the charmed circle, and knelt before her. There she stood, the living lady of his passionate visions, alone beside him, in a thundery twilight, and the glow of a magic fire.

"Why," said the lady, with a trembling voice, "didst thou bring a poor maiden through the rainy streets alone?"

"Because I am dying for love of thee; but I only brought thee from the mirror there."

"Ah, the mirror!" and she looked up at it, and shuddered. "Alas! I am but a slave, while that mirror exists.

252

But do not think it was the power of thy spells that drew me; it was thy longing desire to see me, that beat at the door of my heart, till I was forced to yield."

"Canst thou love me then?" said Cosmo, in a voice as calm as death, but almost inarticulate with emotion.

"I do not know," she replied sadly; "that I cannot tell, so long as I am bewildered with enchantments. It were indeed a joy too great, to lay my head on thy bosom and weep to death; for I think thou lovest me, though I do not know; - but - "

Cosmo rose from his knees.

"I love thee as - nay, I know not what - for since I have loved thee, there is nothing else."

He seized her hand: she withdrew it.

"No, better not; I am in thy power, and therefore I may not."

She burst into tears, and kneeling before him in her turn, said -

"Cosmo, if thou lovest me, set me free, even from thyself; break the mirror."

"And shall I see thyself instead?"

"That I cannot tell, I will not deceive thee; we may never meet again."

A fierce struggle arose in Cosmo's bosom. Now she was in his power. She did not dislike him at least; and he could see her when he would. To break the mirror would be to destroy his very life, to banish out of his universe the only glory it possessed. The whole world would be but a prison, if he annihilated the one window that looked into the paradise of love. Not yet pure in love, he hesitated.

With a wail of sorrow the lady rose to her feet. "Ah! he loves me not; he loves me not even as I love him; and alas! I care more for his love than even for the freedom I ask."

"I will not wait to be willing," cried Cosmo; and sprang to the corner where the great sword stood.

Meantime it had grown very dark; only the embers cast a red glow through the room. He seized the sword by the steel scabbard, and stood before the mirror; but as he heaved a great blow at it with the heavy pommel, the blade slipped half-way out of the scabbard, and the pommel struck the wall above the mirror. At that moment, a terrible clap of thunder seemed to burst in the very room beside them; and ere Cosmo could repeat the blow, he fell senseless on the hearth. When he came to himself, he found that the lady and the mirror had both disappeared. He was seized with a brain fever, which kept him to his couch for weeks.

When he recovered his reason, he began to think what could have become of the mirror. For the lady, he hoped she had found her way back as she came; but as the mirror involved her fate with its own, he was more immediately anxious about that. He could not think she had carried it away. It was much too heavy, even if it had not been too firmly fixed in the wall, for her to remove it. Then again, he remembered the thunder; which made him believe that it was not the lightning but some other blow that had struck him down. He concluded that, either by supernatural agency, he having exposed himself to the vengeance of the demons in leaving the circle of safety, or in some other mode, the mirror had probably found its way back to its former owner; and, horrible to think of, might have been by this time once more disposed of, delivering up the lady into the power of another man; who, if he used his power no worse than he himself had done, might yet give Cosmo abundant cause to curse the selfish indecision which prevented him from shattering the mirror at once. Indeed, to think that she whom he loved, and who had prayed to him for freedom, should be still at the mercy, in some degree, of the possessor of the mirror, and was at least exposed to his constant observation, was in itself enough to madden a chary lover.

Anxiety to be well retarded his recovery; but at length he was able to creep abroad. He first made his way to the old broker's, pretending to be in search of something else. A laughing sneer on the creature's face convinced him that he knew all about it; but he could not see it amongst his furniture, or get any information out of him as to what had become of it. He expressed the utmost surprise at hearing it

254

had been stolen, a surprise which Cosmo saw at once to be counterfeited; while, at the same time, he fancied that the old wretch was not at all anxious to have it mistaken for genuine. Full of distress, which he concealed as well as he could, he made many searches, but with no avail. Of course he could ask no questions; but he kept his ears awake for any remotest hint that might set him in a direction of search. He never went out without a short heavy hammer of steel about him, that he might shatter the mirror the moment he was made happy by the sight of his lost treasure, if ever that blessed moment should arrive. Whether he should see the lady again, was now a thought altogether secondary, and postponed to the achievement of her freedom. He wandered here and there, like an anxious ghost, pale and haggard; gnawed ever at the heart, by the thought of what she might be suffering - all from his fault.

One night, he mingled with a crowd that filled the rooms of one of the most distinguished mansions in the city; for he accepted every invitation, that he might lose no chance, however poor, of obtaining some information that might expedite his discovery. Here he wandered about, listening to every stray word that he could catch, in the hope of a revelation. As he approached some ladies who were talking quietly in a corner, one said to another: "Have you heard of the strange illness of the Princess von Hohenweiss?"

"Yes; she has been ill for more than a year now. It is very sad for so fine a creature to have such a terrible malady. She was better for some weeks lately, but within the last few days the same attacks have returned, apparently accompanied with more suffering than ever. It is altogether an inexplicable story."

"Is there a story connected with her illness?"

"I have only heard imperfect reports of it; but it is said that she gave offence some eighteen months ago to an old woman who had held an office of trust in the family, and who, after some incoherent threats, disappeared. This peculiar affection followed soon after. But the strangest part of the story is its association with the loss of an antique

255

mirror, which stood in her dressing-room, and of which she constantly made use."

Here the speaker's voice sank to a whisper; and Cosmo, although his very soul sat listening in his ears, could hear no more. He trembled too much to dare to address the ladies, even if it had been advisable to expose himself to their curiosity. The name of the Princess was well known to him, but he had never seen her; except indeed it was she, which now he hardly doubted, who had knelt before him on that dreadful night. Fearful of attracting attention, for, from the weak state of his health, he could not recover an appearance of calmness, he made his way to the open air, and reached his lodgings; glad in this, that he at least knew where she lived, although he never dreamed of approaching her openly, even if he should be happy enough to free her from her hateful bondage. He hoped, too, that as he had unexpectedly learned so much, the other and far more important part might be revealed to him ere long.

"Have you seen Steinwald lately?"

"No, I have not seen him for some time. He is almost a match for me at the rapier, and I suppose he thinks he needs no more lessons."

"I wonder what has become of him. I want to see him very much. Let me see; the last time I saw him he was coming out of that old broker's den, to which, if you remember, you accompanied me once, to look at some armour. That is fully three weeks ago."

This hint was enough for Cosmo. Von Steinwald was a man of influence in the court, well known for his reckless habits and fierce passions. The very possibility that the mirror should be in his possession was hell itself to Cosmo. But violent or hasty measures of any sort were most unlikely to succeed. All that he wanted was an opportunity of breaking the fatal glass; and to obtain this he must bide his time. He revolved many plans in his mind, but without being able to fix upon any.

At length, one evening, as he was passing the house of

Von Steinwald, he saw the windows more than usually brilliant. He watched for a while, and seeing that company began to arrive, hastened home, and dressed as richly as he could, in the hope of mingling with the guests unquestioned: in effecting which, there could be no difficulty for a man of his carriage.

In a lofty , silent chamber, in another part of the city, lay a form more like marble than a living woman. The loveliness of death seemed frozen upon her face, for her lips were rigid, and her eye-lids closed. Her long white hands were crossed over her breast, and no breathing disturbed their repose. Beside the dead, men speak in whispers, as if the deepest rest of all could be broken by the sound of a living voice. Just so, though the soul was evidently beyond the reach of all intimations from the senses, the two ladies, who sat beside her, spoke in the gentlest tones of subdued sorrow.

"She has lain so for an hour."

"This cannot last long, I fear."

"How much thinner she has grown within the last few weeks! If she would only speak, and explain what she suffers, it would be better for her. I think she has visions in her trances, but nothing can induce her to refer to them when she is awake."

"Does she ever speak in these trances?"

"I have never heard her; but they say she walks sometimes, and once put the whole household in a terrible fright by disappearing for a whole hour, and returning drenched with rain, and almost dead with exhaustion and fright. But even then she would give no account of what had happened."

A scarce audible murmur from the yet motionless lips of the lady here startled her attendants. After several ineffectual attempts at articulation, the word "*Cosmo!* " burst from her. Then she lay still as before; but only for a moment. With a wild cry, she sprang from the couch erect on the floor, flung her arms above her head, with clasped and

257

straining hands, and, her wide eyes flashing with light, called aloud, with a voice exultant as that of a spirit bursting from a sepulchre, "I am free! I am free! I thank thee!" Then she flung herself on the couch, and sobbed; then rose, and paced wildly up and down the room, with gestures of mingled delight and anxiety. Then turning to her motionless attendants - "Quick, Lisa, my cloak and hood!" Then lower - "I must go to him. Make haste, Lisa! You may come with me, if you will."

In another moment they were in the street, hurrying along towards one of the bridges over the Moldau. The moon was near the zenith, and the streets were almost empty. The Princess soon outstripped her attendant, and was half-way over the bridge, before the other reached it.

"Are you free, lady? The mirror is broken: are you free?"

The words were spoken close beside her, as she hurried on. She turned; and there, leaning on the parapet in a recess of the bridge, stood Cosmo, in a splendid dress, but with a white and quivering face.

"Cosmo! - I am free - and thy servant for ever. I was coming to you now."

"And I to you, for Death made me bold; but I could get no further. Have I atoned at all? Do I love you a little - truly?"

"Ah, I know now that you love me, my Cosmo; but what do you say about death?"

He did not reply. His hand was pressed against his side. She looked more closely: the blood was welling from between the fingers. She flung her arms around him with a faint bitter wail.

When Lisa came up, she found her mistress kneeling above a wan dead face, which smiled on in the spectral moonbeams.

CHRISTINA ROSSETTI (1830-1894) was the younger sister of the pre-Raphaelite rakehell Dante Gabriel Rossetti (1828-1882); their mother was the sister of John Polidori, who had produced the most important precursor of modern vampire stories in *The Vampyre* (1819) before committing suicide in 1821. She conformed more closely to the expectations of the age than these relatives, however; like her elder sister (who eventually became a nun) she became a conscientiously devout Puritan, rigorously ascetic and self-denying. She suffered perpetual ill-health and was always physically frail; she refused various offers of marriage and probably died a virgin. Her moralistic verse parable "Goblin Market" (written in 1859 and first published in book form in *Goblin Market and Other Poems*, 1862) presumably seemed to her to be a straightforward parable of the power and responsibility which the good allegedly have to work for the redemption of their weaker brethren, but modern readers cannot help but see other implications in it. The *double entendres* which leap out at the modern eye can easily be interpreted in such a way as to make it one of the most vividly erotic pieces of writing to have surfaced in England during the entirety of Victoria's reign. The basic pattern of symbolism is certainly the product of calculated artifice, but the author was presumably blissfully ignorant of the lesbian undertones contained in the speeches and actions of the two sisters.

GOBLIN MARKET

By Christina Rossetti

Morning and evening
Maids heard the goblins cry:
"Come buy our orchard fruits,
Come buy, come buy:
Apples and quinces,
Lemons and oranges,
Plump unpecked cherries,
Melons and raspberries,
Bloom-down-cheeked peaches,
Swart-headed mulberries,
Wild free-born cranberries,
Crab-apples, dewberries,
Pine-apples, blackberries,
Apricots, strawberries; -
All ripe together
In summer weather, -
Morns that pass by,
Fair eves that fly;
Come buy, come buy:
Our grapes fresh from the vine,
Pomegranates full and fine,
Dates and sharp bullaces,
Rare pears and greengages,
Damsons and bilberries,
Taste them and try;
Currants and gooseberries,
Bright-fire-like barberries
Figs to fill your mouth,
Citrons from the South,
Sweet to tongue and sound to eye;
Come buy, come buy."
Evening by evening
Among the brookside rushes,
Laura bowed her head to hear,

Lizzie veiled her blushes:
Crouching close together
In the cooling weather,
With clasping arms and cautioning lips,
With tingling cheeks and finger tips.
"Lie close," Laura said,
Pricking up her golden head:
"We must not look at goblin men,
We must not buy their fruits:
Who knows upon what soil they fed
Their hungry thirsty roots?"
"Come buy," call the goblins
Hobbling down the glen.
"Oh," cried Lizzie, " Laura, Laura,
You should not peep at goblin men."
Lizzie covered up her eyes,
Covered close lest they should look;
Laura reared her glossy head,
And whispered like the restless brook:
"Look, Lizzie, look, Lizzie,
Down the glen tramp little men.
One hauls a basket,
One bears a plate,
One lugs a golden dish
Of many pounds' woight.
How fair the vine must grow
Whose grapes are so luscious;
How warm the wind must blow
Through those fruit bushes."
"No," said Lizzie: "No, no, no;
Their offers should not charm us,
Their evil gifts would harm us."
She thrust a dimpled finger
In each ear, shut eyes and ran:
Curious Laura chose to linger
Wondering at each merchant man.
One had a cat's face,
One whisked a tail,

One tramped at a rat's pace,
One crawled like a snail,
One like a wombat prowled obtuse and furry,
One like a ratel tumbled hurry skurry.
She heard a voice like voice of doves
Cooing all together:
They sounded kind and full of loves
In the pleasant weather.

Laura stretched her gleaming neck
Like a rush-imbedded swan,
Like a lily from the beck,
Like a moonlit poplar branch,
Like a vessel at the launch
When its last restraint is gone.

Backwards up the mossy glen
Turned and trooped the goblin men,
With their shrill repeated cry,
"Come buy, come buy."
When they reached where Laura was
They stood stock still upon the moss,
Leering at each other,
Brother with queer brother;
Signalling each other,
Brother with sly brother.
One set his basket down,
One reared his plate;
One began to weave a crown
Of tendrils, leaves, and rough nuts brown
(Men sell not such in any town):
One heaved the golden weight
Of dish and fruit to offer her:
"Come buy, come buy," was still their cry.
Laura stared but did not stir,
Longed but had no money.
The whisk-tailed merchant bade her taste
In tones as smooth as honey,

The cat-faced purr'd
The rat-paced spoke a word
Of welcome and the snail-paced even was heard;
One parrot-voiced and jolly
Cried 'Pretty Goblin' still for 'Pretty Polly';
One whistled like a bird.

But sweet-tooth Laura spoke in haste:
"Good folk, I have no coin;
To take were to purloin:
I have no copper in my purse,
I have no silver either,
All my gold is on the furze
That shakes in windy weather
Above the rusty heather."
"You have much gold upon your head,"
They answered all together:
"Buy from us with a golden curl."
She clipped a precious golden lock.
She dropped a tear more rare than pearl,
Then sucked their fruit globes fair or red.
Sweeter than honey from the rock,
Stronger than man-rejoicing wine,
Clearer than water flowed that juice;
She never tasted such before,
How should it cloy with length of use?
She sucked and sucked and sucked the more
Fruits which that unknown orchard bore;
She sucked until her lips were sore;
Then flung the emptied rinds away
But gathered up one kernel stone,
And knew not was it night or day
As she turned home alone.

Lizzie met her at the gate
Full of wise upbraidings:
"Dear, you should not stay so late,
Twilight is not good for maidens;

Should not loiter in the glen
In the haunts of goblin men.
Do you not remember Jeanie,
How she met them in the moonlight,
Took their gifts both choice and many,
Ate their fruits and wore their flowers
Plucked from bowers
Where summer ripens at all hours?
But ever in the noonlight
She pined and pined away;
Sought them by night and day,
Found them no more, but dwindled and grew grey;
Then fell with the first snow,
While to this day no grass will grow
Where she lies low:
I planted daisies there a year ago
That never blow.
You should not loiter so."
"Nay, hush," said Laura:
"Nay, hush my sister:
I ate and ate my fill,
Yet my mouth waters still:
To-morrow night I will
Buy more; " and kissed her.
"Have done with sorrow;
I'll bring you plums to-morrow
Fresh on their mother twigs,
Cherries worth getting;
You cannot think what figs
My teeth have met in.
What melons icy-cold
Piled on a dish of gold
Too huge for me to hold,
What peaches with a velvet nap,
Pellucid grapes without one seed:
Odorous indeed must be the mead
Whereon they grow, and pure the wave they drink
With lilies at the brink,

And sugar-sweet their sap."

Golden head by golden head,
Like two pigeons in one nest
Folded in each other's wings,
They lay down in their curtained bed:
Like two blossoms on one stem,
Like two flakes of new-fall'n snow,
Like two wands of ivory
Tipped with gold for awful kings.
Moon and stars gazed in at them,
Wind sang to them lullaby,
Lumbering owls forebore to fly,
Nor a bat flapped to and fro
Round their nest:
Cheek to cheek and breast to breast
Locked together in one nest.

Early in the morning
When the first cock crowed his warning,
Neat like bees, as sweet and busy,
Laura rose with Lizzie:
Fetched in honey, milked the cows,
Aired and set to rights the house,
Kneaded cakes of whitest wheat,
Cakes for dainty mouths to eat,
Next churned butter, whipped up cream.
Fed their poultry, sat and sewed;
Talked as modest maidens should:
Lizzie with an open heart,
Laura in an absent dream,
One content, one sick in part;
One warbling for the mere bright day's delight,
One longing for the night.

At length slow evening came:
They went with pitchers to the reedy brook;
Lizzie most placid in her look,

Laura most like a leaping flame.
They drew the gurgling water from its deep.
Lizzie plucked purple and rich golden flags,
Then turning homeward said: "The sunset flushes
Those furthest loftiest crags;
Come, Laura, not another maiden lags.
No wilful squirrel wags,
The beasts and birds are fast asleep."
But Laura loitered still among the rushes,
And said the bank was steep.

And said the hour was early still,
The dew not fall'n, the wind not chill;
Listening ever, but not catching
The customary cry,
"Come buy, come buy,"
With its iterated jingle
Of sugar-baited words:
Not for all her watching
Once discerning even one goblin
Racing, whisking, tumbling, hobbling -
Let alone the herds
That used to tramp along the glen,
In groups or single,
Of brisk fruit-merchant men.

Till Lizzie urged, "O Laura, come;
I hear the fruit-call, but I dare not look:
You should not loiter longer at this brook:
Come with me home.
The stars rise, the moon bends her arc,
Each glow-worm winks her spark,
Let us get home before the night grows dark:
For clouds may gather
Though this is summer weather,
Put out the lights and drench us through;
Then if we lost our way what should we do?"

Laura turned cold as stone
To find her sister heard that cry alone,
That goblin cry,
"Come buy our fruits, come buy."
Must she then buy no more such dainty fruit?
Must she no more such succous pasture find,
Gone deaf and blind?
Her tree of life drooped from the root:
She said not one word in her heart's sore ache:
But peering thro' the dimness, nought discerning,
Trudged home, her pitcher dripping all the way;
So crept to bed, and lay
Silent till Lizzie slept;
Then sat up in a passionate yearning,
And gnashed her teeth for baulked desire, and wept
As if her heart would break.

Day after day, night after night,
Laura kept watch in vain
In sullen silence of exceeding pain.
She never caught again the goblin cry,
"Come buy, come buy;"
She never spied the goblin men
Hawking their fruits along the glen:
But when the noon waxed bright
Her hair grew thin and grey;
She dwindled, as the fair full moon doth turn
To swift decay and burn
Her fire away.

One day remembering her kernel-stone
She set it by a wall that faced the south;
Dewed it with tears, hoped for a root,
Watched for a waxing shoot,
But there came none.
It never saw the sun,
It never felt the trickling moisture run:
While with sunk eyes and faded mouth

She dreamed of melons, as a traveller sees
False waves in desert drouth
With shade of leaf-crowned trees,
And burns the thirstier in the sandful breeze.

She no more swept the house,
Tended the fowls or cows,
Fetched honey, kneaded cakes of wheat,
Brought water from the brook:
But sat down listless in the chimney-nook
And would not eat.

Tender Lizzie could not bear
To watch her sister's cankerous care,
Yet not to share.
She night and morning
Caught the goblin's cry:
"Come buy our orchard fruits,
Come buy, come buy:"
Beside the brook, along the glen,
She heard the tramp of goblin men,
The voice and stir
Poor Laura could not hear;
Longed to buy fruit to comfort her,
But feared to pay too dear.
She thought of Jeanie in her grave,
Who should have been a bride;
But who for joys brides hope to have
Fell sick and died
In her gay prime,
In earliest winter time,
With the first glazing rime,
With the first snow-fall of crisp winter time.

Till Laura dwindling
Seemed knocking at Death's door.
Then Lizzie weighed no more
Better and worse;

But put a silver penny in her purse,
Kissed Laura, crossed the heath with clumps of furze
At twilight, halted by the brook:
And for the first time in her life
Began to listen and look.

Laughed every goblin
When they spied her peeping:
Came towards her hobbling,
Flying, running, leaping,
Puffing and blowing,
Chuckling, clapping, crowing,
Clucking and gobbling,
Mopping and mowing,
Full of airs and graces,
Pulling wry faces,
Demure grimaces,
Cat-like and rat-like,
Ratel and wombat-like,
Snail-paced in a hurry,
Parrot-voiced and whistler,
Helter skelter, hurry skurry,
Chattering like magpies,
Fluttering like pigeons,
Gliding like fishes, -
Hugged her and kissed her:
Squeezed and caressed her:
Stretched up their dishes,
Panniers, and plates:
"Look at our apples
Russet and dun,
Bob at our cherries,
Bite at our peaches,
Citrons and dates,
Grapes for the asking,
Pears red with basking
Out in the sun,

Plums on their twigs;
Pluck them and suck them, -
Pomegranates, figs."

"Good folk," said Lizzie,
Mindful of Jeanie:
"Give me much and many":
Held out her apron,
Tossed them her penny.
"Nay, take a seat with us,
Honour and eat with us,"
They answered grinning:
"Our feast is but beginning.
Night yet is early,
Warm and dew-pearly,
Wakeful and starry:
Such fruits as these
No man can carry;
Half their bloom would fly,
Half their dew would dry,
Half their flavour would pass by.
Sit down and feast with us,
Be welcome guest with us,
Cheer you and rest with us." -
"Thank you," said Lizzie: "But one waits
At home alone for me:
So without further parleying,
If you will not sell me any
Of your fruits though much and many,
Give me back my silver penny
I tossed you for a fee."-
They began to scratch their pates,
No longer wagging, purring,
But visibly demurring,
Grunting and snarling.
One called her proud,
Cross-grained, uncivil;
Their tones waxed loud,

270

Their looks were evil.
Lashing their tails
They trod and hustled her,
Elbowed and jostled her,
Clawed with their nails,
Barking, mewing, hissing, mocking,
Tore her gown and soiled her stocking,
Twitched her hair out by the roots,
Stamped upon her tender feet,
Held her hands and squeezed their fruits
Against her mouth to make her eat.

White and golden Lizzie stood,
Like a lily in a flood, -
Like a rock of blue-veined stone
Lashed by tides obstreperously, -
Like a beacon left alone
In a hoary roaring sea,
Sending up a golden fire, -
Like a fruit-crowned orange-tree
White with blossoms honey-sweet
Sore beset by wasp and bee, -
Like a royal virgin town
Topped with gilded dome and spire
Close beleaguered by a fleet
Mad to tug her standard down.

One may lead a horse to water,
Twenty cannot make him drink.
Though the goblins cuffed and caught her,
Coaxed and fought her,
Bullied and besought her,
Scratched her, pinched her black as ink,
Kicked and knocked her,
Mauled and mocked her,
Lizzie uttered not a word;
Would not open lip from lip
Lest they should cram a mouthful in:

But laughed in heart to feel the drip
Of juice that syruped all her face,
And lodged in dimples of her chin,
And streaked her neck which quaked like curd.
At last the evil people,
Worn out by her resistance,
Flung back her penny, kicked their fruit
Along whichever road they took,
Not leaving root or stone or shoot;
Some writhed into the ground,
Some dived into the brook
With ring and ripple,
Some scudded on the gale without a sound,
Some vanished in the distance.

In a smart, ache, tingle,
Lizzie went her way;
Knew not was it night or day;
Sprang up the bank, tore thro' the furze,
Threaded copse and dingle,
And heard her penny jingle
Bouncing in her purse, -
Its bounce was music to her ear.
She ran and ran
As if she feared some goblin man
Dogged her with gibe or curse
Or something worse:
But not one goblin skurried after,
Nor was she pricked by fear;
The kind heart made her windy-paced
That urged her home quite out of breath with haste
And inward laughter.

She cried, "Laura," up the garden,
"Did you miss me?
Come and kiss me.
Never mind my bruises,
Hug me, kiss me, suck my juices

272

Squeezed from goblin fruits for you,
Goblin pulp and goblin dew.
Eat me, drink me, love me;
Laura, make much of me;
For your sake I have braved the glen
And had to do with goblin merchant men."

Laura started from her chair,
Flung her arms up in the air,
Clutched her hair:
"Lizzie, Lizzie, have you tasted
For my sake the fruit forbidden?
Must your light like mine be hidden,
Your young life like mine be wasted,
Undone in mine undoing,
And ruined in my ruin,
Thirsty, cankered, goblin-ridden?" -
She clung about her sister,
Kissed and kissed and kissed her:
Tears once again
Refreshed her shrunken eyes,
Dropping like rain
After long sultry drouth;
Shaking with anguish fear, and pain,
She kissed and kissed her with a hungry mouth.

Her lips began to scorch,
That juice was wormwood to her tongue,
She loathed the feast:
Writhing as one possessed she leaped and sung,
Rent all her robe, and wrung
Her hands in lamentable haste,
And beat her breast.
Her locks streamed like the torch
Borne by a racer at full speed,
Or like the mane of horses in their flight,
Or like an eagle when she stems the light
Straight toward the sun,

Or like a caged thing freed,
Or like a flying flag when armies run.

Swift fire spread through her veins, knocked at her heart,
Met the fire smouldering there
And overbore its lesser flame;
She gorged on bitterness without a name:
Ah! fool to choose such part
Of soul-consuming care!
Sense failed in the mortal strife:
Like the watch-tower of a town
Which an earthquake shatters down,
Like a lightning-stricken mast,
Like a wind-uprooted tree
Spun about,
Like a foam-topped waterspout
Cast down headlong in the sea,
She fell at last;
Pleasure past and anguish past,
Is is death or is it life?

Life out of death.
That night long Lizzie watched by her,
Counted her pulse's flagging stir,
Felt for her breath,
Held water to her lips, and cooled her face
With tears and fanning leaves.
But when the first birds chirped about their eaves,
And early reapers plodded to the place
Of golden sheaves,
And dew-wet grass
Bowed in the morning winds so brisk to pass,
And new buds with new day
Opened of cup-like lilies on the stream,
Laura awoke as from a dream,
Laughed in the innocent old way,
Hugged Lizzie but not twice or thrice;
Her gleaming locks showed not one thread of grey,

274

Her breath was sweet as May,
And light danced in her eyes.

Days, weeks, months, years
Afterwards, when both were wives
With children of their own;
Their mother-hearts beset with fears,
Their lives bound up in tender lives;
Laura would call the little ones
And tell them of her early prime,
Those pleasant days long gone
Of not-returning time:
Would talk about the haunted glen,
The wicked quaint fruit-merchant men,
Their fruits like honey to the throat
But poison in the blood
(Men sell not such in any town):
Would tell them how her sister stood
In deadly peril to do her good,
And win the fiery antidote:
Then joining hands to little hands
Would bid them cling together, -
"For there is no friend like a sister
In calm or stormy weather;
To cheer one on the tedious way,
To fetch one if one goes astray,
To lift one if one totters down,
To strengthen whilst one stands."

275

WILLIAM GILBERT (1804-1890) was a medical man whose interest in abnormal psychology is elaborately displayed in his collections of imaginary case-studies *Shirley Hall Asylum; or, The Memoirs of a Monomaniac* (1863) and *Dr. Austin's Guests* (1866). His horror and fantasy stories are similarly embedded in two collections, each of which has a linking frame-narrative. *The Magic Mirror* (1866), from which the story below is taken, features a mirror which grants the wishes of those who look into it; *The Wizard of the Mountain* (1867) describes the fates of various visitors who come to beg favours from the mysterious Innominato, and are served according to their desserts. His novels - as is commonly the case with the authors included in this anthology - are much more earnest, devoid of supernatural intrusions, and quite forgotten.

Gilbert was the father of William Schwenck Gilbert (1836-1911) of Gilbert & Sullivan fame; the younger Gilbert also published a collection of stories including several absurd fantasies, *Foggerty's Fairy and Other Stories* (1890), but the ironic impact of the stories tends to be weakened by an over-extravagant silliness which he certainly did not inherit from his father.

THE SACRISTAN OF ST. BOTOLPH

By William Gilbert

Master Walter de Courcey, although an indefatigable man of business, was extremely punctual in his religious observances, and he made a point, both in winter and summer, of attending early mass in his parish church, St Botolph's, Bishopsgate. It has already been stated that his departure for Windsor was very sudden, in fact hardly any one out of his own house was aware that he had left London. The officiating priest at the church was therefore much surprised at his non-appearance two days running; and as Master Walter did not appear on the third, nor in fact for a week, he began to fear he might be indisposed, and one morning, as soon as mass was over, he directed the sacristan to call at the merchant's house and inquire after his health. The sacristan was a certain Geoffrey Cole, a very tall thin man with a low forehead, deep sunk eyes, harsh features, and very large hands and feet. Although something of a miser, intensely selfish, and most uncharitable, both in the matter of giving alms, and in his feelings towards his neighbours, he was extremely punctilious in all the external forms and ceremonies of the Church, and he flattered himself he was not only very religious, but even a model of piety. The more he studied the subject, the more certain of his blissful state he became, till at last he believed himself to be so good that the saints alone were his equals. He would frequently draw comparisons between his life and some of the inferior saints, and he generally concluded he could compare with them most advantageously. On the morning when he was directed to call on Master Walter this train of thought especially occupied his mind, and by the time he had arrived at the house he was certain that in the whole city of London there was not another individual so good as himself.

The person who received him was an old woman half imbecile from age, who had formerly been Master Walter's nurse, and with her the sacristan had frequently conversed on matters of what he called religion. When he had received from her an explanation of the merchant's absence from church, the pair commenced talking on subjects connected with Church affairs, which consisted in fact of the sacristan's explaining to her what a good and pious man he was, and her complimenting him thereon. Before he left the house the nurse asked him if he would like to see the mirror, as she would have much pleasure in showing it to him. He accepted the offer at once, at the same time saying that vanities of the kind had but few attractions for him.

The nurse led the way to the chamber, and when they had arrived there, in spite of his mock ascetic manner, there was no difficulty in perceiving he admired the mirror greatly. Fearing, however, the real state of his mind might be detected by the old woman, he began to speak of it in terms of great disparagement, not indeed finding fault with its form and beauty, but dwelling on the absurdity of mortals setting their minds on such trifles, and neglecting subjects of far greater importance which concerned the welfare of their souls.

"But everybody cannot be so good as you are, Master Geoffrey," said the old woman; "and you ought to have a little feeling for those who are not."

"I do not see that," said the sacristan, taking the compliment without the slightest hesitation. "I condemn all trifles of the kind. What would the blessed St Anthony have said to a vanity of this sort?"

"Ah!" said the old woman; "but it would not be possible in the present day to find so good a man as he was."

"It would be very difficult, I admit," said the sacristan; "but I am not sure it would be impossible. Do not think for a moment that I would attempt to compare myself with him; but I thought, while reflecting on his life as I came here this morning, that I should very much like to be subjected to the same temptations, to see if I could not resist them."

"You surely do not mean that?" said the nurse; "why, they were dreadful."

"Indeed, I do," said the sacristan, looking at himself in

the mirror, "I should like immensely to be subjected to them for a month, and then I could form an idea whether I was as good as I ought to be."

"Well," said the nurse, leaving the room with him, "I trust you will never be subjected to anything of the kind." After a little conversation of the same description the sacristan left the house.

After he had delivered his message to the priest and the functions of the day were over, he sought his own home in the rural district of Little Moorfields. He lived in a room on the top floor of a house occupied by a man and his wife who were employed at a merchant's house in the City. As the merchant and his family were absent, Geoffrey's landlord and his wife were requested to sleep at the house of business, and thus he had for the time the whole abode to himself.

His room, which was comfortably furnished, was the very picture of neatness and cleanliness, for he was very particular in his domestic arrangements; and his landlady, during her temporary absence at the house of business, called every day to put his room in order, and place his supper on the table.

Arrived at home he requested a neighbour's wife to light his lamp and fire for him, and that being done she left him. He then bolted the street door, went up to his own room, and after having a very comfortable and abundant meal went to bed, having, however, left ample food on the table for his breakfast the next morning. He was generally a very sound sleeper, and his slumbers that night formed no exception to the general rule; but, somehow or other, as morning advanced they were by no means so profound. He grew very restless, with a sense of oppression, and occasionally he heard a sound like the tinkling of a bell, which continued till daybreak, when the annoyance became intolerable. At last, when it was fully day, he aroused himself and sat up in his bed. What was his surprise and terror when he saw, stretched across the foot of it, outside the clothes, a large fat pig with a bell fastened round its neck

279

with a leathern strap. His first attempt was to push the brute from the bed, but the only effect produced was that it placed itself in a still more comfortable position directly on his legs, and then went to sleep again. Enraged and in great pain, he immediately began to pommel the pig with his fist on the neck and head, but without other result than a few surly grunts. His passion increased to such an extent that he struck it still harder blows, when suddenly his attention was arrested by a loud peal of laughter, and he saw, sitting on his stool by the fireplace, an imp so intensely ugly that he was almost frightened to look at it. Somewhat recovering himself, he said, "Who are you, and what are you doing here?"

"No matter who I am," said the imp; "but as to what I am doing, I am simply laughing at your ungrateful and absurd behaviour."

"In what way," said the sacristan, "is my behaviour absurd?"

"In attacking in that violent manner your friend and pig."

"My pig?" said the sacristan; "I have no pig. It is none of mine."

"O you ungrateful man," said the imp. "Did you not yesterday say you wished you could meet with some temptations similar to those tradition tells us annoyed St. Anthony? And now, when you have a pig, and a very handsome one too, for your protection and society, the first thing you do is to pommel it as if you would kill it."

"I did not know it was a pig of that description," said the sacristan, with much solemnity of tone, "or I should have treated it with the respect it deserves."

"Well, then, do so now," said the imp. "To all appearance it will give you ample opportunity for a trial of patience."

"But I cannot remain here all day," said the sacristan, "I must go to my duties; I shall be scolded as it is for being late."

Then scratching the pig lovingly on the poll, he

addressed it with much sweetness of tone and manner: "If it is not asking you too great a favour, would you oblige me by getting off my bed? I am really very sorry to trouble you, but you are rather heavy, and I suffer from corns."

But the pig took no further notice of these blandishments than closing its eyes more fast than ever, and falling into a sounder sleep.

"What am I to do?" said the poor sacristan, in a despairing tone.

"Exercise your patience," said the imp. "He is affording you capital practice."

The sacristan was now silent, and for some time the imp said nothing, contenting himself with a quiet chuckle. Presently, however, he said to the sacristan,

"Come, I will assist you if I can. What do you want me to do?"

"To get this accurs.... I mean blessed pig off my bed if you can."

"I can do it easily enough," said the imp; "but you mortals are so ungrateful, it is ten to one you will be angry with me if I do."

"On the contrary," said Geoffrey, "I shall be most grateful to you, I promise you on my word of honour. That is to say," he continued, "if it do not put the dear creature to much pain."

"I promise you that it shall, on the contrary, be much pleased."

"Pray proceed then."

The imp immediately leaped off the stool, and going to the table took from it the food the sacristan had set aside for his breakfast, and placing it on the ground called out, "Pig, pig."

The pig lazily opened its eyes and looked on the ground. No sooner, however, did it see the food than its sleepy fit left it, and it jumped from the bed and commenced a furious attack on the sacristan's breakfast.

Master Geoffrey, in spite of his promise, was now dreadfully angry. He leaped on the floor, and rushing to the pig attempted in vain to push it away from the food, the imp laughing lustily the while.

"Upon my word," he said, "I never saw in my life a man worse adapted for an anchorite than you are. Why, you ought to be delighted to see your pig enjoy itself so heartily."

Master Geoffrey immediately left the pig and cast a very proper look of intense hatred at the imp, who seemed more delighted with it than ever.

"Did I not tell you," he said, "that you would be ungrateful to me for my kindness?"

The sacristan made no reply, but commenced dressing himself. He went on systematically with his toilet, casting occasionally an envious glance at the pig, but by the time he was fully dressed he had contrived to regain his equanimity. He now put on his cap as if to leave the house, and then, going to the pig, he patted it on the back and scratched its head, saying at the time,

"There's a good pig, go on with your breakfast, and when you have finished we will take a pretty pleasant walk together down to St. Botolph's, and there I will leave you in the streets till my duties are over, and then we will walk back together comfortably in the evening."

Here the imp set up a furious laugh, and stamped on the floor with pleasure.

"Bravo! admirable!" he said, "upon my word you are a nice fellow. You know the Lord Mayor has lately published an order that all pigs found in the streets of the City shall have their throats cut, and their flesh given to the poor. Upon my word you are a very clever fellow, and I begin to like you immensely. I could not have done anything better myself."

Master Geoffrey contented himself with casting another look of intense hatred at the imp, but he said nothing.

After a few minutes' silence the imp said to him,

"Now I know you want to ask me a question and are too proud to do it. You would inquire what you must do with the pig during the day?"

282

"I acknowledge it," said the sacristan. "What can I do with it? - of course I cannot take it to the church with me."

"Leave it at home, then, I should if I were you, rather than be bothered with it all day."

"Well, I should like to do that, but if my landlady should come and find it here she would very likely drive it away. Perhaps," he said , after a moment's reflection, "that would be the better way after all."

"Not at all," said the imp, "it would be sure to find its way back again at night, so that would be of no use. I see you want to get rid of it."

"Your base suspicions annoy me."

"Indeed. Now let me advise you. Go round to the house your landlady lives at, and tell her that you do not want your room arranged either to-day or to-morrow. She will be pleased to hear it, as I know she is suffering very severely from an attack of rheumatism. So you see you can leave the pig in your room without the slightest danger of its being found out by anyone. Now you had better go. Do not forget to bring the pig's supper back with you, or it will again be under the unpleasant necessity of eating that which you had reserved for yourself. Now good-bye."

The sacristan then left the house, and after having called on his landlady and assured her that there would be no occasion for her to arrange his room for him either that day or the next, - a piece of news which gave her great satisfaction, as the weather was cold and her rheumatism worse, - he continued his way to the church, where he had great difficulty in making his peace with the priest for being so late. When the duties of the day were over, he first went to an eating-house and ate a most hearty supper, determining that the pig should not deprive him of that meal. He then bought sufficient for his breakfast the next morning, and afterwards some vegetables for the pig. This last investment, we are obliged to acknowledge with great sorrow, caused him much annoyance. He had a violent objection to spend money on anybody but himself, and although he wished to act up to the part of an anchorite as

283

closely as he could, he never had heard of one spending money on a dumb animal, and he almost considered it to be a work of supererogation to waste the money he had done on the pig. However, it was done, and there was no help for it. He sincerely repented his fault, and he could not say more; he would be more cautious another time.

When he arrived at home and had procured a light from a neighbour, he entered his room and found in it the pig and the imp. He showed little delight at the sight of either. The pig, on the contrary, received him with every mark of satisfaction, that is to say, as soon as it perceived the vegetables under the sacristan's arm.

The sacristan took no notice of the imp, but threw the vegetables down on the floor, setting aside, however, enough for the pig's breakfast the next morning, and it was soon occupied with its supper. The sacristan watched it thoughtfully as it fed, not a word being spoken the while either by the imp or himself. When the pig was fully satisfied, the sacristan swept up the remains, and opening the casement threw them into the street. He then closed it quickly as the weather was cold, intending to enjoy, if possible, a comfortable night's rest, when to his intense horror, he found the pig had leaped upon the bed and had stretched itself full length upon it from head to foot, so that it would have been difficult for the sacristan to have placed himself beside the pig even if he had been so inclined.

The sacristan could hardly contain his rage, indeed for a moment it partially broke out, but a roar of laughter from the imp induced him to restrain himself. With great difficulty he put something like an amiable smile on his countenance, and then addressed the pig with much genuine persuasion in his tone and manner.

"Come off the bed, there's a good pig," he said, "and I will make you up another on the floor, where you will be much more comfortable than you are there. Come now, there's a good pig." But the only answer he got was a grunt.

"What in the name of Fortune," said the imp, "do you want the pig to get off the bed for?"

"Why to sleep there myself, of course," said the sacristan.

"Upon my word, you are a pretty anchorite. You slept like a top all last night to my certain knowledge, and you want to go to bed to-night!"

"What am I expected to do then?" said the sacristan.

"Pass the night in meditation on the floor, of course; who ever heard of an anchorite sleeping two nights running? You will now find how invaluable is your pig. It will sleep soundly enough while you meditate, but the moment you fall asleep it will ring its bell. I see you do not like that arrangement, and I begin to suspect you are no better than a sham after all."

"I will prove to you I am," said the sacristan; "that is to say if I am to have the pleasure of your company here all night."

"That you will not have," said the imp, "but you will see me in the morning," and he immediately vanished.

To say the truth, the sacristan passed a most uncomfortable night. Whenever he attempted to sleep, the pig rang its bell until the unfortunate man was fully awake, and then went to sleep himself. Several times in the course of the night did he beg the pig to keep quiet, and once he endeavoured to explain to it that he always meditated best with his eyes shut, but the pig would hear of no compromise, and continued faithfully to do its duty till morning. When day broke the imp made his appearance, and as before seated himself on the stool.

"What sort of a night have you passed?" said the imp.

"A very unpleasant - I mean a very happy one, indeed."

"I do not believe you," said the imp. "I suspect after all you are not the man to resist temptation."

"There you are certainly wrong," said the sacristan. "No man," he continued, casting a most vindictive glance at the pig, "was ever more cruelly tempted than I have been to-night, and yet I successfully resisted it. But after all I candidly admit that, all things considered, it will be exceedingly difficult for me to carry out my wish at present, much as it would disappoint me to relinquish it. You must perceive yourself that in a small room like this, I have no convenience or accommodation for a temptation of the kind."

"O you coward!" said the imp. "What, going to give in already? No accommodation indeed! Why, I should like to know how the anchorites of old managed?"

"They had the desert handy, where they had plenty of room."

"Why do you not go there then?"

"How absurdly you talk!" said the sacristan peevishly. "Why, the desert is so far off it would take me a life-time to get there."

"Try Kennington Common, then," said the imp. "There will be room enough for you there, and I observed the other day at the farthest part a half-ruined shed that would serve you and your pig admirably for shelter."

"If I went there," said the sacristan, "would it be necessary for me to take the pig with me?"

"Of course; its duty is to keep you from relapsing; and besides that, it would not stay behind though you wished it."

The sacristan reflected for some minutes. To say the truth, the proposition of the imp did not altogether displease him. Near that part of Kennington Common resided a buxom widow very well to do in the world, who was rather fond of hearing the sacristan converse on serious subjects. He calculated that if bad weather came on, or if his provisions did not hold out, or if he were cold or dull, he could go to her house and instruct her.

"I think," said he at last to the imp, "your idea an excellent one, and I will carry it out. As soon as my duties for the day are over, I will go to the Common and remain there a week at least, that is to say, if the priest will give me leave of absence for so long a time, of which I have little doubt. I will go immediately and ask him."

So saying he left the house, after giving the pig its breakfast.

In the evening the sacristan returned to the house with a large bundle of warm clothing, some boiled bacon and ham, and bread enough to last him for several days, which he placed on the table, and a very small quantity of food for the pig, which he threw on the ground, and on which the pig began to feed ravenously. The sacristan then seated himself on the bed to recover his breath, for he was greatly fatigued with the exercise he had taken.

"What may those things be for?" said the imp, pointing to the bundle on the table.

"It is warm clothing," said the sacristan, "for the nights are cold."

"That is hardly *en règle*, " said the imp; "you ought to take nothing more with you than you have on. The ancient anchorites never had even a change of linen."

"You forget," said the sacristan, "they lived in warmer climates, where it was not required; here, where it is colder, it would be allowed. I have well studied that question, and I know I am right."

"And that other parcel, what may that contain?"

"Boiled bacon and ham, and bread."

"That is not orthodox."

"Why not?"

"If you are going to live the life of an anchorite, you must live upon herbs and roots, and drink nothing but water; and, by-the-bye, if I am not mistaken, I see something in your bundle the form of which is remarkably like that of a leathern bottle of wine."

"I have received a dispensation from the priest to eat meat for the next fortnight, and the wine is to be taken occasionally on account of my weak state of health."

"You hypocrite!" said the imp; "you have imposed on the worthy priest. You know there is nothing the matter with you."

"I scorn your imputation," said the sacristan with much virtuous indignation in his tone; "I have practised no imposition on the holy man whatever. I went to a leech and told him I felt in a very weak state of health, and I gave him a crown to give me a certificate that a course of animal food with wine was necessary for me, and this certificate I took to the priest, who, on the faith of it, gave me the dispensation. If there is any sin in the matter it is the doctor's, not mine - I took good care of that."

"Upon my word," said the imp, "I begin to respect you. You are evidently a man after my own heart."

"I consider your hatred," said the sacristan, "a far greater compliment than your love."

The sacristan now made preparations for his journey, and left the house with the pig.

"*Bon voyage*," said the imp; but he received no answer.

The sacristan and the pig made their way without much difficulty through the City, and even crossed the crowded thoroughfare of London Bridge without anything occurring particularly worthy of remark. When they arrived at the Borough Market things did not go on so well. The pig had had but a very scanty supper, and the quantity of vegetables he found strewed about in the market offered an amount of temptation he could not resist. The market at the time was crowded, and the pig, in its eagerness to obtain food, ran in the way of the merchants and purchasers, and in return got many and sundry hard kicks, which appeared not to agree with its constitution.

It is well known that even the best pigs, when hungry, have but little of the moral quality of integrity about them, and the one whose history we are recording formed no exception to the rule. Not content with picking up the refuse vegetables which lay strewn about, it had the imprudence to walk off with a fine cauliflower from a trader's basket. This was perceived, however, and the hue and cry was immediately raised. The cauliflower was taken from it, and a perfect shower of kicks was rained on its sides. Some inquired to whom the pig belonged, and one asked the sacristan if it was his. We are sorry to be obliged to say that he replied in the negative, and still more sorry to admit that while his pig was being assaulted in this cruel manner, he looked on without the slightest expression of indignation or compassion on his face, and at last turned on his heel and continued his road, letting his pig disengage itself from the

288

crowd as best it could.

He had hardly arrived at Newington when the pig joined him, grunting in a most lamentable manner. As last the pair reached Kennington Common, and the sacristan made directly for the shed mentioned by the imp. He found it without any difficulty, and without allowing the pig time to make a choice, he appropriated the driest and warmest corner to himself. The pig offered no opposition, for the treatment it had received appeared to have taken every particle of courage out of it, and it threw itself down in an opposite corner, and was soon fast asleep. The sacristan now undid his wallet, and, after having made a hearty supper, he put on some warm clothing and went to sleep, having first hung his wallet and provisions under the roof so as to be out of the reach of the pig.

Next morning he found the imp in the shed, but the pig had sauntered out for the moment into a neighbouring turnip-field.

"So you arrived here safely?" said the imp to the sacristan, who was occupied with his breakfast. "I followed you under the form of a dog the whole of the way, and I must say your conduct was most cowardly and disgraceful. You looked on with perfect indifference when the pig was being so horribly maltreated in the market."

"That is not true," said the sacristan; "I assure you that I felt bitterly for the poor animal. I felt as much pain from every kick it received as if it had been inflicted on my own person; but I said to myself, Here is a trial for me, and it is my duty to support it meekly and with patience. And I flatter myself I did so admirably. When the kicks were being showered so cruelly on its sides I not only made no opposition, but, wishing to see how far my own self-denial would go, I said, Kick on."

"And, pray, why did you deny being its master?"

"That I might not appear proud. Pride is a sin I despise."

"Capital! Now, what do you intend to do this morning? - meditate, I suppose?"

"No," said the sacristan with a sigh; "I would willingly do so, but unfortunately I am unable. I have occasion to go into the City."

"Nonsense, you know you have got leave of absence for a fortnight, and there is no occasion whatever for you to go there."

"You are in error," said the sacristan mildly, "for go I must."

"Might I ask on what errand?"

"To get some wine."

"How preposterous!" said the imp; "you brought enough with you to last a moderate man for three days at least."

"Not under the circumstances in which I was placed," said the sacristan. "You forget how cold it was."

"What, in the name of Fortune, has that to do with it? Do you think the anchorites of old drank wine in that manner?"

"Possibly not, very possibly not; but their case was very different. They did not suffer from cold, for they lived in a warm climate. I do not, and I am justified in taking as much wine while living in this open shed as shall raise the temperature of my body to an equality with that of theirs in the African desert; and that cannot be done under a bottle a day. Now I have only one leathern bottle in my possession, and therefore you yourself must perceive that I am obliged, though sorely against my inclination, to go to London every day."

"That is very sad indeed," said the imp; "but do you not think the anchorites, had they been placed in your position, would have attempted to abstain from wine? Judging from what I have heard of them, I think they would."

"I do not agree with you. Judging from my own conscientious feelings on the subject, I am decidedly of the opinion they would not; nor will I try it, lest I might fall into a grievous and sinful error."

"And what may that be?"

"In thinking that so sinful a mortal as I am could

surpass the sanctity of those venerable men. I am not sure that even making the attempt would not be a mortal sin, and I shall not try it."

"Just as you please," said the imp. "When do you start?"

"Immediately. Now, my faithful companion," he continued, addressing the pig, who had just returned from the turnip-field, where, judging from the rotundity of its person, it had made an excellent breakfast, "let us start off for London at once, that we may have plenty of time to see the sights; that is to say, after I have called on a friend of mine who lives in St. Nicholas in the Shambles."

But the pig took no notice of the invitation, and stolidly prepared a bed for itself in the corner of the shed. Doubtless a vivid reminiscence of the Borough Market, - through which it would have to pass, - was still fresh in its memory.

It was nearly dark when the sacristan returned to the shed that evening. He appeared in perfect good humour with himself and all the world; and if his cheeks were not rosy his nose was certainly slightly so. Altogether he presented the appearance of a person who had drunk a trifle more than was absolutely necessary for him, without being at all intoxicated. He hung up a bottle of wine under the roof, with some ham and some bread, and then, seating himself in his corner, he attempted to meditate, but did not succeed. He felt that evening especially the want of society, for even the pig lay fast asleep beside him, after a hearty supper in the turnip-field. He would have felt more comfortable if the imp had been there, although expressly sent to tempt him. The feeling of *ennui* grew on him till he found it almost unsupportable, and at last he determined, although it was rather late in the day for a person connected with the church to call upon a lone woman, to pay the widow a visit, and talk with her on moral subjects. The resolution was no sooner formed than he rose from his seat to put it in practice, and putting his cap on his head in a jaunty manner, he left the house.

To his sore annoyance, however, the pig, which had been as still as a dormouse while he was in the shed, showed unusual signs of liveliness when he quitted it. It rose up, and, following him, gambolled round in front of him, impeding his walk, and grunting and ringing its bell in a most absurd manner. This enraged him excessively, for although he had nothing to be ashamed of in visiting the widow, still, when a man calls on the woman of his choice, he does not wish it to be trumpeted forth to all the world, in such a very ridiculous manner. He attempted to drive the pig back again without the slightest effect, and we are sorry to add made use of such language on the occasion as any well-disposed sacristan would be shocked to repeat. At the same time it is but just to state that, when he found he could not get the pig to forego its intention by any possible entreaties and threats, he honestly begged its pardon, and allowed it to accompany him.

When they arrived at the widow's door the pig placed itself close against it, so as to be able to enter at the same time with its master. This annoyed the sacristan exceedingly; of course he could not allow the pig to enter, yet how to keep it out he did not know. The widow, who was rather of a timorous disposition, called out before opening the door,

"Who's there?"

The sacristan immediately answered that it was he, and that there was a pig outside which seemed desirous to enter. Was it hers?

"No," she said; "pray drive it away."

"I have tried to do so," said the sacristan, "but I have not succeeded."

"Wait a moment, I will see what I can do;" and a minute afterwards the widow opened the door. Armed with a besom, she dealt the pig a tremendous blow on the snout.

Now it is well known that a pig, which may be as bold as a lion on all other occasions, will not a face a housewife with a besom. So the sacristan's pig started back, and howled terribly, while its master, profiting by its retreat,

292

entered the house.

The sacristan found a warm, blazing fire in the widow's little sitting-room, and the table was spread out for her solitary supper. The place had a look of comfort about it which directly went to his heart, and he regretted that so amiable a person should have no one always at hand to talk to her on serious subjects, and advise her in the management of her affairs. She appeared much pleased to see him, the more so as that evening she had been reflecting on her solitary lot. She immediately placed another platter on the table, and produced some wine, which she kept by her to use medicinally, as occasion required. The sacristan was touched by her kindness. In return he talked to her very comfortably, showing her the folly of setting one's heart on sublunary things, and doing full justice to her provisions the while. He would have been perfectly happy had it not been for the incessant ringing of the pig's bell outside the house. The widow, in the course of conversation, asked him what he was doing in that out-of-the-way part of the world. He told her he had requested leave of absence from his priest, and that during it he was determined to pass the time in meditation amid the solitude of the Common. She admired his resolution, and said that at any time when he might feel dull, she would be happy to see him; for which he thanked her, with evident gratitude, and said he would willingly profit by her offer.

In this cozy manner the conversation continued for some time, till at last the widow asked where he intended passing the night. The sacristan was on the point of telling her about the shed, when he remembered she might call upon him there, and discover that he was the owner of the pig, which still kept up his annoyance by incessantly ringing its bell; so he checked himself, and said that it would be on any part of the Common where he could find a dry spot.

"But, my good soul," said the widow, "you will catch your death of cold there, for you are evidently far from strong. I will tell you what I will do. I will make up a little bed for you in the back room."

Before the sacristan could explain how gratefully he accepted her offer, both he and the widow were startled by what at first they considered an unearthly noise, but afterwards found to be the pig howling tremendously, and furiously ringing its bell at the same time.

"Somebody must surely be killing that pig," said the widow.

"Poor pig!" said the sacristan, with great resignation in his tone; "it is very sad, but we should remember it is the lot of its race, and we ought to smother our feelings."

The widow now left the room to prepare the bed, and in a few minutes again entered, saying that all was ready.

Terrible as had been the cries of the pig before, they were *sotto voce* compared with those it now uttered. They might with ease have been heard as far as Newington; and to add to the discomfort, the sacristan could easily perceive that they were gathering a crowd about the house. What to do he knew not. He was perfectly aware the pig would not cease its annoyance so long as he remained in the house, and he had not the heart to leave, he was so comfortable in it. He endeavoured to support the infliction for nearly an hour longer, when, fearing that the widow would feel irritated if the pig continued its cries, and as he particularly wished to stand well in her good graces, he told her that happy as he was it was hardly becoming an anchorite to indulge in so much luxury, and that with much genuine sorrow he must leave her. She attempted to dissuade him, but in vain; and, with a profusion of thanks for her kindness, he left the house.

He found in the road not only the pig, which was now silent, but a great crowd as well. He pushed through them and was soon lost to their sight in the darkness. He had hardly proceeded a hundred yards when the pig joined him. The sight of the poor animal put him into a great passion, and as a reward for its ill-timed services, he bestowed on its ribs a dozen hearty kicks, resolving in his mind that if he were acting wrongly he would repent of it afterwards.

When he arrived at the shed he went to his corner, and

294

first took down his bottle of wine, which he placed by his side. He passed a large portion of the night in meditation, principally on the good qualities of the widow, with occasional thoughts on the pig. From time to time he put the bottle to his lips and took a hearty draught to keep the warmth of his person up to the same temperature as it would have reached on an African desert.

When day broke he found the imp in the shed, accompanied by two others, more hideous than himself.

"You passed a very respectable night for an anchorite," said one.

"In what was I at fault?"

"Your treatment of your friend the pig was infamous. You know you do not love him."

"I admit it," said the sacristan. "As an anchorite it is my duty to detach myself from earthly affections, and the pig is a mundane animal."

"So is the widow," said the imp.

"But the widow has a soul," said the sacristan, "and it is my duty to talk seriously to her."

"And a pretty face, and money as well," said the imp.

"You may attempt to disturb my meditations by talking of the widow and her attractions as much as you please," said the sacristan, "but you will not annoy me."

"Of that I am perfectly persuaded," said the imp; "but we will talk of something else. How do you intend occupying yourself to-day?"

"I have to go to the City for some more wine."

"Very like an anchorite, indeed," said the imp; reversing the empty bottle, from which but one drop fell.

"If you can prove to me that the anchorites of old would not have done the same during a cold night on Kennington Common, I will leave it off; till then I shall continue it."

So saying, he put on his cap and left the shed, the pig making no attempt to follow him.

The sacristan continued this method of life for two or three days longer. During the time he made several attempts to call on the widow, but each time the pig kept so close to his heels that he was obliged to desist. One calm moonlight night he thought he would take a walk. He strolled in the direction of Camberwell, the pig following him. Presently he saw two female figures a little in advance, and he hastened to overtake them. When he had reached them he found they were dressed like ladies, but so muffled up in coifs and cloaks that it was impossible for him to see whether they were young or old, handsome or ugly. He entered into conversation with them, and they answered him very courteously. He walked by their side, talking of the beauty of the night and other congenial subjects. They continued walking on, conversing very discreetly, the pig from time to time ringing its bell, not in an angry manner, but simply as if in doubt on some subject passing in its mind. They proceeded with their walk till it got very late, and the heavens became covered with thick clouds, which totally obscured the moon from their sight.

At last, when it was at least ten o'clock, the sacristan was on the point of stopping to wish his fair companions good night, as it was time for him to return, when they heard before them the sounds of a violin most exquisitely played, but they could not see the performer. They continued their road onwards, listening to the music (by-the-bye it was the same air the devil played to Tartini in his sleep some hundred years afterwards). A spell seemed to be on them, for they could not stop, but followed the invisible musician. The pig now began to be very uneasy, and rang its bell in an angry manner; the sacristan, however, paid no attention to it, but walked onwards.

In this manner they marched for at least two hours, when at last the sacristan found himself on the borders of Blackheath. One of his lady companions then said to him, "We are going to a very pleasant party to-night a little way farther on. I wish you would accompany us; I am sure you would be well received, and you would have an opportunity of immensely improving the minds of the company."

In spite of the anger of the pig the sacristan consented,

and presently they found themselves in the midst of a circle brilliantly lit up. On one side was a raised orchestra for some musicians, all of whom were of the most extraordinary shapes with instruments as strange. Their music, however, was of the most delightful description, so much so as to dispel all fear on the part of the sacristan, and inspire him with a wish to dance. Presently the whole circle was filled with dancers, all of the most fantastic, and many even of the most horrible shapes; still he felt no fear, but stood aside wishing to join them. At last his two lady companions, who had been standing beside him, threw off their wrappers, and appeared in costumes so disgracefully *décolleté*, that the author declines to describe them. The ladies seized the sacristan each by a hand and drew him gently into the middle of the circle, and then commenced dancing. The orchestra at the time played more brilliantly than ever, while the poor pig ran round and round outside the circle, uttering the most discordant sounds and ringing its bell furiously. The sacristan now danced with all his might, his grotesque figure flying about in all directions, while he performed the most eccentric steps. He became more and more excited with the scene, and danced with still greater vigour. But in a moment the whole vanished, and he found himself in pitchy darkness in the midst of the heath, and in a pouring shower of rain. He listened for a moment for the bell of his pig, but it was no longer heard. The spell under which he had been labouring for some days past was broken, and he found he had been making a great fool of himself. With much difficulty he discovered the high road to London, and arrived at his lodgings about daybreak. The next morning he commenced a new life. He became, not superciliously pious, but a good charitable man, doing his duty in the church, giving alms of all he had to the poor, and contented with being thought no better than his neighbours.

EDWARD LEAR (1812-1888) was the second great pioneer, with Lewis Carroll, of Nonsense Literature. Like the Reverend Dodgson, Lear was somewhat happier in the company of children than that of adults, and he took the side of the children in opposing the tedium of moral instruction. He never achieved the recognition which he sought to win by means of his work as a landscape artist, although his beautifully-detailed studies of parrots and macaws are nowadays highly prized, but his verses - which achieve a marvellous blend of absurdity and euphony which no one has ever managed to imitate - have always been much loved. His first collection, *The Book of Nonsense,* appeared in 1846, signed "Derry Down Derry", and was twice expanded in 1861 and 1863. Some of his most famous poems - including "The Owl and the Pussycat" and "The Jumblies" - were in *Nonsense Songs, Stories, Botany and Alphabets* (1871); the rest - including "The Dong with a Luminous Nose" and "The Pobble Who Has No Toes" - were in *Laughable Lyrics* (1877).

As with Carroll's "nonsense" Lear's work contains a very particular opposition to and rejection of "sense", which is by no means devoid of meaning. His weirdly escapist poems express, in a strangely pathetic fashion, the misery and sense of alienation which he felt throughout his life, which was blighted by epilepsy (for whose effects, which were not at the time understood, he probably thought himself culpable).

THE DONG WITH A LUMINOUS NOSE

By Edward Lear

When awful darkness and silence reign
Over the great Gromboolian plain,
   Through the long, long wintry nights;-
When the angry breakers roar
As they beat on the rocky shore;-
   When Storm-clouds brood on the towering heights
Of the Hills of the Chankly Bore:

Then, through the vast and gloomy dark,
There moves what seems a fiery spark,
   A lonely spark with silvery rays
   Piercing the coal-black night, -
   A meteor strange and bright:
Hither and thither the vision strays,
   A single lurid light.

Slowly it wanders, - pauses, - creeps, -
Anon it sparkles, - flashes and leaps;
And ever as onward it gleaming goes
A light on the Bong-tree stems it throws.
And those who watch at that midnight hour
From Hall or Terrace, or lofty Tower,
Cry, as the wild light passes along, -
   "The Dong! - the Dong!
   "The Wandering Dong through the forest goes!
   "The Dong! the Dong!
   "The Dong with a luminous Nose!"

   Long years ago
   The Dong was happy and gay,
Till he fell in love with a Jumbly Girl
   Who came to those shores one day,
For the Jumblies came in a Sieve, they did, -
Landing at eve near the Zemmery Fidd

Where the Oblong Oysters grow,
And the rocks are smooth and gray.
And all the woods and the valleys rang
With the Chorus they daily and nightly sang, -
"Far and few, far and few,
Are the lands where the Jumblies live;
Their heads are green, and their hands are blue,
And they went to sea in a sieve."

Happily, happily passed those days!
While the cheerful Jumblies stayed;
They danced in circlets all night long,
To the plaintive pipe of the lively Dong,
In moonlight, shine, or shade.
For day and night he was always there
By the side of the Jumbly Girl so fair,
With her sky-blue hands, and her sea-green hair.
Till the morning came of that hateful day
When the Jumblies sailed in their sieve away,
And the Dong was left on the cruel shore
Gazing - gazing for evermore, -
Ever keeping his weary eyes on
That pea-green sail on the far horizon, -
Singing the Jumbly Chorus still
As he sat all day on the grassy hill, -
"Far and few, far and few,
Are the lands where the Jumblies live;
Their heads are green, and their hands are blue,
And they went to sea in a sieve."

But when the sun was low in the West,
The Dong arose and said, -
"What little sense I once possessed
Has quite gone out of my head!"
And since that day he wanders still
By lake and forest, marsh and hill,
Singing - "O somewhere, in valley or plain
"Might I find my Jumbly Girl again!

"For ever I'll seek by lake and shore
"Till I find my Jumbly Girl once more!"

Playing a pipe with silvery squeaks,
Since then his Jumbly Girl he seeks,
And because by night he could not see,
He gathered the bark of the Twangum Tree
  On the flowery plain that grows.
  And he wove him a wondrous Nose, -
A Nose as strange as a Nose could be!
Of vast proportions and painted red,
And tied with cords to the back of his head.
  -In a hollow rounded space it ended
With a luminous lamp within suspended,
  All fenced about
  With a bandage stout
  To prevent the wind from blowing it out; -
And with holes all round to send the light,
In gleaming rays on the dismal night.
And now each night, and all night long,
Over those plains still roams the Dong;
And above the wail of the Chimp and Snipe
You may hear the squeak of his plaintive pipe
While ever he seeks, but seeks in vain
To meet with his Jumbly Girl again;
Lonely and wild - all night he goes, -
The Dong with a luminous Nose!
And all who watch at the midnight hour.
From Hall or Terrace, or lofty Tower,
Cry, as they trace the Meteor bright,
Moving along through the dreary night, -
    "This is the hour when forth he goes,
    "The Dong with a luminous Nose!
    "Yonder - over the plain he goes;
    "He goes!
    "He goes;
    "The Dong with a luminous Nose!"

WALTER BESANT (1836-1901) was a prolific Victorian novelist, knighted late in life, whose early best-sellers were written in collaboration with James Rice (1844-1882). He was a founder member of the Society of Authors and had a lifelong interest in social reform. Several fantasies which he wrote in collaboration with Rice were collected in *The Case of Mr. Lucraft and Other Tales* (1876), including the bizarre title story, in which a young man leases his healthy appetite to an aging sybarite and takes on himself the painful side-effects of the other's self-indulgence, and "Titania's Farewell", an allegory in which the fairies leave England in protest against social injustice. Besant later wrote a few solo fantasies, including the identity exchange story *The Doubts of Dives* (1889) and the multiple personality story *The Ivory Gate* (1892); he also wrote two early futuristic novels, *The Revolt of Man* (1882) and *The Inner House* (1888).

Besant's collaborations with WALTER HERRIES POLLOCK (1850-1926) include a book of drawing-room comedies as well as "Sir Jocelyn's Cap" (1884-5); the latter arose out of a playful conversation in the Savile Club with Charles Brookfield (who actually proposed the idea on which the story turns). The novelette is an important early example of a particular kind of comedy in which magical premises are developed in a sceptical and down-to-earth fashion which mocks and undermines their promise; the formula was brought to full flower by the novels of "F. Anstey", whose success with it called forth scores of cruder imitations by the likes of "R. Andom" and Richard Marsh.

Pollock collaborated with Andrew Lang on a series of parodies of the novels of H. Rider Haggard including *King Solomon's Treasures, It* and *Bess* (all 1887). He also wrote a handful of stories - including the comic fantasy "Edged Tools" (1886) - in collaboration with the American writer and critic J. Brander Matthews. (Matthews was also an inveterate writer of stories in collaboration, and once wrote a comedy called "The Three Wishes" with Anstey, which is so down-to-earth as to have no authentic supernatural intrusions.) Most of Pollock's solo fantasies are collected in *Nine Men's*

302

Morrice (1889), which includes three items reprinted from an earlier collection, *The Picture's Secret* (1883). The title story of the earlier collection, called "Lilith" in the later one, is a novella about a *femme fatale* and a family curse; in the other items, run together as "An Adventure in the Life of Mr. Latimer" in the earlier collection, but separated as "Mr. Morton's Butler" and "Lady Volant" in the later, the Devil's attempts to trick an oblivious young man into signing his soul away are continually thwarted by happy accidents. Other fantasies by Pollock are in his collection *King Zub* (1897), including "Sir Jocelyn's Cap", which can also be found in Besant's collection *Uncle Jack, etc* (1885).

SIR JOCELYN'S CAP

By Walter Besant & Walter Herries Pollock

1

"This," said Jocelyn, throwing himself into a chair, "is the most wonderful thing I ever came across."

Do you know how, sometimes in the dead of night, or even in broad daylight, while you are thinking, you distinctly hear a voice which argues with you, puts the case another way, contradicts you, or even accuses you, and calls names?

This happened to Jocelyn. A voice somewhere in the room, and not far from his ear, said clearly and distinctly, "There is something here much more wonderful." It was a low voice, yet metallic, and with a cluck in it as if the owner had begun life as a Hottentot.

Jocelyn started and looked around. He was quite alone. He was in chambers in Piccadilly: a suite of four rooms; outside there was the roll of carriages and cabs, with the trampling of many feet; at five o'clock on an afternoon in May, and in Piccadilly, one hardly expects anything supernatural. When something of the kind happens at this time, it is much more creepy than the same thing at midnight. The voice was perfectly distinct and audible. Jocelyn felt cold and trembled involuntarily, and then was angry with himself for trembling.

"Much more wonderful," repeated this strange voice with the cluck. Jocelyn pretended not to hear it. He was quite as brave as most of his brother-clerks in the Foreign Office, but in the matter of strange voices he was inexperienced, and thought to get rid of this one as one gets rid of an importunate beggar, by passing him without notice.

"I've looked everywhere," he said.

"Not everywhere," clucked the voice in correction.

"Everywhere," he repeated, firmly. "And there's nothing. The old man has left no money, no bank-books, no sign of investment, stocks, or shares. What did he live upon?"

"Me," said the voice.

Jocelyn started again. His nerves, he said to himself, must be getting shaky.

"He seems to have had no 'affairs' of any kind; no solicitors, no engagements; nothing but the letting of the Grange. How on earth did he -" Here he stopped, for fear of being answered by that extraordinary echo in his ear. He heard a cluck-cluck as if the reply was ready, but was checked at the moment of utterance.

"All his bills paid regularly, nothing owing, not even a tailor's bill running, and the money in his desk exactly the amount, and no more, required for his funeral. Fancy leaving just enough for your funeral! Seems like a practical joke on your lawful heir. Nothing in the world except that old barn." He sat down again and meditated.

The deceased was his uncle, the chief of the old house, the owner and possessor of the Grange. He left, it is true, a formal will behind him, in which he devised everything of which he was possessed to his nephew Jocelyn, who inherited the Grange and the park besides the title. Unfortunately, he did not specify his possessions, so that when the young man came to look into his inheritance, he knew not how great or how small it was. Now, when one knows nothing, one expects a great deal, which accounts for the buoyancy of human youth and the high spirits of the infant pig.

He began with an unsystematic yet anxious examination of the old man's desks and papers. They were left in very good order; the letters, none of which were of the least importance, were all folded, endorsed, and dated; the receipts - all for bills which would never be disputed - were pasted in books; the diaries, which contained the record of daily expenditure and the chronicle of small-beer, stood before him in a long uniform row of black cloth volumes. Even the dinner-cards were preserved, and the play-bills: a most methodical old gentleman. But this made it the more surprising that there could not be found among all these papers any which referred to his private affairs and his personal property.

"He must have placed," said Jocelyn, "all the documents concerning his invested moneys in the hands of some solicitor. I have only got to find his address."

He then proceeded to examine slowly and methodically the drawers, shelves, cupboards, recesses, cabinets, boxes, cases, receptacles, trunks, and portmanteaus in the chambers, turning them inside out and upside down, shaking them, banging them, peering and prying, carefully feeling all the linings, lifting lids, sounding pockets, and trying locks, until he was quite satisfied that he had left no place untried. Yet he found nothing. This was surprising as well as disappointing. For although of late years old Sir Jocelyn's habits had been retired and even penurious, it was well known that in early manhood, that is to say, somewhere in the twenties and thirties, he was about town in a very large and generous sense indeed. He must, at that time, have had a great deal of money. Had he lost it? Yet something must have remained. Else, how could he live? And at least there must be some record of the remnant. Yet, strange to say, not even a bank-book. Jocelyn thought over this day by day. He had taken up his abode in the chambers, which were comfortable, though the furniture was old and shabby. The rent, which was high, was paid by the Grange, now let to a family of Americans of the same surname as his own, who wanted to say they had lived in an old English country-house, and would go home and declare that it was the real original cradle of their race. Cradles of race, like family trees, can be ordered or hired of the cabinet-maker, either in Wardour Street or the College of Heralds. The old man *must* have had something besides the family house. If it was only an annuity, there would be the papers to show it. Where were those papers?

This search among the drawers and shelves and desks took him several days. It was upon the second day that he heard the voice. On the fifth day, which was Saturday, he began with the books on the shelves - there were not many.

First he looked behind them: nothing there; he remembered
to have heard that sometimes wills, deeds, and other proofs
of property have been hidden in the leaves of the Family
Bible: there was no Family Bible, but there was a great
quantity of novels, and Jocelyn spent a long afternoon
turning over the leaves of these volumes in search of some
paper which would give him a clue to his inheritance. He
might just as well have spent it squaring the circle, or
extracting the square root of minus one, or pursuing a
metaphysical research, for all the good it did him. It is only
fair to the young man to say that he would have greatly
preferred spending the time in lawn-tennis, and especially in
playing that game at a place which was adorned with the
gracious presence of a certain young lady. "A Foreign Office
clerk," said Jocelyn bitterly; "a mere Foreign Office clerk is
good enough to dance with. She has danced with me for a
year and a half. The other fellows can't dance. But when
that clerk becomes the owner of a tumble-down Grange,
though there are not twenty acres of ground belonging to it,
and, besides, gets all the property of old Sir Jocelyn, whom
all the world knows, and inherits his title, that Foreign
Office clerk becomes, if you please, a person of consideration
as the other fellows shall see. But where the devil *is* the
property?"

"Property!" It was the same curious echo, in his ear, of
that metallic clucking voice. Remember that it was
Saturday afternoon, when the streets are full; this made
such a phenomenon as a voice proceeding from empty space
all the more striking and terrible. Much more terrible was
the thing which next occurred. You know how in thought-
reading the medium takes your hand, and without your
guidance moves slowly, but certainly, in the direction of the
spot where you have hidden the ring. The phenomenon has
been witnessed by hundreds; it is a fact which cannot be
disputed. What happened to Jocelyn was exactly of the same
kind, and therefore not more surprising. An invisible force -
call it not a hand - an invisible, impalpable, strange
electrical force seized his hand with a kind of grasp. It was

not a strong grasp; quite the contrary. The pressure was varying, flickering, inconstant, uncertain. At the very first manifestation and perception of it, Sir Jocelyn's knees knocked themselves together, his hair stood on end, his moustache went out of curl, and, to use a favourite and very feeling expression of the last century, his jaws stuck. By this feeble pressure or hand-grasp, the young man was pulled, or rather guided gently across the room to a table on which stood, with its doors open, a large Japanese cabinet. It was one of those things with two doors, behind which are two rows of drawers, and below the doors one long drawer. He had already examined every one of the drawers on the first day of the search, when he had opened and looked into all the desks, drawers, boxes, and cupboards in the chambers. He knew what was in the drawers - a collection of letters, chiefly from ladies, written to his uncle and preserved by him. Was it possible that he had overlooked something? He opened all the drawers, turned out their contents, and proceeded to examine every letter. This took him two or three hours, during the whole of which time he had an uncomfortable feeling as if his forefinger were being gently but steadily pulled. At last he threw down the last letter and let himself go, just as a man who is blindfolded and yet finds a hidden object, allows himself to be led by the unconscious guide straight to the place where it has been deposited. Guided by this unknown force, he found himself grasping the lowest drawer - the large one - which he had already pulled out. What did it mean? He turned it round: there was nothing remarkable about the drawer: an empty drawer cannot contain a secret. Surprising: his fingers seemed pulled about in all directions - what was it? By this time, the first natural terror was gone, but his pulse beat fast; he was excited; he was clearly on the eve of making some strange discovery.

He examined the drawer again, and more carefully. He could see nothing strange about. Then he heard again that curious voice which seemed in his own head, and it said "Measure."

308

What was he to measure? If Jocelyn had been a conjuror he would have understood at once: he would even have guessed: the professor of legerdemain is a master in all kinds of craft and subtlety - I knew one of them who, though passionately fond of whist, would never play the game on account of the temptation in dealing to give himself all the thirteen trumps - but above all he understood the value of drawers, compartments, divisions, and recesses which are shorter than they seem. The drawer was in fact only three-fourths the depth of the cabinet. When Jocelyn at length realized this fact, he perceived that there must be a secret compartment at the back, where no doubt something was hidden which it greatly concerned him to find out. Of course by this time he accepted without further doubt the fact that unusual forces - call them forces - were abroad. "A psychic influence," said Jocelyn, though his teeth chattered, " of a rare and most curious description." The communication of it to the Society established as a Refuge for the stories which nobody outside it will believe, would be very interesting: but perhaps it was his uncle who thus - here another impatient jerk of his finger startled him. He turned the cabinet round; the back presented a plain surface of wood without any possible scope for the operation of secret springs; the side was carved with little round knobs in relief. He measured the drawer with the side of the cabinet: there was a difference of three and a half inches, and the drawer was three inches high: as the cabinet was two feet broad, this gave a space of 3 x 24 x $3\frac{1}{2}$, which represents 252 cubic inches. A good deal may be hidden away in 252 cubic inches. How was he to get at the contents? Anyone can take a hammer and chisel and brutally burst open a cabinet, whether of Japanese or any other work. It did strike Jocelyn that perhaps with the poker he might prise the thing open. But then, so beautiful a cabinet, and his late uncle's favourite depository for the love letters of a life spent wholly in making love - 'twould be barbarous. While he considered, the forefinger of his right hand was travelling slowly over the knobs. Presently it stopped, and Jocelyn felt upon the knuckle a distinct tap. He pressed the knob; to his astonishment a kind of door flew open. Jocelyn looked in - there *was* something! At this moment he paused. He did not doubt that the treasure, whatever it was, would prove of the greatest, the very greatest importance to him, perhaps title-deeds, perhaps debentures, perhaps notes of investments, perhaps the address of the solicitors in whose hands Sir Jocelyn, his uncle, had placed his affairs, perhaps - but here he tilted up the cabinet, not daring, through some terror of the supernatural, as if a spirit who could bite might be lurking in the recess, to put in his hand, and the contents fell out without any apparent supernatural assistance, by the natural law of gravity. We may take it as a general rule in all occurrences of the supernatural kind, that the ordinary machinery provided by nature and already explained by Sir Isaac Newton and others, is employed wherever it is possible. In cases where direct interference of another kind is required, no doubt it is always forthcoming. No ghost or spirit would hesitate, of course, to go through closed doors, pass parcels through walls, and so forth; but if the doors are open the plain way is clearly and obviously the safest and best. So that, if a thing will fall from a receptacle of its own accord when that receptacle is inverted, there is really no necessity at all for the assistance of psychic force. This explains why the parcel fell out.

It was wrapped in an old discoloured linen covering. Jocelyn unfolded it with trembling fingers. It contained a cap. Odd; only a cap. It was made of cloth, thick, such as is used for a fez, and formerly no doubt red, but the colour was almost gone out of it, and it was moth-eaten. In shape it was not unlike a Phrygian cap. Round the lower part there ran an edging, an inch broad, of gold embroidery, but this too was ragged and, in places, falling off. There was also a lining of silk, but it was so ragged and worn that it looked as if at a single touch it would fall out.

"A worn-out, old, decrepit cap" said Jocelyn, "All this fuss about a worthless cap!" Just then his little finger received a tap; and Jocelyn, his attention thus directed to the spot, saw a folded paper beneath the cap.

310

"Ah!" he cried, "this is what I have been looking for. But a cap! I never heard my uncle talk about a cap."

He took up the paper, and yet he could not choose but look at the cap itself. As he gazed upon it, he felt himself turning giddy. Cabinet, cap, and paper swam before his eyes. "It is nothing," he murmured, "the heat of the room - the - the --"

"Effendi!" said the voice he knew, metallic and yet quavering. "Excellency! it is - *me* - your servant."

The cap was transformed - it was now of a brilliant hue, while its gold embroideries were fresh and glittering - it no longer lay upon a table, decrepit and falling to pieces, but it now covered the head of a little old man, apparently about eighty or more, so wrinkled and lined was his visage. He seemed feeble, and his knees and shoulders were bent, but his eyes were bright. He was dressed in some Oriental garb, the like of which Jocelyn had never seen.

He bowed, in Oriental style with gesture of the fingers. "I am," he said, "the Slave of the Cap. I am a Jinn, and I am at his Excellency's service, night and day, to perform his wishes so long as he possesses the Cap."

"And at what price?" asked Jocelyn.

"At none. The Effendi's ancestor paid the charges; fees are not allowed to be taken by assistants. Sorcerers and great Effendis like his Excellency are particularly requested to observe this rule."

"Certainly," said Jocelyn. "If there is to be no signing of bonds and terms of years -"

"Nothing, your Excellency, nothing of the kind."

"In that case - " here the faintness came over him again and his eyes swam. When he recovered he looked about him for the Oriental servant. There was no one there, only the furniture in the room and the cabinet, and beside the cabinet the worn and faded cap.

"I think I must be going off my head," said Jocelyn. "I wish I had a glass of water." As he spoke he saw that a glass of water actually stood on the table at his elbow. He took it and was going to drink it. "Faugh!" he cried, setting it down

311

hastily, "it has had flowers in it."

Then he remembered the roll of paper - which he opened. It was a letter on two sheets, addressed to himself by his uncle; but the second sheet had been twisted, and apparently used as a light, for it was partly burned, and had been rolled out again and placed with the unburned sheet as if the writer had been hurried.

"My dear Nephew," it said, - "I have deferred until a late - perhaps the last moment, writing to you. I have long felt that you are ardently desirous of ascertaining what I have and what I should leave to you. In the first place, there is the Grange. You can always, I should think, let that very old and picturesque building for a sum which will give you the rent of your chambers, pay your club subscriptions and your dinners. You have, besides, your clerkship, which ought to pay your tailor's bill. I do not advise you as regards the conduct of your life. My own, it is true, has been chiefly guided by the precepts of the great and good Lord Chesterfield; but I refrain from pressing my examples upon you.

"There is, however, a very curious family possession which I am able to leave you. I am sure you will value it highly, if only on account of its history. It has been in the possession of the chief of our race for five hundred and fifty years and more. Sir Jocelyn de Haultegresse, your ancestor, being one of the later Crusaders under Richard Coeur de Lion, received it for some friendly services, the nature of which is unknown, from his noble and learned friend, the Saracen Sorcerer, Ali Ibn Yûssûf, commonly called Khanjar ed Dîn, or the Ox Goad of Religion. This invaluable cap confers on its possessor the power of having whatever he wishes for. Armed with this talisman, and being all, like myself, men of moderate ambitions, anxious chiefly to get through life as pleasantly as possible, we have not incurred odium by amassing broad lands and great possessions. I bequeath, therefore, to you this cap, in the hope that you will use it with moderation. Ponder carefully before expressing a

312

desire, even in your own mind, the effect of making a wish which will be construed into an order. I must also give you a word of warning. I have observed for some time, to my great regret" - here the page was partly and irregularly burned - "to my very great regret... on many occasions to carry out my wishes promptly ... desirable to exercise modera...no excuse for other than prompt...not fall to pieces, or there may may be alleged some pretext for crying off...ments have long been lost, and it might be difficult in court of law to recover... Well, my nephew, this talisman kept me in luxury for sixty years; perhaps it may yet ...regain, so to speak, its old tone. At least, I hope so.
"Your affect..."

"By Jove!" said Jocelyn.

He might have gone on to ask if anybody had ever seen the like, or if one could have expected it, or if one was really living in an age when such things are discredited. But he did not. He only said "By Jove!" and looked about the room, and at the cap, and at the letter, with bewildered eyes. At last he understood the meaning of this very plain letter. He pushed back his chair and sprang to his feet, crying, "Christopher Columbus! I've got a WISHING CAP!"

II

He stood looking at the faded old cap. The thing fascinated him; the gold embroidery flickered, and seemed to send out sparks and tiny gleams of fire. The rusty stuff glowed and became ruddy again. *Could* the thing be true? But his uncle was a sober man and a truthful; his narrative had nothing wild or enthusiastic about it.

"My ancestor, Sir Jocelyn de Haultegresse," the young man repeated. "Yes; the one who lies with crossed legs in the old church. I wish I knew how he got the cap."

His eyes fell upon a picture. Why, he had seen that picture a hundred times, and never thought what it might mean, or if it had any meaning at all. It hung, among

313

others, on the wall, and represented a Crusader in full armour conversing with a Moslem. The former was a young man; the latter was old, with a long grey beard - an old man who looked impossibly wise.

They were not only conversing, but Jocelyn heard what they were saying.

"I understand, Venerable Ox Goad of Religion," said the Christian, "that with this thing in my possession I can ask for and obtain anything I want."

"Anything in reason," replied Khanjar ed Dîn. "You cannot, for instance, walk dry-shod from Palestine to Dover, but you can sail in safety through a storm."

"And not be sea-sick?"

"Certainly not, if you command it."

"Suppose, for instance - a valiant knight would not ask such a thing - but suppose, for illustration, one were to ask for - say the absence of the enemy when one lands, eh? - terror of the enemy at one's approach - flight of the enemy when one charges - safety when the arrows are rattling about one's armour - eh?"

"All these things," replied the wise man, "you can command and ensure."

"Ha!" Sir Jocelyn smiled . "It rejoices me," he said piously, "that I came a-crusading. All Christendom - ay! and Islam too - shall ring with my prowess."

"Certainly," replied the Sage, "if you wish it."

"Can one also command the constancy of one's mistress?"

The magician hesitated.

"You can command it," he said. "But I know not the Frankish ladies. Perhaps they will not obey even the Slave of the Cap."

"One more question," said Sir Jocelyn. "In my country they have a trick of burning those - even if they be knights, crusaders, and pious pilgrims - burning and roasting, I say, at slow fires those who become magicians, wizards, sorcerers, and those who employ the services of a devil."

"Keep your secret," said the wizard. "Let no one know.

314

And, that none may guess it, let your desires be moderate. Farewell, Sir Jocelyn."

The conversation ceased, but the picture remained. Pictures, in fact, last longer than conversations.

"This is truly wonderful," said Jocelyn.

He threw open the windows and looked into the street. Below him, in Piccadilly, was the crowd of the early London season: the carriages and cabs rolled along the road; on the other side the trees were in their early foliage. It seemed impossible, in the very heart and centre of modern civilization and luxury, that such things as he had heard and witnessed should have happened. Yet, when he looked round the room again, there was the Cap, there was his uncle's letter, and there the picture of Sir Jocelyn's bargain. What had he given this Eastern wizard for a power so tremendous?

Then the young man began to reflect upon the history of his House. They had for generations lived in the ease and affluence of English country gentlefolk: they had never, so far as he knew, turned out a spendthrift: they had not fooled away their small estate: they had neither distinguished nor disgraced themselves: in fact, there was no reason why they should try to distinguish themselves: they had all they wanted, because they could command it. Knowledge? they had the royal road to it: art - skill - strength? they had only to wish for it. Wealth? they could command it. Why, then, should they seek to show themselves better, more clever, stronger, or wiser than their fellows? It would have cost an infinity of trouble, and for no good end; because if they succeeded, how much better off would they have been? The knowledge of this secret made him understand his ancestors. As they had been, so should he be. Except for one thing. The four last baronets were unmarried; in each case the title descended to a nephew. As for himself - and here he murmured softly, "Eleanor" - and choked. Suppose you had set your heart wholly upon one thing, and that thing seemed impossible of attainment, so that the future loomed before you as dull and as grey as noon-tide at a foggy Christmas: and then suppose the clouds lifted, the sun shining, and that glorious, that beautiful Thing actually within your grasp. Anyone, under these circumstances, would choke.

He returned to the table and contemplated the Cap, wondering if the Attendant of the Cap were actually at his elbow.

"It might be awkward," he said, "to wake at night and remember that the dev - I mean Monsieur the Jinn, the Minister of the Cap, was sitting beside one on the pillow. Would he come to church with one, I wonder? And would he be offended with remarks about him?" He half expected some reply, but there was none.

"He was a very old fellow to look at," he went on. "But in these cases age goes for nothing. I suppose he doesn't know, himself, how old he is; as for the Cap, I wish it were a trifle less shabby."

Wonderful to relate, a curious change came over the faded cloth. It looked bright again, and the gold embroidery smartened up; not to look fresh, but a good many years younger.

"Sun came out", said Sir Jocelyn, trying not to be too credulous. Then he thought he would test the powers of the Cap, as mathematicians test a theory, namely, with elementary cases. "I wish," he said, "that my hat was new." Why, as he looked at his hat, it suddenly struck him that it was not so very shabby after all: a mirror-like polish has a got-up look about it. This hat was one which had evidently been worn for a week or two, but was still quite good enough to be worn in the park or anywhere.

"My gloves" - he stopped because, without formulating the wish in words, he instantly became aware that his gloves were by no means as bad as they had seemed a moment before. Not new certainly: but what is so horrid as a pair of brand-new gloves? He had overrated the faults of his gloves. They were an excellent pair of gloves, just worn long enough to make them fit the Fingers, and not make them look like glove-stretchers; the glove should look made for the fingers, in fact, not the fingers for the glove. To be sure, the gloves on the table were not those he had in his mind; and, in fact,

316

he could not remember exactly how he came by those gloves. Later on, he discovered that he had taken up a wrong pair at the Club.

He sat down to argue out this matter in his own mind. All young men try to do this: when they come to realize that "arguing out" leads to hopeless fogging, they give it up. Very few middle-aged men argue out a thing; mathematicians, sometimes; logicians, never; the intellectual ladies who contribute arguments on the intellect of the domestic cat to the *Spectator*, frequently. But the result is always more fog.

A Wishing Cap, at this enlightened period, is absurd.

But tables turn, furniture dances, men are "levitated," thought is read, and there is a Psychical Society, with Fellows of Trinity and Doctors of Letters at the head of it. Nothing, at any time, is absurd.

What evidence had he for the miraculous powers of the Cap? First, the word of his uncle, a most truthful and honourable gentleman. Next, the picture. Thirdly, the two remarkable Visions he had himself received. Fourthly, the gloves and the hat. Lastly, any further evidence the Cap itself might afford him.

By this time he was hopelessly fogged. He began to remember Will, Magnetic Force, Psychic fluid, all the tags of the spiritualistic folk. These phrases are like spectres which come with fog and mist.

Sir Jocelyn was then sensible enough to perceive that he had argued the matter thoroughly out. After all, there is nothing like experiment, especially, as the conjurors say, under "test conditions," that is to say, where collusion, connivance, fraud, and deception of any kind are impossible. I have seen at a fair, under "test conditions," a plum-cake made in a gentleman's hat, and the hat none the worse.

He lit a cigarette and tried to think of other things unconnected with a Wishing Cap. And first he reflected that, although it is bad to be a penniless Foreign Office clerk, with no other recommendations than that of being heir to a Baronet reputed well off, it is worse to have succeeded to the title and to have discovered that there is no money after all.

317

"Hang it !" cried Jocelyn, "there might have been something. I do wish my uncle had left me something - even a single sixpence!" As he spoke a small coin, a sixpence in fact, tumbled out of a forgotten hole in his waistcoat pocket and fell clinking on the floor. At this point Jocelyn gave way to temper. "Damn the waistcoat!" he cried, and at the same moment dropped his cigarette and burnt an irreclaimable hole in the light stuff of which the waistcoat was made.

Then he conceived a strange idea, a kind of trap to catch a demon, or at least to prove him. He leaned his elbows on the table and addressed the Cap.

"You are a poor old moth-eaten thing," he said. "That, so far as I know, you may have been when the Ox Goad of Religion gave you to my ancestor, Sir Jocelyn the Valiant. Now, you give me a test of your powers in a simple and unmistakable way. I am tired of the uniform London dinner. Cause me to have an entirely new dinner. There!" He expected some movement on the part of the Cap: a nod or inclination at least. Nothing of the kind. The Cap remained perfectly still.

"A note for you, sir," said the servant, bringing him a letter.

It was from a man named Annesley, a friend of Jocelyn's who had rooms in Sackville Street.

"If by any lucky chance," it said, "you are disengaged this evening, come here. The experiment in *menus* we have talked of comes off to-night. Courtland has been called away, so we must have it now or perhaps never."

Yes, there had been talk about variety in *menus*. Annesley, a man of invention and ideas, had promised something, vaguely. Well, he would go: he answered the note to that effect.

"I suppose," he said to the Cap, "that you have got something to do with this. I wished for a new kind of dinner, and here is one: on the other hand, Annesley hasn't got a Cap, and I suppose he arranged his *menu* without reference to you. I will now give you another chance. I am going to the Park. I wish to meet the Stauntons. Do you know who the Stauntons are? Find out! Yah! You and your sixpence!"

In spite of his bluster, he was rapidly acquiring confidence in his Cap. Before going out, he carefully placed it, with his uncle's letter, in the secret drawer, which he closed. Then he looked at the picture of his ancestor and the Syrian magician.

"Venerable Ox Goad of Religion!" he said, imitating his great ancestor, "can I command, in truth, all that I desire?"

It seemed as if a voice spoke in answer, but whose voice, or whence it came, he knew not.

"Command!"

Jocelyn heard it and shuddered. Then he took his hat and gloves, and hurried forth.

III

When Jocelyn wished to meet the Stauntons, he should have explained that he wished to meet Nelly, or Eleanor Staunton. This might have saved him a good deal of annoyance. For, first there were Connie Staunton, the actress, and her sister Linda, both of the Gaiety. He met them, driving in a victoria, and heard two young gentlemen, as they lifted their hats, murmur their names in accents of idolatrous emotion.

"Your are a fool," said Jocelyn, addressing the Cap. Then there came rolling along a great yellow chariot, with an old lady and still older gentleman in it.

"That," said one of two girls who were standing beside the railing, "that is Lady Staunton and Sir George - our Hemmer is her lady's-maid. She's a kind old thing."

"This is ridiculous," said Jocelyn. Yet he was pleased to observe the activity of his new servant. Two sets of Stauntons already, though not yet the right set. "I mean the Howard Stauntons."

It was before him, slowly advancing with the throng. He could see the backs of two heads and the parasol of a third. Mrs. Staunton and Caroline, and - yes - Nelly! Hers was the parasol. He would walk on and meet them when they turned.

319

He was conscious that he was regarded with no great favour by the young lady's mamma. Still, he was now a Baronet, with a place in the country, and an income, counting his clerkship, of - Well - was it quite six hundred pounds a year? There was also the Cap, but of that he could say nothing. Yet, oh! the joy of wishing beautiful dresses for Nelly, when Nelly should be his own!

There were two daughters: Caroline, the elder, was now seven-and-twenty years of age, and in her ninth season. As she was beautiful, accomplished, clever, and rich (by reason of a bequest from a rich uncle), it was to all women a most surprising thing that she did not marry. Men, who understand these things better, were not surprised. Her beauty was after the fine old Roman style, and accompanied by a more than classical coldness. She was an advocate of Woman's Rights, an ardent politician, a student of logic, learned in many ways, but she was not, apparently, a devotee of Venus. That goddess loves her worshippers to be soft-eyed, smiling, caressing, lively, willing to be pleased and anxious to please. Caroline was chiefly anxious to be heard. There was also some talk about an early affair which ended badly. Some girls harden after such a disaster. Still, there was no doubt that Caroline desired to convert men into listeners. Of the opposite school was Nelly - younger than her sister by seven good solid years. Not so beautiful - in fact, with irregular features - she was singularly taking, by reason principally of her sympathetic nature. She had no opinions at all of her own, but she was on the other hand very ready to hear those of other people, especially those of young men. That woman is certain to go far who thoroughly understands that young men - indeed, men of all ages - delight in nothing so much as to talk confidentially with women, and especially young women, about themselves. Many a most excellent chance has been lost through not observing and acting upon this principle. Nelly, her mother was resolved, should not be thrown away. As for Jocelyn, he had nothing, and she had nothing, therefore any little tenderness which might arise on the girl's side should be instantly nipped in the bud. A resolute mother, when assisted by an elder daughter, is altogether too powerful for a detrimental. Therefore Jocelyn got next to no chances, and worshipped at a distance and sadly. Whether Nelly ever understood the meaning of his melancholy I know not. Meantime, the young man lost no opportunity of meeting the object of his hopeless passion, though he too often fell into the hands of the elder sister, who made him sit down and hear her opinions. Now, however, he repeated, he was a Baronet, and he had - he had a Wishing Cap.

"I wish they would go slower," he said. There was a block at Prince's Gate, and the whole line was stopped.

"Thank you," said Jocelyn. In another moment he would have reached the carriage, when - oh! - he groaned deeply - as there met him the greatest bore of his acquaintance, a long-winded bore, a cheerful bore, a bore who laughs, a bore who tells very pointless stories, a bore at the sight of whom men fly, plead engagements, and for their sake break up clubs. This creature seized Jocelyn by the button, and told him how he had landed a good thing. And the block was removed and the carriages went on again. At last he broke away, still keeping the Stauntons in sight. But there was another diversion. This time it was a slight carriage accident, but as it happened to friends he could not in common decency pass on without tendering his assistance. Once more he got away, and saw the Stauntons' carriage slowly making its way to the turning at Albert Gate. Then was his last chance: the crowd was thick, but he forced his way through, and was prepared with a ready smile just before the carriage turned homewards. In fact, he had already executed a beautiful bow before he perceived that the vehicle was empty. The ladies had got out without his seeing them. He turned, discomfited, and went home to dress for dinner.

While dressing, in a pretty bad temper, he began to "argue it out" again. Why, after all, he had got his wishes in the most remarkable manner. About the reality of his power there could be no doubt. He had wished for water: it was at his elbow. No doubt, if he had said drinking-water, the Cap would not have brought water in which flowers had been standing for a week. He had wished for a new hat, and his hat suddenly blossomed into such glossiness as is acquired by a *coup de fer* at the hatter's; for new gloves, and his gloves became - not new certainly, but newish. He had foolishly wished that his uncle had left him the smallest coin, and there was a sixpence; he had wished for a new and original dinner, and there had come Annesley's invitation; he had wished to see the Stauntons, and he had seen them.

It was with a feeling of great elation that he went to the dinner. Anybody would feel elated at the acquisition of such a strange and wonderful power.

"You shall have," said Annesley, as if he had actually heard Jocelyn's wish, "you shall have something perfectly new and original for dinner. It is an experiment which will, I think, please you."

The table was laid with the exquisite attractiveness and skill which belonged to all of Annesley's entertainments. He was a young man who had ideas and a considerable fortune to carry them out with. Life is only really interesting when one has both ideas and a fortune. As for Courtland, he was a critic. Not a failure in art and letters, but a critic born: one of the men who are critics of everything, from a picture to a slice of bread and cheese, and from Château-Lafitte to bitter beer.

"I see," said Annesley, with a gratified smile, "I see, my dear fellow, that you are surprised at seeing oysters. It is not the season for oysters, certainly," yet there were six on each man's plate. "But these are Chinese sun-dried oysters. They came to me by a singular chance, in a state resembling shrivelled rags. You put them into salt water for an hour or two, and then, as you observe, they turn out as plump and as fresh as natives. By the Chinese they are esteemed a great delicacy."

Jocelyn tasted one, though with misgiving. Probably he did not share the Chinese opinion of sun-dried oysters, for he turned pale, gasped, and hastily drank a glass of lacryma, which had been chosen by Annesley to accompany the oysters. The other man, observing the effect of the sun-dried oysters upon Jocelyn, prudently abstained from tasting them at all, but began a stream of conversation, under cover of which the oysters got carried away, while Annesley's delight in his experiment prevented him from observing its failure. Indeed, he went on to talk with complacent assurance of the foolish and ignorant prejudices with which many admirable forms of food are regarded.

"I shall proceed," he said, "to give you presently a remarkable illustration of this." Jocelyn shuddered. "Meantime, here is a soup which I can highly recommend; it is a *purée* of cuttle-fish."

It really was an excellent soup, could Jocelyn have rid himself of the horrible imagination of a *poulpe* flinging hideous gelatinous arms about from the middle of the plate, and fixing its suckers on the hand that grasped the spoon.

"The cuttle-fish," said Annesley, who, besides being a man of ideas, was also somewhat of a prig, "the cuttle-fish, which is the actual type of the legendary Kraken - though, by the way, the Kraken is not so very legendary, since the great Squid -"

"That will do Annesley," said Courtland. "We know all about the Squid. Fellow wrote a book about him. Model at the Fisheries."

"The cuttle-fish," continued Annesley, "is a much maligned creature. Not more so, however, than the fish which Williams is now putting on the table - the dog-fish."

"Oh! I say!" cried Jocelyn,

"Dog-fish," said Courtland. "Beasts when alive. Take all your bait. Fishermen roll 'em up and scrub the gunwhale with 'em. Think it will encourage the others."

"My pet fisherman," said Jocelyn, "used to do that till I begged him not to. He told me, I remember, that some people eat them."

"Did he eat them himself?" asked Courtland.

"No, he did not."

"Cooked like this," interrupted Annesley, with a

reassuring smile, "he would have eaten them with enthusiasm. They are stuffed with tinned shrimps."

"Lead poisoning," Courtland murmured in his beard.

The two guests, however, struggled manfully with the dog-fish.

With it, Annesley insisted, must be taken Catalan wine. Little was done with either. Nor was the next course, which consisted of iced potatoes with mulled Moselle, much more successful. It was one of Annesley's whims to find for each course its one peculiar drink: thus with the edible fungus he gave iced negus; and though he provided a sufficiency of dry champagne, he begged his guests so pathetically to try his fancies, that they could not refuse. Long before the unnatural dinner came to an end, all three were excited by the mixture of drinks and the correspondingly small supply of food. By the time when the curried kingfishers - a rare and *recherché* dish - arrived, they were tired of talking about *cuisine*, and were arguing hotly, especially Courtland and Annesley, about things of which they knew nothing: such as the proper method of riding a steeplechase - a thing which none of them had ever tried; the locality of "Swells' Corner" at Eton - all three had been at Harrow - and so forth. At last, Jocelyn, weary of the babble, and perhaps more than a little cross with the terrible failure of the dinner, cried out, "Oh, don't let us wrangle in this way! I wish we had a little harmony!"

He had hardly spoken when a German band, brazen beyond all belief, broke out at the end of Sackville Street, and a piano-organ below their window.

"This is the work" - Jocelyn banged his fist upon the table - "of my ancestor's amazing fool of a devil!"

The others stopped and looked at him. They only half heard the words, but Jocelyn hastily fled.

Everything had gone wrong - the dinner more than anything else. A terrible thought struck him. Could his devil by any chance have gone stupid, or was he inattentive? And, if the latter, how to correct him? Suppose, for instance, Ariel had refused to obey Prospero, and his master had no spells to compel obedience! Now this seemed exactly Jocelyn's case. He sat down and took a cigar. "The dinner," he said, "was the most infernal mess ever set before a man. I've taken too much wine, and mixed it; and I've eaten next to nothing. To-morrow morning I shall have a very self-assertive head; and all through that fool of a Cap." He remembered, however, that he had as yet asked nothing serious of the Cap, and went to bed hopeful.

IV

Perhaps the wine he had taken made Jocelyn sleep, in spite of the many and exciting adventures of the day, without thinking of the Cap, or being disturbed by the thought of the invisible servant who sat beside his pillow. In the morning, which happened to be Sunday, he did think of the Cap when he awoke, but with a sleepy comfortable satisfaction in having got what promised to be a good thing. It was eight o'clock. "Too early to get up," he said; "wish I could go to sleep again."

His eyes instantly closed. When he awoke again it was eleven and he proceeded to get up. It would be wrong to say that he did not think about the Cap; in fact, his mind was brimful of it; but Jocelyn was not one of those who work themselves up to an agony point of nervousness because they cannot understand a thing. On the contrary, once having realized that the thing *was* - an unmistakable and undeniable fact - he was ready to accept it, a thing as difficult to understand as the law of attraction.

"Heigho! he said; "I wish I was dressed."

He then perceived that he had already put on his socks, though he couldn't remember having done so. And, besides, you cannot tub in your socks; so he had to take them off again. He wished for nothing more while he was dressing except once, and that at a most unlucky moment: it was in the process of shaving. He was thinking of the battles round Suakim, and his young heart, like that of his crusading ancestor, glowed within him. "I wish," he said,

325

with enthusiasm, "that I had a chance of shedding my blood for my country." He forgot that his razor was at that moment executing its functions upon his chin; there was an awful gash - and an interval of ten minutes for temper and court-plaister.

He then began to comprehend that, with an attendant ready to carry out every wish, it is as well not to wish for things that you do not want. But no one knows, save those who have had a similar experience, how many things are wished for, carelessly and without thought. Jocelyn had to learn the lesson of prudence by many more accidents.

When his landlady, for instance, brought him his breakfast, she began, being a garrulous old creature, to talk about old Sir Jocelyn and the flight of time, and what she remembered; and presently mentioned casually, that it was her birthday.

"Indeed!" said Jocelyn, with effusion; "then Mrs Watts, I wish you many happy returns of the day and all such anniversaries."

He accompanied the wish with a substantial gift, but was hardly prepared, when the good woman's daughter came up to clear away, to hear that it was also the anniversary of her wedding-day. In fact, in a short time the housekeeper's anniversaries rained, and all of them demanded recognition. Like the clerk who accounted for absence three times in one year by the funeral of his mother, so this good lady multiplied her own birthdays and those of her children as long as their announcement drew half-a-crown from her lodger. After breakfast Jocelyn prepared to sally forth. He could not find his umbrella. "Devil take the thing!" he cried impatiently. It is to the credit of the Cap that the umbrella has never since been found. Therefore the wish was granted, and the devil did take the umbrella. Jocelyn *says* that he must have left it at the Club, but he *knows* otherwise.

He knew the church where the Stauntons had sittings, and he proposed to meet them as they came out, and to walk in the gardens with them - perhaps to have luncheon with them. Nelly would be there, he knew, in the sweetest of

326

early summer costumes - an ethereal creature made up of smiles, bright eyes, flowers, and airy colour. She would smile upon him; but then, hang it! she would smile upon another fellow just as sweetly. Would the time come, he thought, when she would promise to smile on no one but himself? Could one ever grow tired of her smiles? Caroline would be there, too, much more beautifully dressed, cold, superior, and ready to lecture. Fancy marrying Caroline! But as for Nelly - "Oh!" he sighed, thinking of his empty lockers; "I do wish I had some money!"

He instantly felt something hard in his pocket. It was a shabby old leather purse full of money. He took out the contents and counted the money: three pounds, fourteen shillings, ninepence and a farthing in coppers. Jocelyn sat down, bewildered.

"It's the Cap!" he said. "I wished for money. The fool of a Cap brings me three pounds fourteen shillings and ninepence farthing!" He threw the purse into the fireplace. "What can you do with three pounds fourteen and ninepence-farthing? It would not do much more than buy a bonnet for Nelly."

Yet he remembered it *was* money. If he could get, any time he wished, just such a sum, he could get on. Almost mechanically he made a little calculation. Three pounds fourteen shillings and ninepence-farthing every half-hour, or say only ten times a day, comes to thirty-seven pounds seven shillings and eightpence-half-penny; that multiplied by three hundred and sixty-five, come to £13,477 8s. 10¼d. "It is," said Jocelyn, "a very respectable income."

He hesitated, being in fact, a little afraid of testing his new power. Then he said boldly, "I want more money."

There was a click among the coins on the table. Jocelyn counted them again. He found another sixpence and a halfpenny more than he had at first observed.

"The Cap," he said "is a fool."

He remembered the advice given by the Ox Goad of Religion to the first Sir Jocelyn to exercise moderation. The reason for that advice, however, existed no longer. He would not now be burnt if all the bishops and clergy of the Established Church knew to a man that he had such a Cap. On the contrary, it would be regarded as a very interesting fact, and useful for religion in many ways. He must try, however, he said, to instruct his servant in larger ideas. No doubt, in the latter days of his uncle, the tendency to moderate or even penurious ways had been suffered to grow and to develop. It must be checked. Money must be had, and in amounts worth naming. Three pounds odd! and then sixpence halfpenny!

He met his friends coming out of the church - Nelly, as he expected, as sweet as a rose in June; Caroline, perhaps more resembling a full-blown dahlia. He walked through the Park to their house in Craven Gardens; Nelly, however, walked with her mother and Annesley, who also happened to be on the spot, while he walked with Caroline, who developed at some length the newest ideas in natural selection. He was asked to luncheon, and sat beside Caroline, who continued her discourse, while Nelly and Annesley were talking all kinds of delightful and frivolous things. After luncheon Caroline said that, as Sir Jocelyn took so much interest in these things, she would show him some papers on the subject which contained her ideas. She did; and the afternoon passed like a bad dream, with the vision of an unattainable Nelly at the other end of the room, as a mirage in the desert shows springs and wells to the thirsty traveller. He might have wished, but he was afraid. He could not trust his Cap; something horrible might be done; something stupid would certainly be done. The servant might be zealous, but as yet he had not shown that he was intelligent.

He came away melancholy.

"My dear," said Mrs Staunton to Caroline, when he had gone, "Sir Jocelyn seems to improve. He is quiet and - well - amenable, I should say. He comes of a good family, and his title is as old as a baronetcy can be. There is, I know, a place in the country, but I am told there is no money. The last baronet spent it all."

Caroline reflected.

"If a woman must marry," she said, "and, perhaps, as things are, it is better that she should for her own independence - a docile husband with a good social position - But perhaps he is not thinking of such a thing at all."

"My dear, he comes here constantly. It is not for Nelly, who cannot afford to marry a poor man. Therefore -"

She was silent, and Caroline made no reply. There comes a time even to the coldest of women, when the married condition appears desirable in some respects. She had not always been the coldest of women, and now the thought of a possible wooer brought back to her mind that memory of a former lover in the days when she, alas! was as poor as her sister Nelly. A warm flush came upon her cheek, and her eye softened, as she thought of the brave boy who loved her when she was eighteen, and he one-and-twenty; and how they had to part. He was gone. But things might have been so different.

"I shall meet them again on Wednesday," Sir Jocelyn thought. "They are going to Lady Hambledon's. If that Cap of mine has any power at all, it shall be brought into use on that evening. I must have - let me see - first of all, opportunity of speaking to her; next, I suppose, I can ask for eloquence, or persuasive power - the opportunity must not be thrown away. And she must be well disposed - do you hear?" he addressed the invisible servant. "No fooling on Wednesday, or - " He left the consequences to the imagination of his menial, perhaps because he did not himself quite see his way to producing any consequences. What are you to do, in fact, with an invisible, impalpable servant - the laws of whose being you know not - whom you cannot kick, or discharge, or cut down in wages, or anything?

In the evening a thing happened which helped to confirm him in the reality of his Cap, and at the same time made him distrustful of himself as well as of his slave.

It was rather late, in fact about twelve o'clock. Jocelyn was walking quietly home from the Club along the safest thoroughfare in Europe - at least the chief of the Criminal

Investigation Department said so. They used to call it the Detective Department, but changed the name because nothing was ever detected, and the term investigation does not imply the arrival at any practical result. There were still a few passengers in the street. One of them, a shambling, miserable-looking creature, besought alms of Jocelyn, who gave him something, and then fell a-moralizing on the mysteries of the criminal and pauper class in London. "That man," he said to himself, "is, I suppose, a vagrant; a person without any visible means of existence. Fill him with beef and beer, or gin, and he will become pot-valiant enough to think of obtaining more of such things by force or fraud instead of by begging. Then he will become one of the dangerous class. Poor beggar! I wish I could do something to help one of these poor wretches." Immediately afterwards he heard the sound of personal altercation. Two men, both in overcoats and evening dress, were struggling together, and one of them raised the cry of "Police!" Then there was the sound of a well-planted blow, and one of the men broke away and ran as hard as he could towards Jocelyn. The other man, knocked for the moment out of time, quickly gathered himself together and ran in pursuit. Jocelyn, by instinct, tried to stop the first man, who, by a dexterous trip-up with his foot, flung him straight into the arms of the second, his pursuer. He, somewhat groggy with the blow he had received, collared Jocelyn, and rolled over with him.

"I give him in charge," he cried, as a policeman came up. "I give him in charge - robbery with violence."

"But my dear sir," explained Jocelyn, "it is a mistake. You have got the wrong man."

"Dessay," said the policeman. "You can explain that little matter at the station, where you are a-going to."

"Little matter?" repeated the man who had been robbed. "You call it a little matter to be robbed of watch and chain in Piccadilly, by a fellow who asks you for a light to his cigar, and then plants as neat a left-hander between your eyes as you can -"

"Why!" cried Jocelyn. "It's Annesley!"

330

It was.

"Well," said the policeman, when he understood, and ceased to suspect; "as for him, he's got safe enough off, this journey. And as for you, sir," he addressed Jocelyn, "you couldn't have done a better turn to that fellow - I know who he is - than to let him chuck you into the other gentleman's arms."

Again Jocelyn had obtained the wish of his heart. He had, thanks to the Cap, done something to help one of "these poor wretches."

V

Jocelyn reserved his final trial of his power for Wednesday evening. Meanwhile, he thought he would let the Cap rest. But one thing happened which troubled him greatly. His housekeeper's daughter - she was a girl of fourteen or so, all knuckles and elbows - brought up his breakfast crying.

"What is the matter?" he asked.

"Please, Sir Jocelyn, mother's had a terrible loss."

"What has she lost?"

"She's lost her purse, Sir Jocelyn, sir, with three pound fourteen and ninepence farthing in it. I don't know what we *shall* do. And I've lost my lucky sixpence. And Bobby, he's lost his ha'penny."

Jocelyn turned crimson with wrath and shame. His house-keeper's purse! The girl's lucky sixpence! And the child's half-penny! His Jinn had placed them all in his pocket!

"I am very *sorry* , " he stammered. "As for your purse, I can't restore - I mean - find that for you. But - have you looked everywhere?"

"Oh, everywhere, sir."

"Look here, Eliza. Here are four pounds," - he would have handed over the exact sum, but he remembered in time that the lucky sixpence was among the coins in his pocket, and would certainly be identified - "here are four sovereigns. Tell your mother to buy herself a new purse, and if she loses

331

her money again, I shall not find it for her. Turn your lucky sixpence into a shilling, and Bobby's halfpenny into a sixpence."

When she was gone he pulled out the Cap, and set it before him on the table. "You are a common thief," he said, shaking his forefinger. "You are so lazy that, when I ask for money, you go to the housekeeper's room and steal - steal her purse. You are a disgraceful sneak and thief. Another such action, and I will - " here he remembered that he wanted the services of the Cap for Wednesday, and said no more. But he was profoundly disgusted. If money could only be had by stealing, how could he accept any money at all? Then he reflected. There is so much money and no more in the world. All this money has owners. The owners do not part with their money except as pay for services done. How, then, can money be got by any servants of a Wishing Cap except by stealing it? But to steal a poor housekeeper's money! Mean! - mean! Yet for a Baronet to accept money stolen from anybody! Impossible. And so vanished at one blow his income of £13,477 8s 10 $^{1}/_{2}$d. The matter opened a large field for inquiry, which he "argued out" as before. That is to say, he got hopelessly fogged over it.

This matter caused him a good deal of annoyance. There were other things too, which made him suspect the power, or the intelligence, of the Cap. Thus, it was vexatious, when he had merely wished, as so many well-meaning people do sometimes wish, that he was able to send to certain cases of distress, coals or help in other ways, to be told by the housekeeper that the ton of coals he had ordered was come, "and please, here is the bill." He paid it silently. Again, he was in his dressing-room, thinking of Nelly Staunton. "The case is as hopeless," he said to himself, "as if seas divided us. I wish," he added gloomily, "seas did divide us". Was it by accident, or was it by the meddlesome and mistaken action of the Cap - he always called it the Cap, to avoid the somewhat invidious phrase, Slave, or Demon of the Cap - that at this moment he kicked over the can containing his bath water, and made, of course, a great and horrible pool? He sat down and considered. As for the ton of coals, he had ordered them; but then they came at the very moment when he was wishing that he *had* coals to send. He had himself kicked over the can; but then, could it have been zeal on the part of the Cap to carry out, however imperfectly, even impossible orders?

On the Monday evening he met a lot of people who had all at some time or other gone in for spiritualistic business. This was indeed their bond of union. After dinner a good many wonderful stories were told, and there was talk about Volition, Magnetism, Clairvoyance, and the like.

"I am sometimes interested," said a lady, who was present, one of those who believe everything, "in the old stories about Slaves of the Lamp, the Ring, or the Jewel. They seem to me illustrative of the supreme power which the Will of man has been known to achieve in rare cases; that namely, when he can command even senseless matter and make it obey him."

"As, for instance," said Jocelyn, waking up, for this seemed likely to interest him, "if I was to order this glass to be upset. Pardon me, but I did not ask Mr Andersen to upset it."

Yet it was upset. Mr. Andersen, one of the guests, had at that moment knocked it over.

"That certainly," observed the lady, "would be an exercise of Will of a very singular and remarkable kind. It belongs to the class of phenomena which the Orientals accounted for by the invention of their so-called Slaves. Solomon had such Slaves. Mohammed had them. Every great man had them."

"Do you think," asked Jocelyn anxiously, "that they exist now?"

"The Slaves? Certainly not." This lady, it is evident, knew a great deal. "But the power - yes - oh yes! - that exists if we can attain to it." She was a woman about thirty years of age, with large full eyes. "If I choose to exercise my Will, Sir Jocelyn, you will advance towards me whether you like it or not."

333

"I very much doubt that; but ," said Jocelyn recklessly, "if *I* choose to exercise my Will, you shall recede from me."

"Really!" said the lady scornfully; "we will try, if you please. My Will against your Will. You shall advance, but I will not recede."

No one had ever before suspected young Sir Jocelyn of any pretence at supernatural powers, so that they all laughed, and expected instant discomfiture. Yet a remarkable thing happened. The lady sat in a chair before him, and Jocelyn fixed his eyes upon hers, which met his with a dilated glare. He did not advance, but presently the lady's chair began to move backward, very slowly. She sprang up with a shriek of fright, and the chair fell over.

"What have you done?" she cried. "Some one was pulling the chair."

"Very clever indeed," observed a man who was addicted to feats of legerdemain and deception. "Very clever, Sir Jocelyn; you have deceived even me. But you will not do it twice, otherwise I shall find out how you did it."

"No," he replied, half ashamed, "not twice. A trick," he added, "ought not to be done over again."

"A trick?" said the lady. "But no - that was no trick. If the chair were not actually pulled, why, you must have the power, Sir Jocelyn. Yes; you have the Will that causes even inanimate matter to move. It was not me, but the chair that you repelled."

He deprecated, modestly, the possession of so strong a Will. The story, however, without the names, has been preserved, and may be read among the papers of the Psychical Society. It is one of their choicest and best authenticated anecdotes. But the real simple truth is not known to them, and in revealing it one does but set the narrative, so to speak, upon a different platform. It is no longer a mysterious Agent.

"It is a long time," observed the Mr. Andersen who had upset the glass - he was a bright and sprightly Americanised Dane - "it is a long time since I did busy myself with the secrets and mysteries of the unseen world; but, if you please,

I will give you, of the final result at which I arrived, an account."

"You did get a result, then?" said the lady of the strong Will.

"You shall hear. I was out camping one night; all the fellows had gone to sleep except me, and I was keeping watch by the campfire with my six-shooter, and the big dog for company. The sky above us was as clear and pure as a young maiden's heart, and the tall trees stood up against the sky like sentinels, dark and steadfast, and the whole air was as still - as still as a fellow keeps when he want to see if the other fellow will copper a queen or not. But I fell to thinking and thinking; and there was some one far away that I wanted so much to see and to know what ... that person - might be thinking and doing - "

""And you saw her!" cried the lady.

"I remembered," he went on, not regarding the interruption, "how the fellow who taught us the mesmeric passes told me what an ever so strong mesmeric power I possessed, and I thought that here, if ever, was a high old time to try that power. I looked round at the still sky, and the quiet trees, and the sleeping fellows, and I just began to wish. Then the big dog lifted up his head and made as though he'd like to give a howl, and he looked at my face, and it seemed as if he believed he'd best swallow that howl. The more he didn't howl the more I wished; and I wished and I wished and I wished till it seemed as if the whole world was standing still to judge how wonderful I was wishing, and then there came a faint rustle, way off among the tops of the trees, and I thought there was something, maybe, beginning to come out of it all. And I wished and I wished and I wished. And -" here he paused in a manner which thrilled his hearers.

"Well? " asked Jocelyn, giving voice to the general expectation.

"And, by Jupiter, Sir Jocelyn," said the narrator, "by Jupiter nothing never came of it!"

Before coming to the ball at Lady Hambledon's, Jocelyn took the most careful precautions to prevent any possible mistake. He put the Cap before him and lectured it solemnly.

"Now, you understand, there is to be no fooling this evening. I am going to Lady Hambledon's - don't confound her with any other Hambledon - Lady Hambledon in Brook Street; the Stauntons are going to be there: you will arrange an opportunity for me to speak to - the young lady; you will do your best to - to stimulate - to give me a shove if I get stuck; you will also, if that is possible, predispose the young lady in my favour. I don't think there is anything more you can do. See that, this evening at least, you make no blunders. Remember the housekeeper's purse." By this time he had learned to avoid the phrase "I wish" as most dangerous and misleading, when a servant of limited intellect interprets every wish literally.

He went off, however, comforted with the conviction that really he had said all that was necessary to say. If this Cap, or the Slave of the Cap, was not a fool and an imbecile, his orders would be executed to the letter. He was a little excited, of course; anybody would have been so under the circumstances. Not only was his happiness at stake - at five-and-twenty one's whole future happiness is very often at stake - but he was about to test and prove the power of the Cap. Hitherto that power had not been exercised to his advantage in anyway. He should now ascertain exactly whether he was going to be a real wizard, or quite a common person like any other young Baronets. On the stairs he overheard a whispered conversation which made him feel uneasy.

"I saw the Stauntons go up just now," said one.

"And I saw Annesley go up just before them," said another.

"Everybody says that he is hard hit. Came here after her, of course."

Nothing absolutely to connect Annesley with Nelly. Yet he was uneasy. Certainly, Annesley would not be hard hit by Caroline. Two people full of ideas cannot marry and be happy. No, it must be Nelly. He fortified himself with the thought of his Cap, and went on upstairs.

The first thing he saw was Nelly herself, dancing with Annesley. "Confound him!" said Jocelyn, "He is as graceful as an ostrich!" On the other side of the room sat Mrs. Staunton. To her he made his way, and reached her just at the moment when Caroline was brought back to the same spot by her partner in the last dance. He could do nothing less than ask Caroline for the valse which had just begun. She was disengaged.

At this juncture there fell upon him the strangest feeling possible. It was exactly as if he was being guided. He felt as if some one were leading him, and he seemed to hear a whisper saying, "Everything is arranged according to your Excellency's commands." The consciousness of supernatural presence in a London ball-room is a very strange thing. There is an incongruity in it; it makes one act and feel as if in a dream. It was in a waking dream that Jocelyn performed that dance. Presently - he was not in the least surprised now, whatever should happen - he found himself sitting in the conservatory with Caroline. She was discoursing in a broad philosophical spirit on the futility of human hopes and opportunities.

Then he heard his own voice asking her: "What is the use of opportunities unless one knows how to use them?"

"What indeed?" replied Caroline; "but surely, Sir Jocelyn, it is only the weaker sort to whom that happens? The strong" - here she directed an encouraging glance at him - "can always use, and can even make, if need be, their opportunities."

"Yes:" Jocelyn forced the conversation a step lower, "but if a girl won't give a fellow a chance."

"I think," said Caroline, "that any man can find his chance, if he likes to seize it."

There was a pause - Jocelyn felt himself impelled to

337

speak. It was as if some one was pushing him towards a precipice. When he afterwards thought of himself and his extraordinary behaviour at this moment, he could only account for it by the theory that he was compelled to speak and to conduct himself in this wonderful way. "You must have seen," he whispered, "you must have seen all this time, that I have been hoping for a chance and was unable to get one. There was always your mother or your sister in the way. And I did hope - I mean - I did think that the Cap - I mean that I did rather fancy that one might perhaps get a chance here, though it isn't exactly what I ordered and wished. But I can't help it. In fact, I made up my mind last Sunday that it must be to-night or never. But what with the crush, and seeing other fellows cut in - Annesley and the others -"

Caroline interrupted this incoherent speech, which, however, could have but one meaning. "This is not the only place or the only time in the world."

"Well," said Jocelyn, "may I call to-morrow? But then - oh! this isn't what I wanted - may I call -" his eyes wandered, and he began a kind of love-babble, yet with a look of bewilderment.

Caroline listened calmly. She remembered another love-scene years before, when much the same kind of thing was said to her, though her lover then had a far different expression in his eyes. They were burning eyes, and terrified her. Jocelyn's were bewildered eyes, and made her feel just a little contemptuous. Even the coldest women like some fierceness in their wooer.

"Hush!" she said, "you will be overheard. Take me now back to mamma. We are going immediately. You may come to-morrow at five."

He pressed her hand, and took her back. Nelly was with her mother, Annesley in attendance. She glanced at her sister, and caught in reply a smile so full of meaning, that she did not hesitate to bestow a look upon Jocelyn of the sweetest sympathy. Her pretty eyes and this sympathetic look of sisterly - yes! sisterly - pleasure, completed the

338

business. It wanted nothing but Nelly's sympathy to round off the situation and fill up his cup of misery.

Then they went away. Jocelyn retired to a comparatively secluded place on the landing, and there, leaning against a door, he began to curse his fate and folly. He was so absorbed in railing at fortune and in self-pity, that he absolutely forgot the very existence of the Cap. The situation was too desperate; in a lesser stress of circumstances he would have remembered it; but as yet he did not even connect the Cap with the present fearful disaster, of which the worst was that it could not possibly be worse; it was hopeless; he had told a girl to whom he was utterly indifferent, that he was in love with her; without being drunk, or blinded for a space by her charms, he had addressed words to her which he had intended for her sister. "Oh," he groaned, "I wish I were somehow, anyhow, out of this horrible situation!"

As he spoke, he involuntarily straightened his legs and leaned back with a jerk. The door opened, and he fell back with a fearful crash of broken glass upon the back stairs and a tray of ices on the way to the tea-room.

Unlucky Jocelyn! To fall downstairs backwards is at best undignified, but who can describe the indignity and discomfort of falling in such circumstances as this? He was helped to his feet by some of the servants, and slipped away as quickly as he could.

The cool night air restored him a little; he found himself able to think coherently; and he now understood that the whole of this miserable evening's work was due to his infernal Cap.

He took it out of the cabinet as soon as he reached his chambers.

"You fool! you beast! you blind, blundering blockhead!" he thus addressed the Cap. "It is all your doing. The wrong girl? Yes: of course it was the wrong girl. Didn't give you her name? You ought to have known it. Girl you talked so long with?" - All this time he seemed to be hearing and answering excuses. "Talked so long with -" He sank in a

339

chair and groaned. Alas! it was his own fault; he had
forgotten to name the girl; the Slave of the Cap knew that he
wanted one of the Stauntons, and supposed that he wanted
the one with whom he had conversed so much on Sunday.
How should he know?

He mixed a glass of whisky and seltzer.

"I wish," he said desperately, "that the stuff would
poison me."

He drank off half the tumbler. Heavens! it was
methylated spirits, not selzer (the bottles were alike in
shape), that he had poured into the whisky. His wish was
very nearly gratified. Fortunately the quantity he had
drunk proved the cause of his safety. Over the bad quarter
of an hour which followed let us drop the veil of pity.

But he was to have another and as rude a lesson in the
activity of his slave. He awoke in the middle of the night,
with a sort of nightmare, in which Caroline was lecturing
him and saying, "I am to be your companion all your life.
You will never cease listening to the voice of instruction."
The weight of his horrible blunder became intolerable to
him. He threw off the clothes and sat up in the bed. "I
wish," he gasped, "I wish I was dead." Something seized him
by the throat. He could not breathe. He sprang from the bed
and rushed to the window for air. He was choking. He
battled with the fit, or whatever it was, which held him for
three or four minutes and left him purple in the face and
trembling in the limbs.

"It is spasmodic asthma," he said, when he had
recovered a little. "My father had it, and his father had it. I
knew it would come some day." At the same time, it was odd
that it should come just when he was wishing to be dead.
And the constriction of the pipes did seem astonishingly like
the fingers of some one trying to throttle him.

VII

"Dear Sir Jocelyn" (it was a note from Mrs Staunton), - "I
shall be very glad to see you to-day at twelve. Caroline tells

me you have something *important* - may I guess what it is? - to say to me. - Yours very sincerely,

"Julia Staunton"

Jocelyn received this note with the cup of tea which he took in bed, according to vicious morning usage. He read it and groaned. It meant, this harmless note, nothing short of a life-long lecture from a female philosopher; and he a perfectly frivolous young man!

He fell back upon his pillow and groaned. Then he foolishly began to wish, forgetting his Cap, "I wish the confounded letter could be washed out of existence," he said, and with an impatient gesture threw out his arms and upset the cup of tea over the paper. It would take ten minutes to get another cup. "It's that accursed Cap," he said; "it always takes one up wrong. I've a good mind to burn it." He dressed himself in the vilest temper. Had he heard the conversation at that moment going on between Caroline and her mother, he would have been more angry still.

" I do not pretend," said the young lady, "to feel any violent attachment for him - that kind of thing is over for me. There was a time as you know - "

"My dear," said her mother, "that is so long ago, and you were so very young, and it was before your uncle died."

"Yes, it is so long ago", said Caroline "I am seven-and-twenty now - two years older than Jocelyn. Poor boy! he is weak, but I think I shall have a docile husband; unless, to be sure, he turns stubborn, as weak men sometimes do. In that case -" Her face hardened, and her mother felt that if Caroline's husband should prove stubborn, there would be a game of "Pull devil, pull baker."

There was, Jocelyn felt, no way out of it at all, unless the way of flight, which is always open to everybody. And then, what a tremendous fool he would seem! As for the truth it could not possibly be told. That, at any rate, must be concealed; and at this point he began to understand some of the inconveniences, besides that of being misunderstood, in keeping a private demon. It is not, nowadays, that you

341

would be burned if it were found out. Quite the contrary: all the clergymen in the world would be delighted at finding an argument so irrefragable against atheists and rationalists. The thing was wrong, of course, but beautifully opportune. But it would be so supremely ridiculous. A Slave of the Cap, Jinn, or Afreet, who could only find his master money by stealing the housekeeper's purse; who interpreted a wish, without the least regard to consequences, literally and blindly; who led his master into the most ridiculous scrapes, even to getting him engaged to the wrong girl: a blundering, stupid slave - this, if you please, would be simply ridiculous. As for Nelly, his chance with her was hopelessly gone, even if, by any accident, he could break off with her sister. Yet, he thought, he should like to know if there was any truth in the report about her and Annesley. "I wish," he said, "I wish now, that I had never know her."

Then it became apparent to him that he really never had known her at all. She could not suspect his intentions because she had no opportunity of guessing them; and he remembered that though he had known the Stauntons a good while, he had never once got an opportunity of talking with her alone, except at a dance, and then her card was always filled up for the whole time she stayed. Sympathetic eyes are very sweet, but they do not mean an understanding without being told that a man is in love with one. To do Nelly justice, she had never thought of Jocelyn in this way. He was an agreeable young man to dance with; he came to afternoon tea and talked with Caroline, or rather listened; she thought he was not very clever, but he seemed nice.

Mrs Staunton received Jocelyn with great cordiality. "Let me," she said, "hear at once, my dear Jocelyn, what you wish to say to me." It was a sign of the very worst that she addressed him by his Christian name, without the handle, for the first time.

"Caroline has told me that last night -"

"Yes," said Jocelyn. "I wish she hadn't." The last words *sotto voce* .

"She did not tell me all," replied Mrs. Staunton. "In

342

fact, very little; but I gathered. -"

"I told her," said Jocelyn, in a tone most melancholy and even sepulchral - "I told her that I loved her."

"You - I gathered so much - and indeed, I was not surprised. To love my Caroline betrays, as well as becomes, a liberal education. Yet I need not disguise from you, Jocelyn," the young lady's mamma continued, "that from one point of view - the only one, I am bound to confess - the match is undesirable. You are of ancient family; you have rank; you have, I am assured, excellent morals and the best principles; but, my dear boy, you have - pardon me for reminding you of it - so scanty a fortune."

"It is true," Jocelyn said briskly, and plucking up a little hope; "and if you think that obstacle insurmountable - if, I say, Mrs. Staunton, that fact stands in the way - I will at once withdraw." He half rose, as if to withdraw at once.

"It would have been insurmountable in Nelly's case," said Mrs. Staunton, "because my poor Nelly will have but a slender portion. With Caroline the case is different. The dear girl is provided for by her uncle's bequest; and though you will not be really rich, there will be enough No, Jocelyn, the objection is not insurmountable, but I feel it my duty to state its existence and its nature. I want you to understand entirely my feelings. And, in fact, my dear Jocelyn," she gave him her hand, which he pressed, but languidly, "you have my full permission to go on with your suit, and my very best wishes for your success; because I think - nay, I am sure - that you already appreciate Caroline at her true value, and will make her happiness your only study."

Jocelyn murmured something.

"It is not often that two sisters get engaged on the same day," Mrs. Staunton continued, smiling; "yet it will please you to hear that I have this morning already consented to Nelly's engagement with Mr. Annesley."

"With Annesley?" It was true, then. All was indeed over now. Yes: when one is already hopelessly crushed, one more wheel may go over without materially increasing the agony.

"We have not known him long, but he bears, so far as we can learn, as good a character as one can desire. He is an intimate friend of your own, Jocelyn, is he not?"

"He is," said Jocelyn gloomily. "He nearly poisoned me last Saturday."

"That is indeed a proof of sincere friendship," the lady replied, laughing. "He and Nelly have been attached to each other, it seems, for some time, though the foolish couple said nothing to me about it; and at last - Well I hope they will be happy. In addition to other advantages, he has a large private income."

"He has, I believe, about four thousand a year. Frillings did it, in Coventry."

"Yes - yes - so many of our best families have made their fortune in trade. We must not think too much of these things. And he certainly has as good a manner as one would expect in an Earl." Then a smile, doubtless at the thought of the four thousand a year, stole over her motherly face. "It is certainly pleasant to think that the dear girl will have everything that a reasonable person can desire. His principles, too, are excellent. And he is, I am assured, a remarkably clever man."

Jocelyn said nothing; he had, in fact, nothing to say, except that all young men with four thousand a year are believed to possess excellent principles.

"And now," she said, "' you may go to Caroline. My *dear* boy, why - why did not your uncle, or your father, make money in frillings at Coventry?"

He went to Caroline; but it was with creeping feet, as a schoolboy goes to school, and with hanging head, as that boy goes on his way to certain punishment.

"What on earth am I to say to her?" he thought. "Am I to kiss her? Will she expect me to kiss Nelly instead."

Just then Nelly herself ran out.

"Oh, Jocelyn!" she said; "you have seen mamma? Of course it is all right. I am so glad! You are going to Caroline? - poor Caroline! You are going to be my brother! I am so glad, and I am so happy - we are all so happy! Did mamma tell you about me as well? Wish me joy, brother Jocelyn!"

"My dear Nelly," he said, with a little sob in his voice - "I suppose I may call you Nelly now, and my dear Nelly as well - I sincerely wish you all the joy that the world has to give."

She put up her face and smiled. He stooped and kissed her forehead.

"Be happy, sister Nelly," he whispered, and left her.

Nelly wondered why there was a tear in his eye. Her own lover certainly had not shed one tear since he first came a-courting; but then men are different.

Caroline was calmly expecting her wooer. She half-rose when he opened the door, and her cheek flushed. She wished the business over.

"Caroline," he said. But he could say no more; his voice and his speech failed him.

"Jocelyn," she replied. And then, because in another moment the situation would have become strained - and, besides, he was a gentleman, and would not give her pain - and, again, if there was any mistake, it was his own folly that had done it - he took both her hands, and drew her gently towards him and kissed her lips, without another word of love or of protestation.

Then he sat beside her, keeping her hand in his, and she began to talk of marriage and its duties, especially the duty of the husband, from a lofty philosophical point of view. It was agreed that she was to have absolute freedom: to take up any opinion, to advocate any cause, that she pleased. At that moment, because she varied a good deal, she was thinking what a splendid field was open to anyone, especially any woman who would preach Buddhism and the Great Renunciation. She made no allusion at all to her fortune, but Jocelyn perfectly understood that she meant to manage her house in her own way. As for himself, she designed, she said, a career for him. Of course, he would give up the F.O.; and so on. He mildly acquiesced in everything. His own slave had landed him in a slavery worse than anything ever

345

imagined or described. He was to spend his life under the rule of a strong-minded woman of advanced opinions.

VIII

Then followed two or three weeks, of which Jocelyn thinks now with a kind of wondering horror. He was expected to be continually in attendance. He was expected to listen diligently. He was even expected to read a great many books, lists of which were prepared for him. Everything, he clearly perceived, was to be arranged for him. Very well: nothing mattered now. Let things go on in their own way.

The worst of all was the abominable selfish rapture with which Annesley, of whom he now, very naturally, saw a great deal, treated him. The man could talk of nothing but the perfections of Nelly. As poor Jocelyn knew these perfections, and had every opportunity of studying them daily, the words of the accepted suitor went into his heart like a knife. Yet he could not object to listen, or contradict his friend, or show any weariness. To be sure, he might have conversed about Caroline, but it seemed ridiculous. Everybody knew that she was regularly and faultlessly beautiful; everybody also knew that she was strong-minded and held all kinds of views. Besides, he could not trust himself to speak of her. It was bad enough every day to speak with her.

The two weddings were to take place on the same day, which was already fixed for the first week in July. It was arranged where the brides should spend their honeymoon - Caroline and Jocelyn in Germany; Nelly with her bridegroom at the Lakes. Meantime it was impossible not to perceive that Jocelyn, who ought to have been dancing, singing, and laughing, grew daily more silent and melancholy. Caroline, however, either did not or would not see this. Nelly, who did, wondered what it meant, and even taxed Jocelyn with the thing.

"What does it mean?" she said. "You get your heart's desire, and then you hang your head and sit mum. Why, I

346

haven't heard you laugh once since your engagement; and as for your smile, you smile as if you were going to have a tooth out."

"Nonsense!" said Jocelyn. "I suppose men are always quiet when they are most happy."

"Then Jack" - this was Annesley - "must be miserable indeed, for he is always laughing and singing and making a noise. Come, Jocelyn, tell me all about it. Are you in debt?"

"No."

"Are you - have you - " She blushed but insisted, "have you got any kind of previous engagement? Oh! I know young men sometimes entangle themselves foolishly" - what a wise Nelly! - "and then have trouble in breaking off."

"It isn't that, Nelly. It really is nothing."

"Then laugh and hold up your head. Or I will pinch you : I will indeed. You are going to marry Caroline, who is the most beautiful girl in London and the cleverest; and you go about as if you wanted to sit in a corner and cry."

Jocelyn obeyed her, and laughed as cheerfully as a starving clown. When he went home, however, it was with a stern resolve. He would have it out with the Cap

In taking it out of the cabinet, however, he took with it his uncle's letter and read it again. The latter part he read with new understanding: "moderation," "failure to comprehend," "want of obedience." Yes, there was something wrong with this Slave of the Cap. As for the Cap itself, it looked surprisingly shabby - far worse than it had appeared when he first got possession of it.

"Now, " he said - the time was midnight, and he was alone in his chamber - "let us understand this." He took the Cap in his hand. "If you can appear to me, Slave or Demon, show yourself to me and answer for your blunders if you can."

The same sensation of faintness which he had before experienced came over him again. When he opened his eyes, he saw before him the same vision of a tottering, battered old creature, with fiery bright eyes.

"I have done my best, Excellency," said the Slave of the

Cap, in a tremulous quavering pipe.

"Your best! You have done everything that is stupid, blundering and feeble. What does it mean? What the devil, I say, does it mean?"

"I beg your Excellency's pardon. If you had mentioned which young lady - "

"Jinn! You knocked me head-over-heels down the back stairs."

"It was the *only* way out of it. You wished to be out of it."

"Slave of the Ox Goad of Religion! you stole the housekeeper's money."

"I have always stolen money for your Excellency's ancestors. You cannot have other people's money without stealing it. This was the nearest money, and I was anxious not to keep your Excellency waiting."

"You have covered me with disappointment and shame."

"I am old, sir. The Cap is falling to pieces. I have slaved for it for five hundred years. After five hundred years of work no Cap is at his best." He looked, indeed, at his very worst, so feeble and tottering was he. "In love matters," he went on, "I am still, however, excellent, as the late Sir Jocelyn always found me. Up to the very last I managed all his affairs for him. If I can do anything for your Excellency now - "

"You have already done enough for me. Stay -" a thought struck Jocelyn. "You would like your liberty."

"Surely, sir."

"You shall have it. I will throw this Cap into the fire - understand that - on one condition: it is that you undo what you have already done. It is by your blundering and stupidity that I have become engaged to Caroline Staunton. Get me out of the engagement. But mind, nothing dishonourable: nothing that will affect her reputation or mine: the thing must be broken off by her, for some good reason of her own, and one which will do neither of us any harm. For my own part, I don't in the least understand how

348

it is to be done. That is your look-out."

"Excellency, it shall be done. It shall be done immediately."

He vanished, and Jocelyn replaced the Cap in the cabinet. It was with anxious heart that he lay down to sleep, nor did sleep come readily. He was quite sure, now, that the engagement would be broken off somehow, but he could not possibly understand how or why. There had been between them no quarrel nor the slightest disagreement - in fact, Jocelyn always agreed to everything: there was nothing, on either side, that was not perfectly well known; nothing, that is, as sometimes happens with young, men, which might "come out and have to be explained." How - But, after all , it was the business of his servant to find out the way. He went asleep.

In the afternoon, next day, a note came to him at the Foreign Office. It was from Caroline, begging him to call upon her as soon as possible.

"I have," she said, " a very important communication to make to you - a confession - an apology if you please. Pray come to me."

He received this strange note with a feeling of the greatest relief. He knew that she was going to release him. Why or with what excuse he neither knew nor cared.

Caroline was in her own room, her study. She gave him her hand with some constraint, and when he would have kissed her, she refused. "No Jocelyn," she said, "that is all over."

"But - Caroline - why?" A smile of ineffable satisfaction stole over his face which she did not see. He would have been delighted to fall on his knees in order to show the depth of his gratitude. But he refrained and composed himself. At all event he would play the lover to the end, as he had begun. It was due, in fact, to the lady as well as to himself.

"Jocelyn," she said frankly, yet with some confusion in her eyes, "I have made a great mistake. Listen a moment, and forgive me if you can. It is now eight years since a certain man fell in love with me - and I with him. My poor

349

boy! I have never felt - I know it now - towards you as I did towards him. We could not marry because neither of us had any money. And then he went abroad. But he has come back - and - and - I have money now, if he has not - and oh! Jocelyn - do you understand, now?"

"You have met him" - oh! rare and excellent Slave! - "you have met him Caroline, and you love each other still." He wanted to dance and jump, but he did not: he spoke slowly, with a face of extraordinary gravity.

"Oh! Jocelyn." Could this be the same Caroline? Why, she was soft-eyed and tearful, her cheeks were glowing, and her lips trembled. "Oh! Jocelyn. Can you forgive me? You loved me, too, poor boy, because you thought me, perhaps, better and wiser than many other women. Better, you see, I am not, though I may be wiser than some."

He gave her his hand.

"Caroline," he said heroically, "what does it matter for me, if only you are happy?"

"Then you do forgive me, Jocelyn? I cannot bear to think that you will break your heart over this - that I am the cause -"

"Forgive you? Caroline, you are much too good for me. I should never have made you happy. As for me - " he gulped a joyful laugh and choked - "as for me, do not think of me. I shall - in time - perhaps...Meantime, Caroline, we remain friends."

"Yes - always friends - yes," she replied hurriedly. Then she burst into tears. "I did not know, Jocelyn, I did not know! I thought I had forgotten him, indeed I did."

He lifted her hand and kissed it with reverence. Then he left her, went to the Club, and had a pint of champagne to pull himself together. As for what people said, when it became known, that mattered nothing, because, whatever they said, they did not say openly to him.

It may be mentioned that no alteration was made in the date of the double wedding, only that one of the bridegrooms was changed. It was a beautiful wedding, and nobody noticed Sir Jocelyn, who was up in the gallery, his countenance wreathed with smiles.

When he left Caroline, Jocelyn went back to his chambers and prepared a little ceremony. He first lit the fire; then he took out the Cap and wrapped it in his uncle's letter. Then he solemnly placed both Cap and letter in the flames.

"You are free, my friend," he said. "An old Cap and an old Slave are more trouble than they are worth. Perhaps, now that the cap is burned, you will recover your youth."

There was no answer or any sign. And now nothing remains to Jocelyn of the family heirloom, except the picture of Sir Jocelyn de Haultegresse and Ali Ibn Yûssûf, otherwise called Khanjar ed Dîn, or the Ox Goad of Religion.

F. ANSTEY was the pseudonym foisted on Thomas Anstey Guthrie (1856-1934) by the error of a typesetter (he had intended to sign himself "T. Anstey"). In the last decades of the century Anstey established himself as the master of Victorian comic fantasy with a series of novels in which magical objects cause havoc by disrupting the supremely conventional lives of assorted individuals, each of whom is in his own way typical of the mores and folkways of Victorian England. The first of these novels was the much-imitated and much-dramatised *Vice Versa; or, a Lesson to Fathers* (1882), in which a businessman trades bodies with his scapegrace of a son. This was followed by *The Tinted Venus* (1885), in which a hairdresser places a ring on the finger of a statue of Aphrodite and finds the reanimated goddess an extremely inconvenient fiancée; *A Fallen Idol* (1886), in which a young painter suffers the attentions of a malevolent Idol mistakenly elevated to godhood by unwary Jains; and *The Brass Bottle* (1900) in which a newly-liberated genie cannot be prevented from showering his rescuer with an extremely inconvenient embarrassment of riches.

Anstey's shorter fantasies are more various in kind and tone. Early stories collected in *The Black Poodle and Other Tales* (1884) and *The Talking Horse and Other Tales* (1892) includes some broadly comic parodies of the popular ghost stories of the day, most notably "The Wraith of Barnjum" (1879) and "The Curse of the Catafalques" (1882), but later stories collected in *Salted Almonds* (1906) tend more to the grotesque and the sardonic. The early collections also include a number of stories for children, most of which are sentimental to the point of sickliness. "The Siren" is one of a small group of stories which contrive to combine all three of the major modes of nineteenth century fantasy: the moralistic, the comic and the sentimental.

THE SIREN

By F. Anstey

Long, long ago, a siren lived all alone upon a rocky little island far out in the Southern Ocean. She may have been the youngest and most beautiful of the original three sirens, driven by her sisters' jealousy, or her own weariness of their society, to seek this distant home; or she may have lived there in solitude from the beginning.

But she was not unhappy; all she cared about was the admiration and worship of mortal men, and these were hers whenever she wished, for she had only to sing, and her exquisite voice would float away over the waters, until it reached some passing vessel, and then every one that heard was seized instantly with the irresistible longing to hasten to her isle and throw himself adoringly at her feet.

One day as she sat upon a low headland, looking earnestly out over the sparkling blue-green water before her, and hoping to discover the peak of some far-off sail on the hazy sea-line, she was startled by a sound she had never heard before - the grating of a boat's keel on the pebbles in the little creek at her side.

She had been too much absorbed in watching for distant ships to notice that a small bark had been gliding round the other side of her island, but now, as she glanced round, she saw that the stranger who had guided it was already jumping ashore and securing his boat.

Evidently she had not attracted him there, for she had been too indolent to sing of late, and he did not seem even to have seen her, or to have landed from any other motive than curiosity.

He was quite young, gallant-looking and sunburnt, with brown hair curling over his forehead, an open face and honest grey eyes. And as she looked at him, the fancy came to her that she would like to question him and hear his voice; she would find out, if she could, what manner of beings these mortals were over whom she possessed so strange a power.

Never before had such a thought entered her mind, notwithstanding that she had seen many mortals of every age and rank, from captain to the lowest galley slave; but then she had only seen them under the influence of her magical voice, when they were struck dumb and motionless, after which - except as proofs of her power - they did not interest her.

But this stranger was still free - so long as she did not choose to enslave him; and for some reason she did not choose to do so just yet.

As he turned towards her, she beckoned to him imperiously, and he saw the slender figure above for the first time, - the fairest maiden his eyes had ever beheld, with an unearthly beauty in her wonderful dark blue eyes, and hair of the sunniest gold, - he stood gazing at her in motionless uncertainty, for he thought he must be cheated by a vision.

He came nearer, and, obeying a careless motion of her hand, threw himself down on a broad shelf of rock a little below the spot where she was seated; still he did not dare to speak lest the vision should pass away.

She looked at him for some time with an innocent, almost childish, curiosity shining under her long lashes. At last she gave a low little laugh: "Are you *afraid* of me?" she asked; "why don't you speak? but perhaps," she added to herself, "mortals *cannot* speak."

"I was silent," he said, "lest by speaking I should anger you - for surely you must be some goddess or sea-nymph?" "Ah, you can speak!" she cried. "No, I am no goddess or nymph, and you will not anger me - if only you will tell me many things I want to know!"

And she began to ask him all the questions she could think of: first about the great world in which men lived, and then about himself, for she was very curious, in a charmingly wilful and capricious fashion of her own.

He answered frankly and simply, but it seemed as if some influence were upon him which kept him from being dazzled and overcome by her loveliness, for he gave no sign as yet of yielding to the glamour she cast upon all other men,

354

nor did his eyes gleam with the despairing adoration the siren knew so well.

She was quick to perceive this, and it piqued her. She paid less and less attention to the answers he gave her, and ceased at last to question him further.

Presently she said, with a strange smile that showed her cruel little teeth gleaming between her scarlet lips, "Why don't you ask me who *I* am, and what I am doing here alone? do not you care to know?"

"If you will deign to tell me," he said.

"Then I will tell you," she said; "I am a siren - are you not afraid *now?*"

"Why should be afraid?" he asked, for the name had no meaning in his ears.

She was disappointed; it was only her voice - nothing else, then - that deprived men of their senses; perhaps this youth was proof even against that; she longed to try, and yet she hesitated still.

"Then you have never heard of me," she said; "you don't know why I sit and watch for the great gilded ships you mortals build for yourselves?"

"For your pleasure, I suppose," he answered. "I have watched them myself many a time; they are grand as they sweep by, with their sharp brazen beaks cleaving the frothing water, and their painted sails curving out firm against the sky. It is good to hear the measured thud of the great oars and the cheerful cries of the sailors as they clamber about the cordage."

She laughed disdainfully. "And you think I care for all that!" she cried. "Where is the pleasure of looking idly on and admiring? - that is for them, not for me. As these galleys of yours pass, I sing - and when the sailors hear, they must come to me. Man after man leaps eagerly into the sea, and makes for the shore - until at last the oars grind and lock together, and the great ship drifts helplessly on, empty and aimless. I like that."

"But the men?" he asked, with an uneasy wonder at her words.

"Oh, they reach the shore - some of them, and then they lie at my feet, just as you are lying now, and I sing on, and as they listen they lose all power or wish to move, nor have I ever heard them speak as you speak; they only lie there upon the sand or rock, and gaze at me always, and soon their cheeks grow hollower and hollower, and their eyes brighter and brighter - and it is I who make them so!"

"But I see them not," said the youth, divided between hope and fear; "the beach is bare; where, then, are all those gone who have lain here?"

"I cannot say," she replied carelessly; "they are not here for long; when the sea comes up it carries them away."

"And you do not care!" he cried, struck with horror at the absolute indifference in her face; "you do not even try to keep them here?"

"Why should I care?" said the siren lightly; " I do not want them. More will always come when I wish. And it is so wearisome to see the same faces, that I am glad when they go."

"I will not believe it, siren," groaned the young man, turning from her in bitter anguish; "oh, you cannot be cruel!"

"No, I am not cruel," she said in surprise. "And why will you not believe me? It is true!"

"Listen to me," he said passionately: "do you know how bitter it is to die, - to leave the sunlight and the warm air, the fair land and the changing sea?"

"How can I know?" said the siren. "*I* shall never die - unless - unless something happens which will never be!"

"You will live on, to bring this bitterness upon others for your sport. We mortals lead but short lives, and life, even spent in sorrow, is sweet to most of us; and our deaths when they come bring mourning to those who cared for us and are left behind. But you lure men to this isle and look on unmoved as they are borne away!"

"No, you are wrong," she said; "I am not cruel, as you think me; when they are no longer pleasant to look at, I leave them. I never see them borne away. I never thought what became of them at last. Where are they now?"

356

"They are dead, siren" he said sadly, "drowned. Life was dear to them; far away there were women and children to whom they had hoped to return, and who have waited and wept for them since. Happy years were before them, and to some at least - but for you - a restful and honoured old age. But you called them, and as they lay here the greedy waves came up, dashed them from these rocks and sucked them, blinded, suffocating, battling painfully for breath and life, down into the dark green depths. And now their bones lie tangled in the sea-weed, but they themselves are wandering, sad, restless shades, in the shadowy world below, where is no sun, no happiness, no hope - but only sighing evermore, and the memory of the past!"

She listened with drooping lids, and her chin resting upon her soft palm; at last she said with a slight quiver in her voice, "I did not know - I did not mean them to die. And what can I do? I cannot keep back the sea."

"You can let them sail by unharmed," he said.

"I cannot!" she cried. "Of what use is my power to me if I may not exercise it? Why do you tell me of men's sufferings - what are they to me?"

"They give you their lives," he said; "you fill them with a hopeless love and they die for it in misery - yet you cannot even pity them!"

"Is it love that brings them here?" she said eagerly. "What is this that is called love? For I have always known that if I ever love - but then only - I must die, though what love may be I know not. Tell me, so that I may avoid it!"

"You need not fear, siren," he said, "for, if death is only to come to you through love, you will never die!"

"Still, I want to know," she insisted; "tell me!"

"If a stranger were to come some day to this isle, and when his eyes meet yours, you feel your indifference leaving you, so that you have no heart to see him lie ignobly at your feet, and cannot leave him to perish miserably in the cold waters; if you desire to keep him by your side - not as your slave and victim, but as your companion, your equal, for evermore - that will be love!"

357

"If that is love," she cried joyously, "I shall indeed never die! But that is not how men love *me* ?" she added.

"No," he said; "their love for you must be some strange and enslaving passion, since they will submit to death if only they may hear your voice. That is not true love, but a fatal madness."

"But if mortals feel love for one another," she asked, "*they* must die, must they not?"

"The love of a man for a maiden who is gentle and good does not kill - even when it is most hopeless," he said; "and where she feels it in return, it is well for both, for their lives will flow on together in peace and happiness."

He had spoken softly, with a far away look in his eyes that did not escape the siren.

"And you love one of your mortal maidens like that?" she asked. "Is she more beautiful than I am?"

"She is mortal," he said, "but she is fair and gracious, my maiden; and it is she who has my love, and will have it while I live."

"And yet," she said, with a mocking smile, "I could make you forget her."

Her childlike waywardness had left her as she spoke the words, and a dangerous fire was shining in her deep eyes.

"Never!" he cried; "even you cannot make me false to my love! And yet," he added quickly, "I dare not challenge you, enchantress that you are; what is my will against your power?"

"You do not love me yet," she said; "you have called me cruel, and reproached me; you have dared to tell me of a maiden compared with whom I am nothing! You shall be punished. I will have you for my own, like the others!"

"Siren," he pleaded, seizing one of her hands as it lay close to him on the hot grey rock, "take my life if you will - but do not drive away the memory of my love; let me die, if I must die, faithful to her; for what am I, or what is my love, to you?"

"Nothing," she said scornfully, and yet with something

358

of a caress in her tone, "yet I want you; you shall lie here, and hold my hand, and look into my eyes, and forget all else but me."

"Let me go," he cried, rising, and turning back to regain his bark; "I choose life while I may!"

She laughed. "You have no choice," she said, "you are mine!" she seemed to have grown still more radiantly, dazzlingly fair, and presently, as the stranger made his way to the creek where his boat was lying, she broke into the low soft chant whose subtle witchery no mortals had ever resisted as yet.

He started as he heard her, but still he went on over the rocks a little longer, until at last he stopped with a groan, and turned slowly back: his love across the sea was fading fast from his memory; he felt no desire to escape any longer; he was even eager at last to be back on the ledge at her feet and listen to her for ever.

He reached it and sank down with a sigh, and a drowsy delicious languor stole over him, taking away all power to stir or speak.

Her song was triumphant and mocking, and yet strangely tender at times, thrilling him as he heard it, but her eyes only rested now and then, and always indifferently, upon his upturned face.

He wished for nothing better now than to lie there, following the flashing of her supple hands upon the harp-strings and watching every change of her fair face. What though the waves might rise round him and sweep him away out of sight, and drown her voice with the roar and swirl of waters? it would not be just yet.

And the siren sang on; at first with a cruel pride at finding her power supreme, and this youth, for all his fidelity, no wiser than the rest; he would waste there with yearning, hopeless passion, till the sight of him would weary her, and she would leave him to drift away and drown forgotten.

Yet she did not despise him as she had despised all the others; in her fancy his eyes bore a sad reproach, and she

359

could look at him no longer with indifference.

Meanwhile the waves came rolling in fast, till they licked the foot of the rock, and as the foam creamed over the shingle, the siren found herself thinking of the fate which was before him, and, as she thought, her heart was wrung with a new strange pity.

She did not want him to be drowned; she would like him there always at her feet, with that rapt devotion upon his face; she almost longed to hear his voice again - but that could never be!

And the sun went down, and the crimson flush in the sky and on the sea faded out, the sea grew grey and crested with the white billows, which came racing in and broke upon the shore, roaring sullenly and raking back the pebbles with a sharp rattle at each recoil. The siren could sing no longer; her voice died away, and she gazed on the troubled sea with a wistful sadness in her great eyes.

At last a wave larger than the others struck the face of the low cliff with a shock that seemed to leave it trembling, and sent the cold salt spray dashing up into the siren's face.

She sprang forward to the edge and looked over, with a sudden terror lest the ledge below should be bare - but her victim lay there still, bound fast by her spell, and careless of the death that was advancing upon him.

Then she knew for the first time that she could not give him up to the sea, and she leaned down to him and laid one small white hand upon his shoulder.

"The next wave will carry you away," she cried, trembling; "there is still time; save yourself, for I cannot let you die!"

But he gave no sign of having heard her, but lay there motionless, and the wind wailed past them and the sea grew wilder and louder.

She remembered now that no efforts of his own could save him - he was doomed, and she was the cause of it, and she hid her face in her slender hands, weeping for the first time in her life.

The words he had spoken in answer to her questions

about love came back to her: "It was true, then," she said to herself; "it is love that I feel for him. But I cannot love - I must not love him - for if I do, my power is gone, and I must throw myself into the sea!"

So she hardened her heart once more, and turned away, for she feared to die; but again the ground shook beneath her, and the spray rose high into the air, and then she could bear it no more - whatever it cost her, she must save him - for if he died, what good would her life be to her?

"If one of us must die," she said, "*I* will be that one. I am cruel and wicked, as *he* told me; I have done harm enough!" and bending down, she wound her arms round his unconscious body and drew him gently up to the level above.

"You are safe now," she whispered; "you shall not be drowned - for I love you. Sail back to your maiden on the mainland, and be happy; but do not hate me for the evil I have wrought, for suffering and death have come to me in my turn!"

The lethargy into which he had fallen left him under her clinging embrace, and the sad, tender words fell almost unconsciously upon his dulled ears; he felt the touch of her hair as it brushed his cheek, and his forehead was still warm with the kiss she had pressed there as he opened his eyes - only to find himself alone.

For the fate which the siren had dreaded had come upon her at last; she had loved, and she had paid the penalty for loving, and never more would her wild, sweet voice beguile mortals to their doom.

ANDREW LANG (1844-1912) was a poet, novelist, parodist, translator, historian and anthropologist, but he made his best-known contribution to popular literature with the oft-reprinted series of twelve anthologies which he assembled for young readers, beginning with *The Blue Fairy Book* (1889) and proceeding through most of the colours of the rainbow and various more exotic hues to *The Lilac Fairy Book* (1910). Lang's own stories for children include three book-length works; the best of them is *The Gold of Fairnilee* (1888), which draws heavily on Scottish folklore, but most contemporary readers thought it too dour and preferred his lighter and more colourful "Chronicles of Pantouflia", *Prince Prigio* (1889) and *Prince Ricardo* (1893).

The Wrong Paradise and Other Stories (1886), whose title story was first published in 1883, includes a few other sarcastic fantasies inspired by Lang's anthropological interests, as well as the more earnest romance of antiquity "The End of Phaeacia". The classic satirical essay "The Great Gladstone Myth" uses the anthropological methodology of the day to prove conclusively that Gladstone never existed, but was simply a symbolic representation of the sun. Lang's anthropological ideas were an important influence on the later works of Rider Haggard, whose earlier works he had parodied in collaboration with Walter Herries Pollock. Lang collaborated with Haggard on a novelistic sequel to the *Odyssey, The World's Desire* (1890); he also wrote a curious partly-allegorical and partly-satirical fairy romance in collaboration with May Kendall, *That Very Mab* (1885).

IN THE WRONG PARADISE
An Occidental Apologue

By Andrew Lang

In the drawing-room, or, as it is more correctly called, the "dormitory," of my club, I had been reading a volume named "Sur l'Humanité Posthume," by M. D'Assier, a French follower of Comte. The mixture of positivism and ghost-stories highly diverted me. Moved by the sagacity and pertinence of M. D'Assier's arguments for a limited and fortuitous immortality, I fell into such an uncontrollable fit of laughter as caused, I could see, first annoyance and then anxiety in those members of my club whom my explosion of mirth had awakened. As I still chuckled and screamed, it appeared to me that the noise I made gradually grew fainter and more distant, seeming to resound in some vast empty space, even more funereal and melancholy than the dormitory of my club, the "Tepidarium." It has happened to most people to laugh themselves awake out of a dream, and every one who has done so must remember the ghastly, hollow, and maniacal sound of his own mirth. It rings horribly in a quiet room where there has been, as the Veddahs of Ceylon say is the case in the world at large, "nothing to laugh at." Dean Swift once came to himself, after a dream, laughing thus hideously at the following conceit: "I told Apronia to be very careful especially about the legs." Well, the explosions of my laughter crackled in a yet more weird and lunatic fashion about my own ears as I slowly became aware that I had died of an excessive sense of the ludicrous, and that the space in which I was so inappropriately giggling was, indeed, the fore-court of the House of Hades. As I grew more absolutely convinced of this truth, and began dimly to discern a strange world visible in a sallow light, like that of the London streets when a black fog hangs just over the houses, my hysterical chuckling gradually died away. Amusement at the poor follies of mortals was succeeded by an awful and anxious curiosity as to the state of immortality and the life after death. Already it was certain that "the *Manes* are somewhat," and that annihilation is the dream of people sceptical through lack of imagination. The scene around me now resolved itself into a high grey upland country, bleak and wild, like the waste pastoral places of Liddesdale. As I stood expectant, I observed a figure coming towards me at some distance. The figure bore in its hand a gun, and, as I am short-sighted, I at first conceived that he was the gamekeeper. "This affair," I tried to say to myself, "is only a dream after all; I shall wake and forget my nightmare."

But still the man drew nearer, and I began to perceive my error. Gamekeepers do not usually paint their faces red and green, neither do they wear scalp-locks, a tuft of eagle's feathers, moccasins, and buffalo-hide cloaks, embroidered with representations of war and the chase. This was the accoutrement of the stranger who now approached me, and whose copper-coloured complexion indicated that he was a member of the Red Indian, or, as the late Mr. Morgan called it the "Ganowanian" race. The stranger's attire was old and clouted; the barrel of his flint-lock musket was rusted, and the stock was actually overgrown with small funguses. It was a peculiarity of this man that everything he carried was more or less broken and outworn. The barrel of his piece was riven, his tomahawk was a mere shard of rusted steel, on many of his accoutrements the vapour of fire had passed. He approached me with a stately bearing, and, after saluting me in the fashion of his people, gave me to know that he welcomed me to the land of spirits, and that he was deputed to carry me to the paradise of the Ojibbeways. "But, sir," I cried in painful confusion, "there is here some great mistake. I am no Ojibbeway, but an Agnostic; the after-life of spirits is only (as one our great teachers says)' an hypothesis based on contradictory probabilities;' and I really must decline to accompany you to a place of which the existence is uncertain, and which, if it does anywhere exist, would be uncongenial in the extreme to a person of my habits."

364

To this remonstrance my Ojibbeway Virgil answered, in effect, that in the enormous passenger traffic between the earth and the next worlds mistakes must and frequently do occur. *Quisque suos patimur manes,* as the Roman says, is the rule, but there are many exceptions. Many a man finds himself in the paradise of a religion not his own, and suffers from the consequences. This was, in brief, the explanation of my guide, who could only console me by observing that if I felt ill at ease in the Ojibbeway paradise, I might, perhaps be more fortunate in that of some other creed. "As for your Agnostics," said he, "their main occupation in their own next world is to read the poetry of George Eliot and the philosophical works of Mr. J.S. Mill." On hearing this, I was much consoled for having missed the entrance to my proper sphere, and I prepared to follow my guide with cheerful alacrity, into the paradise of the Ojibbeways.

Our track lay, at first, along the "Path of Souls," and the still, grey air was only disturbed by a faint rustling and twittering of spirits on the march. We seemed to have journeyed but a short time, when a red light shone on the left hand of the way. As we drew nearer, this light appeared to proceed from a prodigious strawberry, a perfect mountain of a strawberry. Its cool and shining sides seemed very attractive to a thirsty Soul. A red man, dressed strangely in the feathers of a raven, stood hard by, and loudly invited all passers-by to partake of this refreshment. I was about to excavate a portion of the monstrous strawberry (being partial to that fruit), when my guide held my hand and whispered in a low voice that they who accepted the invitation of the man that guarded the strawberry were lost. He added that, into whatever paradise I might stray, I must beware of tasting any of the food of the departed. All who yield to the temptation must inevitably remain where they have put the food of the dead to their lips. "You," said my guide, with a slight sneer, "seem rather particular about your future home, and you must be especially careful to make no error." Thus admonished, I followed my guide to

365

the river which runs between our world and the paradise of the Ojibbeways. A large stump of a tree lies half across the stream, the other half must be crossed by the agility of the wayfarer. Little children do but badly here, and "an Ojibbeway woman," said my guide, "can never be consoled when her child dies before it is fairly expert in jumping. Such young children they cannot expect to meet again in paradise." I made no reply, but was reminded of some good and unhappy women I had known on earth, who were inconsolable because their babes had died before being sprinkled with water by a priest. These babes they, like the Ojibbeway matrons, "could not expect to meet again in paradise." To a grown-up spirit the jump across the mystic river presented no difficulty, and I found myself instantly among the wigwams of the Ojibbeway heaven. It was a remarkably large village, and as far as the eye could see huts and tents were erected along the river. The sound of magic songs and of drums filled all the air, and in the fields the spirits were playing lacrosse. All the people of the village had deserted their homes and were enjoying themselves at the game. Outside one hut, however, a perplexed and forlorn phantom was sitting, and to my surprise I saw that he was dressed in European clothes. As we drew nearer I observed that he wore the black garb and white neck-tie of a minister in some religious denomination, and on coming to still closer quarters I recognized an old acquaintance, the Rev. Peter McSnadden. Now Peter had been a "jined member" of that mysterious "U.P. Kirk" which, according to the author of "Lothair" was founded by the Jesuits for the greater confusion of Scotch theology. Peter, I knew, had been active as a missionary among the Red Men in Canada; but I had neither heard of his death nor could conceive how his shade had found its way into a paradise so inappropriate as that in which I encountered him. Though never very fond of Peter, my heart warmed to him, as the heart sometimes does to an acquaintance unexpectedly met in a strange land. Coming cautiously behind him, I slapped Peter on the shoulder, whereon he leaped up with a wild unearthly yell, his countenance displaying lively tokens of terror. When he recognized me he first murmured, "I thought it was these murdering Apaches again;" and it was long before I could soothe him, or get him to explain his fears, and the circumstance of his appearance in so strange a final home. "Sir," said Peter, "it's just some terrible mistake. For twenty years was I preaching to these poor painted bodies anent heaven and hell, and trying to win them from their fearsome notions about a place where they would play at the ba' on the Sabbath, and the like shameful heathen diversions. Many a time did I round it to them about a far, far other place -

"Where congregations ne'er break up,
And sermons never end!"

And now, lo and behold, here I am in their heathenish Gehenna, where the Sabbath-day is just clean neglected; indeed, I have lost count myself, and do not know one day from the other. Oh, man, it's just rideec'lous. A body - I mean a soul - does not know where to turn." Here Peter, whose accent I cannot attempt to reproduce (he was a Paisley man), burst into honest tears. Though I could not but agree with Peter that his situation was "just rideec'lous," I consoled him as well as I might, saying that a man should make the best of every position, and that "where there was life there was hope," a sentiment of which I instantly perceived the futility in this particular instance. "Ye do not know the worst," the Rev. Mr. McSnadden went on. "I am here to make them sport, like Samson among the Philistines. Their paradise would be no paradise to them if they had not a pale-face, as they say, to scalp and tomahawk. And I am that pale-face. Before you can say 'scalping-knife' these awful Apaches may be on me, taking my scalp and other leeberties with my person. It grows again, my scalp does, immediately; but that's only that they may take it some other day." The full horror of Mr. McSnadden's situation now dawned upon me, but at the same time I could not but perceive that, without the presence of some pale-face to torture - Peter or another - paradise would, indeed, be no paradise to a Red Indian. In the same way Tertullian (or some other early Father) has remarked that the pleasures of the blessed will be much enhanced by what they observe of the torments of the wicked. As I was reflecting thus two wild yells burst upon my hearing. One came from a band of Apache spirits who had stolen into the Objibbeway village; the other scream was uttered by my unfortunate friend. I confess that I fled with what speed I might, nor did I pause till the groans of the miserable Peter faded in the distance. He was, indeed, a man in the wrong paradise.

In my anxiety to avoid sharing the fate of Peter at the hands of the Apaches, I had run out of sight and sound of the Ojibbeway village. When I paused I found myself alone, on a wide sandy tract, at the extremity of which was an endless thicket of dark poplar-trees, a grove dear to Persephone. Here and there in the dank sand, half-buried by the fallen generations of yellow poplar-leaves, were pits dug, a cubit every way, and there were many ruinous altars of ancient stones. On some were engraved figures of a divine pair, a king and queen seated on a throne, while men and women approached them with cakes in their hands or with the sacrifice of a cock. While I was admiring these strange sights, I beheld as it were a moving light among the deeps of the poplar thicket, and presently saw coming towards me a young man clad in white raiment and of a radiant aspect. In his hand he bore a golden wand whereon were wings of gold. The first down of manhood was on his lip; he was in that season of life when youth is most gracious. Then I knew him to be no other than Hermes of the golden rod, the guide of the souls of men outworn. He took my hand with a word of welcome, and led me through the gloom of the poplar trees.

Like Thomas the Rhymer, on his way to Fairyland -
"We saw neither sun nor moon,
But we heard the roaring of the sea."
This eternal "swowing of a flode" was the sound made by the circling stream of Oceanus, as he turns on his bed, washing

the base of the White Rock, and the sands of the region of dreams. So we fleeted onwards till we came to marvellous lofty gates of black adamant, that rose before us like the steep side of a hill. On the left side of the gates we beheld a fountain flowing from beneath the roots of a white cypress-tree, and to this fountain my guide forbade me to draw near. "There is another yonder," he said, pointing to the right hand, "a stream of still water that issues from the Lake of Memory, and there are guards who keep that stream from the lips of the profane. Go to them and speak thus: 'I am the child of earth and of the starry sky, yet heavenly is my lineage, and this yourselves know right well. But I am perishing with thirst, so give me speedily of that still water which floweth forth of the mere of Memory.' And they will give thee to drink of that spring divine, and then shalt thou dwell with the heroes and the blessed." So I did as he said, and went before the guardians of the water. Now they were veiled, and their voices, when they answered me, seemed to come from far away. "Thou comest to the pure, from the pure," they said, "and thou art a suppliant of holy Persephone. Happy and most blessed art thou, advance to the reward of the crown desirable, and be no longer mortal, but divine." Then a darkness fell upon me, and lifted again like mist on the hills, and we found ourselves in the most beautiful place that can be conceived, a meadow of that short grass which grows on some shores beside the sea. There were large spaces of fine and solid turf, but, where the little streams flowed from the delicate-tinted distant mountains, there were narrow valleys full of all the flowers of a southern spring. Here grew narcissus and hyacinths, violets and creeping thyme, and crocus and the crimson rose, as they blossomed on the day when the milk-white bull carried off Europa. Beyond the level land beside the sea, between these coasts and the far off hills, was a steep lonely rock, on which were set the shining temples of the Grecian faith. The blue seas that begirt the coasts were narrow, and ran like rivers between many islands not less fair than the country to which we were come, while other isles, each with its crest of clear-cut hills, lay westward, far away, and receding into the place of the sunset. Then I recognized the Fortunate Islands spoken of by Pindar, and the paradise of the Greeks. "Round these the ocean breezes blow and golden flowers are glowing, some from the land on trees of splendour, and some the water feedeth, with wreaths whereof they entwine their hands." And, as Pindar says again, "for them shineth below the strength of the sun, while in our world it is night, and the space of crimson-flowered meadows before their city is full of the shade of frankincense-trees and the fruits of gold. And some in horses and in bodily feats, and some in dice, and some in harp-playing have delight, and among them thriveth all fair flowering bliss; and fragrance ever streameth through the lovely land as they mingle incense of every kind upon the altars of the gods." In this beautiful country I took great delight, now watching the young men leaping and running (and they were marvellously good over a short distance of ground), now sitting in a chariot whereto were harnessed steeds swifter than the wind, like those that, Homer says, "the gods gave, glorious gifts, to Peleus." And the people, young and old, received me kindly, welcoming me in their Greek speech, which was like the sound of music. And because I had ever been a lover of them and of their tongue, my ears were opened to understand them, though they spoke not Greek as we read it. Now when I had beheld many of the marvels of the Fortunate Islands, and had sat at meat with those kind hosts (though I only made semblance to eat of what they placed before me), and had seen the face of Rhadamanthus of the golden hair, who is the lord of that country, my friend told me that there was come among them one of my own nation who seemed most sad and sorrowful, and they could make him no mirth. Then they carried me to a house in a grove, and all around it a fair garden, and a well in the midst.

Now stooping over the well, that he might have sight of his own face, was a most wretched man. He was pale and very meagre; he had black rings under his eyes, and his hair was long, limp, and greasy, falling over his shoulders. He

370

was clad somewhat after the manner of the old Greeks, but his raiment was woefully ill-made and ill-girt upon him, nor did he ever seem at his ease. As soon as I beheld his sallow face I knew him for one I had seen and mocked at in the world of the living. He was a certain Figgins, and he had been honestly apprenticed to a photographer; but, being a weak and vain young fellow, he had picked up modern notions about art, the nude, plasticity, and the like, in the photographer's workroom, whereby he became a weariness to the photographer and to them that sat unto him. Being dismissed from his honest employment, this chitterling must needs become a model to some painters that were near as ignorant as himself. They talked to him about the Greeks, about the antique, about Paganism, about the Renaissance, till they made him as much the child of folly as themselves. And they painted him as Antinous, as Eros, as Sleep, and I know not what, but whatever name they called him he was always the same lank-haired, dowdy, effeminate, pasty-faced photographer's young man. Then he must needs take to writing poems all about Greece, and the free ways of the old Greeks, and Lais, and Phryne, and therein he made "Aeolus" rhyme to "control us." For of Greek this fellow knew not a word, and any Greek that met him had called him a κόλλοψ and bidden him begone to the crows for a cursed fellow, and one that made false quantities in every Greek name he uttered. But his little poems were much liked by young men of his own sort, and by some of the young women. Now death had come to Figgins, and here he was in the Fortunate Islands, the very paradise of those Greeks about whom he had always been prating while he was alive. And yet he was not happy. A little lyre lay beside him in the grass, and now and again he twanged on it dolorously, and he tried to weave himself garlands from the flowers that grew around him; but he knew not the art, and ever and anon he felt for his button-hole, wherein to stick a lily or the like. But he had no button-hole. Then he would look at himself in the well, and yawn and wish himself back in his friends' studios in London. I almost pitied the wretch, and, going up to him, I asked him how he did. He said he had never been more wretched. "Why," I asked "was your mouth not always full of the 'Greek spirit,' and did you not mock the Christians and their religion? And, as to their heaven, did you not say that it was tedious place, full of pious old ladies and Philistines? And are you not got to the paradise of the Greeks? What, then, ails you with your lot?" "Sir," said he, "to be plain with you, I do not understand a word the fellows about me say, and I feel as I did the first time I went to Paris, before I knew enough French to read the Master's poems*. Again, every one here is mirthful and gay, and there is no man with a divinely passionate potentiality of pain. When I first came here they were always asking me to run with them or jump against them, and one fellow insisted I should box with him, and hurt me very much. My potentiality of pain is considerable. Or they would have me drive with them in these dangerous open chariots, - me, that never rode in a hansom cab without feeling nervous. And after dinner they sing songs of which I do not catch the meaning of one syllable, and the music is like nothing I ever heard in my life. And they are all abominably active and healthy. And such of their poets as I admired - in Bohn's cribs, of course - the poets of the Anthology, are not here at all, and the poets who are here are tremendous proud toffs" (here Figgins relapsed into his natural style as it was before he became a Neopagan poet), "and won't say a word to a cove. And I'm sick of the Greeks, and the Fortunate Islands are a blooming fraud, and oh, for paradise, give me Pentonville." With these words, perhaps the only unaffected expression of genuine sentiment poor Figgins had ever uttered, he relapsed into a gloomy silence. I advised him to cultivate the society of the authors whose selected words are in the Greek Delectus, and to try to make friends with Xenophon, whose Greek is about as easy as that of any ancient. But I fear that Figgins, like the Rev. Peter McSnadden, is really suffering a kind of punishment in the disguise of a reward, and all through

* Poor Figgins always called M. Baudeláire "the Master."

having accidentally found his way into what he foolishly thought would be the right paradise for him.

Now I might have stayed long in the Fortunate Islands, yet, beautiful as they were, I ever felt like Odysseus in the island of fair Circe. The country was lovely and the land desirable, but the Christian souls were not there without whom heaven itself were no paradise to me. And it chanced that as we sat at the feast a maiden came to me with a pomegranate on a plate of silver, and said, "Sir thou hast now been here for the course of a whole moon, yet hast neither eaten nor drunk of what is set before thee. Now it is commanded that thou must taste if it were but a seed of this pomegranate, or depart from among us." Then, making such excuses as I might, I was constrained to refuse to eat, for no soul can leave a paradise wherein it has tasted food. And as I spoke the walls of the fair hall wherein we sat, which were painted with the effigies of them that fell at Thermopylae and in Arcadion, wavered and grew dim, and darkness came upon me.

The first of my senses which returned to me was that of smell, and I seemed almost drowned in the spicy perfumes of Araby. Then my eyes became aware of a green soft fluttering, as of the leaves of a great forest, but quickly I perceived that the fluttering was caused by the green scarfs of a countless multitude of women. They were "fine women" in the popular sense of the term, and were of the school of beauty admired by the Faithful of Islam, and known to Mr Bailey, in "Martin Chuzzlewit," as "crumby". These fond attendant nymphs carried me into gardens twain, in each two gushing springs, in each fruit, and palms, and pomegranates. There were the blessed reclining, precisely as the Prophet has declared, "on beds the linings whereof are brocade, and the fruit of the two gardens within reach to cull." There also were the "maids of modest glances," previously indifferent to the wooing "of man or ginn." "Bright and large-eyed maids kept in their tents, reclining on green cushions and beautiful carpets. About the golden couches went eternal youths with goblets and ewers, and a cup of flowing wine. No headache shall they feel therefrom," says the compassionate Prophet, "nor shall their wits be dimmed." And all that land is misty and fragrant with the perfume of the softest Latakia, and the gardens are musical with the bubbling of countless *narghilés;* and I must say that to the Christian soul which enters that paradise the whole place has, certainly, a rather curious air, as of a highly transcendental Cremorne. There could be no doubt, however, that the Faithful were enjoying themselves amazingly - "right lucky fellows," as we read in the new translation of the Koran. Yet even here all was not peace and pleasantness, for I heard my name called by a small voice, in a tone of patient subdued querulousness. Looking hastily round, I with some difficulty recognized, in a green turban and silk gown to match, my old college tutor and professor of Arabic. Poor old Jones had been the best and the most shy of university men. As there was never any undergraduate in his time (it is different now) who wished to learn Arabic, his place had been a sinecure, and he had chiefly devoted his leisure to "drawing" pupils who were too late for college chapel. The sight of a lady of his acquaintance in the streets had at all times been alarming enough to drive him into a shop or up a lane, and he had not survived the creation of the first batch of married fellows. How he had got into this thoroughly wrong paradise was a mystery which he made no attempt to explain. "A nice place this, eh?" he said to me. "Nice gardens; remind me of Magdalene a good deal. It seems, however, to be decidedly rather gay just now; don't you think so? Commemoration week, perhaps. A great many young ladies up, certainly; a good deal of cup drunk in the gardens too. I always did prefer to go down in Commemoration week, myself; never was a dancing man. There is a great deal of dancing here, but the young ladies dance alone, rather like what is called the *ballet,* I believe, at the opera. I must say the young persons are a little forward; a little embarrassing it is to be alone here, especially as I have forgotten a good deal of my Arabic. Don't you think, my dear fellow, you and I could

374

manage to give them the slip? Run away from them, eh?" He uttered a timid little chuckle, and at that moment an innumerable host of houris began a *ballet d'action* illustrative of a series of events in the career of the prophet. It was obvious that my poor uncomplaining old friend was really very miserable. The "thornless loto trees" were all thorny to him, and the "tal'h trees with piles of fruit, the outspread shade, and water outpoured" could not comfort him in his really very natural shyness. A happy thought occurred to me. In my early and credulous youth I had studied the works of Cornelius Agrippa and Petrus de Abano. Their lessons, which had not hitherto been of much practical service, recurred to my mind. Stooping down, I drew a circle round myself and my old friend in the fragrant white blossoms which were strewn so thick that they quite hid the grass. This circle I fortified by the usual signs employed, as Benvenuto Cellini tells us, in the conjuration of evil spirits. I then proceeded to utter one of the common forms of exorcism. Instantly the myriad houris assumed the forms of irritated demons; the smoke from the uncounted *narghilés* burned thick and black; the cries of the frustrated *ginns,* who were no better than they should be, rang wildly in our ears; the palm-trees shook beneath a mighty wind; the distant summits of the minarets rocked and wavered, and, with a tremendous crash, the paradise of the Faithful disappeared.

As I rang the bell, and requested the club-waiter to carry away the smoking fragments of the moderator-lamp which I had accidentally knocked over in awakening from my nightmare, I reflected on the vanity of men and the unsubstantial character of the future homes that their fancy has fashioned. The ideal heavens of modern poets and novelists, and of ancient priests, come no nearer than the drugged dreams of the angekok and the biraark of Greenland and Queensland to that rest and peace whereof it has not entered into the mind of man to conceive. To the wrong man each of our pictured heavens would be a hell, and

375

even to the appropriate devotee each would become a tedious purgatory.

OSCAR WILDE (1854-1900) was, of course, Irish by birth and homosexual by nature, and his attempts to take English society by storm were doomed to fail. There is, however, every reason to include him in a history of British fantasy; although he was aided and abetted by Richard Garnett, Vernon Lee and Laurence Housman it was he who conspicuously brought to rebellious fruition the covert moral unease which fantasy had contrived to preserve throughout the long years when the British Isles were tyrannised by that appalling species of sanctimonious puritanism which was symbolised and enacted by its unhappy and unfortunate queen.

Wilde published three classic volumes in a single year (1891). *Lord Arthur Savile's Crime* contains two fine comic fantasies: the title story, which deals with an ironically self-fulfilling prophecy; and the best of the many Victorian parodies of ghost stories, "The Canterville Ghost". *The Picture of Dorian Gray*, though conventionally regarded as a horror story, is actually an allegory revealing and regretting the folly of trying to live one's life as a work of art; it unwittingly prefigures the eventual fall of its creator, crucified by forces of repression which he had finally driven to vengeful outrage. *The House of Pomegranates* follows Wilde's earlier collection of unorthodoxly-moralistic children's stories, *The Happy Prince and Other Tales* (1888) with four longer and more sophisticated parables, each of which combines consummate stylistic elegance with considerable depth of feeling; all four are bitter parables in which human folly, vanity and infidelity cause considerable misery.

"The House of Judgement" is one of a series of poems in prose which appeared in the *Fortnightly Review* in 1894.

377

THE HOUSE OF JUDGEMENT

By Oscar Wilde

And there was silence in the House of Judgement, and the Man came naked before God.

And God opened the Book of the Life of the Man.

And God said to the Man, "Thy life hath been evil, and thou hast shown cruelty to those who were in need of succour, and to those who lacked help thou hast been bitter and hard of heart. The poor called to thee and thou did'st not hearken, and thine ears were closed to the cry of My afflicted. The inheritance of the fatherless thou did'st take unto thyself, and thou did'st send the foxes into the vineyard of thy neighbour's field. Thou did'st take the bread of the children and give it to the dogs to eat, and my lepers who lived in the marshes, and were at peace and praised Me, thou did'st drive forth on to the highways, and on Mine earth out of which I made thee thou did'st spill innocent blood."

And the Man made answer and said, "Even so did I."

And again God opened the Book of the Life of the Man.

And God said to the Man, "Thy life hath been evil, and the Beauty I have shown thou hast sought for, and the Good I have hidden thou did'st pass by. The walls of thy chamber were painted with images, and from the bed of thine abominations thou did'st rise up to the sound of flutes. Thou did'st build seven altars to the sins I have suffered, and did'st eat of the thing that may not be eaten, and the purple of thy raiment was broidered with the three signs of shame. Thine idols were neither of gold nor of silver that endure, but of flesh that dieth. Thou did'st stain their hair with perfumes and put pomegranates in their hands. Thou did'st stain their feet with saffron and spread carpets before them. With antimony thou did'st stain their eyelids and their bodies thou did'st smear with myrrh. Thou did'st bow thyself to the ground before them, and the thrones of thine idols were set in the sun. Thou did'st show to the sun thy shame and to the moon thy madness."

And the Man made answer and said, "Even so did I."

And a third time God opened the Book of the Life of the Man.

And God said to the Man, "Evil hath been thy life, and with evil did'st thou requite good, and with wrongdoing kindness. The hands that fed thee thou did'st wound, and the breasts that gave thee suck thou did'st despise. He who came to thee with water went away thirsting, and the outlawed men who hid thee in their tents at night thou did'st betray before dawn. Thine enemy who spared thee thou did'st snare in an ambush, and the friend who walked with thee thou did'st sell for a price, and to those who brought thee Love thou did'st ever give Lust in thy turn."

And the Man made answer and said, "Even so did I."

And God closed the Book of the Life of the Man, and said,

"Surely I will send thee into Hell. Even into Hell will I send thee."

And the Man cried out, "Thou canst not."

And God said to the Man, "Wherefore can I not send thee to Hell, and for what reason?"

"Because in Hell have I always lived," answered the Man.

And there was silence in the House of Judgment.

And after a space God spake, and said to the Man, "Seeing that I may not send thee into Hell, surely I will send thee unto Heaven. Even unto Heaven will I send thee."

And the man cried out, "Thou canst not."

And God said to the Man, "Wherefore can I not send thee unto Heaven, and for what reason?"

"Because never, and in no place, have I been able to imagine it," answered the Man.

And there was silence in the House of Judgment.

VERNON LEE was the pseudonym of Violet Paget (1856-1935), who was born in France and lived most of her life in voluntary exile, but who was English nevertheless. She was the half-sister of the poet Eugene Lee-Hamilton, who spent most of his life as a chronic invalid but eventually recovered his health by mysterious means (only to be accused by some of his friends of having been a hypochondriac all along). Violet also became a habitual sufferer of nervous breakdowns, and her life was further complicated by her ill-concealed lesbianism.

Lee's supernatural fiction includes some vivid horror stories as well as several notable fantasies. She makes extensive use of the figure of the *femme fatale*, which is featured in the intense "Amour Dure" and "Dionea" (both in *Hauntings* , 1890), the flamboyant extravaganza "The Virgin of the Seven Daggers" (written in 1889), and the bitterly sentimental *Yellow Book* fantasy "Prince Alberic and the Snake Lady" (1896; reprinted in *Pope Jacynth and Other Fantastic Tales,* 1904). She also wrote an excellent comic fantasy, "The Gods and Ritter Tanhuser" (1913), which - like "The Virgin of the Seven Daggers" - was belatedly reprinted in a book dedicated to Maurice Baring (who was himself a writer of some delicately ironic fantasies), *For Maurice: Five Unlikely Stories* (1927).

"St. Eudaemon and his Orange-Tree" is one of a small group of sarcastic fantasies by Lee which make subtle mockery of Christian mythology in order to support a more liberal morality; the others are "Pope Jacynth" and "Marsyas in Flanders". These, together with certain stories by Richard Garnett, belong to a curious *fin de siècle* sub-genre first popularised by Anatole France in stories collected in *Mother of Pearl* (1892; tr. 1908) and *The Well of St. Clare* (1895; tr. 1909).

ST. EUDAEMON AND HIS ORANGE-TREE

By Vernon Lee

Here is the story of St. Eudaemon's Orange-Tree. It is not among the *Lives of the Blessed Fathers,* by Brother Dominick Cavalca of Vico Pisano, still less in the *Golden Legend* compiled by James of Voragine; nor, very likely, in any other work of hagiography. I learned it on the spot of the miracle, and in the presence of its ever-blossoming witness, the orange-tree. The orchards of the Caelian and the Aventine spread all round, with their criss-cross of reeds carrying young vines, and you see on all sides great arches and vague ruins: Colosseum, Circus Maximus, House of Nero, and the rest; with, far beyond, modern Rome, St. Peter's dome and the blue Sabine Mountains . There is a little church - one of a dozen like it - with chipped Ionic columns, and a tesselated pavement lilac and russet like a worn-out precious rug, and a great cactus, like a python, winding round the apse. The orange-tree stands there, shedding its petals over vines and salads, immense and incredibly venerable; what seems the trunk, in reality merely the one surviving branch, the real trunk being hidden deep below the level of the garden. Here did I learn the legend; but from whom, and how, I must leave you to guess. Suffice that it be true.

Long, long ago, before the church was built, which has stood, however, over twelve hundred years, there settled on the Caelian slopes a certain saint, by name Eudaemon. The old Pagan Rome was buried under ground, great boulders and groups of columns only protruding; and the new Christian Rome was being built far off, of stones and brick quarried and carted from the ruins. Weeds and bushes, and great ilexes and elms, had grown up above the former city, and it was haunted of demons. Men never came near it, save to quarry for stone or seek for treasure with dreadful

381

incantation; and it became a wilderness, surrounded, at uneven distances, by the long walls, and the storied square belfries of many monasteries.

The place to which this Eudaemon came - and no one can tell whence he came, nor anything of him save that he had a bride, who died the eve of their wedding - the place to which Eudaemon came was in the heart of the ruins and the wilderness, very far from the abode of men; and indeed he had but two neighbouring saints like himself, a theologian who inhabited a ruined bath to avoid the noise of bell-ringing; and a stylite, who had contrived a platform of planks roofed over with reeds on the top of the column of the Emperor Philip.

Eudaemon, as above stated, was a saint; persons who did not molest their neighbours were mostly saints in those days; and so, of course, he could work miracles. Only, his miracles, in the opinion of other saints, particularly of the Theologian and the Stylite (whose names were Carpophorus and Ursicinus), were nothing special, in fact, just barely within the limits of the miraculous. Eudaemon had planted a garden round about the ruins of the circular temple of Venus; and vines and lettuces, roses and peaches had replaced within a very few years the scrub of ilex and myrtle, and the mad vegetation of wild fennel and oats and wallflower which matted over the masonry; and this, of course, since he was a saint, must be a miracle. He had cleared out, also, the innermost cell of the temple, and turned it into a chapel, with a fair carved tomb of the pagans for an altar, and pictures of the Blessed Virgin and the Saviour, with big eyes and purple clothes, painted on the whitewash. And he had erected alongside a belfry, three stories high, circular and open with pillars quarried from the temple, and stuck about with discs of porphyry (out of the temple floor), and green Cretan bowls for ornament; which, of course, was also a miracle. Moreover, at the end of the orchard he had erected wattled huts for poor folk, to whom he taught gardening and other useful arts; also sheds for cows and goats, and a pigeon-cot; and he had constructed out

382

of osier a cart, and broken in a donkey's foal, in order to send his vegetables to distribute in Rome to the indigent, together with cans of milk and rounds of goats' cheese. And to the wives of the poor whom he lodged he taught how to weave and cure skins, and to the children he taught the abacus and the singing of hymns. And for the poor folk he made, near their wattled huts, a bowling-green, and instructed them to play at that game. And indeed the matter of the orange-tree arose out of the making of the bowling-green; all of which were plainly miracles. Meanwhile Eudaemon lived all alone in a shed closed with reeds, and roofed by one of the vaultings of that temple of the Pagans; and he was a laborious man, and abstemious, and possessed a knowledge of medicine, and was able, though but little, to read in the Scriptures; and Eudaemon was a saint, though but a small one.

But Carpophorus the theologian, and Ursicinus the stylite, did not think much of Eudaemon and his saintlings, nay, each thought even less of him than of the other. For Carpophorus, who had translated the books of Deuteronomy from the Hebrew, and the gospels of Nicodemus and of Enoch into Latin, and written six treatises against the Gnostics and Paulicians, and a book on the marriage of the Sons of God; and who, moreover, had a servant to wash his clothes and dust his rolls of manuscript, and cook his dinner, thought Ursicinus both ignorant and rustic, living untidily on that platform on the column, as shaggy and black as a bear, and constantly fixing his eyes on his own navel; while Ursicinus the stylite, who had not changed his tunic or touched cooked food for five years, and had frequently risen to the contemplation of the One, looked down upon the pedantry and luxurious habits of Carpophorus, and esteemed him a man of fleshly vanities.

But Carpophorus and Ursicinus agreed in having a very poor opinion of Eudaemon; and often met in brotherly discourse upon the likelihood of his being given over by Heaven to the Evil One. And this opinion they made freely manifest to himself, on the occasions when he would invite them to dinner in his orchard, regaling them on fruit, milk, wine, and the honey of his bees; and whenever either came singly to borrow a wax taper, or a piece of fair linen, or a basket, or a penn'orth of nails, he made it a point to warn Eudaemon very seriously against his dangerous ways of thinking and proceeding, and to promise intercession with the Powers above.

The two saints would have liked a fine theological set to. But Eudaemon only smiled. Eudaemon was always smiling; and that was one of the worst signs about him: for a man, let alone a saint, who smiles, expresses thereby satisfaction with this world and confidence in his salvation, both of which are slights to Heaven. Moreover, Eudaemon talked in a profane manner; and there was far too much marrying and giving in marriage among the poor folk he had gathered round him. He showed unseemly interest in women in labour, even assisting them with physic, and advising them on the rearing of infants; he rarely chastised young children, and allowed the lads and maidens to tell him their love-affairs, never exhorting either to a life of abstinence and celibacy. He attended to the ailments of animals, and was frequently heard to address speech to them as if they had been possessed of an immortal soul, and as if their likings and dislikings should be considered; thus he made brooding nests for the doves, and placed dishes of water for the swallows, and was surrounded by birds, allowing them to perch on his shoulders and hands, and calling them by name. Various things he said might almost have led you to suspect - had such suspicion not been too uncharitable - that he considered birds and beasts as the creatures of God and brethren to man; nay, that plants also had life, and recognised the Creator; but when he came to speak of such matters, calling the sun and moon *brother* and *sister*, and attributing Christian virtues, as humility, chastity, joyousness, to water, and fire, and clouds, and winds, his discourses were such that it was more charitable to consider them as ravings, and himself as one of the half-witted; and this, indeed, Eudaemon probably was, and not utterly damned, otherwise Carpophorus could scarcely have borrowed his altar clothes and tapers, or Ursicinus accepted his lettuces and honeycomb.

The two saints were devoured by curiosity to know what might be the secret relations of their fellow saint with the world of devils. For these delicate matters gave a saint his position; and on these it was customary to show a subtle mixture of reticence and bragging. Had Eudaemon ever had encounters with the Prince of Darkness? Had he been tempted? Had lovely ladies burst in upon his visions, or large stones been rained down through his roof? Carpophorus, feigning to speak of a third person, made some extraordinary statements concerning himself; and Ursicinus led to even more marvellous suppositions by refusal to go into details. But Eudaemon showed no interest in these discourses, neither courting nor evading them. He stated drily that he had undergone no temptations of an unusual sort, and no persecutions worth considering. As to encounters with devils, and with heathen divinities, upon which his fellow-saints insisted upon explicit answers, he had nothing to report that concerned anyone. He had, indeed, on the coast of Syria once come across a creature who was half man, half horse, of the sort which the pagans called *Centaur*, of whom he had asked his way in the sand and grass, and who had answered with difficulty, making whinnying noises, and pawing, and cocking his ears; and some years later, among the oakwoods round the lake of Nemi, he had met a Faun, a rustic creature shaped like a man, but with goat's horns and legs, who had entertained him pleasantly in a cool brake of reeds, and given him nuts and very succulent roots for a midday meal; and it was his opinion that such creatures, although denied human speech, were aware of the goodness of God, and possessed some way of their own, however different from ours, of expressing their joy therein. Indeed, was there aught in the Scriptures which affirmed or suggested that any one of God's creatures was destitute of such sense of His loving-kindness? As regards the gods of the heathens, what manner of harm could they do to a Christian? Can false gods hurt any except their believers? Nay, Eudaemon actually seemed to hint that these Pagan divinities were deserving of compassion, and that they also, like the sun and moon, the wolves and the lambs, the grass and the trees, were God's children and our brethren, if only they knew it...

Of course, however, Carpophorus and Ursicinus never allowed Eudaemon to become quite explicit on this point of doctrine, lest they should have to consider him damned beyond remission, and therefore, unfit for their society. As things stood, the two saints were comfortably persuaded that those little visits, with accompanying loans and gifts, were probably poor Eudaemon's one chance of salvation.

And now for the miracle.

It happened that in digging the ground for a fresh piece of vineyard, a spade struck upon an uncommonly large round stone, which being uncovered, disclosed itself to be a full-length woman, carved in marble, and embedded in the clay, face upwards. The peasants fled in terror, some crying out that they had found an embalmed Pagan, and some, a sleeping female devil. But Eudaemon merely smiled, and wiped the earth off the figure, which was exceedingly comely, and mended one of its arms with cement, and set it up on a carved tombstone of the ancients, at the end of the grass walk through the orchard, and close to the beehives.

Carpophorus and Ursicinus heard the news, and hastening to the spot, instantly offered Eudaemon their help in breaking the figure to bits and conveying it to a limekiln by the Tiber. For it was evidently an image of the goddess Venus, by far the wickedest of all the devils. The two saints examined the statue with holy curiosity, and quoted, respectively, several passages of Athenagoras, and Lactantius, and many anecdotes of the Hermit St. Paul, and of other anchorites of the Thebais. But Eudaemon merely thanked them very sweetly for their exhortations, and sent them away with a pair of new sandals and a flask of oil as a gift. After this, the two saints did not consider themselves free to call upon him any longer, and took no notice of the presents he continued to send. They would greatly have liked to behold that idol again, not on account of its comeliness, which neither recognised, but from intense curiosity to see devils a little closer. But having preached openly against it, and tried to stir the peasants to knock it down and break it, they were ashamed of entering the orchard; and merely sought for opportunities of looking across the narrow valley, and seeing the figure of the goddess, shining white among the criss-cross reeds and the big fig-trees of Eudaemon's vineyard.

This being the case, judge of the joy of the two holy men when one June evening - and it was the vigil of the Birth of John Baptist - the news was brought that Eudaemon had at last been caught hold of by the Devil! All other considerations vanished, for brotherly charity required that they should fly to the spot and behold the catastrophe.

The two saints were rather disappointed. The Devil had not carried off Eudaemon, whom, indeed, they found peaceably watering some clove-pinks; but he had carried off, or a least appropriated, a notable piece of Eudaemon's property. For Eudaemon, of all the worldly goods he had once enjoyed, had retained one only, but that surely the most sinful, a wedding-ring. It was quite useless to his neighbours, and a token of earthly affections, having been bought by him to stick on the hand of the girl he had been about to marry. The ring had been a subject of scandal to Carpophorus and Ursicinus, the more so that Eudaemon had flown into a rage (the only time in their experience), when they suggested he should exchange it in the city against a chapel bell; and it was highly satisfactory that the Devil should have opened his campaign by seizing this object above all others.

The way it had happened was this. It being the vigil of the Birth of John Baptist, Eudaemon had, according to a habit of his, which was far from commendable, allowed his peasant folk to make merry, nay, had spread tables for them in the vineyard, and arranged games for young and old; a way of celebrating the occasion the less desirable, that it was said that the vigil of John Baptist happened to coincide with the old feast of the devil Venus, and that the rustics still celebrated it with ceremonies connected with that evil spirit, and in themselves worthy of blame, such as picking bundles of lavender for their linen lockers, making garlands of clove-pinks and lighting bonfires, all of which were countenanced by Eudaemon. On this occasion Eudaemon thought fit to open the bowling-green, which he had just finished building up of green sods, carefully jointed and beaten, with planks to keep the balls from straying. He was showing the rustics how to bowl their balls, and had, for this purpose, girt up his white woollen smock above his knees, when he was stung by a wasp, a creature, no doubt of the Devil. Seeing his finger begin to swell and unwilling to be prevented from continuing the game, he had, for the first time on record, removed that gold wedding-ring, and, after a minute's hesitation how to dispose of it, stuck it on the extended right annular figure of the marble statue of the devil Venus; and then gone on playing. But that rash action, so unworthy of a Christian saint, and in which so many blameable acts culminated - for there should have been neither ring to remove nor idol to stick it on - that altogether reprehensible action was punished as it deserved. After a few rounds of the game, Eudaemon bade the peasants fall to on the dinner he had provided for them, while he himself retired to say his prayers. So doing, he sought his ring. But - O prodigy! O terror! it was in vain. The marble she-devil had bent her finger and closed her hand. She had accepted the ring (and with it, doubtless, his wretched sinful soul) and refused to relinquish it. No sooner had a single one of the rustics found out what had happened, than the whole crew of them, men, women, and children, fled in confusion, muttering prayers and shrieking exorcisms, and carrying away what victuals they could.

It was only when Carpophorus and Ursicinus arrived, armed with missals and holy-water brushes, that a few of the boldest rustics consented to return to the scene of the wonder. They found, as I have already mentioned,

Eudaemon placidly watering some pots of clove-pinks, which he had prepared as gifts for the maidens. The tables were upset, the bunches of lavender lying about; the lettuces and rosebushes had been trampled. The frogs had begun to wail in the reed-brakes, and the crickets to lament in the ripe corn; bats were circling about and swallows, and the sun was sinking. The last rays fell upon the marble statue at the end of the bowling-green, making the ring glimmer on her finger; and suddenly, just as the two saints entered, reddening and gilding her nakedness into a semblance of life. Carpophorus and Ursicinus gave a yell of terror and nearly fell flat on the ground. Eudaemon looked up from his clove-pinks at them, and at the statue. He understood. "Foolish brothers," he said, "did you not know that Brother Sun can make all things alive?"

And he continued watering the flowers and going to the well to re-fill his can.

Carpophorus and Ursicinus had not recovered from their terror; but it was spiced with a certain delight, for were they not about to witness some dreadful proceeding on the part of the Evil One? Meanwhile, they kept at a respectful distance from the idol, and splashing holy water right and left, and swinging censers backwards and forwards, they set up a hymn in a shaky voice, not without some lapses of grammar. But the idol took notice of none of it; she shone out white in the gathering twilight, and on her bent finger, on her closed hand, twinkled the little gold circlet.

When Eudaemon had finished his watering, he let the bucket once more down in to the well, and took a deep drink of water. Then he dipped his hands, ungirt his white woollen robes, the day's work being done, and walked leisurely down the bowling-green, calling the birds, who whirled round his head; but taking no notice of his fellow-saints and their exorcisms. Before the idol he stood still. He looked up, quite boldly, at her comely limbs and face, and even with a benign smile. "Sister Venus," he said, "you were ever a lover of jests; but every jest has its end. Night is coming on, my outdoor work is over; it is fit I should retire to prayers and to

389

rest. Give me therefore my ring, of which I bade you take charge in return for the hospitality I had shown you."

Carpophorus and Ursicinus quickened the time of their hymn, and sang much at cross purposes, looking up at the idol with the corner of their eyes.

The statue did not move. There she stood naked and comely, whiter and whiter as the daylight faded, and the moon rose up in the east. "Sister Venus," resumed Eudaemon, "you are not obliging. I fear, Sister Venus, that you nurture evil designs, such as mankind accounts to your blame. If this be, desist. Foolish persons have said you were wicked, nay a devil; and like enough you have got to believe it, and to glory, perhaps, in the notion. Cast it from you, Sister Venus, for I tell you it is false. And so, restore me my ring."

But still the idol did not move, but grew only whiter, like silver, in the moonbeams, as she stood above the green grass, in the smoke of the incense. Carpophorus and Ursicinus fixed their eyes on her, wondering when she would break in two pieces, and a dragon smelling of brimstone issue from her with a hideous noise, as a result of the exorcism.

"Sister Venus," Eudaemon repeated, and his voice, though gentle, grew commanding, "cease your foolish malice, and, inasmuch as one of God's creatures, obey and restore to me my ring."

A little breeze stirred the air. The white hand of the statue shifted from her white bosom, the finger slowly uncrooked and extended itself.

With incredible audacity Eudaemon ran into the trap of the Evil One. He advanced, and, rising on tiptoe, stretched forth his hand to the idol's. Now indeed would that devil clasp him to her, and singe his flesh on the way to Hell!

But it was not so. Eudaemon took the ring, rubbed it tenderly on his white woollen sleeve, and stuck it slowly and pensively on his own finger.

"Sister Venus," he then said, standing before the

statue, with the finches and thrushes and ortolans perching on his shoulders, and the swallows circling round his head, "Sister Venus, I thank you. Forget the malice which foolish mankind have taught you to find in yourself. Remember you are a creature of God's, and good. Teach the flowers to cross their seeds and vary their hues and scents; teach the doves and the swallows and the sheep and the kine and all our speechless brethren to pair and nurture their young; teach the youths and the maidens to love one another and their children. Make this orchard to bloom, and these rustics to sing. But, since in this form you have foolishly tried to give scandal as foolish mortals had taught you to do, accept, Sister Venus, a loving punishment, and in the name of Christ, be a statue no longer, but a fair white tree with sweet-smelling blossoms and golden fruit."

Eudaemon stood with his hand raised, and made the sign of the cross.

There was a faint sigh, as of the breeze, and a faint but gathering rustle. And behold, beneath the shining white moon, the statue of Venus changed its outline, put forth minute leaves and twigs, which grew apace, until, while Eudaemon still stood with raised hand, there was a statue no longer at the end of the bowling-green, but a fair orange-tree, with leaves and flowers shining silvery in the moonlight.

Then Eudaemon went in to his prayers; and Carpophorus and Ursicinus returned each in silence, one to his cavern and one to his column, and thought themselves much smaller saints for ever in future.

As to the orange-tree, it still stands on the slope of the Caelian, opposite the criss-cross reeds of the Aventine vineyards, beside the little church with the fluted broken columns and the big cactus, like a python, on its apse. And the pigeons are most plentiful, and the figs and clove-pinks most sweet and fragrant all round; and there is always water in plenty in the well. And that is the story of St. Eudaemon and his Orange-Tree; but you will not find it in the *Golden Legend* nor in the Bollandists.

RICHARD GARNETT (1835-1906) worked for the greater part of his life in the British Museum Library, serving as Supervisor of the Reading Room and as Keeper of Printed Books. Most of his writings were scholarly, but he produced one extraordinary book of stories, *The Twilight of the Gods*, which is one of the landmarks of British fantasy. It was first issued in 1888 but was enlarged from sixteen stories to twenty-eight in the second edition of 1903. Most of the stories in it are romances of antiquity or historical fantasies, often based in obscure legends; they are carefully embellished with all manner of exotica, stylistically highly-polished, neatly ironic and brilliantly witty. The title story, which describes the later career of Prometheus, reprieved from his horrible punishment following the abdication of the Olympians, is one of several parables which subtly champion liberal humanist values against the excesses of ascetic religion - although such cautionary tales as "The City of the Philosophers" insist that we must be sceptical even of our best and most humane intentions.

The urbane and flirtatious surfaces of Garnett's stories excuse the fact that their subject matter is mischievously and extravagantly opposed to Victorian ideas and ideals. "Alexander the Ratcatcher" was first published in *The Yellow Book* in 1897; it is one of several cynical anti-clerical satires recalling the most calculatedly heretical of the tales in Anatole France's *The Well of St Clare* (1895; tr. 1909). Vernon Lee's fantasies in a similar vein are restrained by comparison, and those of Laurence Housman are even more so.

ALEXANDER THE RATCATCHER
by Richard Garnett

"Alexander Octavus mures, qui Urbem supra modum vexabant, anathemate perculit." *Palatius. Fasti Cardinalium,* tom. v. p. 46

I

"Rome and her rats are at the point of battle!"

This metaphor of Menenius Agrippa's became, history records, matter of fact in 1689, when rats pervaded the Eternal City from garret to cellar, and Pope Alexander the Eighth seriously apprehended the fate of Bishop Hatto. The situation worried him sorely; he had but lately attained the tiara at an advanced age - the twenty-fourth hour, as he himself remarked in extenuation of his haste to enrich his nephew. The time vouchsafed for worthier deeds was brief, and he dreaded descending to posterity as the Rat Pope. Witty and genial, his sense of humour teased him with a full perception of the absurdity of his position. Peter and Pasquin concurred in forbidding him to desert his post; and he derived but small comfort from the ingenuity of his flatterers, who compared him to St. Paul contending with beasts at Ephesus.

It wanted three half-hours to midnight, as Alexander sat amid traps and ratsbane in his chamber in the Vatican, under the protection of two enormous cats and a British terrier. A silver bell stood ready to his hand, should the aid of the attendant chamberlains be requisite. The walls had been divested of their tapestries, and the floor gleamed with pounded glass. A tome of legendary lore lay open at the history of the Piper of Hamelin. All was silence, save for the sniffing and scratching of the dog and a sound of subterranean scraping and gnawing.

"Why tarries Cardinal Barbadico thus?" the Pope at last asked himself aloud. The inquiry was answered by a wild burst of squeaking and clattering and scurrying to and

393

fro, as who should say, "We've eaten him. We've eaten him!"

But this exultation was at least premature, for just as the terrified Pope clutched his bell, the door opened to the the narrowest extent compatible with the admission of an ecclesiastical personage of dignified presence, and Cardinal Barbadico hastily squeezed himself through.

"I shall hardly trust myself upon these stairs again," he remarked, "unless under the escort of your Holiness's terrier."

"Take him, my son, and a cruse of holy water to boot," the Pope responded. "Now, how go things in the city?"

"As ill as may be, your Holiness. Not a saint stirs a finger to help us. The country-folk shun the city, the citizens seek the country. The multitude of enemies increases hour by hour. They set at defiance the anathemas fulminated by your Holiness, the spiritual censures placarded in the churches, and the citation to appear before the ecclesiastical courts, although assured that their cause shall be pleaded by the ablest advocates in Rome. The cats, amphibious with alarm, are taking to the Tiber. Vainly the city reeks with toasted cheese, and the Commissary-General reports himself short of arsenic."

"And how are the people taking it?" demanded Alexander. "To what cause do they attribute the public calamity?"

"Generally speaking, to the sins of your Holiness," replied the Cardinal.

"Cardinal!" exclaimed Alexander indignantly.

"I crave pardon for my temerity," returned Barbadico. "It is with difficulty that I force myself to speak, but I am bound to lay the ungrateful truth before your Holiness. The late Pope, as all men know, was a personage of singular sanctity."

"Far too upright for this fallen world," observed Alexander with unction.

"I will not dispute," responded the Cardinal, "that the head of Innocent the Eleventh might have been more fitly graced by a halo than by a tiara. But the vulgar are incapable of placing themselves at this point of view. They know that the rats hardly squeaked under Innocent, and that they swarm under Alexander. What wonder if they suspect your Holiness of familiarity with Beelzebub, the patron of vermin, and earnestly desire that he would take you to himself? Vainly have I represented to them the unreasonableness of imposing upon him a trouble he may well deem superfluous, considering your Holiness's infirm health and advanced age. Vainly, too, have I pointed out that your anathema has actually produced all the effect that could have been reasonably anticipated from any similar manifesto on your predecessor's part. They won't see it. And, in fact, might I humbly advise, it does appear impolitic to hurl anathemas unless your Holiness knows that some one will be hit. It might be opportune, for example, to excommunicate Father Molinos, now fast in the dungeons of St. Angelo, unless, indeed, the rats have devoured him there. But I question the expediency of going much further."

"Cardinal," said the Pope, "you think yourself prodigiously clever, but you ought to know that the state of public opinion allowed us no alternative. Moreover, I will give you a wrinkle, in case you should ever come to be Pope yourself. It is unwise to allow ancient prerogatives to fall entirely into desuetude. Far-seeing men prognosticate a great revival of sacerdotalism in the nineteenth century , and what is impotent in an age of sense may be formidable in an age of nonsense. Further, we know not from one day to another whether we may not be absolutely necessitated to excommunicate that factor of Gallicanism, Louis the Fourteenth, and before launching our bolt at a king, we may think well to test its efficacy upon a rat. *Fiat experimentum.* And now to return to our rats, from which we have ratted. Is there indeed no hope?"

"Lateat scintillula forsan," said the Cardinal mysteriously.

"Ha! How so?" eagerly demanded Alexander.

"Our hopes," answered the Cardinal, "are associated with the recent advent to this city of an extraordinary

395

personage."

"Explain," urged the Pope.

"I speak," resumed the Cardinal, "of an aged man of no plebeian mien or bearing, albeit most shabbily attired in the skins, now fabulously cheap, of the vermin that torment us; who, professing to practise as an herbalist, some little time ago established himself in an obscure street of no good repute. A tortoise hangs in his needy shop, nor are stuffed alligators lacking. Understanding that he was resorted to by such as have need of philters and love-potions, or are incommoded by the longevity of parents and uncles, I was about to have him arrested, when I received a report which gave me pause. This concerned the singular intimacy which appeared to subsist between him and our enemies. When he left home, it was averred, he was attended by troops of them obedient to his beck and call, and spies had observed him banqueting them at his counter, the rats sitting erect and comporting themselves with perfect decorum. I resolved to investigate the matter for myself. Looking into his house through an unshuttered window, I perceived him in truth surrounded by feasting and gambolling rats; but when the door was opened in obedience to my attendants' summons, he appeared to be entirely alone. Laying down a pestle and mortar, he greeted me by name with an easy familiarity which for the moment quite disconcerted me, and inquired what had procured him the honour of my visit. Recovering myself, and wishing to intimidate him:

" 'I desire in the first place', I said, 'to point out to you your grave transgression of municipal regulations in omitting to paint your name over your shop.'

" 'Call me Rattila,' he rejoined with unconcern, 'and state your further business.'

"I felt myself on the wrong tack, and hastened to interrogate him respecting his relations with our adversaries. He frankly admitted his acquaintance with rattery in all its branches, and his ability to deliver the city from this scourge, but his attitude towards your Holiness was so deficient in respect that I question whether I ought to report it."

"Proceed, son," said the Pope; " we will not be deterred from providing for the public weal by the ribaldry of a ratcatcher."

"He scoffed at what he termed your Holiness's absurd position, and affirmed that the world had seldom beheld, or would soon behold again, so ridiculous a spectacle as a Pope besieged by rats. 'I can help your master,' he continued, 'and am willing; but my honour, like his, is aspersed in the eyes of the multitude, and he must come to my aid, if I am to come to his.'

"I prayed him to be more explicit, and offered to be the bearer of any communication to your Holiness.

" 'I will unfold myself to no one but the Pope himself,' he replied, 'and the interview must take place when and where I please to appoint. Let him meet me this very midnight, and alone, in the fifth chamber of the Appartamento Borgia.'

" 'The Appartamento Borgia!' I exclaimed in consternation. 'The saloons which the wicked Pope Alexander the sixth nocturnally perambulates, mingling poisons that have long lost their potency for Cardinals who have long lost their lives!'

" ' Have a care !' he exclaimed sharply. ' You speak to his late Holiness's most intimate friend.'

" 'Then,' I answered, ' you must obviously be the Devil, and I am not at present empowered to negotiate with your Infernal Majesty. Consider, however, the peril and inconvenience of visiting at dead of night rooms closed for generations. Think of the chills and cobwebs. Weigh the probability of his Holiness being devoured by rats.'

" ' I guarantee his Holiness absolute immunity from cold,' he replied, ' and that none of my subjects shall molest him either going or returning.'

" 'But, ' I objected, ' granting that you are not the Devil, how the devil, let me ask, do you expect to gain admittance at midnight to the Appartamento Borgia?'

" ' Think you I cannot pass through a stone wall?' answered he, and vanished in an instant. A tremendous scampering of rats immediately ensued, then all was silence.

"On recovering in some measure from my astounded condition, I caused strict search to be made throughout the shop. Nothing came to light but herbalists' stuff and ordinary medicines. And now, Holy Father, your Holiness's resolution? Reflect well. This Rattila may be the King of the Rats, or he may be Beelzebub in person."

Alexander the Eighth was principally considered by his contemporaries in the light of a venerable fox, but the lion had by no means been omitted from his composition.

"All powers of good forbid," he exclaimed, "that a Pope and a Prince should shrink from peril which the safety of the State summons him to encounter! I will confront this wizard, this goblin, in the place of his own appointing, under his late intimate friend's nose. I am a man of many transgressions, but something assures me that Heaven will not deem this a fit occasion for calling them to remembrance. Time presses; I lead on; follow, Cardinal Barbadico, follow! Yet stay, let us not forget temporal and spiritual armouries."

And hastily providing himself with a lamp, a petronel, a bunch of keys, a crucifix, a vial of holy water, and a manual of exorcisms, the Pope passed through a secret door in a corner of his chamber, followed by the Cardinal bearing another lamp and a naked sword, and preceded by the dog and the two cats, all ardent and undaunted as champions bound to the Holy Land for the recovery of the Holy Sepulchre.

II

The wizard had kept his word. Not a rat was seen or heard upon the pilgrimage, which was exceedingly toilsome to the aged Pope from the number of passages to be threaded and doors to be unlocked. At length the companions stood before the portal of the Appartamento Borgia.

"Your Holiness must enter alone," Cardinal Barbadico admonished, with manifest reluctance.

"Await my return," enjoined the Pontiff, in a tone of

more confidence than he could actually feel, as, after much grinding and grating, the massive door swung heavily back, and he passed on into the dim, unexplored space beyond. The outer air, streaming in as though eager to indemnify itself for years of exile, smote and swayed the flame of the Pope's lamp, whose feeble ray flitted from floor to ceiling as the decrepit man, weary with the way he had traversed and the load he was bearing, tottered and stumbled painfully along, ever and anon arrested by a closed door, which he unlocked with prodigious difficulty. The cats cowered close to the Cardinal; the dog at first accompanied the Pope, but whined so grievously, as though he beheld a spirit, that Alexander bade him back.

Supreme is the spell of the *genus loci*. The chambers traversed by the Pope were in fact adorned with fair examples of the painter's art, most scriptural in subject, but some inspired with the devout Pantheism in which all creeds are reconciled. All were alike invisible to the Pontiff, who, with the dim flicker of his lamp, could no more discern Judaea wed with Egypt on the frescoed ceiling than, with the human limitation of his faculties, he could foresee that the ill-reputed rooms would one day harbour a portion of the Vatican Library, so greatly enriched by himself. Nothing but sinister memories and vague alarms presented themselves to his imagination. The atmosphere, heavy and brooding from the long exclusion of the outer air, seemed to weigh upon him with the density of matter, and to afford the stuff out of which phantasmal bodies perpetually took shape and, as he half persuaded himself, substance. Creeping and tottering between bowl and cord, shielding himself with lamp and crucifix from Michelotto's spectral poniard and more fearful contact with fleshless Vanozzas and mouldering Giulias, the Pope urged, or seemed to urge, his curse amid phantom princes and cardinals, priests and courtesans, soldiers and serving-men, dancers, drinkers, dicers, Bacchic and Cotyttian workers of whatsoever least beseemed the inmates of a Pontifical household, until, arrived in the fifth chamber, close by the, to him, invisible picture of the Resurrection, he sank exhausted into a spacious chair that seemed placed for his reception, and for a moment closed his eyes. Opening them immediately afterwards, he saw with relief that the phantoms had vanished, and that he confronted what at least seemed a fellow-mortal, in the ancient ratcatcher, habited precisely as Cardinal Barbadico had described, yet, for all his mean apparel, wearing the air of one wont to confer with the potentates of the earth on other subjects than the extermination of rats.

"This is noble of your Holiness - really," he said, bowing with mock reverence. "A second Leo the Great!"

"I tell you what, my man," responded Alexander, feeling it very necessary to assert his dignity while any of it remained, "you are not to imagine that, because I have humoured you so far as to grant an audience at an unusual place and time, I am gong to stand any amount of your nonsense and impertinence. You can catch our rats, can you? Catch them then, and you need not fear that we shall treat you like the Pied Piper of Hamelin. You have committed sundry rascalities, no doubt? A pardon shall be made out for you. You want a patent or a privilege for your ratsbane? You shall have it. So to work, in the name of St. Muscipulus! and you may keep the tails and skins."

"Alexander," said the ratcatcher composedly, "I would not commend or dispraise you unduly, but this I may say, that of all the Popes I have known you are the most exuberant in hypocrisy and the most deficient in penetration. The most hypocritical, because you well know, and know that I know that you know, that you are not conversing with an ordinary ratcatcher: had you deemed me such, you would never have condescended to meet me at this hour and place. The least penetrating, because you apparently have not yet discovered to whom you are speaking. Do you really mean to say that you do not know me?"

"I believe I have seen your face before," said Alexander, "and all the more likely as I was inspector of prisons when I was Cardinal."

"Then look yonder," enjoined the ratcatcher, as he pointed to the frescoed wall, at the same time vehemently snapping his fingers. Phosphoric sparks hissed and crackled forth, and coalesced into a blue lambent flame, which concentrated itself upon a depicted figure, whose precise attitude the ratcatcher assumed as he dropped upon his knees. The Pope shrieked with amazement, for, although the splendid Pontifical vestments had become ragged fur, in every other respect the kneeling figure was the counterpart of the painted one, and the painted one was Pinturicchio's portrait of Pope Alexander the Sixth kneeling as a witness of the Resurrection.

Alexander the Eighth would fain have imitated his predecessor's attitude, but terror bound him to his chair, and the adjuration of his patron St. Mark which struggled towards his lips never arrived there. The book of exorcisms fell from his paralysed hand, and the vial of holy water lay in shivers upon the floor. Ere he could collect himself, the dead Pope had seated himself beside the Pope with one foot in the grave, and, fondling a ferret-skin, proceeded to enter into conversation.

"What fear you?" he asked. "Why should I harm you? None can say that I ever injured any one for any cause but my own advantage, and to injure your Holiness now would be to obstruct a design which I have particularly at heart."

"I crave your Holiness's forgiveness," rejoined the Eighth Alexander, "but you must be aware that you left the world with a reputation which disqualifies you for the society of any Pope in the least careful of his character. It positively compromises me to have so much as the ghost of a person universally decried as your Holiness under my roof, and you would infinitely oblige me by forthwith repairing to your own place, which I take to be about four thousand miles below where you are sitting. I could materially facilitate and accelerate your Holiness's transit thither if you would be so kind as to hand me that little book of exorcisms."

"How is the fine gold become dim!" exclaimed Alexander the Sixth. "Popes in bondage to moralists! Popes nervous about public opinion! Is there another judge of morals than the Pope speaking *ex cathedra,* as I always did? Is the Church to frame herself after the prescriptions of heathen philosophers and profane jurists? How, then, shall she be terrible as an army with banners? Did I concern myself with such pedantry when the Kings of Spain and Portugal came to me like cats suing for morsels, and I gave them the West and the East?"

"It is true," Alexander the Eighth allowed, "that the lustre of the Church hath of late been obfuscated by the prevalence of heresy."

"It isn't the heretics," Borgia insisted. "It is the degeneracy of the Popes. A shabby lot! You, Alexander, are about the best of them; but the least Cardinal about my Court would have thought himself bigger than you."

Alexander's spirit rose. " I would suggest, " he said, "that this haughty style is little in keeping with the sordid garb wherein your Holiness, consistent after death as in your life, masquerades to the scandal and distress of the faithful."

"How can I other? Has your Holiness forgotten your Rabelais?"

"The works of that eminent Doctor and Divine," answered Alexander the Eighth, "are seldom long absent from my hands, yet I fail to remember in what manner they elucidate the present topic."

"Let me refresh your memory," rejoined Borgia, and, producing a volume of the Sage of Meudon, he turned to the chapter descriptive of the employments of various eminent inhabitants of the nether world and pointed to the sentence:

"LE PAPE ALEXANDRE ESTOYT PRENEUR DE RATZ"

"Is this indeed sooth? " demanded his successor.

"How else should François Rabelais have affirmed it?" responded Borgia. "When I arrived in the subterranean kingdom, I found it in the same condition as your Holiness's dominions at the present moment, eaten up by rats. The attention which, during my earthly pilgrimage, I had devoted to the science of toxicology indicated me as a person qualified to abate the nuisance, which commission I executed with such success, that I received the appointment of Ratcatcher to his Infernal Majesty, and so discharged its duties as to a merit a continuance of the good opinion which had always been entertained of me in that exalted quarter. After a while, however, interest began to be made for me in even more elevated spheres. I had not been able to cram Heaven with Spaniards, as I had crammed the Sacred College - on the contrary. Truth to speak, my nation had not largely contributed to the population of the regions above. But some of us are people of consequence. My great-grandson, the General of the Jesuits, who, as such, had the ear of St. Ignatius Loyola, represented that had I adhered strictly to my vows, he could never have come into existence, and that the Society would thus have wanted one of its brightest ornaments. This argument naturally had great weight with St. Ignatius, the rather as he, too, was my countryman. Much also was said of the charity I had shown to the exiled Jews, which St. Dominic was pleased to say made him feel ashamed of himself when he came to think of it; for my having fed my people in time of dearth, instead of contriving famines to enrich myself, as so many Popes' nephews have done since; and of the splendid order in which I kept the College of Cardinals. Columbus said a good word for me, and Savonarola did not oppose. Finally I was allowed to come upstairs, and exercise my profession on earth. But mark what pitfalls line the good man's path! I never could resist tampering with drugs of a deleterious nature, and was constantly betrayed by the thirst for scientific experiment into practices incompatible with the public health. The good nature which my detractors have not denied me was a veritable snare. I felt for youth debarred from its enjoyments by the unnatural vitality of age, and sympathised with the blooming damsel whose parent alone stood between her and her lover. I thus lived in constant apprehension of being ordered back to the Netherlands, and yearned for the wings of a dove, that I might flee away and be out of mischief. At last I discovered that my promotion to a higher sphere depended upon my obtaining a testimonial from the reigning Pope. Let a solemn procession be held in my honour, and intercession be publicly made for me, and I should ascend forthwith. I have consequently represented my case to many of your predecessors: but, O Alexander, you seventeenth-century Popes are a miserable breed! No fellow-feeling, no *esprit de corps* . *Heu pietas! heu prisca fides!* No one was so rude as your ascetic antecessor. The more of a saint, the less of a gentleman. Personally offensive, I assure you! But the others were nearly as bad. The haughty Paul, the fanatic Gregory, the worldly Urban, the austere Innocent the Tenth, the affable Alexander the Seventh, all concurred in assuring me that it was deeply to be regretted that I should ever have been emancipated from the restraints of the Stygian realm, to which I should do well to return with all possible celerity; that it would much conduce to the interests of the Church if my name could be forgotten; and that as for doing anything to revive its memory, they would just as soon think of canonising Judas Iscariot."

"And therefore your Holiness has brought these rats upon us, enlisted, I nothing doubt, in the infernal regions?"

"Precisely so: Plutonic, necromantic, Lemurian rats, kindly lent by the Prince of Darkness for the occasion, and come dripping from Styx to squeak and gibber in the Capitol. But I note your Holiness's admission that they belong to a region exempt from your jurisdiction, and that, therefore, your measures against them, except as regards their status as belligerents, are for the most part illegitimate and *ultra vires*."

"I would argue that point," replied Alexander the Eighth, "if my lungs were as tough as when I pleaded before the Rota in Pope Urban's time. For the present I confine myself to formally protesting against your Holiness's unprecedented and parricidal conduct in invading your country at the head of an army of loathsome vermin."

"Unprecedented!" exclaimed Borgia. "Am I not the

modern Coriolanus? Did Narses experience blacker ingratitude than I? Where would the temporal power be but for me? Who smote the Colonna? Who squashed the Orsini? Who gave the Popes to dwell quietly in their own house? Monsters of unthankfulness!"

"I am sure, " said Alexander the Eighth soothingly, "that my predecessors' inability to comply with your Holiness's request must have cost them many inward tears, not the less genuine because entirely invisible and completely inaudible. A wise Pope will, before all things, consider the spirit of his age. The force of public opinion, which your Holiness lately appeared to disparage, was, in fact, as operative upon yourself as upon any of your successors. If you achieved great things in your lifetime, it was because the world was with you. Did you pursue the same methods now, you would soon discover that you had become an offensive anachronism. It will not have escaped your holiness's penetration that what moralists will persist in terming the elevation of the standard of the Church, is the result of the so-called improvement of the world."

"There is a measure of truth in this," admitted Alexander the Sixth, " and the spirit of this age is a very poor spirit. It was my felicity to be a Pope of the Renaissance. Blest dispensation! when men's view of life was large and liberal; when the fair humanities flourished; when the earth yielded up her hoards of chiselled marble and breathing bronze, and new-found agate urns as fresh as day; when painters and sculptors vied with antiquity, and poets and historians followed in their path; when every benign deity was worshipped save Diana and Vesta; when the arts of courtship and cosmetics were expounded by archbishops; when the beauteous Imperia was of more account than the eleven thousand virgins; when obnoxious persons glided imperceptibly from the world; and no one marvelled if he met the Pope arm in arm with the Devil. How miserable, in comparison, is the present sapless age, with its prudery and its pedantry, and its periwigs and its painted coaches, and its urban Arcadias and the florid

405

impotence and ostentatious inanity of what it calls its art! Pope Alexander! I see in the spirit the sepulchre destined for *you*, and I swear to you that my soul shivers in my ratskins! Come, now , I do not not expect you to emulate the Popes of my time, but show that your virtues are your own, and your faults those of your epoch. Pluck up a spirit! Take bulls by the horns! Look facts in the face! Think upon the images of Brutus and Cassius! Recognise that you cannot get rid of me, and that the only safe course is to rehabilitate me. I am not a candidate for canonisation just now; but repair past neglect and appease my injured shade in the way you wot of. If this is done, I pledge my word that every rat shall forthwith evacuate Rome. Is it a bargain? I see it is; you are one of the good old sort, though fallen on evil days."

Renaissance or Rats, Alexander the Eighth yielded.

"I promise," he declared.

"Your hand upon it!"

Subduing his repugnance and apprehension by a strong effort, Alexander laid his hand within the spectre's clammy paw. An icy thrill ran through his veins, and he sank back senseless into his chair.

III

When the Pope recovered consciousness he found himself in bed, with slight symptoms of fever. His first care was to summon Cardinal Barbadico, and confer with him respecting the surprising adventures which had recently befallen them. To his amazement, the Cardinal's mind seemed an entire blank on the subject. He admitted having made his customary report to his Holiness the preceding night, but knew nothing of any supernatural ratcatcher, and nothing of any midnight rendezvous at the Appartamento Borgia. Investigation seemed to justify his nescience; no vestige of the man of rats or of his shop could be discovered; and the Borgian apartments, opened and carefully searched through, revealed no trace of having been visited for many years. The Pope's book of exorcisms was in its proper place, his vial of holy water stood unbroken upon his table; and his chamberlains deposed that they had consigned him to Morpheus at the usual hour. His allusion was at first explained as the effect of a peculiarly vivid dream; but when he declared his intention of actually holding a service and conducting a procession for the weal of his namesake and predecessor, the conviction became universal that the rats had effected a lodgment in his Holiness's upper storeys.

Alexander, notwithstanding, was resolute, and so it came to pass that on the same day two mighty processions encountered within the walls of Rome. As the assembled clergy, drawn from all the churches and monasteries in the city, the Pope in his litter in their midst, marched, carrying candles, intoning chants, and, with many a secret shrug and sneer, imploring Heaven for the repose of Alexander the Sixth, they were suddenly brought to bay by another procession precipitated athwart their track, disorderly, repulsive, but more grateful to the sight of the citizens than all the pomps and pageants of the palmiest days of the Papacy. Black, brown, white, grey; fat and lean; old and young; strident or silent; the whiskered legions tore and galloped along; thronging from every part of the city, they united in single column into an endless host that appeared to stretch from the rising to the setting of the sun. They seemed making for the Tiber, which they would have speedily choked; but ere they could arrive there a huge rift opened in the earth, down which they madly precipitated themselves. Their descent, it is affirmed, lasted as many hours as Vulcan occupied in falling from Heaven to Lemnos; but when the last tail was over the brink, the gulf closed as effectually as the gulf in the Forum closed over Marcus Curtius, not leaving the slightest inequality by which any could detect it.

Long ere this consummation had been attained, the Pope, looking forth from his litter, observed a venerable personage clad in ratskins, who appeared desirous of attracting his notice. Glances of recognition were exchanged, and instantly in place of the ratcatcher stood a

tall, swarthy, corpulent, elderly man, with the majestic yet
sensual features of Alexander the Sixth, accoutred with the
official habiliments and insignia of a Pope, who rose slowly
into the air as though he had been inflated with hydrogen.

"To your prayers!" cried Alexander the Eighth, and
gave the example. The priesthood resumed its chants, the
multitude dropped upon their knees. Their orisons seemed
to speed the ascending figure, which was rising rapidly,
when suddenly appeared in the air Luxury, Simony, and
Cruelty, contending which should receive the Holy Father
into her bosom. Borgia struck at them with his crozier, and
seemed to be keeping them at bay, when a cloud wrapped the
group from the sight of men. Thunder roared, lightning
glared, the rush of waters blended with the ejaculations of
the people and the yet more tempestuous rushing of the rats.
Accompanied as he was, it is not probable that Alexander
passed, like Dante's sigh, "beyond the sphere that doth all
spheres enfold"; but, as he was never again seen on earth, it
is not doubted that he attained at least as far as the moon.

APPENDIX

Notes on authors not represented in the Anthology.

RICHARD HARRIS BARHAM (1788-1845) was a clergyman who adopted the pseudonym Thomas Ingoldsby in order to write *The Ingoldsby Legends: or, Mirth and Marvels.* These began to appear piecemeal in the early issues of *Bentley's Miscellany* in 1837, and were eventually collected in three volumes in 1840, 1842 and 1847. The prose tales are in much the same vein as the comic fantasies included in Dickens', *Pickwick Papers;* they include "The Spectre of Tappington", about a trouser-stealing ghost, and "The Leech of Folkestone"' about a murder unsuccessfully attempted by magical means. The witty verses, rich in overblown wordplay, carry forward a tradition of humorous poetry whose fashionability was renewed by the more light-hearted works of THOMAS HOOD (1799-1845); some of the Ingoldsby legends appeared in the *New Monthly Magazine* during the period of Hood's editorship (1841-43).

MARIE CORELLI was the name adopted by Minnie Mackay (1855-1924) for her literary endeavours, which included several best-selling occult novels. *A Romance of Two Worlds* (1886) describes the revitalization of an effete young woman by a Chaldean magician. *Ardath* (1889) is a fantasy of reincarnation mostly set in the fabulous prehistoric city of Al-Kyris. *The Soul of Lilith* (1892) features a girl whose soul is imprisoned in her body after death so that she may be used as an instrument of occult enlightenment. *The Sorrows of Satan* is a Faustian parable in which Satan, depressed by the ease with which men fall prey to his wiles, finally meets his match in a saintly novelist called Mavis Clare. Marie Corelli was the perfect embodiment of late Victorian values: her unorthodox piety, moralistic fervour and monumental vanity combined to preserve in her the illusion that she was far too good for this

409

world, much more suited to life among the angels.

F. MARION CRAWFORD (1854-1909) produced a rather rough-hewn *Arabian Nights* fantasy, *Khaled* (1891), and a number of romances containing occult elements, including a long and somewhat laborious *femme fatale* story, *The Witch of Prague* (1891).

JAMES DALTON (dates unknown) is credited by various bibliographers with having produce a number of anonymous works, including an early comic fantasy about an incautious deal with the devil, *The Gentleman in Black* (1831) and other items with some fantasy content. These other items include one of the very few fantasy novels to be produced in the three-decker format which dominated Victorian publishing - a remarkable moralistic comedy called *The Invisible Gentleman* (1833). This stands at the head of a rich Victorian tradition of cautionary tales of invisibility, which also includes Charles Wentworth Lisle's *The Ring of Gyges* (1886), James Payne's *The Eavesdropper* (1888), C. H. Hinton's *Stella* (1895) and H. G. Wells' *The Invisible Man* (1897). The British Museum Catalogue gives separate listings to "James Dalton, novelist" and the *Blackwood's* writer James Forbes Dalton, but the latter was active in the same period and his story "The Beauty Draught" (1840) has exactly the same moral as *The Invisible Gentleman,* so he may well be the same person. The bibliographical confusion is further compounded by the fact that some sources identify the author of *The Gentleman in Black* etc. simply as "Dalton", a signature which was also used by Richard Harris Barham's son Richard Harris Dalton Barham on various pieces published in *Bentley's Miscellany* in the late 1830s.

LADY EMILIA FRANCES DILKE (1840-1904) wrote two volumes of allegorical prose poems, *The Shrine of Death and Other Stories* (1886) and *The Shrine of Love and Other Stories* (1891). The stylistically ornate and distinctly morbid stories are among the more curious *fin de siècle* fantasies produced in Britain.

GEORGE DU MAURIER (1834-1896) produced three eccentric sentimental fantasies, of which the best is *Peter Ibbetson* (1891), whose eponymous hero, condemned to life imprisonment, achieves a kind of escape by sharing his dreams with a girl he knew in childhood. *Trilby* (1894) is more famous because of the sub-plot involving the heroine's subjugation by the mesmerist Svengali. *The Martian* (1897) is a moralistic fantasy of reincarnation.

HENRY RIDER HAGGARD (1856-1925) wrote numerous lost race stories set in Africa, many of which have fantasy elements - most conspicuously the best-selling *She* (1886), whose unlucky heroine loses her immortality but is conveniently reincarnated in *Aycoha* (1906) and other sequels. Haggard also wrote a mock-Icelandic saga, *Eric Brighteyes* (1891) and several other romances of reincarnation. In collaboration with Andrew Lang he wrote *The World's Desire,* in which Odysseus goes in search of Helen of Troy.

JAMES HOGG (1770-1835) was a prolific contributor to *Blackwood's Magazine,* and a leading member of its editorial coterie, within which he was affectionately nicknamed "The Ettrick Shepherd"; his aggressiveness and hard drinking were continually caricatured in the magazine's "Noctes Ambrosianae" section. He is best-remembered today for his phantasmagoric study in paranoia *The Private Memoirs and Confessions of a Justified Sinner* (1824), but he also wrote a number of historical novels (which were virtually eclipsed by Scott's) and he became one of the leading conservationists of Scottish folklore by means of his various supernatural tales and the anecdotes and legends which he recorded in his regular *Blackwood's* column "The Shepherd's Calendar".

LAURENCE HOUSMAN (1865-1959) produced several books of sophisticated children's fantasies in the same quasi-allegorical vein as George MacDonald and Oscar Wilde, including *A Farm in Fairyland* (1894), *The House of Joy,* (1895), and *The Field of Clover* (1898). His early fantasies for adults include the highly unusual *Gods and their Makers* (1897), whose young protagonist belongs to a tribe where every man must make his own personal deity, and is eventually banished to the realm where those gods come to life following the deaths of their creators. His carefully reverent Christian fantasies, collected in *All Fellows: Seven Legends of Lower Redemption* (1896) and *The Cloak of Friendship* (1905) are the best examples of their kind, and though they refuse to flirt deliberately with heresy after the fashion of the anti-clerical fantasies of Vernon Lee and Richard Garnett they are nevertheless drawn by degrees towards a warm Epicurean liberalism. Housman met Oscar Wilde in Paris shortly before Wilde's death, and his memoir of their conversation, *Echo de Paris* (1923), includes two brief fantasy parables which Wilde recited to his listeners. His sister CLEMENCE HOUSMAN (1861-1955) wrote the fine erotic fantasy *The Were-Wolf* (1890) and a more languid *femme fatale* story *The Unknown Sea* (1898).

DOUGLAS JERROLD (1803-1857) was a noted humourist who produced for the satirical magazine *Punch* a bizarre moralistic comedy, *A Man Made of Money* (1848-9), in which a man with a spendthrift wife wishes he were made of money, and finds himself able to peel banknotes from his heart - but his substance dwindles away as he spends himself. The story was presumably inspired by Balzac's *La*

412

Peau de Chagrin (1831; tr. as *The Magic Skin*).

CHARLES KINGSLEY (1819-1875) produced one of the classic Victorian children's fantasies in *The Water-Babies* (1863), a very peculiar story in which a chimney sweep's boy succeeds in learning after death the moral lessons which he never had a chance to absorb in life. The book displays the author's interest in evolutionary theory as well as his evangelistic fervour, and is said by some Freudian critics to feature an extended (but presumably unconscious) extrapolation of Victorian anxieties regarding the perils of masturbation.

RUDYARD KIPLING (1865-1936) wrote several notable children's fantasies, including a series of stories featuring the feral child Mowgli, raised by wolves and educated by a panther and a bear, which first appeared in *The Jungle Book* (1894) and *The Second Jungle Book* (1895). Kipling's *Just So Stories* (1902) boldly carry forward the Victorian tradition of sensible nonsense, offering fanciful fabular explanations of "How the Leopard Got His Spots", "How the Camel Got His Hump" and so on.

FIONA MACLEOD was the pseudonym used by William Sharp (1855-1905) for most of his tales based in Scottish folklore, some of which are historical fantasies, some occult romances and some metaphysical allegories. They include the novels *Pharais* (1894), *Green Fire* (1896) and *The Divine Adventure* (1900) and the collections *The Sin-Eater and Other Tales* (1895), *The Washer of the Ford and other Legendary Moralities* (1896) and *The Dominion of Dreams* (1899). Sharp wrote a few fantasies under his own name, including the title story of *The Gypsy Christ and Other Tales* (1895).

ROBERT MACNISH (1802-1837) was a regular contributor to *Blackwood's Magazine,* where his contributions were usually attributed to "A Modern Pythagorean". The pseudonym derives from his first and most significant contribution to the magazine. "A Metempsychosis" (1826), an early identity-exchange story which claims descent from the Pythagorean theory of the transmigration of souls. All MacNish's work (which was assembled for posthumous publication in volume form in 1838) partakes of an unusually heavy sense of irony and a remarkable flair for grotesquerie, displayed to its best advantage in such hallucinatory stories as "The Man with the Nose". His penchant for describing altered states of consciousness was presumably connected with the condition which led to his premature death, which he had elected to study scrupulously from within for his doctoral dissertation, entitled "The Anatomy of Drunkenness".

GEORGE MEREDITH (1828-1909) wrote one humorous fantasy novel of note at the beginning of his career: the baroque Oriental fantasy *The Shaving of Shagpat* (1856). The story has allegorical pretensions, but these may be part-bluff. Meredith's novella *Farina* (1857) is a historical romance with some fantasy elements.

JOSEPH SHIELD NICHOLSON (1850-1927) wrote three anonymously-published fantasy novels. *Thoth* (1888) is a curious historical fantasy which features a scientifically-advanced lost race. *A Dreamer of Dreams* (1889) is a moralistic Faustian fantasy. *Toxar* (1890) - the best of the three - is an extended *conte philosophique* cast as a romance of antiquity.

MRS. MARGARET OLIPHANT (1828-1897) wrote numerous moralistic ghost stories which stand on the borderline between fantasy and horror, the most interesting being *A Beleaguered City* (1880), in which the inhabitants of a French town are briefly driven from their abode by the disappointed spirits of their ancestors. She also wrote some of the most famous and most successful consolatory fantasies about the afterlife, following the posthumous exploits of a saintly woman; two such stories are combined in *A Little Pilgrim in the Unseen* (1883) and two others are in *The Land of Darkness* (1888). The title story of this second collection is far less reassuring, offering a tour of the Hell which parallels the little pilgrim's Heaven, and her later contributions to the sub-genre, *"Dies irae;" the story of a Spirit in Prison* (1895) and "The Land of Suspense" (1897) offer distinctly uneasy contemplations of Purgatory and Limbo.

THOMAS LOVE PEACOCK (1785-1866) made a significant contribution to the development of native British folkloristic materials in his two historical fantasies, *Maid Marian* (1822) - which popularised the modern version of the story of Robin Hood - and *The Misfortune of Elphin* (1829), which developed themes from the Mabinogion, including its references to Arthurian legend.

JOHN RUSKIN (1819-1900) wrote the most celebrated example of a British *kunstmärchen, The King of the Golden River* (1851) simply to demonstrate that he could. It follows a classic pattern, allowing the youngest of three brothers to find appropriate supernatural aid in order to repair the damage done to their beautiful valley by his selfish siblings.

BRAM STOKER (1847-1912) went on to write one of the classic Victorian horror stories in *Dracula* (1897), but his first book was a collection of downbeat allegorical fairy tales, *Under the Sunset* (1881). Like George MacDonald's tales they mirror the author's psychological problems in a rather peculiar fashion.

WILLIAM MAKEPEACE THACKERAY (1811-1863) was an early contributor to the sub-genre of Christmas fantasies, under the pseudonym M. A. Titmarsh. *The Rose and the Ring* (1855), subtitled "a fireside pantomime", is an uninhibited exercise in parodic slapstick.

HERBERT GEORGE WELLS (1866-1946) was the parent and presiding genius of the British tradition of scientific romance, but he also wrote a number of excellent fantasies.
The Wonderful Visit (1895) is a scathing moralistic fantasy in which an angel from the Land of Dreams finds Victorian England an ugly place ruled by sanctimonious hypocrisy and frank injustice. "The Man Who Could Work Miracles" (1898) is a classic cautionary tale which Wells later turned into a notable film script. *The Sea Lady* (1902) is a calculatedly unconventional *femme fatale* story which seems in the end to reach a compromise with the sentimentality which it originally set out to undermine. "The Country of the Blind" (1904) and "The Door in the Wall" (1906) are classics of allegorical fantasy.